I didn't have much to go on—an image that Pasha had given me of the young man in the office, boy even.

Dusky yet paler than he could have been, should have been, not unlike myself or a thousand others. Not the blue-white undertones of a Downsider who'd spent his life in the dark, but more like an Upsider from the wrong side of Trade, who saw the sun perhaps for a few minutes a day as it stood at noon and shone straight down, and for the rest of the time saw it only second- or third-hand, bounced down on mirrors and through cobwebbed light wells. He'd been thin too, like we all were, and getting thinner. A man like thousands Under Trade, except for the smell of the Stench on him and in his mind the inexplicable events he'd seen, perhaps inadvertently caused.

A boom-shudder rattled the walls, made dust drift on to my face and stick to the clammy sweat there. Another reminder of why I needed to find this man, and soon. The sound had become part of the city over the last days, echoing along the walkways and haunting every level from the darkest depths of Boundary right up to the rarefield and sun-drenched air of Top of the World to rattle even the Ministry. And with every boom-shudder, you could almost see the thought run through the heads of everyone, Upsider and Downsider alike.

The Storad were at the gates.

The Storad were lurking Outside . . . waiting for their chance.

BY FRANCIS KNIGHT

Fade to Black

Before the Fall

Last to Rise

FRANCIS
KNIGHT

www.orbitbooks.net

Orbit
Hachette Book Group
237 Park Avenue, New York, NY 10017
HachetteBookGroup.com

First U.S. Edition: November 2013

Orbit is an imprint of Hachette Book Group, Inc. The Orbit name and logo are trademarks of Little, Brown Book Group Limited.

Library of Congress Control Number: 2013947176
ISBN: 978-0-316-21774-3

10 9 8 7 6 5 4 3 2 1

RRD-C

Printed in the United States of America

To Nerisse;
More awesome than Hit Girl.
And no, you are not getting a butterfly knife
for your birthday.
We can negotiate on nunchucks.

Chapter One

There is, perhaps, some universal truth that no one has seen fit to tell me about. Namely that if I have to find someone they are always in the shittiest place I can imagine, and I can imagine a lot of shit.

This place had to take the prize though. Right down in the bowels of Mahala, where the sun never shone. It didn't get much of a breeze either, which was a pity because it could have used one.

Down past No-Hope-Shitty, on into even-worse Boundary and across towards the base of the Slump, its mangled remains reminding everyone what can happen when a mage goes bat-shit crazy. That was where you'd find the Stench – it's above the 'Pit but not by much – and the people who made sure we didn't drown in our own waste. There's a few people who might say that I belonged there too.

I picked my way carefully past the dripping girders, under

the newly lit Glow lights that still gave me a thrill to look at. Their light didn't pierce much of the darkness – down here wasn't considered priority for Glow, and the lights were sparse – but at least I could see where I was going and what not to step in, which was most of it.

I moved past vast, evil-smelling vats of who-knew-what except that it was lumpy, a gruesome brown-green that was bright even in the gloom, and was giving off fumes that smelled like they could kill at ten yards. I was grateful I didn't have a curious bone in my body, because nobody *wanted* to know what was in them, surely. Guessing would be enough.

Water kept on drip-drip-dripping from the ceiling, filtered down through a hundred or more levels of city above us, through cracks and crevices and light-wells. At least, I hoped it was only water, because it sidled down the collar of my coat like it had found a home. The faint chemical tang of synth overrode other, more earthy smells, and I wondered how many of the Stenchers had succumbed to the synthtox.

There didn't seem to be anyone about but I knew my man was down here somewhere. Since the Glow had come back on, mages were needed to power it rather than be hunted down and executed for being unholy (among other things). So now we were free to get killed for more prosaic reasons, though mages were still pretty shy about coming forward. After all, it might have been a bluff – the Ministry had tried that one before, and no one Under Trade trusted the Ministry, even when they were in temple, praying the proper, sanitised prayers.

With mages actually needed now, the new archdeacon had issued a notice of reward for anyone coming forward with information on . . . unusual occurrences. So now we had people falling over themselves to offer up their fellow man. Mostly it was out of petty vengeance of some sort or another – men dobbing in someone they thought was having an affair with their wife, or a professional rival, or just that snobby bastard from the next level up who kept dumping his rubbish over the walkway instead of sending it down the bucket lifts to the Stench. Often the dobbers-in did it for the money too – money meant food, and food was hard to come by, what with the siege on one side of the city and neighbours of doubtful intent on the other, with nothing much in between except level upon level of starving people all hemmed in by the ring of mountains that kept us safe, or had done up till now.

Given that siege, any food was difficult to find. *Good* food, something edible that wasn't watery mush or riddled with beetles, was almost mythical. By this point, when we'd been under siege for long enough that rats were looking mighty tasty, I'd have sold my soul for bacon and my left arm for anything that didn't taste like sawdust and mouse droppings. Except my soul wasn't worth a bent copper in the state it was in, and, due to a small incident involving how my magic works and me feeling rather vengeful, my left arm wasn't up to much either; at least my hand wasn't. What it was, was screwed.

Of course, everyone was trying to take advantage of the

money the Archdeacon had offered by reporting each other for such things as "looking funny", "walking strange", "having a wart" or, on one memorable occasion, "talking shit". A lot of more serious accusations flew about as well, but I didn't care about them because some pretty serious allegations can be laid at my feet too.

But in among all that, we'd had a few useful reports. Yesterday a man, thin as a stick and still with the stink of this place on him, had sidled into the office, looking askance at the sign on the door:

LICENSED MAGES, ALL MAGICAL THINGS ATTEMPTED.
SPECIALITIES INCLUDE INSTANT COMMUNICATION, MIND-READING, PEOPLE FOUND AND THINGS REARRANGED.
FEES AVAILABLE ON REQUEST.

It was a good sign, all the better because now we were legal and casting a spell no longer meant getting arrested, a term that had long been a euphemism for "dying messily". Still, the Ministry had spent a couple of decades telling everyone how evil and unholy we were, and it was taking time for people to adjust.

The thought of mages had made the thin man pause. The sight of Pasha, with his Downsider pallor under dusky skin that to an Upsider meant "heretic" or worse, had him running away like Namrat himself was chasing him, wanting to eat his soul before he crapped it into hell. The man hadn't escaped before Pasha had used his magic to lift the information from the man's mind – a series of inexplicable events down here in the Stench. Inexplicable was what we were after, hence why I was down here trying not to breathe, in case it was possible to die from inhaling the smell.

I didn't have much to go on – an image that Pasha had given me of the young man in the office, boy even. Dusky yet paler than he could have been, should have been, not unlike myself or a thousand others. Not the blue-white undertones of a Downsider who'd spent his life in the dark, but more like an Upsider from the wrong side of Trade, who saw the sun perhaps for a few minutes a day as it stood at noon and shone straight down, and for the rest of the time saw it only second- or third-hand, bounced down on mirrors and through cobwebbed light-wells. He'd been thin too, like we all were, and getting thinner. A man like thousands Under Trade – except for the smell of the Stench on him and in his mind the inexplicable events he'd seen – perhaps inadvertently caused.

A boom-shudder rattled the walls, made dust drift on to my face and stick to the clammy sweat there. Another reminder of why I needed to find this man, and soon. The sound had become part of the city over the last days, echoing along the walkways and haunting every level from the darkest depths of Boundary right up to the rarefied and sun-drenched air of Top of the World to rattle even the Ministry. And with every boom-shudder, you could almost see the thought run through the heads of everyone, Upsider and Downsider alike.

The Storad were at the gates.

The Storad were lurking Outside, waiting for their chance, and they had a parade of big, smoking machines that were making a creditable attempt at blasting the crap out of said gates. The boom was the machine firing what looked like enormous bullets. The shudder was what happened when the bullets struck the gates, a tremor and terror that vibrated through the whole city.

I reached the end of the vats with relief and, hoping I might be able to take a deep breath without throwing up, braved the echoing cavern at the end. The smell didn't get any better. Instead it got worse so that my eyes watered. I'd have happily killed any number of people for a fresh breeze. Where the hell was this guy? Where was anyone?

A series of smaller tanks and vats filled the cavern, larger feeding into smaller, overspill running into a channel that carved its way down the centre. Greenish froth bubbled and steamed on the surfaces of some of the tanks, but the run-off looked surprisingly clear. The liquid – I hesitate to call it water except in the most generous sense – splashed down the channel with a cheerful prattle until it slid over a lip and out of sight.

I still hadn't seen anyone and I was starting to get cranky. We had no time to spare, not with the Storad Outside, wearing down the gates a chunk at a time. Churning out Glow was wearing Pasha and me down a chunk at a time too. No time to spare and we needed every mage we could find, whether they knew they were mages or not. I tried calling out, tried poking around, but all I got for my trouble was more smell and green stuff on my coat. It was hovering around noon up at Top of the World, and I needed to be somewhere else as soon as I could. No time to mess about, and that made me swear because it meant I had to use my magic. I'd been hoping I'd get away with it. No such luck.

I found a wall that wasn't dripping too badly, leaned against it for support and hoped like hell that this time I wouldn't end up on my knees, because a ruined pair of boots was enough without ruining my allover too. I shut my eyes and pulled my nicely buggered hand out of my pocket. Usually I needed a prop of some kind, a link to whoever I was going to find, unless I knew them well. A lock of hair, a scrap of clothing, a picture. This time all I had was the face that Pasha had shown me, a picture in my head if you will, along with a name and being fairly certain the guy was down here. It might work. I hoped it would, because this was going to hurt and I don't like to hurt, especially for no purpose.

My hand was slowly getting better since I'd completely screwed it, but pumping out enough magic to run the Glow lights and everything else over the last few weeks hadn't really made it easier. The generator was helping, taking the magic and magnifying it, but Trade is a hungry beast. Purple-blue and swollen doesn't even begin to cover how damaged my hand was, but it was a fact of my life. If I was lucky the hand wouldn't drop off any time soon.

I took a deep breath and clenched my fist. First the pain came, familiar and unwanted, a silver-red line of agony in my hand, my arm, my head. After that, from the pain came the juice, the surge of magic that would show me the way, and that also tempted me, taunted me. Pain was the least of my worries when I cast a spell, because the black was always waiting, watching, hoping I'd fall in and never get back out. It scared the crap out of me, if I'm honest, because part of me *wanted* to fall in, into warm comfort and fearless wonder, to be free of everything, to care about nothing.

The face, I concentrated on the face. I'd been getting a fair bit of practice at find-spells just lately, cast more in the last week than I'd done in the previous decade, as my poor hand could attest, and I was getting better, honing it. A face wasn't much to go on, but I could feel a pull, a tug on my arm. A raised voice echoing in my head, another against it, though I couldn't tell if it was the guy I was after, not yet. Better than nothing though, so I followed the tug of my throbbing arm, the pulse of the juice and the knowledge in my head that *this* way was the way to go. My magic, at least this part of it, had rarely steered me wrong before – it was almost the only thing I could rely on.

The tug led me down a leprous gap between two vats, one I'd never have noticed on my own. I'd never have gone down there even if I *had* noticed, if not for the pull, because being sandwiched between two of the vats, sideways because my shoulders wouldn't fit, gave me an extra special blast of stench. Probably a good job I'd not been able to find any food for breakfast. I held my breath and squeezed through.

The other side opened out into a dark and grimly dripping tunnel that perhaps had once been an alley before someone built over the top. That was the thing with Mahala: someone always built over the top – there wasn't anywhere else *to* build, not any more. The tunnel wasn't much wider than the gap between the vats, but at least the smell faded a touch as I went in. I kept my good hand on the butt of my pulse pistol, just in case.

The echoing voices became louder and I was thankful I'd not have to use any more magic for now, though the aching throb of my hand meant at least I'd have plenty of spare juice if I needed it. The tunnel wound on, a glow flickering along the damp walls. Not Glow, but the subtler light of a rend-nut-oil lamp, last chance of the poorest of the poor – the smell of day-old farts and rotting fish mingled with the more pervasive smell from behind.

I was getting close, the tug told me. A last corner and the tunnel opened out, became a wide corridor, well lit by stinking lamps and with walls that looked like patches of damp held together by mould. A series of doorways lined with ragged drapes opened off the right-hand side.

Stenchers lived whole lives down here, rarely ventured anywhere outside their little domain. The voices became clearer –

a man and a woman arguing violently, though their words were still indecipherable. I didn't need to know what they were saying to get the gist though. Things seemed to be at the "Bitch!", "Bastard!", "My mother always said—", "Your mother is a—" phase, and I hesitated to intervene. Caught in domestic crossfire is never a good place to be, because like as not they'll *both* turn on you. I have the scars to prove it.

My hesitation – all right, craven sense of self-preservation – flew out of the window at the unmistakable sound of an open hand cracking against a cheek. The woman screamed like hell had just opened up a portal at her feet and Namrat had leapt out and started eating her face. I had my pulse pistol out and was round the corner of the doorway before the scream had a chance to die away. I may be self-serving, and I may try to avoid responsibility at all costs, will do almost anything to outrun it, but I have this other little failing, one that annoys Erlat no end.

I was round the corner in a heartbeat, pulse pistol out and ready to zap the guy in the head, short-circuit his brain with a concentrated blast of magic. He might be a mage, might be the guy I was after, but even so—

I didn't get any further than that thought before he slammed into me, knocking us both out into the corridor and up against the wall in a tangle of limbs and knocked heads. I landed on my bad hand, naturally, and bit back a scream. Bit back too the surge of juice that rattled my brain and made me want to flail around with my magic. I didn't quite hold on to all of it and it went wild. Without direction it did what it wanted to. A pair of rags serving as curtains in the doorway morphed into two rippling puddles of brown gloop on the floor before they grew stubby, gooey wings and half flew, half flopped off down the corridor. Oops.

When my head cleared a little, I realised that it hadn't been the guy attacking me as I'd thought. He'd been thrown against the wall, had hit me instead, and now lay dazed and confused on the floor.

In the room opposite us, clearly visible because some idiot had rearranged her curtains, a woman stood in utter outrage, fists clenched, eyes hot, a curving, satisfied smile on her lips. It might seem odd that the first thing I noticed about her wasn't that she was flying, or rather hovering a foot above the floor. Given that it's me we're talking about here, the *first* thing I noticed was that the shapeless rag of a tunic she wore couldn't hide the fact she had a stupendous figure, all round and curvy in the best places, and some of those places were heaving in a very distracting manner. Noticing the hovering only came quite far after that, and smacked me in the head with the thought. It wasn't the guy with the thin face, crumpled at the bottom of the wall, that I was looking for.

He wasn't the mage.

She glared at me, one side of her face red with a handprint, her head held high and her chin almost regal in the way it lifted, as though she was goading me. Try it, go on, I dare you, that look said. You try it and I'll slam you too. Just you see if I don't.

I lived for this kind of challenge – that is, ones involving women.

I got slowly to my feet, trying my best to look as non-threatening as possible. It was hard when, even with her hovering, I was still a touch taller. I was also substantially broader across the shoulders and dressed in a black allover that purposely mimicked the uniforms of the deadly Ministry Specials. It's helpful in putting the fear of the Goddess into my more usual clients – runaways, men with a bounty on their heads, small-timers for the most part, nothing too dangerous because I liked my face where it was. Tracking down possible mages was a new sideline, and I wasn't even getting paid for it.

It was pretty hard not to stare at all the heaving, but I made a valiant effort to roll my tongue back in.

She tensed, ready to let something else go I was sure, maybe slam me into the wall next to the other guy, so I turned on the old Rojan never-fails smile. I'd sworn off women and had been doing well for at least two, almost three days – a new personal record of which I was quite proud – but I was bound to fall off the wagon at some point. If that point made it easier to stay alive, well, that's always a bonus.

The smile didn't fail me now because the tension in her shoulders relaxed, just a touch.

"So, I'm a mage," she said, defiance in every drip of a

vowel. "What you going to do about it? Turn me in for the reward?"

I shoved the pulse pistol back in my pocket, though I kept my hand on it just in case, and racked up the smile another notch. Screw it, I was sworn off women, but never turn an opportunity down, right? Besides, the way she held herself, the waft of her as she hung in the air . . .

My other little failing is that I'm a sucker for women. All of them. Tall, short, big, small, pretty or plain, it's not any of those things that are my undoing. But I can't resist a show of grace in movement, the way they hold themselves. Gets me every time. It doesn't usually last long, granted, because resisting temptation isn't a strong point of mine. Also, once I have what I want, I have the attention span of a small beetle and I'm really world-class at screwing things up, but by the Goddess's tits it still gets me.

Besides, if she was a mage, we needed her, especially as she seemed to have a handle on it, unlike most of our other recruits. So I wasn't being *entirely* selfish when I said, "I was wondering if you were free for lunch?"

Chapter Two

Once the offer of food was on the table, she didn't take much persuading – with a siege on, everyone was hungry, more than hungry, at least everyone Under Trade. A bit of a blow to the ego that it was the food and not me that held the appeal, but probably for the best. Even more trouble with women was the last thing I needed, and I had a fair bit already – my life was such that I'd have been worried if I didn't.

She called herself Halina and she was suspicious and wary and so cynical she made me look like a beacon of hope. She battered me with questions and sneered at the answers as I led her through the ragged recesses of Boundary. Past dripping concrete houses all crammed together like mangy puppies huddling for warmth, all in a pile on top of each other, squeezing each other at the sides, squashing all the even worse places below. Damp and dingy houses that had seen better days – hell, better decades. Walkways launched themselves across yawning gaps between crumbling buildings or crept around them like naughty children. Near-constant rain pattered through their mesh, sliced into a million tiny misting droplets, every one of which seemed to delight in aiming itself down the neck of my jacket. Stairwells led off into twisting darkness up and down, most likely with a mugger on every turn that didn't have a Rapture junkie. The walkways, stairwells and the streets that were bolted more firmly to buildings were all but empty, always seemed empty in those desperate days when people were more concentrated on food, on what was at our gates and trying to come in. A few of the more dissolute wandered the walkways in a haze, from starvation or desperation I could never be sure. A single dark figure drifted along a street on the other side of the chasm, a level down, his face pale as it turned up to look at us.

When we crossed over up into No-Hope and she broached the mage subject, Halina stopped dead halfway across a walkway so that it jiggled and swayed and I almost had a heart attack.

"Is it true, then? About the mages? I thought it was just me," she said while I hung on surreptitiously and tried not to look like I was about to cry. It was a long way down from there, even at the arse end of No-Hope. Long enough for some serious screaming before I hit the bottom. Maybe I'd rattle around a few of the safety nets first but I didn't trust them to save me. They were old and frayed and had never been efficient to start with because people had a tendency to bounce. They'd just give me more time to scream.

"Which bit? Look, can we get across?" I inched my way forward, but she made a grab for me that had the walkway lurching under my feet. My initial reaction – a yelp of terror I kept clenched behind my teeth – wasn't helped by another boom-shudder from the gates, or the fact that the walkway was black at one end from the fires that had raged here during the recent riots. For the second time that day I was glad I hadn't managed breakfast. I stopped with the surreptitious and just hung on, acutely aware that hanging on would do me no good whatsoever if the walkway decided to become detached from the scabby buildings it linked.

Halina raised an eyebrow and a corner of her mouth into a sneer. With a quick twist of something I couldn't see, she levitated off the walkway. That was rubbing it in. I ignored her, took the deepest breath I could manage and got across to a more solid-seeming stairwell, where I waited for the world to stop swimming in front of my eyes and be sensible.

She floated over to me with a grin that would have floored me if I'd been in any proper state to appreciate it. Made funny things happen to my stomach too, or maybe that was still the thought of the drop that had so very nearly been mine.

"What's the matter with you? And you didn't answer my question." She landed lightly on the stair above me. What I wouldn't have given for that ability – I'd never have had to fear a long drop ever again.

"Nothing. What was the question again?"

"I see the news-sheets, you know. Even down in the Stench

we see them, once everyone else is done with them. I can read too. Is it true, about the mages?"

She sounded unbearably proud of that reading, but hey, why not? Few enough Under could read anything other than their own name, if that – that's how my colleague Dendal made his living: reading and writing for those who couldn't. The news-sheets were sponsored mostly by the cardinals and therefore spouting their own rather individual versions of events. Facts weren't important; simple words for the simple readers to recite to those who couldn't manage were. Mages had, well, a pretty shit reputation in the sheets. We were legal, most of them said, because the Archdeacon was too pure and holy to understand how evil we were, and also he was cursed with a merciful nature and a mage for a brother. Actually, that was true enough, Perak *was* of a very merciful nature, and I probably did curse him by being both his brother and a mage. The sheets, though, often went on into glorious detail about just how evil we were. Are.

"Some of it's true," I started, wary of going too far because, well, because some mages had been very evil indeed. "The sheets don't mention who's supplying the Glow though, do they? Or much at all about the Storad, which seems both odd and stupid to me. Why's that, do you think? I mean, Storad at the gate, trying to get in, everyone wants to know why, right?"

She laughed at that, and it made my stomach go flippy-flop all over again. "Because of the mages, that's what everyone says. Mages and Downsiders. And you want me to go with you? Set myself up as a fall-girl perhaps? Well maybe I want to leave the Stench anyway – who wouldn't? And maybe this is far enough before you tell me what I'm letting myself in for."

My stomach went flippy-flop for an entirely different reason – she'd managed to manoeuvre herself so that one quick shove and I was over the edge. I tried my best smile and shuffled over a bit so my back was to a wall.

"Look, now . . ." Stammering is not a good way to flirt, so I tried not to look down and pulled myself together. "How about I show you? Then you can make up your mind. And even if you say no, you get one free meal."

She regarded me appraisingly, looking me up and down real slow with a raised eyebrow that seemed to say, You have got to be kidding me. I straightened up, ran a hand through my hair and tried to look like I was good boyfriend material – not easy, all things considered, but heck, you have to try.

Finally she grinned again, though I didn't like the way it seemed to hint at her knowing more than I thought. "All right. Hell, I wouldn't have come with you at all if I believed half what the sheets say. Besides, be nice to go somewhere that isn't the Stench. I'm not promising anything though."

"Fair enough. After you. Maybe no levitating though – we might be legal, but that doesn't mean anyone likes us." I waved her in front of me on the stairs and followed her up.

"I don't give a shit who knows what I am. Anyone doesn't

like it, they'll feel the whack of my magic on their arse. And speaking of arses, if you don't stop staring at mine," she said over her shoulder, "I'm going to show you what happens when I get *really* pissed off."

Do you know, the fretwork on the walkways round there was really quite something, all curly stuff and little icons of the Goddess's face interspersed with stylised versions of the saints and martyrs. I concentrated on remembering what the hell their names were and barely even glanced at Halina or her arse the whole way there.

Chapter Three

We got up to the pain lab sitting at the edge of Trade. Halina curled her lip at the sight of it, its fire-blackened exterior, the mess of mechanicals and electricals that was Lise's workbench, the straggle of teens and youths – my merry band of magelets – in one corner going through their paces. Then she saw the grey, watery mess that was all we had to call food and dived in like it was steak and eggs.

All the new recruits were being housed at the lab or in the building directly below. Easier to keep an eye on them, especially as most were still learning about their magic, and that usually came with a few surprises. We'd even moved our office there, and that suited me a damn sight better than the old one. I left Halina eating like the world was about to end, and headed for my desk.

I didn't get far. For one thing, Lise wasn't at her workbench, which was odd. Not just because we were relying on her expertise at inventing things that might help us fend off the Storad, but because she was only ever really happy when she was tinkering. It had to be something pretty important to drag her away. The raised voices through the door were a clue – I could hear her and Perak and a whole jumble of other voices all talking over each other. I wasn't entirely sure I wanted to get involved, but figured it was too late for that.

The pain room was full. Lise stood protectively in front of the rig we used to suck out magic, a screwdriver in her hand like she thought someone was about to sabotage it again. Pasha was there, looking rumpled and angry, but then again he often did. Archdeacon Perak, my and Lise's brother, not looking his calm and serene self but more frazzled and pissed off than I thought I'd ever seen him. When I saw who else was in the room, I wasn't surprised.

A whole Ministry delegation: fat, smug cardinals resplendent in their robes, bishops only slightly less chubby or gaudy, advisers lurking at the back, whispering in ears. Even without the robes, you could tell they were Ministry. In a city where food was at a premium, where finding breakfast could be a day-long and expensive job and everyone Under had got to know the sight of their rib bones, these guys all looked sleek and well-rounded.

"And I told you, that's non-negotiable," Perak was saying. "I'm not handing over one of my best mages to the Storad, especially when Glow is at a premium. No mages, no Glow, no nothing. I wouldn't negotiate with them before, and I'm not going to start now."

A disgruntled murmur from the assembled clergy. Perak was . . . well, he wasn't what anyone was used to in a Ministry man. The bishops and cardinals were used to what they called discretion and Perak called weaselling about with the truth. Tact and diplomacy Ministry-style do not run in our family, and Perak's straight way of talking was a breath of fresh air that had most of them reaching for the smelling salts. Entertained me enormously, though.

One of the bolder cardinals glared at Lise. "What about electricity? You said that you could use it, make it. So make it! Then we won't have to rely on these damned mages. We could destroy all these infernal mage-powered machines. Maybe we should anyway."

Lise glared at him and brandished her screwdriver. It might not have seemed much of a weapon but it wasn't all she had, and I had no doubt these cardinals knew what she was like with booby traps. That is, excellent. Then again, it wasn't going to be cardinals trying anything with her machines, they liked their hands and other bits and pieces attached.

Across the room, I could see Pasha struggling not to say anything. It was a struggle for me too, but Perak got in before I could unleash anything.

"I told you, it'll take months to build a non-magic-powered electricity generator a tenth as powerful as what Rojan and

Pasha can produce in half an hour on this rig. For the future, yes. But we won't *have* a future if the Storad get in."

"What about the Mishans then? We're running out of things to trade and they're getting ready for the day the Storad take over – maybe he'd do to trade with." A second cardinal, not as bold as the first, with a smooth, bland sort of face, the sort used to saying what he thought people wanted to hear. A face used to weaselling around with the truth and calling it diplomacy. "Any of them, perhaps. A mage or two would be no great loss, surely?"

"The mages are the best defence we've got. I'm not trading them with anyone!"

Only one or two cardinals looked anywhere near agreeing with Perak. The rest, no matter how they tried to hide it, had varying degrees of mutiny in their glance.

"Perak, you don't seem to realise that the only person who thinks we can win this is you." The bold cardinal again. "We're not going to stop working in the best interests of the city just because he's your brother and you can't – *won't* – see that he's the best bargaining chip we have if we want to survive."

Perak drew himself up to his best, admittedly not very imposing, height. "Best interests of the city? For your own hides, that's what you're working for, I'm not blind to that. I'm working in the best interests of the Goddess, as the mages are, as you should be. Pray on it, why don't you? Now, if you don't mind . . . ?"

They left in dribs and drabs, a good half of them giving me a wish-you-were-dead glare on the way. The bolder cardinal stopped next to me and whispered, "If you weren't his brother, would he still defend you, do you think? Or would he throw you to the Storad? If he doesn't tread carefully, he may not have a choice. And if you don't, neither will you."

He left before I had a chance to answer, or think much more than *That didn't sound good*. Perak's face when they'd gone looked like bad news too. As if to underline the trouble we were all in and bring my mind back to why Perak was here, another boom-shudder shook the room. Those boom-shudders seemed to punctuate everything, every moment, to the point where if they stopped for long my shoulder blades started to itch, wondering when the next would come.

Half a step behind Perak, a position she seemed welded to since she'd become the new captain of his personal guard, stood Jake. I tried not to stare. The uniform really suited her too – a moulded breastplate that showed off every curve, a pair of trousers that fitted her very snugly indeed, the swords that were never far from her reach and that she knew how to use with devastating and clinical effect. On the outside she was cool and collected, her glance like calculated ice. Underneath she was a volcano waiting to happen, all bubbling fervour. I lived in hope of seeing it again.

All that stuff I said about women and what I like about them? Jake was like all of that rolled up into one glorious package that made me go all tingly in diverse parts of my anatomy. Which was a shame, because she was in love with Pasha and he was in love with her and . . . yeah, I didn't have so many friends I could afford to screw them over.

So I dragged my eyes away from her, to Perak as he inclined his head in a come-with-me manner and went to stand by the window. I followed and together we looked out across Trade, which shuddered with its own kind of boom – I could feel it as a hum through my feet. Trade was working again, properly, at last. It had taken a lot, a lot of pain – a lot of blood – to get it going again. It wasn't going to be enough. Not for the machines that camped outside our gates.

We stared out over the backs of the hulking factories, the boutiques and arcades, the once-teeming shops of Trade that could sell you anything you could think of and a few things you couldn't. I let my gaze follow the Spine up, Over, on towards Heights, where the aspiring classes lived, looking up and wishing that they too could afford to live in Clouds – vast platforms that lurked over the city, stole the sun from underneath. Just visible above them in the dusk was Top of the World, now Perak's domain. Where Ministry had long ruled with a jackboot and a prayer. It was changing, but too slowly.

Another boom drew our gaze northwards, over the bulk of Trade where they'd never build. There were mountains over there, which had hemmed our city in, made us grow up rather than out. There were Storad there too now.

"How long, do you think?" I didn't need to say what I

meant; it was all anyone thought about, the question on everyone's lips. How long until we starved or they broke the gates down, whichever came first.

Perak stared out, his face a study in misery, in the responsibility I tried – and failed – to avoid. I had a sinking feeling in my stomach that he was here to do his usual trick of "dump Rojan in the shit". He never *meant* to. But he did it just the same. And just the same, no matter how much I ran from responsibility – and believe me, I tended to run like fuck – when little brother came asking, big brother didn't, couldn't, turn him down. I was too tired to run any more.

"Not long enough," he said.

"It was me they wanted handed over, I take it?"

"Hmm? Oh, yes. The Storad made a list of demands. That we open the gates, that we let them in peaceably, dismantle the factories, neutralise the mages, and also that we first hand over you for public execution as an indication of our good faith. In return they won't completely destroy the city. I think Dench is going to hold a grudge until the day he dies."

Ah, yes, the redoubtable Dench, he of the careworn face and the drooping moustache. Ex-head of the Specials, ex-right-hand man of Perak. Ex-friend of mine, I think it was safe to assume, partly because I'd dumped the bastard right into the Storad camp he was working with anyway. No real loss, except . . . except he'd have been a handy guy to have around right now because he was a sneaky, devious and downright underhand fighter. The kind that's great to have on your side, but not on theirs.

"But I told them, again, that we aren't negotiating," Perak said. "Not on any of it. The cardinals thought we could maybe appease them with you and talk about the rest. I said no. I don't think they're going to let it rest there, though. I think you need to be careful, Rojan."

"When don't I? But you've got a plan, right?"

It probably came out more sarcastic than I intended, because Perak always had plans, which was part of the trouble. Like the time he spent days "planning" a firecracker display that ended up taking out the front of the house, part of the walkway in front of it and the façade of the shop opposite. Having successfully scared the crap out of himself and everyone within about a mile's radius, he'd promptly fainted. Which left me, dazed and confused, to take the tongue-lashing of a lifetime from said shop's owner and, later, Ma. At first I'd been too groggy to protest, and by the time I wasn't it didn't matter – the shopkeeper thought I was guilty, so I was. Ma was too sick from the synthtox by then to disagree, and I didn't want to make things any worse for her than they already were.

So I spent six weeks refurbishing that sodding shop in payment, repairing things that had been broken even before Perak's little escapade. That shopkeeper really laid the screws on me, threatening to go back to Ma if I looked like I was slacking, threatening to make up all sorts of shit. Ma couldn't take it, so I did. And Perak? Perak said he was sorry, and meant it, and then went back to daydreaming about what other chemicals he could mix together to explode.

At the time it made me want to strangle him, made me desperate not to be the adult in that family when I was barely in my teens. Made me desperate to run away from my responsibilities, which I duly did just as soon as Ma died. Looking at Perak now though, I thought that his daydreams were just his escape from what was happening to us, to Ma, same as running away from responsibility was mine. Because he wasn't dreaming any more.

"I have a plan, or rather Lise does," he said now.

"That explains the smell in the lab."

Lise's speciality was chemicals, and the stench of whatever she was brewing up pervaded the lab, the pain room and our offices. The colours were quite pretty, if you didn't mind an accompanying whiff that could make your eyeballs pop out of their head. Today's brew had been a particularly acrid-smelling choke that threatened to make my throat close up. Hell only knew what she meant to do with it.

Perak's smile was thin, like he was, like we all were. "But that's not why I'm here. Or maybe partly. I need you to go to the 'Pit."

"What? What for? I've got enough to deal with, what with trying to find mages, trying to keep them fed, everything else, without traipsing off to the 'Pit." That wasn't why I didn't want to go, naturally. The 'Pit held memories I wasn't sure I wanted to revisit but I wasn't about to say that out loud, especially not with Jake within earshot. I like to at least pretend I'm heroic in front of her.

"Look at me, Rojan. I've got a city load of starving people, Outside I've got Storad trying to batter their way in; inside I've got a load of cardinals that are worse than useless, they're actively trying to counteract everything I do. I'm fairly sure half of them are trying to work out how to bribe their way out of the Mishan gate on the other side. They pretty much all want to hand you over to buy some time. I've got guards who are afraid to guard anything, Specials who are still smarting over what you did to Dench, and Dench telling the Storad all our little secrets. And down in the 'Pit I have tunnels. I don't know how many, or where most of them are, but I do know that if we don't find them the Storad will, and they'll use them, because that'll be one of the secrets Dench will have mentioned. Storad have been poring over the mountainsides; I've been watching them. So have the cardinals, and they're panicking. The Storad are going to find those tunnels eventually and I want to be prepared for when Dench uses them."

A long time ago, when we were just a castle in a handy pass through the mountains with a warlord who could serve as the definition of "sneaky", he'd had a load of tunnels made. Devious tunnels that you wouldn't find unless you fell into them, tunnels that not coincidentally led straight from the keep of the castle to the rear of where any army stupid enough to try to siege us would camp. Which would be great, if we knew where they all were.

I sighed inwardly – I had the feeling I knew what was coming, that I'd already lost this battle. I skipped over the predictable argument and went straight to the "What is it you want me to do?"

Perak's smile became more genuine, and he looked less tired. "Go to the 'Pit. Find whatever tunnels you can, so we can have them blocked up. Lise has a plan in mind for one of them, if you can find one that opens out near where the Storad are camped. With a bit of luck, getting you out of the cardinals' sight for a while may help too."

"When you say 'find whatever tunnels', can I take it this means even you don't know where they are?"

"Not all of them, no."

"Perak, I really don't know if I'm the best guy for this job. A structural engineer would be better, surely?"

"I need you out of the way *right now*, before you get bundled off and sent to Dench. It might give me some time to smooth things over with the cardinals, especially if I can tell them the tunnels aren't a problem any more. Where better to be out of the way than the 'Pit?"

"Surely you've got men down there already? Men who'd be better at it than me?"

"Look, those tunnels are our weakest point bar the gates. I want to be *sure*, and for that I need to use someone I can trust. I wouldn't trust a guard further than I could spit him, and the

Specials . . . well, after Dench, trust isn't something I have in them. You, Pasha, Dendal, Lise, Jake . . . you're all I've got that I can truly rely on. It was Dendal's idea. He said the thought of bacon would be enough to persuade you, and it'd make a handy training exercise for some of the younger mages."

There was that word again, "rely". Much as I hated it, it was flattering in a way.

"Well, I suppose— Wait, did you say bacon?" If there is one thing in this world that may, perhaps, persuade me there is a Goddess and she looks down on us with something approaching kindness, it's bacon. Hot, crispy, fat bacon, all golden and crunchy around the edges. My stomach contracted painfully at the thought, and the remembrance of what I was actually going to be eating later – half a bowl of mouldy-looking mush, if I was lucky. If I wasn't lucky, it would have weevils in it.

"The Storad had a supply train in yesterday. It brought about a hundred pigs, among other things." Perak tried to suppress a smile. This was his big persuading move. Which was annoying, especially when you considered that it was, in fact, persuading me.

I stared at him while my mouth daydreamed. A hundred pigs. A *hundred*. That was a lot of bacon, and I'd have forked my own eye out just for one measly, glorious rasher. So it was my stomach rather than my brain that said, "All right, we'll do it."

*

It needed a bit of arranging, so I was left to my own devices for a while. Black shapes kept swimming past my eyes, the voice kept on in my head. I needed sleep, but my stupid conscience would give me lots of lovely dreams that I didn't want to think about. It was starting to get dark, and that meant that at least one person of my acquaintance would be around, one person who might be able to help me with those shapes.

A frigid wind swept into the city, crept through every crack and crevice so I was frozen to the bone long before I got to Erlat's.

Erlat's house wasn't far away from the lab, in the area Under Trade where the rich boys came to play if they were feeling a bit adventurous but not quite so brave as to try Under proper. It's a haven for smooth bars that sell – all right, used to sell – overpriced "authentic" beer, set to the beat of dancers that at least probably didn't have the pox and probably weren't out of their heads on Rapture. You know, kind of fake shabby, just so people could say they'd tried Under and lived to tell the tale. I often wanted to take one of the patrons down to the real Under, but I suspected they'd last about half a heartbeat before they had no clothes on their backs, and possibly no lips to brag with.

Erlat's place isn't a bar, but home to one of the other reasons the rich boys came down to play – women. Over Trade, well, it's all pious and Ministry-run, the Goddess looking over everyone's shoulder to make sure they behave. Not exactly conducive to Erlat's business. Frankly, I'm surprised the Buzz didn't get more trade than it did, given that. But it got enough and Erlat's house, being fairly new and full of "exotic" ladies from the 'Pit with that blue-white undertone to their skin and oddly alluring accent, had been a hit.

Kersan met me at the door with the news that Erlat wasn't in, but also told me where she was and that he was sure she would be pleased to see me. So I took myself off to a small and discreet bar not far into the Buzz proper. Not too bad, this one: it had actual carpet on the floor, even if was so stained I couldn't tell the colour. Or maybe that was the "discreet" lighting that meant I had to grope my way to the bar to find a drink.

I sat at the bar, tried to look into murky corners without seeming obvious about it, and wished Erlat had been at home instead.

The place wasn't full, unsurprisingly. They didn't have much behind the bar that didn't have a good chance of making me blind, even in a place as up-market as this. Shortages were really starting to bite. For most of us anyway – Ministry men still had money, food, probably whatever they wanted. They were conspicuous down here the same way a slug is conspicuous in your dinner. Chubby soft hands waved money, more money that I'd seen in months, perhaps even years. The girls – classy and tastefully dressed but still working, and still wanting to get themselves fed – clustered round them.

A boom-shudder made the barman hang on to his glasses. One escaped and flew off a shelf to shatter on the floor. By the look of things, it wasn't the first. One of the girls let out a little scream of surprise at the noise, but the drunken Ministry boys laughed and groped and promised them the world, promised them a way out of this, out of Mahala. The girls laughed in return but there was no mistaking the fear in their eyes – that this was the only way out they had, sucking up to smug pricks like this.

The barman finished sweeping up the glass and came over. He checked me out, took in the imitation-Specials look with an air that said he didn't believe it for a second, before he raised an eyebrow inviting me to state my drink. I considered my finances, and what he had behind the bar. Screw it, you only live once. "Whatever won't kill me."

A conspiratorial wink, a quick check to make sure the Ministry boys weren't watching, and the barman slid out a bottle. Something brown and rich-looking flowed into the glasses.

"I'm shutting up after tonight," he said, as though to thin air. "Got nothing left to sell any more. Except moonshine that'd take the varnish off the saints and martyrs, and this one bottle. Fed up with Ministry coming to rub our faces in it, even more than usual too. Been promising the girls everything – not just money, no, the chance to get out, the chance to live. They don't actually follow through, naturally. They're just using it for a chance at free girls. And the girls are desperate enough to take a gamble that they might come through. Some of them, anyway."

We raised a glass each, and I savoured the taste of real, good booze. It'd been a while. Then I saw where the barman was looking.

A far dark corner. Erlat was sitting with a guy, Ministry perhaps because he was smooth and fat and smug as hell. He patted her hand and she laughed, and she looked like she meant it too. I turned back to my glass of heaven and left her to it.

Erlat is . . . I find it hard to say what Erlat is, or was. One of the most beautiful women I'd never tried to take to bed. Not because of what she did for a living – I was no better and the only difference was I didn't charge – but because of the way she had of unbalancing me, taking what I thought I knew about myself and the world around me and turning it on its head.

After a second swig, the barman and I weren't alone as Erlat joined us, but he knew his job well enough and went off to count the pieces of glass left on the floor or something.

Erlat looked tired today, but still had the serene grace that I so admired in her. She'd seen more, endured more than I'll ever have to and she took it all with barely a ripple in her calm – a smooth and polished piece of jade, reflecting you back at yourself.

I often thought she was the strongest woman I knew. No, she didn't have Jake's swords or the ability to slice a man to ribbons, but it was there, none the less. A strength that sometimes was hidden, but was even stronger because of it. Which was why, when my brain wanted to rebel, run amok and perhaps eat me alive, it was Erlat I turned to.

The basis of my and Erlat's relationship was simple. No, I was not and never had been a customer. The thought of it made me itch, somehow, though she'd offered me freebies often enough, probably because it made her laugh when I stumbled out a "No thanks." No, the basis of it all was that she could be herself with me, and I could be myself with her. We didn't need to pretend, though we often did anyway.

I never heard the black at Erlat's house, I didn't know why, but we weren't at her house today, and she was – I don't know. Perhaps seeing her somewhere else, seeing her laughing at someone else like she did with me . . . the black was bad, a constant seething in my head, and it wasn't going away, it was getting worse.

"Rojan, how surprising to see you in a bar." Her mouth taunted me with an impish grin and she smoothed the dark hair elegantly coiled at the nape of her neck. "What brings you here?"

I watched her client shrug an expensive-looking coat on and leave. He looked shifty, glancing all around before he braved the door.

"You, naturally."

Her smile became strained. "Can I have some of that?"

I handed over the glass and wondered what was wrong.

Definitely something up. Erlat took a delicate sip, licked her lips at the taste and set the glass down. "Is he gone?"

"Who, your friend? Yes, he's gone."

A subtle alteration in her, the slight relaxation of her shoulders and her mouth didn't look quite so set. "Good. Gives me the creeps, but luckily he's just a talker, mostly anyway. Pays me to listen to him and laugh at his jokes. Pathetic, really. But I'm glad you came. It was you he was talking about today."

"Well, why not? I'm a popular man."

That got me a glare so I caught the barman's eye and another glass appeared next to Erlat. The barman retired with his drink and kept an eye on the last few Ministry men down the end of the bar.

Erlat poured herself a good slug of the booze. She seemed to be gathering herself for something, so I let her.

"The Storad want you dead, you know that, of course? Of course. You stopped their previous plan, they don't want you messing with this one. But that man, my creepy talker, isn't Storad, and isn't working for them either. But he still wants you dead or, if not dead, then in the hands of people you probably don't want to be in the hands of. Good thing it's dark in here or the evening could have ended before it's begun."

"He can join the queue." I suspected I sounded far more blasé than I felt, but people wanting me dead was getting old, though no less worrying. "What's his reason?"

One shoulder went up in a subtle shrug. "He's not Storad; he's Mishan. One of their ambassadors, as it happens. They've been coming in dribs and drabs, negotiations and so on. Ministry likes to keep them entertained, and we were hired. He's got a fondness for my girls, me, so he's kept on coming even though most of the rest are back the other side of their gate. This one is a liaison supposedly, between the Mishans and the Ministry. Trade, food, what we're bartering, all that sort of thing. Including cardinals."

"We're bartering cardinals? I don't suppose we get much for them."

"For the Goddess's sake!" Erlat slammed her glass on the bar, bringing a few drunkly interested looks from the Ministry boys down the other end. "Can't you take this seriously? *Me* seriously? I'm trying to help you here, help us all, and all you're doing is making fun."

I shut my eyes and tried not to see the things swimming there before I snapped them open again and nodded a sorry. "All right. Mishan liaison wants me, dead or not so dead. What for?"

Erlat settled down again. "Some of the cardinals are, well, in talks shall we say? Not official ones either. One or two have already sneaked their families over, and they're just waiting for the right time to run themselves, before the Storad get here. The Mishans want the best deal in return. Money, goods, guns – you name it, they're trying to get the cardinals to pay it. But they aren't forgetting that if the Storad win, the

Mishans might well be next on the list of places and people for them to destroy. They've hated each other a long time, and until now Mahala has been the only thing that's kept them from trying to rip each other's throats out. How we made all that money, right? So one of the prices the Mishans are demanding in return for saving a few cardinal skins is you and Lise."

"Lise? But—"

"But nothing. Lise is a damned genius and they know it as well as you do. If Perak wasn't Archdeacon but was still inventing guns and all the rest, they'd ask for him too. As it is, he'd just be a bonus. The Mishans need someone to make things for them, or to show them how to make guns and whatever else so they can defend themselves when – and as far as they're concerned it is a when, not an if – the Storad destroy us and start threatening them. And they want you handed over as an initial peace offering, so they can give you to the Storad if they need to."

The only word that came to mind was "Shit."

"Quite."

"Does Perak know about this?"

"I suspect so, or at least he guesses. Jake's mentioned it once or twice – I think she was hoping I'd find out what I could. I'll tell Perak as soon as I can; at least he might be able to keep Lise safe."

All of a sudden that bold cardinal's snide words didn't seem quite so much bluster, and Perak wanting me out of harm's way made a lot more sense. So did getting out of this bar about now.

I slapped down the last of my money on the bar, took what was left of the bottle and offered my arm to Erlat.

"Perhaps you'd like an escort home?"

She took my arm and I got a proper smile out of her at last. "Only if you promise to finish that bottle with me. Maybe take me up on my offer for once, and let me ruin you for other women. And to be *careful*, whatever it is you're planning on doing. A corpse would suit them just as well."

"I promise faithfully on the Goddess's fictional arse to both finish the bottle and be as careful as I can. That do?"

And there, a laugh that lightened all the black thoughts in my head. "It's all I'm going to get, isn't it?"

The streets were lonely and dark, but I was sure I saw a pale face turned up to watch me as we passed.

That pale face bothered me, a lot. I couldn't be sure it was the same one that I'd seen earlier when I was with Halina, but in light of what the cardinals had argued, and what Erlat had told me, taking chances seemed stupid. Especially if it wasn't me the Mishans were after – there was Lise to warn too. So, reluctantly because Erlat's house was a safe haven and I wanted that right then, I didn't stay there once that bottle was finished. I made sure I didn't have too much of it too.

I even kept part of my promise to Erlat about being careful and rearranged my face, just a touch, so that I didn't look like me but instead like some blandly forgettable guy from Under.

Pale Face was still there, lurking, but I was pretty sure I fooled him – men came and went at an alarming rate from Erlat's house so I was just one of several, even at that hour. But he was still there, and that opened up a whole load of possibilities in my head. I hurried as quickly as I could without looking suspicious and got to the lab.

The office was quiet as I passed, dark except for the flicker of Dendal's candles. The lab was quiet too – it was the middle of the night. That hadn't stopped the boom-shudders from keeping on coming though, and another one rocked the lab just as I got there. A few heartbeats later something smashed inside – call it a gut feeling or paranoia, but I was pretty sure it wasn't the usual sort of smash that came after the boom-shudders.

I had my pulse pistol out and the door half open even before I thought about it. Another smash, and someone swearing – Lise.

"Oh, you Goddess-fucked bastard, do you know how long it took me to make that?"

By the time I got to her, whoever had been doing the smashing was regretting it. The lab was in near-darkness, just one faint Glow globe hanging over Lise's desk. At the edge of its light, a man hunched over his stomach, holding on like he thought it'd fall out otherwise. The blood was very dark on his hands, and it was on the long screwdriver that Lise had taken to keeping with her at all times. I don't suppose he'd have been all that comforted to know she could have called upon any number of torturous instruments if she'd wanted.

Lise herself stood under the light, looking pale but furious in a blizzard of bits of machine, even worse than normal. Two of Perak's guards whom he'd assigned to protect Lise and the lab lay unconscious a bit further in. They obviously weren't up to the job.

Lise caught sight of me and stepped back from the man on the floor, from her screwdriver sticking out of his stomach. "Rojan, I – oh, I – I – he broke my gyroscope! Bastard. It took me *days* to get it all aligned properly. And he wanted me to leave, he kept grabbing me and . . . "

She sat down in the chair behind her desk, hard enough I thought the legs might snap, a hand over her mouth as the man on the floor looked up, still with a faint look of surprise. By the time I got to her, he'd keeled over and stopped breathing, and the pool of blood had reached Lise's feet. She stared down at it like she couldn't work out what it was.

"Rojan, I – I—" Normally all poise and technical know-how, Lise was reduced to a stammer. Shock, most certainly, and I couldn't say I'd be any better if I'd just stabbed a man with a screwdriver. Especially not at just-turned-sixteen. I definitely wouldn't have pulled myself together as quickly as Lise did.

"He said Perak sent him," she said. Without saying anything about it, we held hands. Hers was cold, with a faint tremor, but her voice was steady enough once she got going, started to think in that logical way that always left me floored. "The orders even had Perak's seal on, look. Only . . . only Perak never *sends* for me. He comes here – I think he likes it in here with all the machines. Better than cardinals, he says. More reliable, less likely to argue. Even if he did want me to go to Top of the World, he wouldn't *order* me. And he needs me here now, more than ever, so I knew something was odd. But when I said something, and one of the guards went to take a look at the orders, he, he – I don't know, it's a blur really. But he took out the guards and said I was going with him whether I liked it or not. He grabbed me and that's when the gyroscope broke. I just meant to keep him away from me. I didn't mean to kill him."

I pulled her in and gave her a hug, and she let me for once, even hugged me back. Not for long, but it was enough to know this had scared her, badly. Scared me pretty bad too.

First things first. I made sure the door was bolted and secure – since the last time someone had tried for the lab, I'd made sure there was extra security, and so had Perak, though we'd had to be subtle because Lise wasn't keen on being mollycoddled as she called it. Then I checked the guards – both out cold, who knew how. Finally, the body. He didn't have anything on him that was any use for working out who he was, but it didn't take much to guess, at least broadly.

"One of the cardinals' men, isn't he?" Lise said. "I thought it was you they were after, to give to the Storad. Or the machines, you know, try to sabotage them like they did before."

"It's not just the Storad who're after me. Or you. The Mishans are quite keen on acquiring us both, so I hear." I sat back and thought for a minute. "All right. A cardinal's man, probably, or perhaps working for the Mishans. Hard to say, or if it's a cardinal which one. I could find out, but dead bodies are hard. So we concentrate on what we do know. We need you here, no doubt about it. Without you doing your thing, we're screwed. Without me, there's only going to be so much Glow to go around. We can't just go and hide. Well, I can in the 'Pit for a while tomorrow, but not forever. What's the most secure room in this place?"

Lise indicated a door in the far corner, which as far as I knew was always kept locked. "In there, only—"

"Only nothing. Firstly, you're going to go in there and stay in there until I can get some better guards. Keep working, because we need you to do that. But I can make you less . . . findable, at least for now. And you can play with chemicals to your heart's content. Make this place a death trap for whoever you don't want in here, and that's anyone you don't know, OK?"

She took a deep breath and squared her shoulders. That donkey line of hers, the stubborn crease in her forehead, was good for more than just thwarting her brothers. "OK. What are you going to do?"

I sat back. What could I do about cardinals? Or Mishans even? Not much, or not right away. I wasn't going to say that. "First, I'm going to change your face, just a bit. Make you less of a target. Then I'm going to let Perak know. If he warns the cardinals off, perhaps . . . I don't know. We'll think of something. It's just for long enough, right? Just until we finish this thing. To do that, we need you now more than anyone – we can't do this without you."

I thought she was going to say something else for a moment – "Are you sure we *can* finish this?", perhaps. She had that kind of look on her face, but not for long.

"All right. Will it hurt?"

"Not you," I said, and wished I hadn't when she flinched at the reminder of where all the juice was coming from. "Not much, no. No more pain than my hand is giving me anyway. How many warts do you want?"

She smacked my shoulder but I got a laugh. "None! Now do it."

So I changed her face. Not much, but enough that she didn't look like my sister any more. It almost certainly wouldn't work for long, because the cardinals – hell, everybody by now – knew that I could disguise myself and other people. Then again, it wouldn't last all that long without me concentrating on it. Long enough for Perak to sort something out, I hoped.

Lise ran her hands over her face. "That feels really bizarre."

"Welcome to Rojan's world. Now get yourself in that room. I'm going to get in touch with Perak and see what we can do."

I helped her get all her bits together, all the plans and tools and Goddess-only-knew-what else. She wouldn't let me in the room though. "Not yet. The machine might not work. I don't want to get anyone's hopes up."

I waited until she'd locked the door behind her, and went to find some guards to hopefully do a better job of guarding the lab before I woke Dendal and got him to contact Perak.

Chapter Four

Another night with no sleep was just what I needed. Not. Perak hadn't been asleep either when I'd got hold of him, but he was incandescent when he found out what had happened. That was clear despite the tinny echo of Dendal's communication conduit, as was a bone-deep despair of ever being able to do anything, anything at all, without the cardinals trying to fuck it up.

"But Lise is safe, you say?"

"For now. She doesn't look like her, and she's locked herself in. But for anyone determined enough, that won't be a problem."

I was fairly sure I heard some muffled swearing at the other end. "Fine. Leave the cardinals to me. Oh, and Erlat's Mishan-liaison friend – I got her message a few minutes ago. I'd incur some of the Goddess's displeasure and lie through my teeth, but they expect that. Maybe Erlat can help . . . yes. She'd be perfect. Listen – you need to get out of the way, even more so now. Get down to the 'Pit as soon as you can. With any luck – no, I won't have the cardinals in line, I doubt I ever will. But I should have something worked out. Look, the sooner we get going, the sooner you two will be safe, the sooner we'll *all* be safe. In the meantime I'll do what I can for Lise, with what men I can spare. I'll sort something. You know I will. But while she can stay in the lab, I need you out of the way. I'll tell everyone . . . well, I'll tell them that Lise isn't at the lab any more, that I've moved her somewhere. You too. Maybe they'll believe it, maybe they won't. But I need you down there, finding me a tunnel I can use."

He was as good as his word, and Specials were swarming over the lab long before the sun rose. Lise was as safe as anyone was going to be.

So there I was, early the next morning, cursing the stomach that had made me agree to this particular escapade, and it had a lot to answer for.

We didn't take most of the new mages down to the 'Pit – as nursemaids go, I am crap. After a quick run through their paces, Pasha and I decided that taking the younger ones would be madness. Half of them didn't even know what their talents were yet, and the other half were at the perilous stage of knowing just enough to be dangerous to themselves and everyone else around them. But Halina proved to be as capable as I'd thought, and levitation might be handy when you were planning a quick pig-snatch-and-grab. So Pasha and I had asked her and she'd looked blandly curious and said OK.

We made our way down to Boundary, trying to be unobtrusive. I'd disguised myself a bit, a quick remoulding of my features. My conversation with Erlat was playing on my mind, along with about a thousand other things. Pasha and Halina noticed the change, but Pasha knew enough not to say anything and maybe Halina thought I did it all the time. Even disguised, I was twitchy. Was that man on the corner watching me? Was that bold cardinal hatching a neat little plan to hand me over to the Storad, or one of his comrades planning the same to hand me over to the Mishans? Was that junkie on the corner one of their men? It would almost be a relief to get to the 'Pit.

From Boundary, we rode down in the lift that lived in a once-hidden access point to a place most had believed was sealed off and free of people, a cesspit of synthtox and chemicals that could eat you up from the inside. It hadn't been quite as bad as that – the chemicals would probably take ten times as long to kill you as the people that had, in fact, lived in the 'Pit.

I shut my eyes and concentrated on the thought of food, real food, beef and gravy and all those things I'd probably never see again, had become addicted to over a very short space of time when they'd been available to me down in the 'Pit. The thought of fat, crispy bacon on the hoof – trotter, whatever – in the Storad camp took my mind off the fact that the lift was coffin-shaped. And badly maintained. And a long, *long* way from the bottom.

Pasha looked surprised when I offered to go first, but that was purely a face-saving move. I'd have at least five minutes to have a little gibber of terror and relief at the bottom while the lift fetched the next person. I managed to pull myself together by the time Halina stepped out and looked round with a wide-eyed stare and a wrinkled nose. The smell of synth was pretty strong down there, enough that it felt like it was stripping the inside of my throat of its skin.

While we were on our own, as Pasha came down in the jolting lift, Halina gave me a sideways glance that spoke volumes, mostly of a series of books called "You Look Like Something That Just Dropped Out Of My Nose, Only With Less Charm".

She was looking pretty fine. Lastri had dug out some of her old clothes, or so she said. I really couldn't imagine Lastri in this little number though – a clingy shirt in a blue bright enough to have an eye out, cinched at the waist to show off Halina's figure in all the very best ways, and a pair of close-fitting trousers that brought me out in a sweat.

She'd not forgiven me for luring her away from the Stench under false food pretences; at least I assumed that's why she kept giving me the old side-eye. Then again, she and Lastri had been very chatty, and no doubt Lastri had given her a highly colourful and probably not especially accurate character assassination of me and my ways. I say inaccurate – Lastri only knew the half of what I got up to, so any assassination attempt would be manslaughter at best.

What Halina said in the end, given that, came as a surprise. "Dendal says you're pretty good at this magic. Says I should look at what you and Pasha do, and try to follow it. But he said a lot of stuff, and not all of it made sense."

"That sounds like Dendal. I—"

"He also said I should ignore any of your attempts to take me out or sweet-talk me. I'm inclined to agree with him on that point. So no funny business, all right?"

I tried the old faithful, never-fails smile. "Business will be strictly unfunny, I guarantee. I have sworn off women." I tried to intimate with only facial gestures that I would fall off that wagon at the first hint of provocation.

My smile failed: she looked distinctly underwhelmed by my promise.

"And don't you forget it," she snapped. "I've had two cardinals have their flunkies ask me to lure you somewhere dark and out-of-the-way already. I'm no fan of the Ministry but I'm not beyond actually doing it, if you piss me off."

It looked like I was behaving for the time being, which was a shame because there's nothing like a flirt to take your mind off the damnfool thing you're about to do.

We made our way out into the 'Pit proper, a maze of streets and scrunched-up buildings that hid behind a curtain of the constant rain – run-off from above which never stopped, which ran and dripped and pooled in glorious decay among the roots of Mahala. Towers loomed over us, dark and forbidding now, just shells that held up the rest of the city above, with girders criss-crossing, buttressing. No one manned the cages that dangled uselessly above us, which had once whirled and clanked in a complicated dance as they took people where they needed to go. The 'Pit was a husk, empty of life and sound and all the vibrancy that had once made me think I could quite enjoy life down here, even if said life was cheaper than shit.

Pasha didn't say anything – this was home to him, or had been, and now it was nothing. His face lost that contented, secret little grin I'd got used to just lately and he looked sallow and gaunt under the sparse rend-nut-oil lamps that lit the street. He took out a floppy old hat I recognised, slapped it on to protect him from whatever the hell was in the water that dripped on us, then shoved his hands in his pockets, hunched his shoulders and went on.

Halina had no such qualms. She looked about with calculating eyes, maybe assessing the value of everything she saw. What she did see wasn't much – the Downsiders had abandoned their homes when the 'Pit was unsealed, gladly, but they'd brought everything that they could up with them. All that was left was what even they didn't think was worth anything.

We trudged the streets, heading for the tunnels, the few that we knew of. For the castle that lay at the heart of them, at the heart of Mahala. Halina stopped dead when the castle loomed out from behind a huge tower that supported the weight of the city above it. From here, mostly all you could see was the curtain wall, with the keep rising up out of the top like some demented bread that had been overloaded with yeast, but the sheer size of it was enough to batter the brain into submission. I'd seen the castle before, and wished I hadn't, so Pasha and I merely carried on. Halina ran to catch up after a while.

"Is it true?" she asked me in a whisper, as though she didn't want to disturb the ghosts that lay thick about us.

"Which part?"

She gave me that sideways look again, like the worth she was assessing was mine. I probably equalled half a rat, by her sneer.

"The pain factories. They were down here, right, like the sheets said? The mages? Dendal said not all of the mages, but still, enough, right? And the Downsiders helped them, and the Little Whores. And they – I mean, Pasha's a Downsider and a mage and—"

She yelped when I gripped her wrist so hard my knuckles cracked. "Shut the fuck up. Especially shut the fuck up in front of Pasha. You don't rate me much, I get that. But don't talk about that in front of him, don't even think it because he can hear that too. Don't think of him in the same thought as them – hell, don't even think about him at all, especially not with that sneer on your face. Or you'll rate me much, much lower. Or higher, depending on if you're scoring on how much

I will zap your arse, because I will. You know nothing about him, all right?"

Her face looked like I already had zapped some tender part of her. "But, I—"

"You know what you think you know from the sheets you saw every day down in the Stench, when people were done with them. The sheets tell you shit, excepting what a few cardinals want you to think. You know crap-all." I took a deep breath. "Look, I don't really want to go in there again, and I know that Pasha doesn't, for reasons that would blow your mind if you knew the half of them. But we have to, so we're going to. It would help if you kept your mouth shut about the rest until you have half a clue what you're talking about."

I'll give her this: she shut up, though I could tell she didn't like it. That sideways glance fell on me more and more often as we went, the lip never ceased to curl, but she carefully avoided looking at Pasha and every now and again a frown would crease her forehead like she was really thinking.

The closer we got to the castle, the quieter Pasha got, the more his shoulders hunched. I couldn't say I blamed him – the place didn't exactly hold happy memories for me either. Halina walked behind us, subdued and thoughtful.

We reached the massive bulk of the outer wall. The main gate – an arching monstrosity bedecked with statues of what had presumably once been great warriors, now blank-faced with time and synth – was still blocked off, but one of the smaller ones had been freed up and two guards lounged at either side looking bored. A glance at the official pass Perak had given us and we were through into one of the closes – a series of squares surrounded by buildings that looked like they should be falling down. Houses crammed into spaces too small, bleeding into each other in an incestuous orgy of bricks, gently rusting girders and stone blocks, broken tiles and crumbling mortar. Narrow, twisting alleyways snaked between the squares, taking whichever path they could in the tangle. Cracked cobbles were slick under our feet, but the air, while harsh and ferociously cold, was mercifully free of the sounds that had long reverberated around the stone. I could see the echo of them on Pasha's tight-lipped face none the less.

"So where are these tunnels?" Halina asked.

A fair enough question. "Most of the ones we know about lead from these squares. Some are pretty short, and now only lead out into the 'Pit, where the city grew after they were made. But some – maybe six or seven, maybe more, maybe less, maybe none – will take us Outside. If we can find them."

"Outside," she said. "Doesn't seem possible. I mean, they always said there was no Outside . . . but it's got to be real now, right? Where else are the Storad coming from? It just doesn't *feel* real."

"It will." Pasha shook out the map that Perak had given us – he'd had his men scour this castle thoroughly since the 'Pit had opened up, and especially since Dench had defected, more or less willingly. The old archdeacon had kept down here a secret from all but a few Upside, and except for a couple of shorter tunnels that he'd used and those that Perak's men had found, no one knew where they all were.

So the map was sketchy, but it was better than nothing.

"Where do we start?" Pasha asked.

A few hesitant dotted lines on the map showed where there might, possibly, be tunnels. Fewer bold lines showed where some had been found and blocked.

"Perak's had his guards searching, and they've found some, but he needs most of his men up elsewhere, at the gates," I said. "Things are getting tricky down by the Mishan gate, so I heard. Let's just hope we don't get another riot, because that's all we damned well need. Perak's left us a few men though. They're based in the barbican."

Luckily the map showed us the route to get there too, because the castle was a maze of squares and alleys that looked like they went in the right direction before they doubled back on themselves. When the mages had been based here, it had all been closed off, and things added to make getting in, or around, harder – doorways bricked up, false doorways added, alleys that led to nowhere.

Halina's silky shirt, and the way it was moving over the more obvious parts of her anatomy, was doing very strange things to me. To distract me, and in the interests of knowing who the hell you're working with, and maybe having them not hate your guts for threatening them, and not *just* because she looked stupendous, I got talking to her. I had a hope that if I was at least nominally nice, maybe she wouldn't think of taking those cardinals' flunkies up on their offer. I was even fairly gentlemanly and asked her about herself, which earned me a knowing raised eyebrow from Pasha.

"I'd never been out of the Stench before you came," she said in answer to my question. She kept looking at me askance, as though I wasn't what she'd expected or the wastrel she'd been told about. She got over it. "Most of us never leave – never get the chance, which is pretty much the only reason I came with you. You didn't tell me I'd be working for Ministry though."

"Would it have made a difference? I mean, for the chance to get out, do something. Eat, for example."

She cast me a sharp glance and thought about it for a while. "Maybe not. Pasha's already taught me more about using magic than I'd managed to teach myself over the years." She even managed to keep the sneer at him being a Downsider out of her voice.

"For someone who taught herself, you're pretty good," he said. He hadn't seemed to notice her antipathy, though I knew he had, that it burned him inside, but he never let it colour his words. He wasn't that kind of guy. "Wonder why we haven't found any more women mages?"

A softening of her sneer at the compliment, and then a wry laugh from Halina. "I expect there have been more of us, but maybe they all fall into the black."

"I'm not sure—" I said.

"Well, women tend to have more pain in their lives as a

matter of course." She laughed at what was probably a comical look of confusion on my face. "You know, monthlies and such. Don't cross me then, I warn you, because that constant ache makes me formidable, not to mention touchy. You may not survive the encounter, for all your super-duper magic power. Then there's childbirth. I mean, sure, the doctors have painkillers, but no reputable doctor would come Under, and especially not to the Stench. And there's ways and ways of not going through it, but all the docs give you is something for the guy to take, and who's going to believe them when they say, 'Hey, babe, I'm safe'? Not me, that's for damned sure. I've seen too many girls caught out by that one."

I was pretty sure she didn't see my guilty flinch – I'd been known to use those words myself in the, ahem, heat of the moment.

"I figured out about the black fairly early on," Halina continued, "and no way am I going to just take some guy's word for it. So, I got pretty good at fending off attention. I don't want to go crazy popping out a baby. Dendal said he thinks that's what happens to women mages, or perhaps that's why we're rarer, because we're more likely to fall in. Best way to avoid that is to avoid men, the way I look at it."

My first thought was, naturally, *What a waste*, followed by *Well, that explains it*. Then I gave myself a mental slap, because she was the most experienced of the mages we'd found, and we needed her. Which was quickly followed by the thought that she'd be one hell of a challenge, and that's what I live for.

I must have given it away somehow, because she fixed me with a glare that promised I'd find out just how good she was at her magic if I tried anything. A reply to my own little threat earlier, and she meant it just as I had. So I didn't try a damn thing. I certainly thought about it though.

By the time we reached the inner gate to the keep – as hideously decorated with faceless statues, and as black with synth as the outer gate – and the guards that Perak had left there, I was impressed by more than just her shirt and what filled it. She was sharp, very sharp, and she had a firm grip on just what she could and couldn't do with magic. She also had a caustic tongue that made me feel like an optimist in comparison. In other words, I liked her – opinions about Downsiders excepted, and maybe that was just a matter of time – even if she didn't like me. I felt pretty confident that she was going to be a great addition to our little gang of mages. Maybe that would be enough, but I doubted it. Even down here, we could feel the boom-shudders as a tremor through our feet, a slight shaking of the walls around us that made my shoulder blades itch.

But for now, a simple little job of blocking tunnels, a smart, attractive woman next to me who presented the best kind of challenge. What could go wrong?

It started off all right – it always does. The guards, bored at being left to wander around down here where there wasn't much chance to bribe anyone and simultaneously grateful they weren't up by the gates where they could get shot at, had found several tunnels and made a start of blocking them from the castle end. They'd also done a few quick and dirty sorties to figure out where the tunnels led – mostly down by the gates of the castle leading out into the 'Pit, though they'd been overtaken by the growth of the city and led to places that were now inside its walls.

It didn't take much for Halina and me to block them more thoroughly. Me via rearranging a few bits of rock and wall into interesting shapes and her by levitating a few bits of handy rubble – otherwise known as what was left of some nearby houses – into place. She really was very good. It didn't hurt too much, and I made sure not to overdo it. We still had the pain lab to visit later on again, and overdoing it would be a bad, bad idea.

While we were doing that Pasha had a look around and managed to find one of the tunnels tentatively marked on Perak's map. Like all of them, it was cunningly disguised – what made them such a bitch to find, all thanks to our sneaky bastard warlord ancestor.

"It's a lot bigger than the rest," Pasha said as he led the way.

He wasn't joking either. The rest of the tunnels were narrow at the castle end, with slits for arrows, or nowadays guns, to shoot through, and bigger ones for a handy boulder or some hot oil to drop on an unsuspecting enemy. Perfect for defence. Even if they weren't now blocked up, it would take a handful of men to hold them against a hundred. The problem being, of course, that we'd never expected anyone from inside Mahala – the defected Dench – to use the knowledge of their existence against us, or that we'd need so many men up by the gates at the same time.

The tunnel Pasha had found would take a battalion to hold. The entrance, like most of the others, was hidden in what appeared to be a solid wall, in this case a blank three-storey-tall affair in one of the inner closes nearer the main keep. The mechanism that opened it was hidden inside a hollow brick – even if you knew where a tunnel was, finding the mechanism was like trying to find a fresh breeze in the Stench. When Pasha pulled on the lever for this one, half the wall rolled away on silent . . . hinges? Rollers? Who knew? Behind it the tunnel yawned off into darkness. No defences here, just wide-open tunnel, which was odd. A frigid wind made the skin on my face tighten and something else – no idea what, but in hindsight perhaps telling the future – made my balls shrivel.

"Much as I don't like to suggest it, I think we may need to check this one out before we seal it," Pasha said. "See where it goes. Why it's different. Maybe it'll be right for whatever Perak and Lise want to use it for. There's no one in it, anyway, I can tell you that."

"Much as I hate to admit it, I think you're right." The thought of it didn't fill me with confidence. I allowed myself one concession to self-preservation. "Perhaps taking a guard or two might be prudent?"

Pasha raised an eyebrow at that, but in the end he conceded it might be wise. A half-dozen guards lounged around the entrance looking bored, and when Pasha asked, four of them looked glad of the chance to do something. The other two waited at the entrance, ready to close the tunnel up, seal it as best they could if everything went tits-up. Not an inspiring thought. Slightly better was the fact that since Trade had started pounding out guns, all the guards had them.

The differences were plain to see inside the tunnel as well as at the entrance. The other tunnels were, shall we say, less crappy-looking than this one. They had dressed stone lining them, at least most of the way, frescos and murals all along the walls, a flat, paved road underfoot. This one had lumpy rock walls that looked half finished and an earth floor that had turned to dust so that little clouds puffed up with every step. Even with the breeze that brought goose bumps up all over, the air felt flat and dead.

"Hey, look." Halina bent down by one wall, just by the entrance. "I wonder what these do."

Pasha held his Glow light where she was looking. A series of what looked like lumps of stone poked out from the wall. I wouldn't have thought anything of it if they hadn't been so regular, like they were put there.

Halina reached out to tug on one, but I was quicker and grabbed her hand away. "The man who had these built was one sneaky little fucker. For all you know, that could bring down a ten-ton slab of rock on our heads."

We all looked up, but there was nothing to see except more rock. That didn't make me feel any better about those little lumps of stone.

"Let's just see where this goes, shall we?" I said. "And not touch anything on the way."

We crept on in, quiet as we could be, listening always for other footsteps ahead, for the sound of furtive breathing or the clank and jingle of the armour all the Storad wore. Every now and again Pasha would twist a finger and we'd stop while he listened, but each time he'd say they seemed far away – far enough to be at their camp probably, though not knowing how much this tunnel twisted it was hard to tell.

The tunnel seemed to go on for an age, mostly straight but with sudden twists and turns that appeared out of the gloom as we went forward, all with guns out, just in case. Every turn brought my heart into my mouth. What if there were Storad just around the corner, what if Pasha couldn't hear them, what if Dench had found a way to block him, what if, what if till my eyes went screwy.

The air got colder, the breeze brisker. The boom-shudder of the guns was felt more than heard in the castle, but the shudders got fainter and the booms got clearer as we went on. We had to be getting close to Outside. I could smell meat crisping already, though I brushed that off as wishful thinking. But the end of the tunnel meant Storad, though we'd heard nothing so far. Pasha handed me the lamp so he could twist his knuckles again and try to hear how far away the camp was.

Sadly, he should have tried about a hundred steps earlier. Then maybe we'd have had more notice and we could have retreated in style. Instead, the first we knew about anything was when Pasha's eyes flew wide open about half a heartbeat before something – a bullet as it turned out – pinged off the rock right by my head and zipped off down the tunnel behind us. I didn't even have time to say, "Shit," before a whole bunch of Storad appeared round the next bend, looking menacing in some weird sort of armour I'd never seen before and dark, twisted helmets. We were near the end, it seemed, and they'd snuck in since Pasha had last listened, or he'd been fooled by the twisting nature of the tunnels. Or maybe Dench really had discovered how to block him at close range.

Whatever, there was a brief, frozen moment in time as we all stared at each other before reality kicked in. We were seven. They were about twenty, with more coming round the corner, no longer caring about being quiet or sneaking. Big, nasty-looking men with guns in their hands.

We ran.

I'll say this about Halina, that girl could really shift, fast enough that I began to wonder if she'd bypassed those cardinals' flunkies and decided to leave me to the Storad herself. Probably helped that she wasn't actually on the ground but propelled herself through the air. I'd have given my left bollock to be able to do the same. I very nearly did give it too, when a bullet grazed the top of my thigh, leaving a burn, a rush of juice and a quick thanks that it hadn't been just that bit higher, thereby putting an end to my favourite hobby. I could have rearranged myself out of there, of course, but that took time and I had to sit down while I did it or I'd fall down. There was no way in the world I was sitting down while a bunch of Storad came for me with guns, so I ran with everyone else.

Unfortunately, it's quite hard to outrun a bullet. Pasha did his best to plant the idea in the shooters' minds that they might want to aim somewhere else, but I reckon it wasn't too easy while running away, plus the Storad language wasn't ours. Bullets zipped about all over the place. One of the guards fell just as we came to the next twist, and had no hope of getting out of the field of fire. Pasha and I picked him up by the shoulders and half dragged, half carried him around the bend, but he was already dead.

"Where in hell did they come from?" Pasha was wheezing like an old man and something, a bit of bullet or a scrap of shattered rock, had sliced a cut across one eyebrow. "One minute they weren't there, the next they were."

"I was hoping you'd tell me. Best answer, Dench is a tricky bastard. Now what?"

His eyes took on the dreamy look that meant he was listening in to people's thoughts. "They're slowing down. I can't hear them properly for some reason – they sound far away even though they aren't, and I don't know much Storad, but I *think* they don't want to come round that corner and find a bunch of guns in their faces."

"Can't say I blame them. How about we use the time to get the fuck out and see if we can block the tunnel? At least jam the door."

"Good plan."

I suppose we could have left a couple of people to slow them down in a rearguard action, but the guards were all piss-scared – this wasn't their usual kind of work. Now they were getting shot at, and while Pasha and I had grabbed their comrade and spent a few seconds deciding what to do, they'd been legging it as fast as they could.

Being the brave and heroic kind of guy I am, I ran after them. We played cat-and-mouse with the Storad, running between twists in the tunnel, hoping they wouldn't catch sight of us, or catch us with a bullet before we rounded another corner. Luck held out, mostly. One of the guards got a bullet in the arse, but he managed to stagger on out of sheer terror: mages weren't the only things lied about in the newssheets, the Storad had a pretty fearsome reputation as baby eaters and captured-person buggerers, and this time I had no idea how true any of it was. I didn't want to stop to find out either.

The Storad still weren't far behind when we got within sight of the entrance, though I'm sure hearing their breathing was just my imagination. The guards were already running for their lives across the close, leaving Halina by the mechanism. She shouted a few choice words after them, but she didn't run.

I was almost having an apoplexy by the time I made it to

the door, and that wasn't helped by the thought of a score of guns coming round the last twist. Halina didn't wait until we were fully through before she yanked on the door mechanism, but the damned thing wasn't built for speed. It glided across the opening like it had all the time in the world.

Too damned slow – the first bullets took a chunk of masonry out, scattering bits of shrapnel all over. More by luck than judgement a cloud of them took out the delicate mechanism, and the whole contraption ground to a halt.

"Fuck," Pasha muttered as he threw himself through the doorway and around a corner, out of the line of fire.

"You got that right." I was half a step behind him.

Halina yanked on the mechanism, but the door stayed where it was and laughed at us. More bullets whizzed past, making us all duck for cover.

"There was another lever inside to shut the door," I said from behind the false safety of a wall.

Halina shook her head. "The whole thing's jammed – there was a coupling inside it and that got smashed. What about the other ones? That you told me not to touch? Bet your life those do something."

"Got to be worth a go."

Only, naturally, getting to them meant crossing the line of sight of the guns that were rapidly approaching. Unless I used my juice.

I slid down the wall and worked as fast as I could. They weren't big, it shouldn't take much. A clench of my buggered hand, a quick spike of pain, a call of the black that I could shove back and down, for now, and the first lever moved. Nothing happened except the Storad got closer and I got more desperate. If they got inside the castle, or even if they got back to their camp and told everyone where this tunnel was, we were screwed. Worse than screwed.

How old were these levers? It didn't matter, all that mattered was whether they worked. Another burst of pain, another surge of juice. I overdid it, and the second lever snapped in two.

Pasha muttering behind me didn't really help, though I thought I could hear something odd down the tunnel, like two of the Storad had decided to get into a fist fight.

"Oh, for fuck's sake," Halina said, twisted her fingers and glared at the third lever as though it was personally thwarting her. It slid down like a dream, trailing a rumbling noise in its wake, followed rapidly by a thud like worlds colliding. A cloud of dust billowed out of the tunnel. Pasha swore violently to one side of me and clutched his head in his hands.

Nobody was shooting any more, which was a relief. Pasha didn't seem capable of talking – he was moaning fit to bust – as I took my life in my hands and peered into the dust.

"I thought you were going to leave us in there for a moment," I managed to pant out at Halina.

"Considered it," Halina said with a grin that could have felled angels. "You're a pain in the arse, but not that much. I may be tempted if that changes."

"Thanks. I think." The dust began to clear, and I began to wish it hadn't. Pasha's moans took on a whole new meaning.

I looked back to where the Storad had been about to leap out of the tunnel. "You know what I said about a ten-ton slab of rock?" I said. "I think I was right." Then I threw up.

Chapter Five

That sneaky old warlord who built the castle and its attendant tunnels knew what he was about all right. Turned out this particular tunnel was constructed, not to be found exactly, but to be just that little bit more findable than the rest. A sort of false hope for anyone looking, to lure them in and kill them with a series of fiendish traps, deadfalls, spikes and other nasty surprises which the Storad had been patiently dismantling or finding ways round. It also turned out that the lever I'd snapped, when fixed, raised the ten-ton slab. What was left underneath wasn't pretty.

The rest of the tunnel had various ingenious devices all along its length, at every twist and turn, all set to spring on anyone coming *in*, but not on anyone going *out*. If not for them, we'd have had about twice as many Storad to deal with as we had.

Goddess's tits, that ancestor of ours had a mean streak and

a very inventive mind, which had saved our arses for now, or at least slowed the Storad down. Perak had doubled the number of guards searching for the rest of the tunnels too, and Lise had an afternoon of fun dreaming up a few chemical traps that would terminally deter anyone wandering in.

Once Pasha had got over the shock of having all those voices suddenly scream in his head and then go deathly quiet, we had a bit more to go on too. We met Perak at the lab to fill him in.

"I'm fairly certain where the tunnel comes out," Pasha told him. "Right near their camp. Pretty close to one of the machines too. I don't speak much Storad and what I did get was fuzzy somehow, like someone was blocking me perhaps? Dench knows what I can do, so they'll be trying anything to stop me figuring out what they're up to. But I could hear some, and I could see the pictures in their heads."

Perak paced up and down. Jake watched him impassively, with Malaki, Dench's replacement as head of the Specials, next to her. I didn't much care for Malaki – he had an effortless "hard-arse bastard" look to him that recalled those not far-off days when I was likely to get arrested every time I cast a spell. That is, he looked like he could kill you without losing sleep over it, in fact he might even relish it. His face was impassive, grey and slab-sided like a badly made granite crypt. It made an interesting contrast to the smooth and sleek Specials uniform that was perfectly designed to help the wearer kill quickly and quietly while looking very scary indeed. His eyes took in everything and gave away nothing, and I'd yet to hear him say anything other than "Yes, Your Grace" when taking orders from Perak. All in all, a perfect specimen of Specialness, and enough to give me the heebie-jeebies.

"We're losing men left and right," Perak said. "Or about to. A number of guns have gone through the Mishan gate already, along with two cardinals. I've had a few subtle words with the remaining ones, but don't expect much joy from that – Mahala is falling apart and they know it. Half the remaining cardinals are in talks with the Mishans – secretly, so they think: I didn't let on that we knew, though they have to know we suspect. Some of the same ones are still hoping I'll turn you over to the Storad, or the Mishans, or don't care as long as they can get rid of you to *some*one. You keep that disguise on, Rojan, and stay where I can find you."

"They want Lise too," I said. "She—"

"Is constantly guarded, best I can spare. The Storad aren't interested in her as yet, as far as I know. That leaves the Mishan liaison, who we know does want Lise and is trying to find a cardinal to help him out. I've, er, my liaisons have talked with him and hinted *very* strongly that it's in the Mishans' best interests that Mahala stands, in which case we need both you and Lise. I think he got the message."

I raised one eyebrow. "Hinted very strongly? I'd have preferred an example of what would happen should they find themselves in possession of me or Lise."

That got me a frazzled smile. "The liaisons in question were Jake and Erlat. Very persuasive, in differing ways, and they will continue to be so. Erlat I may have to appoint as an actual liaison."

I tried to imagine a very strong hint from Jake and the swords that were never far away, coupled with Erlat and her beguiling smile. "OK, fair point, but that's not going to stop the cardinals."

"I don't suppose it'll stop the Mishans either, but at least they know we're looking out for them, and they know that Lise will be harder to get to now. I've also told them that you're down in the 'Pit and likely to stay there. But that's not the really pressing thing, is it?"

Anther boom-shudder to rattle our bones. The Storad seemed particularly good at punctuating a conversation, and reminding us that, above all else, the *really* pressing thing was keeping them out of the city.

"No food coming in now, either," Perak said. "Not a thing left to trade for it except guns, and we can't trade those or we're dead anyway. Whatever we're going to do, it needs to be now. The tunnel, is it safe?"

"You mean *apart* from the fact it's full of traps, we aren't sure we've found them all and we daren't go to the end because we'll tip the Storad off to exactly where it is if they aren't aware already, which they probably are? Sure, Perak. Safe as houses. I'm surprised Dench hasn't come up it to find the men who've gone missing. He will."

Perak glanced at Jake and Malaki, who both nodded. I didn't like the way this was going. It had the smell of drop-Rojan-in-the-shit.

"We need to do something to end this quickly," Perak said. "But first we need to slow them down – the Storad's machines will have the gates down in a few days otherwise, and then it doesn't matter about all the rest. Look, let us get all the information we can, see what we can come up with. In the meantime . . . "

"Yeah, yeah, I know. In the meantime keep my head down, rearranged and out of sight, try not to piss off any cardinals, keep pumping out Glow, get on with finding more mages, teaching them, see if we can get them firing up some Glow too. Check if any of them have a handy ability for making a whole damn army disappear. Right?"

Perak looked apologetic, but there it was. We all had to do things we didn't want to, except of course those cardinals who felt it was more useful to be a bunch of dissenting and/or running-away bastards.

I was seriously starting to feel tied to the damned pain lab, to Glow, like it was the only reason I was here and anyone was putting up with me. A fleeting – and very tempting – thought said that if the pain machine went belly-up, no one would need me. I could go and have a nice sleep, maybe drink myself insensible if I could find anything that would do the job. The only problem with that was that I'd probably fail to wake up due to a Storad bullet in the head.

Compared to that, a little pain, a little bit of teaching, would be a breeze.

There were often days when I wondered why the hell I bothered getting up. This was turning into one of them. Not that I'd actually got up as such, because I hadn't really slept, but still. Lise and Perak were tweaking her mysterious machine while Jake and Malaki did some reconnoitring and tried to figure out a plan. In the meantime I was left to keep my head down and try not to foam too much at the mouth about it.

The trickle of leads on new mages had dried up, so other than pumping out Glow I tried to keep myself busy training the mages we did have while looking over my shoulder all the time for a cardinal's man to come and stick a bag over my head, knock me out and drag me off.

The training wasn't going so well – I am not a natural teacher. Allit was a sulky mess, all knees and elbows as boys his age are. Allit, however, wasn't wholly as other boys, and if he carried on like this, there was a good chance we'd end up as part of the decor. Uncontrolled magic is a delicate thing, hence what made the Slump.

We were outside because this was a tricky business and, if it all went tits up, well, I didn't want it scaring the crap out of the other magelets. Or exploding any of Lise's experimental chemicals. The downside was that I was still smelling food cooking and it was almost enough to drive me crazy, especially as no one else seemed to be smelling it. My mind had taken against me, in league with my stomach.

Clouds hovered gently over the city like a murderer lowering a suffocating pillow, making Top of the World seem ghostly and indistinct. The wind blew straight down from mountains that were sprinkled with the first snow of the year, but for once it wasn't raining, so we sat on a frigid walkway overlooking the huge bulking factories of Trade. I made sure I was nice and close to a wall, because it was a long way down.

The factories' rumble shivered our bones, both comforting and odd. Comforting because, for a while there, we'd had no trade and that meant no food. Odd because, well, because it wasn't for trade that the factories were rumbling. The factories were working flat out, producing guns as fast as they could, bigger and better. But the very people we usually traded with for our raw materials were the ones who were sat outside the gates trying to batter their way in.

So, despite my genius little sister busting her arse to try to get more power out of the magic we *could* produce, and working on whatever gizmos she could think of on the side, we had to go with what we'd got and try every angle. Hence, a frustrating and painful morning for both me and Allit. At least I wasn't in a tunnel, getting shot at.

"It's stupid," Allit said, nursing a cut thumb.

"Not *just* stupid," I said. "Stupid, painful and a one-way road to madness, if you let it. That's why we start small, not try the big stuff straight away. Do that again and I'll toss you over the walkway. Lesson one – you don't use it lightly. *I* prefer not to use it at all."

"Why?"

"Because dislocating your own thumb to cast a spell is a ridiculous way to do things. And it hurts. I do not like to hurt. I also do not wish to go completely crazy, which is always a possibility." Of course, there was a good chance that it had already started on me.

Allit looked at me sideways, trying for guile but failing. "But you still do it. Why's that then?"

I wasn't going to be totally honest with him – I'm not even totally honest with myself most of the time – so I said, "Because sometimes even I have to. Like now. We make the magic, make the Glow or we all die. That simple. Doesn't mean I have to *like* it."

He gave me the sort of "Yeah, right" look that only works when teenagers try it. To distract him from the fact he was dead on right, I started him on another bit of practice.

We hadn't worked out what his talents were exactly. Not yet. Every mage has a Minor and a Major. Took me years to figure out that what I'd thought was my Minor – the way I could mould my face to look like other people – was in fact part of my Major, and the rearranging of things was just a matter of wanting to enough, and being able to stand the pain I needed to make it. My Minor – finding people, how I'd made my living in the recent past – didn't hurt so much, which is all relative because it still hurt like a damn bitch.

But Allit hadn't figured out what either of his talents was yet – all he'd managed was moving a cup about an inch, which might mean everything and nothing. As it went, not exactly helpful, though he could probably work it up to something useful in time.

We needed him to find out what else he could do, round about yesterday. As Dendal's and Pasha's more logical methods hadn't worked, I was getting him to try anything we could think of to see if we could stumble on it by accident.

I'd started by looking at the sorts of spells he'd accidentally cast when his magic first showed itself. Around about puberty, a proto-pain-mage knocks himself, or gets hurt in some way, and the magic leaks out, often in a way that might give a clue to his emerging talents.

Allit hadn't shown anything much, or not much he'd talk about anyway. There were other ways of finding out, but they weren't so pleasant, and I had a soft spot for cocky little Allit, whose bravado was covering up a whole shedload of fear. So we tried everything else, and it was slow, very slow. We didn't have time for slow.

After another few fruitless attempts, I had him stop before his thumb started squirting blood all over me. A boom-shudder rocked us, harder than the comforting rumble of Trade. Perak said he was working on it, which filled me with bone-deep dread. Another reason to be out here freezing my arse off with Allit. I didn't want to think what shit Perak was going to drop me in this time – the tunnels had been bad enough.

"All right then, Allit," I said. "Look out over the city. Really look at it. What do you see?"

He muttered under his breath, something about it being "unfair".

"Tell you what I see. I see Top of the World, where Ministry looks down on people like us because of where we're from, see us as just ways to get them what they want, money, power, all that happy horseshit. I see Clouds overhead, stealing our sun. I see Heights, see the people there look up with hope. I see Trade, see what made us great and also made us arrogant and led to us being weak. Look down, though, Allit. Look down at No-Hope Shitty; further, look into Boundary, in the Slump, the Stench, all the other crappy little places full of people with crappy little lives just doing the best they can to stay upright. See all those poor bastards down there. No sun, no food, no fucking hope. People like us. Well, like you perhaps, because the only hope they can find is to believe in a ministry that's done little except squeeze them dry, sucked their souls, made them want what it offers whether they like it or not. Whether it's helpful or hopeful or not. 'Believe in us,' they say, 'believe in us, do as you're told, get a nice life from the Goddess after you're dead, there's a good boy.' Well, don't know about you, but I'd prefer a nice life right now, and I believe that the Goddess is a crock of shit."

I swallowed the bile back down – it was getting easier to do that, or maybe I was mellowing a bit in my old age – and sneaked a look at Allit. His mouth hung open like I'd just told him I liked to bugger goats. I used to hide it, the fact that I don't believe in the Goddess, in all that Ministry tells us. Mainly because Ministry had this distressing habit of disappearing anyone they didn't like, and they *really* didn't like disbelievers. I used to hide it, hide a lot of things, but I was done hiding now. It hadn't done me a whole lot of good.

"But, Rojan—"

"But nothing. Just look. Look up, then look down."

He did, reluctantly at first, with hesitant little side glances at me every now and again. I didn't really expect much, at least not for him to see what I saw. He'd been filled with every sermon, from Dendal's essays on morality to Pasha's passionate rants about the 'Pit's version of the Goddess. None of this sanitised, soulless crap down there. In the 'Pit she was all blood and glory, enough to turn a boy's head.

So I wasn't expecting much, maybe just a new perspective for him, outside himself and into the world. Make him *think*. That's what Ministry has traditionally hated, above all else – someone who thinks for themselves rather than swallowing what they are fed. Maybe what they hated about pain-mages. If there's one thing to be said for dislocating your thumbs to cast a spell, it's that it really makes you think about what's necessary and what's just fluff.

Allit looked up with longing, as anyone from Under might. A wintry sun managed to break through a gap in the clouds. And then he saw something else. His eyes jerked wide and he snapped back towards me, away from the edge. When he tried to speak, nothing came out for a moment, until a breathy, horrified whisper. "I can see them. They're coming, more machines, bigger machines. I can see them. Mountains, men, machines. They're coming."

The ragged edge to his voice made rivulets of ice run down my back. I didn't need to be Pasha, rummage in his head with my magic, to know that Allit was so scared he was about to piss himself. And this was a boy who'd taken to hurting himself on a regular basis like a bird took to the air. It was about then that I noticed what he was doing with his hand – he had hold of his cut thumb and was pinching the two edges of the wound together, tighter and tighter, twisting as he went. Pain, meet magic.

"Allit?" I grabbed his shoulder with my good hand. "Allit, what are you seeing? Where are you seeing it? Allit?"

He shook himself like a boy waking from a bad dream, his hands trembling so hard they looked in danger of falling off. "We need to go find the others. Find Perak. Tell them. More Storad coming, no good, it's no good. More machines. Bigger ones, with, with . . . "

He rubbed a shaking hand over his eyes and I realised he was trying not to cry, trying to be a man about it. When I was a kid I always loved being big brother to Perak, though I came to loathe it later, to fear it, to run from it whenever I could. Events and people were trying to cure me of that, with varying success. But when Perak was small, when Ma was alive and our father still lived with us, and Perak looked at me like I knew everything . . . Yeah, I loved being big brother *then*. Looking at Allit, at the fear in his thin, hunched shoulders, the way he looked at me like I had the answer to everything, like I was some sort of god, well, maybe it turned my head. Who doesn't like to be thought of as a god? Big brothering slid back into me like it was coming home.

I got him to his feet and draped an arm over his shoulder. "It's all right, Allit. I'm going to make sure it's all right."

I've always been a superb liar.

Chapter Six

By the time we got back to the offices, Allit had himself under control, of sorts. I really was starting to like this kid because he reminded me of me, when I still had stars in my eyes and hope in my by now grubby little soul.

I told Allit to go see if there was anything to eat in the kitchen – not because I thought there was anything worth eating in there (I knew there wasn't) but more to keep him out of the way while I talked to Pasha. Lastri gave me a glare like I'd tried to poison the kid or something, and went to see what she could do about fattening him up. Not a lot, probably.

Of course, with Pasha being the way he was, the way his magic ran, I didn't need to tell him much. He cast a surreptitious glance at Dendal, who was oblivious to anything but what was dancing in his head. Unspoken, we'd taken to not telling him everything. Most of it, but not everything. Whatever else he might be, and he's a lot of things, Dendal was a gentle soul and these were not about to be gentle times. Crazy perhaps – I mean, when he remembered, he was a powerful mage, the strongest we had – but he also had an in-built faith in people that I couldn't quite bring myself to destroy. That's without the wandering through his days humming to himself and playing with imaginary fairies, which could be fatal if he lost concentration at a vital point. We told ourselves we were keeping him in reserve, and perhaps we were.

I checked for any traps my desk might have laid for me and sank warily into the chair behind it. Pasha came and took up his customary position on the corner of the desk, his back to Dendal and his candles so that his outline seemed to flicker with a halo of light.

"I caught bits," he said in an undertone. "Did he really see it, do you think?"

I shrugged and played with a pen, adding to the doodles on my blotter. "I think he's found one of his talents, yes. Makes me wonder – the first time, when his magic started. I wonder what it was he saw that's left him so jittery."

"I could take a look? No, all right, maybe not. So if he saw it, if it's real . . . *He* thinks it is, at the least. Here, look, I caught this much."

I could see the office, the cobwebs in the corner, the array of candles in weird shapes, the top of Dendal's head as he bent to start another letter, Pasha's monkey face and the way he was twisting his finger out of its socket with a hiss of pained breath. Overlaid on all that, I could see . . . machines, mountains, men. Just like Allit had said. I tried to shut my eyes against it, but Pasha's little insertion into my brain was still there.

I'd seen the machines at the gates from far away, through a telescope at Top of the World. Monstrous guns on wheels, and they'd been bad enough. These machines were different. Imagine a spider got drunk and mated with a – hell, I don't know, a lion *and* a giraffe or something. And then had some twiddly bits grafted on. They had too many legs, too many nasty, brutal-looking protuberances and weird twisting parts that looked like teeth at the same time as they looked like guns. Smoke oiled its way around them, making them vague and all the more disturbing. I was pretty sure I knew what I was going to be having nightmares about when I slept next, though they'd have a fight on their hands with all the other crap my brain liked to throw at me when I was weak.

Maybe Dench had been right all along: maybe we should have allied with the Storad, should have bent the knee, swallowed our pride. Maybe I shouldn't wait for the cardinals' men to find me but hand myself over now, as long as the Storad promised not to use these things in anger. From this news of more machines, if not from the things already here, it was obvious that this had been long in the planning. They'd just been waiting for the best time, the time when we were weak.

But now maybe we had an edge. If the boy could really farsee, then that might be all the edge we needed.

Perak was there in minutes when I called him – he'd been

in the lab, looking very secretive as he discussed something with Erlat. She gifted me a wink before she left, leaving me with the feeling that something funny was going on there. No time to think about it right then though.

Pasha showed them what he'd showed me of Allit's vision. Perak looked pale and shaky, kind of how I felt.

"Are you *sure*?" he kept asking. "It couldn't be a mistake, could it?"

"Allit certainly seems sure," I said, with a shrug that probably made me look a lot more unconcerned than I was. "But then, it's only the first time this has happened to him that we know of."

"So perhaps—"

"Perhaps we don't want to take that chance, Perak."

He sat on the other edge of my desk and ran a hand through his hair. "No. No, you're right. But by the Goddess, just when I though we might be able to do something, get this over with. I thought we had a chance, but with that on the way . . ."

When I looked up, Allit was standing in the doorway to the kitchen, Lastri's hand on his shoulder. He looked very young all of a sudden.

"Allit," Pasha asked in a soft voice, "do you think you could do it again? Just to see if – well, if it's still the same."

Allit's voice was full of teenage belligerence and a hint of bewilderment. "I didn't lie." He looked at me, as though I had all the answers. "I didn't."

"No one says you did," I said. "But – first proper spell and all, well, first intentional one, it's difficult. Maybe you aren't farseeing. Maybe you are and it's the other side of the world, not Storad in *our* mountains. Maybe a hundred things, but we have to be sure."

He looked between me and Perak, seeming to weigh it all in his mind. "All right. I'll try it again."

Perak nodded firmly. "Good. In the meantime, at least I've got something to go on. Jake and Malaki, I've got some work for them to do, and I've got a few things to deal with myself – all these people who want you dead, for starters. Let me know what you find."

Pasha and I settled down with Allit, and got on with the business of him trying again. It didn't go well.

Finally, after blood had got everywhere, we'd got nowhere and Allit seemed on the verge of tears, I said, "Allit, when you . . . well, when you first found out you were a mage. What was it you saw?"

Colour seemed to drain away from his cheeks, leaving him ashen, shaken. "Nothing."

"Look, you can farsee, perhaps; that's good. That's great. But I need you to able to do it again. You need to as well, or you're going to end up one big ball of frustration." Not to mention he'd end up in the black, or going kablooie when it all went tits up, as it would.

Pasha, standing where Allit couldn't see him, got that dreamy look he took on when he was listening in on someone's thoughts. "You know, first time I heard anyone's voice in my head, I thought I was going mad. Scared me stupid, so I didn't want to try again. Or at least I tried, but it wouldn't come."

Allit twisted round to look at him. "You were scared?"

I laughed, more at the memory of myself at this point than anything. "We all were, Allit – I had no idea what the hell was going on, all I knew was things kept changing and I knew where people were without knowing how I knew. Made life a real challenge for a while, and then when I tried to do it on purpose, it all went wrong, when it went at all, which it mostly didn't for a long time. Still don't know what the hell I'm doing, really. But it's going to happen sometime, whether you want it to or not. Best if you know how to manage it. Be its master rather than the other way round."

He took it a damn sight better than I'd taken that little speech from Dendal, way back when: I'd ended up not using my magic unless I really had to, and of course when it came to it I was out of control. Thing was, we were all right to be afraid. When I'd first joined up with Dendal I'd looked at him, slave to his magic, addicted to it like a junkie to Rapture, and thought, *I don't want to end up like that*.

I was beginning to think that it was inevitable. We were all slaves to it in one way or another, and I felt a twinge of guilt at bringing Allit into that fold, into that slavery. Yet the choice wasn't much of a choice – if we didn't help him, chances were pretty good he'd end up dead of it. Dendal had some really gruesome stories about mages who hadn't faced up to their magic, ones he used to tell me over and over. I'd started to dream about them too just lately.

The really scary thing is, I was starting to sound like Dendal, always banging on about mastery.

Allit sat for a while, still pale and shaking, but in the end he took a deep breath and gave me a determined nod. Once he started, it seemed like he couldn't stop till it all came out.

"I saw lots of things, the first time. I found myself in the wrong end of the 'Pit, and, and I got knocked about pretty bad. Still had the last of the bruises when you found me and that was weeks later. And . . . and when you found me, I already knew who you were. I saw you, before. I saw what you did at the pain factory, with all the Glow. How it all ran, and you were full of it, full of Glow and you seemed to light up, it was running from your hands, from your eyes and there was glass everywhere and you were smiling, Goddess, the most awful smile, like you were Namrat coming to eat me. And then your father, you left him to die. On purpose, I saw you. Not clearly – it was vague and blurry, but I saw, and I saw you bring him up to be tried by Ministry too, and I saw you join him in the factory, and I saw him kill you. All those things, but only one happened. And I saw Pasha all whacked out, like his mind wasn't his any more, and I knew you were both using magic, and I thought I might be and I didn't want it. Not if that's what it was, and when I met you it scared me because I thought that was you, that man with Glow running out of his eyes, and I didn't want to be one of *them*. I saw other things too, before, the pain factory, the screaming and . . . and . . . later I think . . . I don't want to see it any more! Only I was trying because you weren't that man, you weren't that scary, or all lit up with Glow. You helped me, that day you found me. You didn't have to, but you did. I *wanted* to help you back, I did, I do, but . . . not the seeing. I don't want to do the seeing."

Pasha was quicker off the mark than me when Allit finally came to a stop. A soft hand on his shoulder, and I knew Pasha would be in the boy's head, talking to him, soothing him. Playing with what was inside there, taking away the fear perhaps. If only he could do that for good.

Pasha was looking at me when he spoke, that little contented smile that he'd got lately just visible. "That's not a choice we get. This is who we are, what we are. And it's crap, and I hate it, and I love it too. But if you have it, you need to know how to keep a lid on it, or you'll be just another mage who fell into the black, whether you mean to use it or not. And to do that, you need to know how it works, how to use it. We'll be here with you, OK? I'm not going anywhere and neither is Rojan, or Dendal or any of us."

Pasha's voice in my head. *You taught me that, that this is what we are and we should be proud of it. So stop thinking otherwise. We need these kids, all of them, and they need us to show them. It's us, all together. This is your way back into the world, instead of being apart from it. Remember that.*

Yes, Ma, I thought back and he laughed. But he was right, and I knew it.

"So, you saw all that," I said to Allit, "and that shows to me at least you really do see true, at least some of it. I thought only I knew what happened between me and my father, but you saw me join him too and that didn't happen." I pondered on that for a moment. "So you saw when I, we, took the pain factory down?"

Allit shook his head. "No, before, a couple of days before, I think. Then I saw you and Pasha do all these different things, and it was blurry, but they were all . . . real? Only I didn't know what it was I was seeing to start with so I didn't know what it meant. Then I saw you and the Glow, and that was clear as anything, like I was there. At first I thought it was some dream perhaps, but then we came Upside and everyone was talking about mages and what had happened to the Glow so I knew it had really happened. I saw things after too, a couple more times when I hurt myself. So I thought maybe it was, you know, magic, only I didn't want it to be, because of the mages at the factory. Because of when I saw you."

"Show me," Pasha said. "Remember it and show me."

So Allit shut his eyes and Pasha twisted a knuckle and cocked his head as though he was listening.

"Well?" I said when Allit opened his eyes.

"Odd – I'm not sure he saw you from a distance, exactly, but he saw you all right. Goddess's tits, I never realised – no wonder he was scared of you. I'm starting to think I should be."

I shrugged that away. "So is he farseeing? Or what? What about all those things he saw that didn't happen? If he isn't farseeing, then what *is* he doing? What's he seeing?"

"Look, I've known a few mages, more than you perhaps, from the 'Pit. I've seen men who could fly, men who could control fire, men like your father who could make others do things by the power of their voice, all manner of things. Who knows if there are any limits to what can happen, what we can do? Each mage is different, you know that. He saw you in the factory, but he saw you *before* you did it, and he saw lots of things that might have happened, how it might have turned out only it didn't. What if . . . what if . . . "

I knew what he was about to say and opened my mouth to say something cutting, like that was stupid thinking, but stopped just in time. What if it wasn't stupid?

"What does it mean?" Allit sounded panicky.

"Goddess's tits," Pasha said.

Quite. "What it means, I think," I said, "is that you're not just seeing far away, sometimes you're seeing a different when. You can see the future."

Chapter Seven

"So what you're saying is, yes, he can farsee, but then again, it might not be now that he's seeing?" Perak asked.

"That's about it," I said, though the latest boom-shudder almost drowned me out.

We were holed up in the lab again, and Perak kept fiddling with the pain rig as we talked – he might be Archdeacon but he was always going to be an engineer first. I was beginning to wonder when he was sleeping, when he was doing anything at all except be Archdeacon. He had a daughter, a niece I'd still not met, and I had to wonder if he ever saw her either.

I was pleased to see this news energised him though, brought a bit of life back to his eyes. "So those machines are definitely on their way, or will be, but we can't say for sure when? They might be further away, but then again they might be closer?"

He stopped fiddling and started to pace, his hands gripping his hair like he was trying to pull the answer out of his head.

"Namrat's bollocks, Rojan." When the Archdeacon uses words like that, you know you're in trouble. "All right. This can still work – mine and Lise's little plan. We need to be sure how close the machines are. Is there any way Allit or anyone else can pin it down? Are they coming over the pass now, next week, or did they come yesterday?"

"We can't give you anything reliable," Pasha said from where he was leaning up against the pain rig and watching Jake with that contented smile on his face. She caught him watching and there was a hint of a blush on her cool façade, which just made him smile more. At least someone was happy. "I can't reach that far, I've tried. Allit – maybe in time he'll be able to be more precise. For the moment, he *thinks* it's either now, or very close to. Things seem to get blurry and vague when they're too far forward, from what I can tell."

"Right. OK. Whatever, wherever they are, we still need more *time*. More – well, more everything. Glow, mages, information. Some cardinals to help – you know more than a quarter have left the city? Bribed their way through the Mishan gate and taken what they could with them? The rest, well . . . they want volunteers for down by the Storad gate, for when, inevitably, they finally batter it down. Only despite the fact we're pumping out guns as fast as we can, they won't let just anyone have them. One cardinal has a man down there checking everyone with a gun, giving them an informal inquisition. Testing their faith. Just in case they might use that gun on anyone other than Storad. Ridiculous." Perak stopped pacing and took a deep breath. "Sorry. The cardinals are my problem, one I'm hoping will be sorted soon, at least as far as them wanting to hand you over goes. As for this problem . . . Jake, we found another tunnel, we think it comes out up by the pass. Can you—"

Jake cocked her head, cool as ice despite what Perak was asking of her. I wouldn't have done it. "Of course. I'll see what I can do."

"*Carefully*."

A cryptic smile, a shrug as she smoothed her hands over the scabbards of her swords.

"Thank you. Because we need information," Perak said. "And because we've got a little plan, or rather Lise has. Even more urgent now, if Allit is right. Take as many men as you think you'll need. Specials, the rest of my guard, whatever you need. I'd rather you came back with nothing than didn't come back."

Jake didn't waste time or words, just cast a glance at Pasha – a glance full of words I was sure were being spoken in their heads – and left.

"Right then," Perak went on. "Let's see . . . we need to assume it's now Allit saw, to be on the safe side. Lise and I had this plan . . . yes. Yes, it should still help, might give us time at least. Wherever those machines are, it won't hurt and might help. I'll see what Lise has ready. In the morning we'll try it, or rather you will. A bit of rearrangement, if you're up to it?"

I'll give him this – he could have laid it all out, laid it all on thick. How ultimately it was my actions that had led us to this mess, when I'd shut down the pain factories that were supplying all our Glow. But he didn't. He never did. He was never one to hold a grudge – that was me, but even I couldn't this time. I did suppress a big-arsed sigh though.

"What do you need me to do?"

When Perak told me the reason for our previous little escapade into the tunnel and how it worked so very well with what he wanted to try, I didn't hesitate to say yes. It could hardly be worse than being shot at.

We couldn't start Perak's plan right away because it was getting dark and we were going to need light, so when he left I headed for the office and settled down at my desk to contemplate a new note Lastri had left about another possible mage. It might make a nice distraction and, with more cardinals having left, there were fewer to try to drag me off. Hopefully. I intended to be careful anyway, but by now the thought of any young mage left to do himself a mischief was just another thing taking chunks out of my stupid new conscience. I couldn't leave him to blow himself up, and it'd stop me having to think too much and end up choking on my own bile.

To sleep first, or not? My brain said, Yes, sleep, if you don't you'll be batshit any time now and the city doesn't need another Slump, especially given what you're going to be doing come sun-up. My poor purple hand said, Hah, fat chance, I'm going to keep you up all night; and the black chimed in and said, Yes, might as well use that juice, twist your hand some more, fall in, come back . . .

I came to with a start when Pasha sauntered in, whistling. Whistling? Normally he was a bunch of jittered nerves, burning anger and electric energy just waiting to get out. Not today. He looked . . . relaxed, which, all things considered – like Jake was off into who knew what kind of shitstorm – was surprising. Then again, Pasha always did tend to surprise me.

Like I said, he was usually burning up with anger at some injustice somewhere, but today his eyes didn't have their normal smoulder. And come to think of it, Jake had looked unusually relaxed too. Usually she was buttoned up tighter than a virgin's knickers, ice queen all the way. Yet despite the seriousness of what Perak and I had been talking about, the seriousness of everything, of tunnels, slabs of rock, Storad and massive machines blowing the crap out of our gates, there had been a soft little smile and a faraway look to her, to them both. I could imagine a few reasons for that, but in the interests of not getting an ulcer I decided not to think of them.

They may have made me a little sharp though – that or the lack of sleep; or Perak's plan, which was *bound* to involve me hurting myself; or perhaps it was just my natural charm. "What the fuck are you so happy about?"

Even that couldn't dim his stupid smile. He cocked his head, made to twist a finger in its socket – all the better to peer inside my head – but my glare stopped him. In the end he grinned his monkey grin, shrugged and said, "And who twisted your nipples today?"

He was such a dick, but my peeved anger evaporated. "No one, that's the problem."

Another boom-shudder rattled the door, but couldn't rattle his laugh. I'd never really heard him laugh before, not like that, like he was happy, and the last of my resentment vanished.

While we were waiting for Jake to come back, or at least for Pasha to be able to hear what she'd seen, Perak had asked us to concentrate our efforts on Allit. Being able to see the future had to be an advantage somehow, but he needed to learn to focus, to decipher what he was seeing, and not drive himself doolally while he was doing it.

So Pasha and I spent a less heavy-minded hour watching Allit go through his paces, twisting a finger then lifting small objects about an inch off my desk, floating them across and getting them to land gently on the blotter among my doodles. Doodles that, when Allit saw them, made him blush redder than brick.

After those few small exercises, we started on what we needed.

"OK," Pasha said. "We're going to start small, and I'm going to watch where you are, where you go in your head, all right? We know where Jake is, sort of. See if you can find her. If a focus helps. If not, just show me what you can see."

Allit nodded, his face screwed up, half scared shitless, half determined to prove he could do this, and twisted a finger. It came out of its socket with a pop that seemed very loud, and his face lost everything but a grimace of pain.

I felt left out, to be honest, with Allit concentrating on what his head was showing him and Pasha keeping an eye on that. Nothing really happened for a minute or two except Allit went red in the face and Pasha put an encouraging hand on his shoulder.

A sudden gasp – not from Allit, which I was expecting, but from Pasha. His dark face drained of all colour until he looked as grey as the mush we'd had for breakfast and he stepped back from Allit.

"What?"

"I – wait, wait a minute."

Pasha took a few deep breaths and shut his eyes against what he'd seen. Allit came back from wherever he'd been, looking embarrassed and scared. "I'm sorry, I didn't mean to, I'm sorry."

"It's all right," Pasha managed. "But I'm not sure what it means. Not what I think, I hope."

"Is someone going to tell me?" I asked. "Or do I have to guess? Allit, what did you see?"

Allit tried to pull himself together, but he looked pretty shaky. "I saw Jake."

"Well then, that's good? Right?" I looked at Pasha's stricken face. "Right?"

"Dench had her," Pasha said in a whisper, but some colour had come back to his face. "He caught her and he was about to— But he *hasn't* caught her. I can hear her right now, I shot off a question and she's telling me not to be so stupid, of course she's fine, she's having a damned ball. I think she's even hoping to run into a Storad or two, just for practice."

My heart had almost stopped at the first part, and I could only imagine what that had done to Pasha. The relief at the second part made me giddy and the third made my heart falter again.

Pasha sat down and ran a relieved hand through his mess of hair. "Allit saw her in a death match – you remember the one you watched, against the Storad? Just a glimpse of her there, like he did the first time. That was his focus. And he saw her in the tunnel too, that one was clear as anything, in the tunnel like I know she is in right now with half of Perak's guard with her. *Safe*. Well, safe for now anyway. Only Allit saw her with Dench too, in the Storad camp, I'm sure of it. He was going to—" Pasha shook his head as though trying to shake out the memory. "Never mind, she's not there. It was, I don't know, sort of fuzzy compared to the others."

"Like it was less real," Allit said. "And behind it I could see something else – see Jake somewhere else at the same time. It was like a possibility, in my head." He struggled to say more, but in the end gave up – it was all too new for him. I remembered how that felt.

"Well, it isn't real as far as we know. Yet. Is it?" I asked.

"No!" Pasha said, almost like he was trying to convince himself, and perhaps he was.

"Blurred, like when Allit saw me do all those different things in the 'Pit?"

Allit nodded, looking relieved as he saw what I meant.

"All right then. So let's make sure it doesn't happen. Any ideas? Where's Jake now?"

Pasha shot me a relieved look. "In the tunnel – they haven't had time to get far. We're pretty sure that tunnel comes out near the pass. And that's a fair way to travel."

"Well, tell her to be extra careful when she gets to the end."

That made him laugh, though there was a harsh edge to it. "You think she'll listen to me? That's what worries me. You know what she's like – caution is for other people."

"No, that's what she used to be like, back when she didn't care if she lived or died. She cares now. You made her care." I thought back to that soft little smile of hers when she looked at Pasha, at how the two of them seemed to be growing into each other, being happy together for once in their screwed-up lives. It hurt me to watch it, but I couldn't begrudge it to either of them.

He opened his mouth to say something, but I caught the whiff of gratitude in the offing so I cut him off.

"Right, so, Allit, you work on this as best you can. Keep

practising and tell us if you find anything else. Try to concentrate on the clearer things if you can, but if you see anything blurry that might help us, tell us."

Pasha grinned at the way I neatly sidestepped any chance of a thank you, but didn't mention it. "And Rojan, if we're going early tomorrow, you need to get something to eat and some sleep. I don't want you wigging out on me. Time for dinner and bed."

All very well for him to say – he had a nice warm bed, usually with a nice warm Jake in it. I had a lumpy sofa, and Griswald the stuffed tiger, but I nodded like I was going to do either of those things. He didn't believe me. He knew me far too well.

"Come on, why don't you go and see if Erlat's got a bed free? You're always in a better mood after you go and see her." He laughed again, for no reason that I could see, almost like he knew something about me that I didn't know myself.

"Maybe." It was tempting, and he was right – I always did feel better after I saw Erlat – but I had other things to do. I should have slept, really, but my sleep was littered with things I didn't want to revisit if I could help it. "I'll go later. Really."

He still didn't believe me, but shrugged and left with Allit, whistling. That happy sound could really get on a guy's tits.

At a loose end, with too much to think about, I wandered through to the lab, where Lise started in on me, but at a shake of my head at least she left me alone. With something like relief, she started work on her machines. Being kept in the lab by Perak for her safety didn't seem to bother her too much; it was driving me stir-crazy.

"For the Goddess's sake, will you stop pacing?" she said now. "It's like being trapped with a tiger."

I sat down with bad grace and watched her as she tinkered. "You don't mind being cooped up, do you?"

She shrugged. "Doesn't make a lot of difference to me. Hand me the pliers, would you? No, the long ones. I'd rather be cooped up here than dragged off to the Mishans, wouldn't you?" She looked up over the tangle of wires she was working on. "No, I don't suppose you would. Safest place to be is here."

While it was good to know she was safe, or as safe as anyone could be, it didn't stop my legs from jiggling, or me from feeling I should be out there, doing . . . well, *something*.

"Allit and some of the others have started on the smaller generators," she said. "Halina is pretty good – I think she can start on this machine tomorrow. It's not for long, Rojan. I've got a new machine too. I think it might even stop the Storad."

That perked me up. "Explain it to me. Simply."

She rolled her eyes, but she was smiling. I think she loved the fact she could lord it over her older brother in the technical department. "Wait till tomorrow. I'm still getting the finishing touches done. But I think you're going to love it. In the meantime . . . " What was it with everyone looking at me like that? Like I was a bomb waiting to go off? "You need to start looking after yourself. Please. If for no other reason than you'll be useless otherwise."

"Vote of confidence so noted."

"And ignored, right?"

I shrugged – she had me there. But she was my sister, still young enough to worry about me, and it shone plain as plain in her eyes. So, being a good big brother, I said, "I will, I promise. Later," and gave her shoulders a squeeze with my good hand. "You too."

"Hmph. *I* will, because I know I can't work right if I don't. You, I'm not so sure."

She glared at me, promising a future tongue-lashing should I dare to ignore her, but she said nothing else before I left. And not for my lumpy sofa.

Chapter Eight

The office was quiet at that time of night, which I was grateful for. Lastri had gone home; the walkway outside was empty. The only sounds were Dendal humming and scratching away in his corner and a series of boom-shudders that made all the pens on my desk roll on to the floor.

It was all very well for everyone to tell me to sleep, to eat. But there was almost nothing *to* eat, nothing I wanted to eat certainly, only the half-dream, half-dastardly promise of Perak's that out there, somewhere, was bacon walking around. Sleep wasn't going to happen either. So I dunked my head in icy water from the tap in the kitchen to wake myself up, grabbed the note with the possible address of a possible mage on it and headed out. At least having an address meant I shouldn't have to fire up any more juice, my hand could have a rest and I was doing something to take my mind off everything else. Sod Perak telling me to stay put, to stay safe.

I did a little bit of rearrangement, made my face someone else's, and went.

Going down into Boundary was an education. I'd lived in those shitty parts of the city most of my life, seen all sorts, from murders and gangs running wild to riots and priests going crazy because they couldn't believe the Goddess would allow such awfulness. But I'd never seen the walkways so full of silent fear, never smelled it so sharply in the crappy air, and long before I made it into Boundary.

I made a slight detour – there was something I wanted to see. On the other side of the city from where the Storad were camped there was another gate, a mirror of it. Small, almost unnoticed until recently. Not unnoticed now, because everyone I saw on the street was heading towards it, towards what they'd until lately thought was just a dead end, because Outside officially didn't exist. Far-off, mythical, unreal. But with missiles arrowing their way in from what was patently not inside the city, the populace had rapidly accepted the unofficial idea that Outside was real, and if there was an Outside, there must be a way to get to it that didn't involve getting shot by the Storad.

There was. The Mishan gate.

The streets on the city side of the inner gates were a heaving crush of people that cringed together at every boom-shudder that came across from the Storad gate. The Mishan gate itself wasn't open – if it were, those people would have been through in a flash – but a small postern was, with a heavy metal grille across it. Mishan guards stood behind the grille, and a string of them kept the crowd away from the front, though they were in danger of being crushed by the sheer panic of the press behind them. Being in Mahala was being a rat in a trap just then, and this gate was the only hope for thousands, though it was hope for almost none. No one was being let through. Not here at least. I had no doubt there was another entrance somewhere else, somewhere quiet, somewhere Over. Somewhere the cardinals could sneak through and hand over their bribes, get the hell out before everyone died. At least I hadn't been one of the bribes. Not yet anyway.

Rumours abounded in the crowd – the Mishans would let you through if you had money, if you had connections. The Mishans weren't letting anyone through. The Storad would leave Under alone, had no desire to attack the downtrodden masses. The Storad would rip through Under like fire in a forest. The Storad ate babies. We should let the Storad in, let them kill every Ministry man they found, and then we'd all be all right. The moon was made of cheese.

These and other even more outlandish rumours flashed along the cramped streets and walkways that shivered with the load, the whispering of them the only sound. The gate looked half formed and vague in the darkness. Once it had looked much like any other part of the city, hidden in plain sight, but now it was laid bare so all could see what it was. Like an optical illusion, once you saw the trick you wondered how you couldn't have seen it before. Because people hadn't believed in Outside or ways to get to it, the gate hadn't been there. Now they did believe, now no one was hiding it but flaunting it, it was obvious.

Frost-rimed arrow slits disguised as light-wells. Heavy, clanking gates that had once looked like the entrance to just another secured factory but now, when you looked a certain way, just had to be something more. Little puffs of chilly breath marked the guards – ours and theirs – that now stood openly in front of it.

News-sheets made their way from hand to hand among the crowds, saying much the same as the rumours. The news-sheets were – well, they weren't unbiased, let's put it like that. They were unofficial rumour mills for the things certain cardinals wanted people to believe, or would be prepared to believe, rather than actual truth. Propaganda. And while not everyone believed all of it, enough believed enough of it. Funny how Perak's really officially official news-sheet, detailing calmly and rationally what was going on, what he intended to do and what people could do to help themselves and Mahala, was mostly ignored as being the far-fetched ravings of a loony. We'd had all the other stuff shoved down our necks for so long, people found it hard to believe the truth when it bit them on the nose.

Someone thrust a copy of one of the more virulent sheets into my hand and I stopped dead when I saw my own ugly mug there, down near the bottom.

Wanted: Rojan Dizon, pain-mage and heretic.
All information received in confidence, and paid for in cash.

I glanced over it, noted the name of the cardinal who had sponsored the sheet – that bold cardinal from before, who wondered whether Perak would protect me if I weren't his brother – and ripped that sucker into bits. The bit about me was bad enough, if not a shock. That cardinal must be getting desperate. The rest though – what a load of old bollocks. The people Under were safe, it said, the guards and Specials had everything in hand. The Storad had no interest in destroying the city, only debilitating our trade – this at least was a hope I had, but I didn't set much store by hope, from long and dark experience. The sheet went on to tell people how to protect themselves in their own homes, to trust in Ministry, and to iterate very strongly indeed that the Mishans would let no one through their gates. Similar spiels had been spouted at many a temple over the last days, cardinal-propelled sops to keep the rabble quiet. Perak had tried to get it to stop, but each temple had its own patron cardinal and they toed that cardinal's line like it was a lift into heaven.

If the spurious news-sheets were saying all this then it meant that the Mishans *would* let a few people through – the cardinals who sponsored the news-sheets and temples almost certainly. Anyone who couldn't afford to pay through the nose, which meant anyone from Under, was fresh out of luck.

After the sheets had made their rounds, and after a few

choice words from some of the Mishan guards, the crowd loosened its stranglehold on the gates. Some stayed, but more drifted away. Murmuring about what they could do now, speculating on what the sheets had said, that they'd be safe if they stayed Under, wouldn't they? Then looking at a different sheet, sponsored by a different cardinal, reading about all the things the Storad would do to them when they got in . . .

I threw the ripped sheet away and made my way down.

Another boom-shudder – it was worse down here, a hundred times worse, for all that the sound was fainter. The rumble shook through me and all the buildings that crowded around. Reminded me how many buildings sat above, waiting to crush the life out of me if they fell. The walkway beneath my feet swayed – not as solid down here, more likely to be rotten with rust, more likely to break, tip me down a couple of dozen or so floors. Less far to fall this far down, but that was still enough to splat me. I grabbed hold of the nearest building and held on for grim death. Something pinged past my face and I hoped like hell it wasn't one of the bolts holding the walkway in place. I kept my eyes shut. Stupid, I know, because it was as dark as Namrat's heart all around me, but that didn't stop the image of a long drop making me want to scream. Almost took my mind off keeping an eye out for any would-be kidnappers. Almost.

After a time the walkway settled and so did my heartbeat, though I made sure I kept hold of something solid as I carried on. I was glad when I came to one of the few Glow globes that lit the walkways. Even gladder when I got to the house I was after. Inside I'd be able to pretend long drops were things that didn't happen.

Another boom-shudder. Was it me or where they getting closer together? It didn't really matter because the walkway lurched under me and I fell into the door rather than knocking on it. I tried to hold myself together when the door opened, because I wasn't going to give a good impression by screaming like a baby. It kind of worked. The scream came out as a squeak, which still wasn't very professional but better, and I managed to avoid falling through the doorway too.

"What do you want?" The door opener didn't look a welcoming sort of guy. He was big and beefy, or perhaps had been before starvation had taken hold. He still had wide shoulders that now had no spare flesh on them, and a face that seemed like life had chipped its way into it with chisels and a hammer, his dark hair crudely shorn and patchy. Not a Downsider – must have been one of the few Upsiders still left in this area. Probably too damned poor to get anywhere else, because the Downsiders had been shoved into all the very worst places, naturally. Also possibly one of the "poor but proud so don't give me any of your charity or I'll feed it to you, with your teeth". Careful handling would be required. I wondered whether I was up to it.

He caught sight of my allover in the dim light of a rend-nut-oil lamp that was busy stinking the place up behind him.

His face changed from not welcoming to a mix of outright fear and barely suppressed anger.

"It's . . . delicate," I said. "Can I come in?"

That seemed to throw him. He obviously thought I was a Special, and Specials didn't need to ask, but at least he opened the door wide enough for me to squeeze past.

"We haven't done nothing," he said behind me as I took in the one-room hovel he called home. Synth-tainted damp dripped from the walls, though someone had tried their best with some whitewash that was now streaked with black. "And you can't prove otherwise."

A teenage boy shot up from what was presumably his bed – a damp and ragged collection of blankets. A large bandage, spotted with blood and more grey now than white, had been clumsily wrapped around his right hand.

"If I was a Special, I wouldn't need to prove much at all," I said without turning. "So it's probably good that I'm not one, isn't it? Though you might prefer that I was when I'm done. Hurt yourself?"

The boy shot a look at what was presumably his father, seemed to get an OK to answer and said, "Yeah. Climbing in the Slump. There's some good salvage if you know where to look. Cut my hand on a bit of metal."

If nothing else, that was enough to show me just how screwed-over these guys were. The Slump was a mangled mess of metal and wood, a nest of squirming, plump rats and the bodies they fed on – the Ministry used it as a dumping ground for anyone who died whose family couldn't afford a proper crypt, which was pretty much everyone. If you needed to salvage in amongst that, you were as desperate as it gets.

"Bet some really weird shit has been happening since, right?" I said.

The boy shot another glance at his father, terrified this time. His father seemed to feel it too, because all of a sudden the feeble light was blocked out while he loomed over me. Enough to make me wonder why I'd been stupid enough to come on my own.

"Who've you been talking to? That bitch down on the stairwell corner? I told her I'd pay her back. Goddess's tits, it was only a spoon! Not half as bad as what happened to the cat. Old bag said she'd dob us in, and I suppose she has, but you're on your own and I reckon I could take one Special, especially a piss-ant little one like you. You aren't arresting either of us."

I backed up a step – he looked really pissed off and, now I came to look, his knuckles seemed well used. I didn't want him using them on me, so I tried a placating smile, which made his face twist even further. His fists seemed to be twitching too, like he was contemplating using them.

"I'm not a Special. I promise." Something by the crappy little stove caught my eye. A mound of bones that still had slivers of cooked meat on them. Small bones, with a long, thin, fur-free tail attached. Namrat's arse, I'd known there wasn't much food, but this? Still, it gave me a tiny bit of leverage. "I'm not taking you anywhere, or at least, not anywhere you don't want to go. And if you go, you should get something other than rats to eat."

A guilty, shamed look between the two of them, and the father backed off.

They didn't look like they'd hand me over to a cardinal any time soon, so I took a risk, and to hell with it. "My name's Rojan." I gripped my pulse pistol, my lucky charm, with my good hand and shuffled round so the door was within reach – you never knew how someone was going to take this and getting the fuck out is certainly the better part of not getting your head stove in. "I'm a pain-mage."

It was touch-and-go there for a while, whether the father was going to kick my bollocks off for being a mage or laugh in relief I wasn't a Special there to arrest them. In the end he settled for a spat: "And?"

I cast a glance over at the boy, who looked like a light had just gone on in his head.

"And so's he, I think."

Before I knew what was happening, the father had grabbed the front of my allover and lifted me off the ground. I had to try, very hard, not to lash out, with pistol or with magic.

"My boy's no hell-damned mage." He rattled me against the wall with every word. I hoped like hell the wall could take it. "You hear me? He's a good boy, not some dirty mage, and you aren't taking him away."

As previously noted, I am not a tactful man and I'd used up the day's supply, plus my hand was throbbing like a bastard.

I had all this juice sloshing round and a black chuckle in the back of my head saying *Do it, go on, show the stupid sod*. And, well, I had this inexplicable aversion to being called dirty, unholy or all those other things they called mages. Made me cranky.

The spell was going to be something small but impressive. I'd discovered that rearranging air could have some pretty spectacular effects and it was just a little thing – use a blast of air to push him away, maybe rearrange my face from my disguise to look like his for a moment. Nothing much, just enough to show him what I was about, and perhaps shut him up about how mages were dirty.

I've never been one for restraint, though, and Dendal's sermons on mastery and control couldn't quite overcome my stinging ego, so what *actually* happened was he ended up blasted into the other wall, bringing down a shower of damp plaster and knocking a small and badly done picture of the Goddess face-first on to the pile of rat bones. The lack of restraint hadn't done wonders for my head either. Little black spots kept swimming past my eyes on their way to somewhere.

The father glared up at me with his mouth open, and looked at his own face on mine. It's handy for freaking people out, satisfying if petty. Another boom-shudder pierced the sudden silence, brought another shower of plaster raining on his head and made the hovel shiver like an old man with ague. A chunk of ceiling made a bid for freedom, smashed the picture of the Goddess through the rat bones, and I wondered just how safe this building was. The superstructure should be all right – barring a catastrophe such as me going batshit, it had been built to withstand a lot. But individual buildings, bolted on an age ago, bolts probably rusty, or synth-eaten . . . maybe not so much. I began a swift calculation of how far it would be to fall if the floor gave way. Too far for my liking.

But after a few heart-stopping moments of absolute terror, everything settled back to almost normal. The boy sat, gobsmacked and speechless, his gaze pinging between me and his father. I had less luck with the father as he got up.

I used my best weapon: my oversized mouth. "Yes, I think he's a mage, and no, we aren't dirty, or unholy or any of those other things Ministry told you to believe. We're men and women who can . . . do a little extra. Bet you get a bit of work in Trade when you can, right?"

A moody shrug, wary but belligerent still. Then again, I was feeling pretty belligerent myself.

"Who do you think got the factories running again so you *could* work? So you could earn a pittance, yes, I know, but better than the fuck-all you earned while they weren't running. Who do you think is lighting the streets? Helping heat this place so we don't all freeze our bollocks off? It's not much, but it's something. I don't know how much you know about what happened with the Glow, with the 'Pit, but most of it's probably crap. The news-sheets print what their patron cardinals tell them to, and it's bullshit. What isn't bullshit is: mages make Glow. Mages power Trade. Mages might be all we've got to beat the Storad off and we need them. *Need.* Right now. So are you going to tell me how dirty I am, in which case I shall showcase some of my better spells, which you will regret, quite possibly over a protracted period of time? Or will you let me train your son so he can help us all out of this mess? If not, you let the Storad just walk in and fuck us all over, worse than even Ministry. Because they will if they get the chance. They care about Trade, about machines, and factories. Maybe they don't eat babies, but they don't give a shit about what's down here, or who, and while they may not come down and kill us outright, I don't see them coming over all charitable and feeding us."

This little speech seemed to terrify the boy even more, but the father beetled his brows like he was really thinking. Another boom-shudder that rattled the walls – they were definitely getting closer together – gave a bit of added weight to what I'd just said.

The father's fists clenched and unclenched a few times and his face creased but I got the impression it wasn't me especially that he was pissed off with. Made a change anyway, and a good job too, because using my magic had made me a bit light-headed, except in the places it was very dark indeed. Things seemed to swim in and out, up and down, and I was very nearly sick on the floor. I tried to get a grip on myself, but only partially managed it. Something big and black swam past my vision and I was sure only that it had glowing eyes, striped skin and big, hungry teeth.

Concentrate, for fuck's sake. Hold on, because the last thing we need is to demolish anything.

It took a few minutes, but given my state of mind I was happy to wait. The father finally seemed to come to a decision and I braced myself. It didn't really help against what he said.

"Beat the Storad." He snorted in disgust. "Yeah, that's what they *say*. We all need to beat the Storad to survive, 'our patriotic duty', do what the Goddess tells us – what the priests want us to do, more like, save their skins for them. Cardinals are sending everything they can out through the Mishan gate, getting themselves out too because they can. Because they can pay and the Mishans aren't taking anyone who can't. Storad are coming, got to be strong, keep our heads down, pray for help, that's what the priests are saying. The Goddess will help. But who else is helping?

"I volunteered, you know. Went up far as they'd let me, said I'd fight. And they said, 'Sure, you can fight.' Wouldn't give me no weapon though. All the guards and Specials, *they* got guns. And I know we've got guns and to spare – I did a couple of days' work next to one of the factories that's making them. Saw some get shipped out to – well, not to *our* guards, let's put it like that. But give a gun to a man from Under? No. They don't know who we might shoot. They want us to fight, but those same cardinals, they aren't letting us, except as the poor bastards that'll be first to die. Well they're going to find out, oh yes, sure as shit stinks, because I'm not the only one thinking this way: that this could be an opportunity. All right, so you're a mage. And the boy too. You mages fighting for them, for Ministry? Or for us?"

I opened my mouth to say, "Not for Ministry, are you crazy?", and then had to stop. Because I was, in a way. Perak *was* Ministry, Archdeacon, Mouth of the Goddess, though he wasn't representative of all those cardinals. He had pretty much the same opinion of them as I did. I was still working for Ministry. When had I gone from hating them so bad I'd happily kill them all, to this? When it was my brother. It made this tricky though, so I did the best I could. My best is usually lying, so I went with that.

"Not for them, for everyone. Without Glow, you're dead, and so am I, from the damned cold if nothing else. We beat the Storad, *then* we can fuck over every cardinal we can find, and I promise you I'll take great pleasure in it. But will you let me take the boy? Even if I don't, he'll still be a mage and without knowing what he's doing . . . it could be messy."

A look passed between father and son, and it was hard to say what kind of look Perhaps a regret on the father's part – that he thought he had more time before his boy made his way into the world, and that this wasn't what he'd hoped for. On the boy's part, it was part dread, part hope perhaps. I remembered the feeling vividly – knowing there was something different about me, something awful and wonderful, and not knowing how to control it, or even what it was. At least he didn't have to hide it, not as I had when mages were illegal. A small consolation perhaps.

"All right," the father said at last. "Cabe, you go with him. He screws you over, you come back home." Then to me, "You'll look after him, right? You said food too. Proper food."

"Proper food. It's not much, but it isn't rats."

Not yet anyway – it might come to that, but there wasn't any point saying that part. And then, because I couldn't get the thought of those rat bones out of my head, and because my conscience was getting to be a pain in the arse just lately, "Look, what's your name? Quillan, all right. You take him there, say I sent you. And if you get hungry, you come visit your boy and maybe I can squeeze an extra place at the table."

Simple as that, I had yet another poor sap roped into a life of hurting themselves for the good of everyone else.

Chapter Nine

Clearly, we were up to our necks in shit. Given that we were a hundred levels above the bottom of Mahala, that's a lot of shit.

It was the next morning, though you wouldn't have been able to tell from me sleeping or anything so sensible. Instead I was perched on a stupid rock far too high up for my liking, and trying not to look down, with varying success.

This city outgrew its walls a long time ago. What we had was mountains. Mahala had grown to fit the space in between like a fungus, spilled out over the top in a welter of concrete and steel. I wasn't looking out over walls, and glad of it.

Outside, a pair of machines were firing out smoke and missiles. They were taking it in turns to pound out what looked like very big bullets. Each salvo began with a hollow boom as the engines geared up and ended with a shudder as the projectiles battered into the stone gates, and each time more of that stone chipped away. The machines belched out black smoke which twined among the buildings close by the gates, made every breath a choke and left its mark in sooty smudges over everything.

From where I stood – OK, crouched behind a handy outcrop, hanging on for dear life – I was almost directly above one of only two identical concessions to the truth that Outside did, in fact, exist despite Ministry's protestations and probably disgust. Under the platforms of Clouds and Top of the World, just above Heights and Trade and tucked out of the way so it couldn't be seen unless you were looking for it, there *was* a small wall. Small but very, very thick, between two arms of a mountain where they ran down to meet each other, making a natural chasm that just begged for a wall. On this side of it lay a wide space filled with abandoned crates and Glow-driven machines for moving cargo that sat dead and sad-looking in the rain. The remnants of the life-blood of Mahala, trade. Below us, in that small wall, a set of gates. Fifty feet high and maybe three or four thick, they sat at the end of a short tunnel, almost an arch, to keep them from prying eyes. From inside the city, anyway. On the other side of the wall and gate, further up a small valley that seemed it could barely contain them, was an army.

If it had just been men, we'd have been laughing. Mahala, with her coat of mountains, was nigh-on impregnable, and where the structure was weak, like the tunnels, we were sneaky. Sneaky was no damned good against what the Storad had brought with them.

I lowered the telescope. "How long, do you think?" The question on everyone's lips.

Pasha twisted his fingers beside me, hissed in pain and screwed up his eyes. "They think a week, maybe less. So do I. That's if the rest don't turn up too soon."

Pasha looked a bit sick, but determined all the same. I was pretty impressed by him being able to rummage in heads over that distance, and said so.

"Not so hard – it's all they're thinking about. That and, well, I know Dench so it's easier to get a fix on him."

We waited a while in the freezing dawn rain – the Storad had certainly picked their time, and I didn't envy those men out there under canvas with sleet slicing down at odd angles so that it got under even the best coat. Under usual circumstances, just before winter set in would be a stupid time for a siege, but they had to strike while we were weak. If they waited till spring, when the snow melted off the pass, we might have built our strength back up. A risk for them but frankly, at that point, my money was on them. The really heavy snow of true winter wasn't due for a month or more, and Pasha was right – it wouldn't be a week before those gates were down. Not unless we did something about it.

I flipped up my coat collar, but as was usual the bastard rain managed to sneak its way in and down my back. As the day grew greyer and colder and the rainclouds thicker, what we were waiting for came.

Dench's men hadn't come back from their little sortie down in the tunnels, and he must be wondering why, or where, exactly – or maybe he knew *exactly* where. Maybe he was planning another attack, only it would be careful and precise if I knew Dench. We were hoping to beat him to it.

We weren't using that tunnel we'd discovered, or rather not in the way Dench would expect. Because he knew about them and he wasn't daft, so he'd have them covered if he knew where the entrances were, and I was sure he knew where the entrance to that one was because his men had been down it once already. Jake had been lucky – Pasha had talked to her before we'd made the climb up here. Dench hadn't found the tunnel she was currently in as she looked for Allit's machines. It was too far up the pass perhaps. That was the good news. The bad news was that not only were the new machines really real and really coming over the pass, they were closer than we'd hoped too. Jake had been all gung-ho about trying a bit of sabotage and mayhem, but Pasha had managed to talk her out if it. For now. He'd managed by telling her that if, or more like when, it all went tits-up she could use her swords as much as she liked.

Back down by the gates, Dench would have the tunnels he knew about covered against attack, by people waving weapons at least.

Pasha muttered under his breath as we waited, and waited. "Come on, come on, what's keeping them?"

"I know this sounds like a stupid question, but can you smell bacon?" I could, again, but I couldn't be sure it wasn't my shrivelled stomach playing tricks on me.

I used the telescope to look out over the camp. Behind the nearest machine belching out missiles, behind the swathe of tents that might have been white once but were now a uniform mud-grey, there was definitely some sort of corral arrangement. It had some animals in it, I couldn't really tell what – most animals I had only seen in books – but perhaps even pigs. Goddess's tits, I'd have sold my soul to have just one, crisping nicely. I swallowed a mouthful of drool and told my stomach to shut the hell up.

Pasha gave me a funny look, but he sniffed and shook his head. "You're imagining it. I wish you weren't though."

Another salvo, another boom-shudder that made me drop the telescope and hang on to the outcrop with my good hand. It really was a long way down. I tried not to look, but it was like telling yourself not to think about marshmallows – suddenly that's all you can think about. The rock we were sitting on wasn't very wide. It was also steeply sloping, and slippery, the freezing rain turning to slushy ice as it hit the rock, which wasn't ideal for holding-on purposes. And there was me with only one hand that worked. Down there, where I was sure I'd drop, were a lot more rocks. Eventually, anyway.

So I was glad when it all kicked off – took my mind off a messy death. Lise's cunning little plan started with what looked like mist drifting across the narrow valley the Storad were camped in. Only mist isn't usually green. It didn't take long for the gas to plume out of the tunnel, and we could hear the sudden choking faintly from here. Not lethal, the gas, but nasty, with a horrendous stench that seemed to coat all your airways. An invention of Lise's and one she'd used on me once upon a time, in a different life.

I picked up the telescope from where it had rolled, balanced it on the outcrop and, taking my life in my one working hand, looked through it. Took me a minute to find the right place, but then Dench staggered out of his muddy tent, his moustache stiff with anger before he clamped a cloth over his nose and mouth. He waved his free arm about and men staggered to obey whatever orders he'd just given. They found it hard, because coughing so much you feel like your guts are going to come up does that to a person. Good luck to them fighting that gas, because that was all they would find.

"Well?" I laid the telescope down and grabbed back hold of the mountain.

A small wet crack as Pasha dislocated a finger, then a pained chuckle. "Oh yes, he's distracted as shit. Not thinking about anything except clear the gas, check for attackers coming through it while they're weak. He's swearing at you too. Quite a lot."

"Good. All right, let's see if I can do this."

It was a long shot, at best. I didn't think it would work and it was going to hurt – a lot – but it had to be worth a try. Even if it only slowed the Storad down. Time was what we needed, what Lise needed to get her genius in gear and find something that would give us the edge in this war, to finish the mysterious gadget she was working on.

I let go of the outcrop – reluctantly, it has to be said – and got myself settled as best I could, leaning up against a wall of rock at my back. I kept my eyes on the Storad machines, which were quiet now, with their crews concentrating on breathing rather than firing. But the gas wouldn't last long before it blew away, and then it would be back to blasting the shit out of the gates again. I didn't dare try this while they were firing – crap only knows what would have happened.

It didn't take much. With my hand as screwed as it was, I only needed a little twist for the pain to bloom, bright and large, in my head. And with the pain came power. It fizzed in my blood, sparked in my head and, as always, it brought its friend along for the ride. The black was getting harder and harder to ignore, but I did my best and concentrated on the machines.

Another twist, another burst of juice, another sing-song in my head. *Come on, Rojan, come in. Let it all go and sink into me. You know you want to.* I gritted my teeth against it, against the pull of the pain, the pull of glorious nothingness to fall into.

The machines were like nothing I'd ever seen before, but Lise had studied them as well as she could from this distance and she'd explained them to me in words of one syllable. I knew what part I had to go for, the easiest to find and rearrange. The long barrel that was pointing at the gates. Just a little rearrangement, nothing fancy. Mould the metal, pinch the barrel. Block those big-arse bullets. With any luck, it'd backfire too. Take that boom-shudder, you bastards.

I pulled the pain in, up my arm, sharpened it to a point in my head. A long way away, those guns. Maybe too far. The metal was thick too, but I started to get a feel for it, to persuade it that actually, what it *really* wanted to do was soften and bend. Using as little magic as possible, because falling over the edge into the black is not a good plan, especially when precariously perched atop a rock. Subtle stuff, and I am not noted for my subtlety.

Twist those fingers again, let the magic flow through you, take you. Make that barrel tie itself in a knot. Show everyone that you're a god among men. You and me, Rojan. Come on, fall in and show the world.

Sweat slicked my face, dripped unheeded into my eyes. Pain throbbed through me but I was past the point of it hurting, exactly. It was red-black warmth inside, an aching comfort, what I knew, like it or not. Pain was part of who I was, who I still am, will always be. Before, I'd always thought I was afraid of my magic because using pain was a stupid way to do things, because who wants to dislocate a thumb just to cast a simple find-spell? Not me, I was too smart, that was what I'd told myself. There watching the gates, I began to know the truth. It wasn't the pain that had me scared. Maybe it wasn't even the black I was afraid of, but the fact that I couldn't give it up, any of it. That pain would become the core of me, and that I'd like it, need it.

It was Pasha who brought me back this time. It always was. His soft voice in my head, using his own pain for his own particular form of magic. I'd lost count of the times he'd pulled me back, given me a mental slap around the face and told me to stop being so stupid.

I blinked back into daylight, into grey clouds and freezing rain and sleet mingling with the sweat on my face, dribbling down my neck. Yet not fully back. Part of me stayed out there, keeping my black company. The edges of my vision were ragged with dark, tattered flaps of my sanity.

"Not yet. The sacrifice isn't worth it, not for this," Pasha said. I've often wondered since if he knew, somehow, how this would all end. His monkey face scrunched into a wry grin. "I think you screwed them good and proper though. Look."

A glance down at the Storad camp and I didn't need to see Dench's face to know he was as pissed off as I'd ever seen him. He stumped around the front of the machine, jabbed his finger at the half-dozen men who worked the thing, and I could almost hear the shouts from here.

"That should give us a day or two," Pasha said. "Might be enough."

I didn't care so much about that, because watching an ant-sized Dench have an apoplexy of rage was more than enough to keep me amused. I really should grow the fuck up.

Men clustered round the machine, noses and mouths covered, some with arms flailing, some stroking at a beard or with a flustered hand rubbing on the back of their neck in the attitude of stumped men everywhere.

"It'll do," I said, and caught Pasha's fleeting look of worry. Not really a surprise. Laconic I am not, among many, many other things, but I was too tired, too sick with a pain that I wanted more and more, to say anything else.

There was no doubt in my mind at that point. We were screwed six ways from hell.

Chapter Ten

By the time we got back to the office, I was ready to fall on the sofa behind my recalcitrant desk, nurse my hand with a shot of something medicinal and perhaps sleep for Mahala. Sadly, I wasn't going to get the chance. Again.

The office was looking the worse for wear. Soot stained the glass of the single window. Even Griswald the tiger, battered and grey with age and moths, looked tattier than normal.

Dendal sat in his usual spot in the corner and Pasha slumped behind his desk, looking even shittier than I felt. It been a long, hard week and it was only going to get longer and harder. We were living on the edge of the worst thing ever to happen to this city, and I think we all just wanted it over with. The Storad making it into the city might even be a relief. At least it would end this feeling of dangling over a precipice with nothing but sharp rocks to fall on to.

A single boom-shudder, weaker than the others. We'd

taken out one machine but the other, further away up the little valley where I didn't have a hope of reaching it, was still going. The only consolation was that the extra distance made the shots weaker. The narrowness of the valley meant that if they wanted to move it nearer, they'd have to dump the closer one over the lip of the valley. Time, we'd gained a little time. How long till they fixed the closer machine or gave it up as a bad job and dumped it? Who knew? Maybe a day. Maybe a week. Without a plan, it didn't matter because we were going to be screwed.

Of course, Perak had a master plan – he always did, that was the problem. The other problem was, he was being all cagey about said master plan. All I knew was it involved our sister Lise and some contraption she had in mind. I trusted her ingenuity more than I trusted Perak's planning, if I'm honest. Perak is far too fair-minded to be properly sneaky. While being fair-minded is useful in some, probably most, situations, when you're about to plunge into a war it's a hindrance. But hey, Perak was Archdeacon. Who was I to argue? Of course, that didn't mean I hadn't. But still, Perak was being distressingly obstinate and vague, while Pasha and I were whacked out on pain and juice.

Speaking of obstinate, here Perak was now, breezing up to the office like an old statesman, saying goodbye to Erlat at the door with a knowing look, making me wonder what was going on when I wasn't looking. Perak came in, glad-handing Lastri, putting her on the back foot – oh yes, didn't I love that! – taking the time to ask after Pasha, and apologising for keeping Jake away from home so much.

Jake herself was a step behind him, freshly back from her reconnoitre of the pass. I tore my eyes away because I could feel Pasha's gaze burning a hole in my neck, and concentrated on Perak. He looked nervy now, like he was strung out on something. Stress, no doubt – I wouldn't have swapped places with him for anything. Storad at the gates and half his remaining cardinals at his back, either hating him or hoping to sneak their way into his job when he fucked up. The other half of the cardinals were ratting it out, and I could hardly even blame them, though naturally I did, at vitriolic length.

"A good job at the gates," Perak said, but there was an edge to his voice, a suppressed . . . something. "Should give us some extra time." He lowered his voice so that Dendal and Lastri – despite her loitering with intent to eavesdrop – couldn't hear. "We've got something to show you."

There was something in the way he said it that jerked me back to full awakeness. Like we were boys again and he wanted to show me something he'd discovered – what happened when he mixed these two chemicals together, or some little gizmo he'd not only repaired but improved. The look in his eye for his big brother, and surrogate father, that said "Look at what I did!" I'd missed that, and had forgotten I'd missed it.

He glanced at Pasha and nodded towards the door. He took us through the pain room, through Lise's work room which was a riot of bits of metal, brightly coloured cables and cans of oil, racks of tools that looked like instruments of torture, half-built gadgets and machines. On the other side of her work room was a door that was, or always had been when I'd noticed, kept locked. Perak glanced my way with a conspiratorial grin and took out a key.

The room the other side of the door was just as incomprehensible to me as all the rest of Lise's gadgets and gizmos. A contraption stood in the centre of the floor. I'd be more specific but it looked like a big pile of complicated metal to me. I could see about half of Lise – her top half seemed to be inside the machine and I could hear the tinkle of metal being adjusted and her cursing under her breath.

She pulled out when she heard us come in, her face smudged with oil and her dark hair tied back tight so as not to get in the way. "I think it's done," she said to Perak. "But I'm not sure about the couplings."

They launched into a conversation that I only understood about half the words of, so Pasha and I took a closer look at the machine. It came up to about my chest, and like the pain-room generator it had a seat attached and a rig for taking magic – that is, for siphoning off a mage's pain. It isn't pleasant and this rig in particular looked even less so, a nest of cables around shining pistons and toothed cogs and other things I have no name for. It reminded me of nothing so much as a tiger, of Namrat, Death, always chasing us, wanting to eat us. Death was never far away. It made my stomach turn.

"That thing scares the shit out of me," Pasha whispered.

"Me too."

Lise started to talk in a language I could understand – she knows how I feel about alchemy and all the rest.

"I think we've got it right. I think this is what we need, what will keep us safe till we can make something, or do something, to fend off the Storad for good. I've got some plans for some machines like theirs. Got a factory working on them, but it'll take longer than we have, and even longer to scrounge up the raw materials we need. So, to give us some time, I made this. It might even help against the machines Allit saw, the ones on their way."

"What is it?" Pasha asked, and he sounded as disturbed as I felt. Genius machines though Lise's contraptions were, they tended to be centred on one thing – our pain and how to use it.

Lise grinned like the kid she was only just starting to grow out of. Nice to see her smile again, and only this, these things, would do it for her. Since Dwarf had died, she'd retreated into her work until it was all she saw, all she thought about. It worried me, but we needed her to do just that too.

"This will take your pain, yes, sorry," she said. "Magnify it like the generator. But it does something very specific with it. It's . . . " She hesitated, and gave me one of her looks, the one that makes it very clear how dense she thinks I am about mechanicals. "It's like your pulse pistol. Sort of. Only a lot bigger. I've even built in some directional controls, look.

Should be able to pinpoint who you want, or spread it over an area. Like the front of the gates." She pointed at a couple of dials like I was likely to understand.

I must have looked dubious – I certainly felt it – because she started to defend her contraption before I'd said a word.

"It's like electricity. Magic is, I mean. We can't seem to get a way to make enough electricity to be useful except this way, not in time anyway. It's . . . Rojan, this is hard to explain when you don't know what the hell I'm talking about. We can use it as a shield. Sort of. You know how electricity arcs . . . No, I don't suppose you do. Look, just, just believe it, all right? You could use this to spread a pulse right across the gates, or anywhere you can reach. Probably to the lip of the valley. Maybe further."

"All right, I believe it. Does it work?"

That got me a pout and a glare. "Not yet, but soon. I think. Only . . ."

That didn't sound good. "Only what?"

Lise threw her screwdriver into the toolbox at her feet. "Only, I don't know! The theory is sound, I'm sure of it, but I don't know what the effects might be. I can't be *sure*."

"Sure of what?" Perak asked quietly.

Lise turned away to stare at a picture that peeked out of the toolbox. A face that only a mother, and perhaps Lise, could love. Dwarf's weird-ugly features stared up out of the picture, from beyond the grave. Lise's mechanic hero, and perhaps more. "*He'd* have known. But I can't be sure."

"Lise, sure of what?"

"What it'll do to the mage in the rig."

Oh, *fantastic*. Three guesses who was going to end up in that rig. "I don't think—"

That was as far as I got because an ominous crack sounded from what seemed like under our feet and the remaining faint boom-shudders stopped. The sudden, if relative, silence was like a razor down the spine.

Lise paled and ran to the main lab, to the telescope she'd set at the window where she studied the Storad and their machines as best she could. Perak shut his eyes and murmured what could only be a prayer under his breath before he followed her.

I followed more hesitantly and was rewarded with Lise's "Oh shit, fuck and *arse*."

The near gun was still out, thank crap. But the far gun, the one I couldn't reach from inside Mahala, had stopped because the Storad had finally done what they set out to do. My little shenanigans down at the gates had bought us bugger-all extra time. A crack split the left-hand gate right down the middle and it hung from its great hinges like a leering drunk.

The Storad were no longer at the gates. They were on their way through them.

Chapter Eleven

We were back on that stupid rock again, high above what was left of the gates. I held on for grim death and Pasha and Allit looked out and told me what they could see and hear above what I could see for myself.

The left-hand gate was a mess of metal and stone, chunks of both strewn across the gap inside. Across the chaos came the Storad, a stream of dark-haired, pale-faced men who looked as hard as the mountains they came from. The far machine which had taken the gate down stood Outside in the distance, quiet now, looking smug.

Men dropped down on the path from the narrow valley, came through the ruined gates in a regimented flood, distinct groups heading for distinct areas. One group to the dead Glow machines that had been used to lift and carry all our wares, where they began to strip anything we'd left, which wasn't much. Another group set up what looked like some kind of command centre just inside the gates, Dench in among them. Still others checked out the furthest reaches of the compound, or tested the inner gates that led inside. Not as strong as the outer gates, but it might take a day or two to get through them.

Some of the guards shot at them, though their aim wasn't great and most of the Storad stayed well out of the guns' current range in any case. Perak said the last lot of guns down at Factory Three could shoot more than double the distance. Until then, or until a decision as to what the hell to do had been reached, Malaki ordered the guards to stop shooting.

"Well?" I asked.

Pasha's monkey features scrunched up in concentration as he surveyed below. "It's . . . ah, there. Dench. He knows, Rojan. He knows what you and I can do. That I'm looking in their heads right now, trying to work out what they're about. Got them all repeating a phrase over and over in their heads so I can't see past it. Currently, said phrase is 'Fuck Rojan.'"

"Nice. He doesn't know about what Allit can do though, does he? Allit?"

The kid was pale but stoic, his eyes shining with hero worship of Pasha and, dare I say it, me. It felt good, but part of me knew I was going to have to let him down gently, because a hero I ain't.

He shuffled forward and grabbed at a finger as he'd seen

Pasha and I do countless times. A twist, a crack that made me grimace along with him, a whimper from a voice not yet broken properly. But he was made of stern stuff.

His eyes went far away, as though he was looking somewhere else, and I suppose he was.

"Almost here," he said in a whisper, and we knew what he meant. More Storad machines, more men. Then his mouth cranked up into a one-sided smile. "Not just them. Others too. Below."

"What do you . . . ? Oh."

From up here we could see the inner gates, see where the Storad had noted our lack of shooting and had sent a small sortie to check them for strength, for weaknesses. We could see this side too, see what the Storad couldn't. A barrel-load of men. Guards in their tabards, milling restively, waiting for the order to shoot.

The guards had always been an arrogant bunch of bastards – I swear it was on the application form: "Please rate your arrogance from 1 to 10" and only someone putting 11 had a hope of getting in. I suppose it came with the territory. They got to do things most of Under only got to dream about. Like having a decent wage without having to bust a gut for it. They were damned good at not busting a gut to solve any crimes, certainly. Instead they revelled in their small rise above the masses, in the freedom to do whatever the hell they liked to a suspect as long as he wasn't Ministry, and Goddess help them if they arrested a Ministry man.

They hadn't signed up for this, I could almost see that thought radiate off them. They'd signed up for a uniform that meant they got to bully people in their normal course of work, for a steady stream of bribes, for the little extras that being a Ministry man, however menial, could give them. They were just your regular guys with a tabard and not much else. I could hardly even blame them for joining up – a job's a job and you do what you can for you and yours. Perak had brought about enough changes as it was, ones that screwed with their nice, contained little lives. New captains, ones who frowned very hard indeed on bullying, bribery or extras. On top of that, now they had to risk their arses in a way they never had before, in a way few of us had ever had to, and they had to be shitting bricks down there. I almost felt sorry for them. Almost.

Even without the different uniforms, you could tell the Specials from the regular guards. While the guards shuffled about like naughty children told to stand in the corner, the Specials stood serene, on the surface at least. Waiting with an infinite patience that was somehow even more bollock-clenching to look at than the uniforms or any amount of bravado would have been.

But bravado wouldn't have helped then. The guards were crapping themselves and, looking the other side of the gates, I couldn't blame them. All of the guards and Specials had guns now – Trade had been pumping them out as fast as its factories could, at least until the raw materials ran out. The

Storad, though, had come for war. Had prepared for it, must have done, must have just been waiting for the right time. Every damn one had a gun or something like it, most had two. Some had other contraptions that grew on their backs like weird metallic monkeys. I didn't know what they did, but I did know I didn't want to find out. And behind them, perched in the top of the valley and looking over them like a watchdog, they had the machine that had already taken down gates that were strong as mountains. It was silent now, presumably so as not to blow up its own men, but it was still there, and it still worked. The other machine, the one I'd bent, looked neglected and bleak, but it didn't matter. A few people wouldn't be a problem for the machine that was left. No, they'd soon be a big fat mess.

All in all I was glad I'd never taken up that career in the guards, and that I'd have made a really crap Special. Then again, at least I wouldn't have been perched on that rock like an idiot, trying not to think about falling off.

The three of us were silent as we each surveyed what was below us.

"What do you think?" I said in the end. I'd twisted one of the big guns, but the other had been beyond me, too far, too much. One was a start but I knew we'd have to sort the other sooner rather than later, because at some point the Storad would finish their inspection and the boom-shudders would start all over again, against the inner gates this time. I had no idea how I was going to sabotage that machine – there was no way I could reach it from inside the city, and I didn't fancy the tunnels again one little bit.

"I think we're screwed," Pasha said. "Can you do the same again with that machine? Or something worse? Worse would be better."

"Doesn't matter," Allit said in a dreamy voice. "More on the way. *Lots* more. We won't do it in time . . . I think . . . I . . . " He shook his head and went quiet.

"I can try," I said, and I'd had a few evil plans hatch in my head. "But . . . " Shit, I couldn't believe I was saying this. "I can do a bit from here, same as before, though that one's too far really. Like you said, Dench knows what we can do. Or at least, thinks he does. But if we got close, I could make it so they couldn't repair it, or not without a lot of replacement parts."

"You want to go down there, in that lot?"

"No. No, I really don't. But I think I might have to."

Pasha gave me a funny look, like I'd grown an extra head or something. "All right," he said in the end. "We'll see what Perak's plans are first. And then we'll *both* go. If I let you go on your own, no telling what might happen."

We made our way back, and I was glad to have a few buildings between the gate and me so I couldn't see the drop any more. Perak wasn't down in the office though, of course. He was up in Top of the World. We stopped off to see Lise, who was staring through the telescope.

"Well?" she demanded.

"Well, I'd get that thing going if I were you, and preferably so it doesn't screw over the mage in it. Look, have you had any other ideas? Any other plans? You know, better guns? Something nice and explosive? We could really use something explosive about now."

"One or two, over and above the guns we've got coming, but they aren't ready. They'll take a day or two to make, more, even if I can find enough raw materials, and even then I can't make many – not enough, that's for sure. Then the factories need a pattern set before they can churn stuff out. But that's not the main problem. It's steel we're short of. They may not work even then, and I should really be concentrating on the shield."

An idea struck me, harmonising quite nicely with my idea for attacking the working machine perched up in the valley. I couldn't help what was probably quite an evil grin. "I might be able to help you out there. With the steel, that is. See what you can do, because I think we're going to need everything you can give us, as soon as the factories can make it."

She frowned at me but for once she didn't argue and we left her muttering under her breath about tensile strength and minimum carbon content. Or something.

Top of the World was a long way from the lab, but with the Glow back on I managed to snaffle a vial to power up my carriage. It was a pretty shit ride, with knackered suspension and ripped upholstery that had been torn out by unhappy "customers" in my former life as a bounty hunter, but it beat walking, or screwing with my hand any more to rearrange myself and Pasha up there.

Away from Trade, up into Heights and past the want-to-haves, through neighbourhoods that got to see the sun at least twice a day for perhaps an hour at dawn and sunset, lucky bastards. Up along the twisting Spine that led from the bottom of Boundary, threading its way through every layer till it broke free of the city and surged past the vast estates of Clouds that balanced precariously over the grubby unwashed of Under, and on like a thread of hope to Top of the World.

The Archdeacon's Palace was the part of Mahala that everyone looked up to – we didn't have a lot of choice really. Atop a platform that from Under looked mythical, it was as different from the rest of the city as I am from a model of chastity. I'd been up there a few times by then, but it still got me, every time. The sense of space, of buildings with room to breathe rather than squashed in together, squeezed by the buildings above, below, to either side. No squashing here. Here was space and beauty. Glow lights in the shape of flickering birds in cages and fluttering rainbow moths. Even flowers, real ones. The ones I hadn't accidentally lopped off, that was.

On two sides of the main plaza, a maze of spire-topped buildings that looked spun out of light and air, outlined by Glow-moths so they almost seemed on fire. On another side, nothing but space and the long drop – from there you could look down over the city if you were brave enough to get close to the edge, could see the dark smudge of it spreading beneath you like an oilstain, sticky and black.

On the last side, what had been the Home of the Goddess

was now a sad pile of rubble, stripped of anything we could rip out to trade with the Mishans for food and raw materials. Wherever I go, I always like to make a lasting impression, and what I'd done to the Home of the Goddess was no different. She was going to have to find somewhere else to sleep.

It was nice being able to saunter past the Specials on the gate – well, nice for us. They looked like they'd been force-fed their own entrails, but they let us past with nothing more than a sour look. Still, no one was executing anyone up here today so I tried to stay jaunty. Got to take it while you can.

We found Perak at the true Top of the World, a circular platform that soared above everything else, seemingly over and above even the very tops of the mountains that looked far-off and yet very real from there. There wasn't even a nice handrail to hang on to, and with that and the wind that whipped my coat out behind me, I got a bit watery around the courage bone. I sucked it up and put a face on it, because looking weak in front of your little brother, well, I just didn't like to. Besides, Jake was here too, fresh from her little jaunt down the tunnel and looking like she'd loved every minute of it. I wasn't about to look chickenshit in front of her. Pasha bit his lip to stop a grin, and had to turn away when I glared at him, but I made it without screaming or gibbering to where Perak stood, looking into a telescope he'd had set on to a tripod, and the tripod set into the stone right at the edge of the platform.

I kept my eyes on Perak rather than look at the drop – if I

looked that way, it would all end in tears. Mine. Naturally, Perak's first words made sure I had to sodding well look.

"Use the telescope, there where I've set it. Tell me what you think."

I put my big boy's pants on, held on to the tripod like it was a long-lost friend, and took a look. I'd thought I was going to see a bird's-eye view of the shattered gates. That would have been bad enough. Instead I got an eyeful of the bulky shoulder of one of the mountains to the north, about on a level with Trade, where the buildings broke free of stone and the mountains receded into craggy spires to rival Top of the World. Across this bulky shoulder, a path had been carved. The pass that they said our city was founded on.

My knees went as watery as my courage bone. I think I may have sworn, quite nastily, because Pasha said, "What?" though he must have had an idea.

Luckily I was saved from answering in what would have been a rather squeaky little voice. I know doom when I see it.

"What Allit saw," Perak said. "Whatever his precise talent, this is what he says he saw, what Jake confirmed for me as I'm sure she's told you. And it's coming. Sooner than we thought."

Men, machines, mountains. I'd thought the Storad already at the gates were bad enough – they darkened the small valley that they'd camped in, left nothing but men and tents all across it. There were perhaps twice that number on the pass, maybe more. Not just men either. Oh no, that would be too easy. Machines they already had, one of which we'd totally scuppered, one they'd finally taken down the outer gates with. I could see two more of those on the pass, as well as one of the mutant machines, or whatever it was, from Allit's vision. Allit had seen more than that, but the cavalcade at the other end of the telescope hadn't finished coming around the cold shoulder of the mountain.

Pasha took his own look through the telescope, and when he'd finished he'd gone a pale shade of gutted – must have been different seeing it through his own eyes rather than someone else's.

"What's the plan, Perak?" I asked. "You do *have* a plan, right?"

Perak paced up and down, far too close to the edge for my liking, but he didn't seem to notice the drop. Too busy thinking. "This changes things. A lot. But I've been thinking on it since Jake confirmed it. Taking advisement, from Jake, Malaki, Guinto even. Sadly some of the cardinals have suggested a thing or two but, well, let's not talk about that except to say I'm not sending anyone against them unarmed, I don't care if the Downsiders do want to shoot all the cardinals too. *I* want to shoot half of them." He took a calming breath. "It'll take the Storad time to get down to their camp. Those machines aren't moving fast. Lise's shield, if we can get that working . . . but still, the Storad already through will need dealing with."

"I might have a little plan for that. Could help all round."

Perak shot me a look. I didn't really like the way he leapt on my idea – I've never been known as an ideas man, and for him to jump on it so quick meant he was out of plans himself.

"Tell me."

So I did, while his eyebrows shot up into his hairline and kept on going as I outlined it.

"We don't have enough men to take them on as it stands, right? You've got guards down there, and Specials, and . . . it won't be enough, and you say the cardinals won't take anyone else if they're armed. Lise needs more raw materials too. I think . . ." Again, I could not believe I was saying this. Usually I'm out of the room before anyone even thinks of asking for me to help, but this time I was dropping myself in it. "I think we can solve both in one go. If we're careful."

I had their attention.

"The machine further away, up in the valley. It's still covering the gate area, which leaves us hamstrung. Anyone trying to move out of the inner gates will be mincemeat. We need to take it out. Permanently. Maybe . . . maybe move it, or some of it. Rearrange it to where we can cannibalise it for metal."

Perak said nothing but went to the telescope again, training it on the mass of Storad now camped between two sets of gates, then up to the valley where the machine sat silent and brooding for now.

"You really think you could manage it?" Pasha asked.

"Probably not the whole thing. But enough of it that it won't work plus Lise will have some metal to play with. The engine perhaps? She could see how it functions. I'll need to get close though." And someone to help me out afterwards, because I'd be thoroughly screwed. Rearranging really takes it out of me, and I was pretty screwed to start with.

"It's risky," Perak muttered without taking his eye from the telescope. "Too risky."

"What else can we do?"

Perak stood straight with a sigh. "I don't know. But if we lose you, then what about the Glow? It's hard enough now, even with Lise's generator. Too few mages. If we lose one . . . That's what the archdeacon in me says. The brother in me says I lost you for long enough years. I'm not losing you for good if there's another way."

Jake's thoughtful glance my way, and my stupid need not to look like a complete coward in front of her, put a stop to any back-pedalling on my part. "Name me this other way then." I consoled myself with the meagre thought that if it all went wrong, at least I wouldn't have to worry about the cardinals' men grabbing me and taking me to the Storad, because I'd already be there.

It took a lot more than that, of course, but I won't bore you with the details. Suffice to say that, with so few guns available, with so few Specials and the small amount of guards we had, and them not keen on doing the guarding that was suddenly necessary, with the cardinals that hadn't run away in full voice about no one else getting any guns because who knew whom any Under man might shoot but it'd probably be cardinals, we didn't have much choice.

I say "we". What I mean is "I".

Chapter Twelve

I managed a doze while Perak and his advisers, Guinto, Jake, Malaki and a couple of the better bishops, talked logistics. I should have tried to stay awake, I suppose, but that kind of thing makes me sleepy at the best of times, and it certainly wasn't that. I was going to need my strength too, so I dozed and tried not to dream, which is harder than it sounds.

By the time they'd finished, the grey clouds massing over Top of the World had a nasty bruised look to them and had started a short test run of finely powdered snow blowing about on the knife-edge wind. Early in the season, maybe to our advantage. We might be short of food, but *we* weren't camping out. Or trying to bring in men and supplies over a high mountain pass. A spiteful thought – a sudden white-out entombing the Storad in drifts of snow, not to be found till spring, when they'd turn up like frozen rocks when the snow melted. Unlikely, more's the pity, but the early harsh weather could work our way. It was maybe the only thing that would.

Perak and the rest seemed to have come up with a plan of sorts. Malaki was of the opinion that it was a stupid risk but, as he couldn't think of anything better, we were on. Perak had a few provisos though – he *said* they were because he wasn't taking any chances with the two mages who put out the most, almost the only, Glow.

"Most of the Storad have moved down from the valley into the compound between the gates," he said. "Malaki here will get some of his Specials to start sniping them – Lise has managed to get some extra range on a few of the guns. Enough to keep everyone busy, hopefully. At least get them looking at the gates and not where you're going to be."

"The tunnels?"

"Exactly. I had all but one blocked off – hoping it would take them a while to figure out which one. Those tunnels are built for defence, but I can't spare any more men than it takes to hold that one. As far as we can make out – Pasha's been listening to what he can for me – they don't know which it is yet, so you should be able to get right up to their camp without them seeing you. If you're careful."

"OK, that's good, we'll—"

"Take someone with you."

"What?"

"You'll take someone with you. As Pasha has pointed out,

Dench knows you both very well, knows what you're capable of. He's bound to try something on the tunnels anyway – an obvious weak point if you know where they are, and he does, or at least some of them. So, take one of your young mages. One whose abilities he won't know. Allit perhaps?"

"Perak, he's thirteen. He's a good lad, but he's not ready for that. *I'm* not ready for it."

"It was your idea."

"That doesn't mean I like it. Look, I'm not taking a kid out there, not Allit, he's got enough on his plate right now. All right?"

"What were you doing at thirteen, Rojan?" Perak looked all artful, like he was trying to get one over one me.

"Trying not to blow myself up with magic I didn't know how to use!"

"All right then, who else have you got? Because you need some edge, or you aren't going."

"I'll go." Jake's voice was soft but determined, as was she, by the look on her face. "You're going to need someone."

"No," Pasha said quickly, too quickly. He looked paler than ever and I thought back to what Allit had seen, which Pasha had never really outlined in detail except that Dench got hold of Jake. "No, you can't."

She raised a cool eyebrow his way and there seemed to be some sort of silent argument going on. Pasha didn't look to be winning either, if the way his face screwed up was anything to go by, until Perak interrupted smoothly.

"Jake, I'm going to need you here with me now. Don't worry, I'll send a few men to help them, guard the tunnel at their back. Besides, Dench will expect you, be prepared for you. But we need someone else, someone they won't know."

Jake looked about to protest – her hands, as always when threatened, went straight to the hilts of her swords – but it seemed Pasha made some last silent plea and she subsided with bad grace.

"Any ideas?" Perak dropped artlessly into the lull.

I clammed up – no way was I going to volunteer anyone for this. That would make me responsible, so I kept my fat mouth shut for a change. It didn't matter, because a relieved Pasha was ticking off the nos on one hand and the possible yeses on the other.

"I think the most likely is Halina. She's smart, she's got a handle on her magic, as she showed on our last jaunt down there, and I think levitation would be a handy thing to have in our bag of tricks. Most of the rest are too young, or too volatile."

"Yes," Perak said. "Only, um, well, I hesitate to send a lady. I mean, we all hear what soldiers are like, and if they catch you—"

"We'll be dead, Perak. Once you're dead, gender doesn't really matter, don't you think?"

"Yes, but . . ."

Next to him, Jake shifted. A hand on a sword, a jingle of the buckles that held her breastplate on, a half-smile that was anything but friendly. Subtle but unmistakable. A reminder that actually, Perak, you have a lady as head of your guard and she could beat the snot out of anyone in this room and I bet you wouldn't stop her now would you? Or perhaps you might try, but you'd probably lose an appendage or two, besides which hadn't you already sent her into the tunnels? Hadn't she come back safe?

"Well, yes, Jake." Perak answered the unspoken statement. "I know, and I know *you* went down the tunnel, but that was you, who knows one end of a sword from the other and is more than happy to use them. Not some girl who . . . I don't think of you as fem— I just hesitate . . . Look, Pasha, do you think she's the most capable? OK, how about we ask her?"

So we did, and Halina almost bit Perak's hand off in her haste to accept.

After a long and tedious discussion, Perak came to a difficult decision.

"Tonight," he said firmly, with a glare to the most vocal cardinal, who'd tried to make everyone go, right now damn it, before the Storad invaded his personal estate. An extra-special glint to the cardinal's argument had seemed to intimate that if any mages died, that would count as a win-win situation. And this was one of the better cardinals. At least the bold one who wanted to hand me over to save his skin was conspicuous by his absence.

"Malaki is quite right," Perak went on. "Going in daylight

would be out of the question, and I'm not about to lose my two best mages. If nothing else, we need them for Glow. Besides which, I quite like having them alive, thank you."

It's nice to have someone on your side, especially when he's in charge. Both Pasha and I let out long breaths at his words – it was going to be our arses on the line, and any reprieve is better than none.

"You should get some sleep," Perak murmured to me, though he looked like he'd not slept in a week himself. I was sure I could see new strands of grey in his hair and his face looked sallow.

But he was right, so I thought about it. I thought about the office, with the sofa that also served as my bed jammed up behind my desk, and Dendal humming a happy song in the background. I thought about the dreams too, the ones that left me all sweaty with terror and with a hand jammed in my mouth to stop the scream. I needed sleep, but I wasn't sure any of that appealed.

So instead I half took Perak's advice and went to see Erlat. I wasn't expecting to sleep, but you never knew. Besides, she probably had a spare bed I could borrow if I felt like bathing myself in fear-sweat.

Hopefully she'd be here this time – over the last couple of days I'd tried a few times to see her but Kersan kept saying she was "busy". I knocked on the door and restrained the urge to lie against it. I almost fell asleep in the two seconds it took before a familiar face opened it. Kersan smiled to see me, his clothes pristine as always, his smile perhaps a bit too practised, and told me in his smooth voice that "Madame is with a client. Would you care to wait?"

I would, although the thought of "with a client" always made me come over a bit funny. I'm not sure why but . . . Instead of thinking about that, about any of what was struggling in my brain, I studied the paintings on the wall, the nudes draped with bits of velvet, their bodies in new and, um, interesting positions. I must have fallen asleep without realising it, because Kersan's voice made me sit up abruptly and wonder where in hell I was. I levered myself up, sweaty from some half-remembered dream, because the half I could remember was scaring the crap out of me.

Kersan ushered me into Erlat's room. As always, no sign of anyone else ever having been here. Erlat was her polished self, her dark hair smoothed back into an elegant coil at the base of her neck, her movements slow and sensual, her mouth quick to laugh, at least when she saw me. Yet she seemed worn down somehow, tired and just that little bit frazzled, though she favoured me with a teasing smile and a wink, so whatever had her ruffled couldn't be too bad.

"Well, if it isn't my hero." Her mouth taunted me with an impish grin and she smoothed her dark hair. "Don't tell me, you've come to take me up on my offer. About time too."

It felt good, better than good, just to be here where I knew my own mind wouldn't gang up on me, so I let her teasing pass and even, for once, didn't blush. "Not today."

A boom-shudder rattled the teacups on the low table between us.

"How long, do you think?" Erlat asked. The question everyone asked of everyone else, the only question. Unanswerable. It was all people would say, could say, keeping everything else under wraps, locked up tight.

When I didn't reply, Erlat raised an eyebrow and regarded me solemnly. "What, lost for words? That's not the Rojan I know."

I couldn't seem to get any words out – how do you say, "Hey, I think I'm cracking up"? Tell her that I didn't want to talk about it, any of it, and I most certainly wasn't telling her what Pasha and me were doing later and what was bound to follow? When I didn't answer, her frazzled look grew stronger as she sat on the lounger and waved a hand for me to join her. Being Erlat, she didn't start with what was really worrying her but worked up to it gradually.

"How's Lise?"

"Well enough. At least she isn't going stir-crazy cooped up in the lab. *I* am. Well, when I stay cooped up anyway."

"I'd bet that isn't often. Perhaps I have a little good news on that score." Her smile was wicked, almost secretive, and made me wonder, once again, what she'd been up to. The last time I'd seen her she'd been taking her leave of Perak with a knowing look. I had a funny feeling one of his plans was to blame.

"What have you done?"

She laughed, and the sound of it did me the power of good.

"Oh, not much, not much at all. Only, one of my girls, she's a regular visitor to my friend the Mishan liaison. Remember him?"

"He wants me dead. How could I forget?"

She flapped a hand, as though that was inconsequential. "Anyway, we hatched a little plan with Perak. One of my girls has been whispering in his ear about the cardinals who want to turn you over to the Storad. Naturally, this would put a crimp in his plan. I, on the other hand, have dropped plenty of hints about how you can disguise yourself. And that he might want to triple-check anyone who makes it through the gate. You know, anyone who might be pretending to be a cardinal . . . "

I must have sat with my mouth open for a full minute.

"No problem, no need to thank me," Erlat said with a raised eyebrow. "I even went so far as to describe your usual disguise. Which I seemed to think looked deceptively similar to the cardinal who was most vocal about handing you over to the Storad. A cardinal who, I hear, is even now on his way to the gate in a fit of terror at the Storad breaking through the gate."

I came very close to kissing her at that point, but restrained myself. If I did that, one thing would lead to another, and before you knew it I'd have screwed things over. "That's . . . that's . . . "

"Clever of me, I thought."

"Yes, but—"

"But what? You do realise other people talk to each other

when you aren't around? That you aren't the only one doing things? One of Perak's plans, though he left the details to me. We didn't want to worry you. I thought I was quite creative. You owe me, mister."

The hunch in my shoulder, the one that seemed to feel eyes watching me wherever I went, that twitched when I thought about how close Lise had come to being spirited away, relaxed a touch. That's when weariness came back in a rush.

"I can think of a few ways you could pay, too." A lewd wink that I tried to ignore, a short silence and then we came to it – what was really worrying her.

"Please tell me it isn't true."

"Which part?" I resisted the temptation to lean back and fall asleep, but only barely.

"What Allit saw. Is it – is it true, do you think? Can he see it, and does that mean it's real? Jake's back but I didn't have much of a chance to talk to her yet. Is it true?"

"He saw it all right, and yes, they are coming. Jake confirmed it."

She paled at that, and rubbed at her wrists, at the faint trace of scars where once she'd been branded – owned, made into what she was now – and it was the thought of that which caused my itch. Probably.

"Can you stop it?"

I frowned at the undertone of her voice. Erlat is, I've often thought, as polished as a gemstone, smooth and gleaming, no flaws, just mirrored lights that reflect you back at yourself rather than revealing anything. A gemstone, and as hard to get to know. It was misleading, and I sometimes forgot myself, or her. I forgot that she wasn't much more than a girl, really. I forgot because she had such a poise to her you'd think she'd seen everything. Maybe she had – she'd seen far too much of what people are capable of, and yet she bore it all with a grace that was almost invisible.

"Maybe," I said, because I didn't like to lie to Erlat. I'd lie to anyone else, to Namrat and the Goddess themselves, but not to her. A guy's got to have a least one crappy standard. "We're going to try. Tonight. Give ourselves more time, and get Lise some of the raw materials she needs. Maybe."

She got up and paced across a delicate silk rug, done in patterns that twined in her favourite green and gold. "Going to try what?"

"Erlat, can you stop? You're making me dizzy. And I'm not really sure yet, except try to rearrange part of the machine up to the lab. That might bugger them up a bit. Nothing to worry about. Look, would you mind if we talked about something else?"

Because right then it was the last thing I wanted to talk about, or think about, because I was scared to the point of pissing myself at what I'd agreed to. *Suggested.* I should really learn to shut the fuck up when I thought I had a good idea.

Peace was what I wanted, a respite from the ever-present fear, a respite that I'd only ever found in two places. Here at

Erlat's, and in the black. That's why it called to me, why I listened. Only it could give me no fear for the rest of my life, and it was tempting. Maybe that's why I never heard the black here at Erlat's – it had less purchase on me because I had no fear here either. Maybe.

She smiled, but it looked slick and fake and I was sure there'd be more later, more questions, more worry. I couldn't blame her – half the city was stiff with fear. The other half just didn't realise how bad things were. But for now I just wanted to sleep and maybe, hopefully, not dream. At least, asleep, I could pretend I wasn't almost pissing myself wondering what I'd got myself into. But I was too jittery for sleep, and so was Erlat.

"Let's talk about something else," I said in the end. "You, perhaps."

A laugh burst out of her, trailing off into little giggles when she saw I was serious. "What, Rojan Dizon, walking advert for the male ego, wants to talk about something other than himself? Oh, I love it when you make me laugh."

It was hard to be offended when she was right, and that's why I loved going there.

And there, just as it had sneaked up on me, threatened to drown me, it all went away. I was at Erlat's, drinking tea, and she was laughing at me, with me, poking fun and teasing, and everything else was very far away. It was almost as good as sleep.

As always, Erlat knew what to say, how to get me out of my

own head. I tried to do the same for her, told a few scathing and sarcastically drawn stories to make her laugh some more. That laugh did wonders for me, it always had. Showed me just how ridiculous I was. We ignored the boom-shudders and forgot the world outside, just for a few hours.

We only touched on the rest once, when Erlat said with sudden seriousness, "Sometimes you scare me. What the hell do I do with a man who won't let me seduce him?" She tried to laugh, but it came out wrong and she tried to cover it with more words. "What are you scared of, Rojan?"

"You seducing me" brought a smile, but that night . . . it was a rare thing for me. A time when I felt I could be as truthful as true gets. Something about sitting there with Erlat, drinking tea like we didn't have a care in the world, like the Storad weren't at the gates and nothing was wrong, even though everything was wrong. Something about the way she looked at me, and how just being there knocked me sideways so I almost wasn't me. Maybe this was what templegoers felt when they went to confess their sins to the priests. "Screwing it up, that's what I'm scared of. Failing when people are relying on me. That part scares me witless, because I am world-class at screwing it up."

What I didn't say, because there are some truths that are too true to be said out loud, was that I was coming to realise that that was why I was in love with Jake. Partly because I admired her – I loved the way she fought back against every crappy thing life had thrown at her, had scratched and clawed to get a hint of happiness, wouldn't, couldn't give up. But also I was beginning to see that I wouldn't make a play for her, and not just because of Pasha, because he was my friend and I couldn't do it to him, even if I'd had a hope in hell. That was my excuse, but it wasn't the reason. If I couldn't or wouldn't try, I wouldn't fail, wouldn't bugger it up in my usual style. She was safe to be in love with.

Erlat said nothing, and I was glad because I didn't want to think about it any more, the prospect of failing. Instead she smiled a secret little smile, poured more tea and changed the subject.

Maybe confession is good for the soul after all, because the next thing I recall is Erlat shaking me, and me all but falling off the lounger with treacle for brains and what felt like a slug for a tongue.

"You do say some strange things while you're asleep," she said while I tried to remember which way was up. An odd tone to her voice that I couldn't quite pin down.

I got myself arranged in something like normal order, and realised I actually felt halfway to decent, bar the ever-present hollow ache in my belly. "Like what?"

She didn't answer but made herself busy with hot water and tea, with setting out two plates on the low table. I steeled myself for grey mush, but it wasn't too bad. At least it had the texture of real food, even if it tasted like ashes. At that point it was almost luxury.

"Good thing I didn't have any more clients booked," she

said. "You snoring and whiffling on about Jake would have quite put them off their stroke."

I could feel the blush starting round my ears, but I didn't even get the chance to defend myself, because Erlat was clearly enjoying this.

"Didn't even have the decency to share my bed. Of course, you'd be ruined for other women then. Maybe that's why, hmm? Or you're just scared. I bet that's it."

She was chattering – not like her, too quick, too smooth, covering up some nameless fear perhaps. Even so, there was a possibility my face might boil off in embarrassment – hell, even talking about what I was going to be doing in an hour or two, creeping behind enemy lines, exposing myself to crap-only-knew-what, seemed preferable. Actually, right then, Namrat turning up and offering to eat my soul seemed preferable to talking about why I wouldn't take Erlat to bed.

She raised an eyebrow, obviously waiting for an answer. And maybe it was the way she'd said it, or that I wanted to think about pretty much anything apart from down there, outside the gates, in a *war*, for fuck's sake – that made me blurt out something close to the truth.

"I'm scared, that's it."

Of course I regretted it as soon as I'd said it, because she cocked her head on one side like a little bird and waited for me to go on.

I wasn't going to let her fool me that way. There were things I would rather die than say, and that was one.

"Lise has built a new machine," I said instead. "Like my pistol, only bigger. Could really help, a lot. Only Perak won't let us use it."

She laughed at my obvious tactic, but didn't push things and took up my strand of thought. "Why not?"

"Too dangerous. Lise says she's not sure what it'll do to the mage in question."

"Then Perak's right."

"Maybe. And maybe we should try it anyway. If the Storad get in, it won't be one mage we'll be worrying about. It's everyone."

Erlat began clearing the plates and cups away. "Ah yes, but it's you he's worried about."

"Then why exactly am I due to go down there, right in among a load of Storad? I'd rather risk the machine, thanks for asking. Lise is pretty good at machines. I am crap at sneaking about in the middle of a group of men with guns who would all like to shoot me."

Then it was time to go, and it was strange. I had this odd sense of weight in my stomach, a dread of leaving, of thinking that if I left now it would be too late to say or do any of things I needed too. Only . . . only I didn't know what the hell those things were, I only knew that they were scaring me badly.

Erlat was odd too, more nervy than I think I'd ever seen her. She seemed half about to say something, then changed her mind and saw me off with a luscious smile and a soft "Come back."

I couldn't help thinking that, if that was it, the last time I saw her, I'd missed some golden opportunity, missed some cue in our conversation that would have perhaps made me see what I was supposed to see.

I stepped out into the frigid air of the Buzz, watched my breath freeze in a cloud in front of me and pushed it all away. Whatever it was, I'd have time, lots of time, to figure out later.

I made it back down to the 'Pit without screaming in the lift, which counted as a win. Perak'd had all the blocked-off tunnels marked on the map, and there was just one left that led Outside. Well, one we knew about other than the booby-trapped one, which I really wasn't going to risk. "Fingers crossed" isn't really a good tactic in anything other than kids' games, let alone a war, but it seemed about all we had.

Luckily, said tunnel wasn't anywhere near the bad memories encased in a room of broken glass in the heart of the keep. Instead Pasha, Halina and I found ourselves at an innocuous building near to the inner wall of the castle. If the piles of fossilised crap were anything to go by, this had once been stables. Or maybe those piles counted as art for our illustrious ancestor.

A half-dozen guards eyed us suspiciously and came towards us with that look I'd come to know so well – the "I-don't-like-you-so-I-think-I'll-arrest-you" look. Quite satisfying to show them the official bit of paper that said they weren't allowed to, see the look of smug superiority bleed off their faces as they realised that no, we weren't just some scum from Under they could do what they wanted with.

They were all as tense as hell, if the way their shoulders were up round their ears was anything to go by, and I couldn't blame them. There wasn't much between them and an invading army, just ingenuity and a hidden tunnel that might not be hidden for long. Worse, Perak's note indicated that some of them would be coming along for a little rearguard action.

Bizarrely, the smell of cooking food was everywhere, strong enough to send me mad with it, make my stomach growl like Namrat. I shook my head. Ridiculous, but that didn't stop me smelling it. Maybe Dench was using it as a form of torture – I wouldn't have put it past the bastard. Actually, I wouldn't have put anything past him, up to and including tap-dancing through the gates dressed in nothing but a hat and a modestly placed hand, if he thought it would give him an edge. He never liked to lose. Who does?

Like most of the other tunnels I'd seen, this one started, or finished, no wider than your average man. The walls either side were sheer and slick, except where handy little holes, far above where any man could reach, allowed arrows or guns to poke through; larger holes had boulders teetering on the edge, relics of a simpler kind of warfare. Ones that gave me a tickle of an idea, which I saved for later.

We looked at each other in the near-dark, and wondered

what the hell we were doing. Well, *I* did anyway. One day I will learn to keep my stupid mouth shut, I really will.

It should have been a rare and magical experience, my first time Outside. But the prospect before me, of getting close enough to all those Storad who would quite like to see me publicly executed, big and mean, with bigger, meaner-looking weapons, put rather a crimp on it. I reminded myself that this was my suggestion, and all I could come up with in response was a new rule: stop making stupid suggestions that might get you killed.

We took the tunnel, left the guards about halfway along where they could come and rescue us if it all went tits up (or scarper, more likely). After that it was just Pasha, Halina and me, nice and quiet. Secret. Pasha's sort of magic had a few very useful applications in a situation like this, especially as I made Halina take the lamp and had him listening at all times. No repeat of last time. This time we'd come prepared with a plan. I like to think I learn from my mistakes.

Being able to look through people's brains had its advantages. Especially when a quick rummage could lead to a small suggestion to any guards who might be lurking that, you know, there aren't really three people sneaking past. Honest.

Of course, if that was all, it would have been too easy and if the Goddess exists I'm fairly sure she makes it her personal mission to ensure my life is as complicated as possible.

Once we got close, I had Halina douse the lamp and we felt our way forward. The tunnel led right behind the Storad camp, out into a gully full of broken rocks and moss and shadows. The entrance was hidden among a tangle of broken mountains and stunted trees, the tunnel so narrow and bent here that from the outside it looked like just another bit of rock.

Dench knew the tunnels were there somewhere, if not the exact locations of all of them. Dench was not stupid. He'd once been head of the Specials, and he knew tactics like I knew the ten best ways to talk a woman into bed. Shame, really: would have made the whole day go a lot better if he hadn't.

So I was pretty sure he'd figure we'd try something – Pasha's rummages, what little he could do over the range, had said as much. Dench knew at least in part what Pasha and I were capable of, so he had to expect we'd try something like this, if not exactly when or where. Plus, the last time we'd tried the tunnels . . . yeah. It made the whole journey an exercise in simultaneously looking for every possible way he could try to stop us, and trying not to overthink it. Because if I thought about it too much, I could recall just how pissed off Dench must be with me, and what he'd do to me if he found me. It was not a comforting thought, so I didn't think it.

Instead, we made our quiet way to the end of the tunnel, easy enough thanks to Pasha making sure no one was ahead the whole time. Calmed my nerves just a tad, especially if I forgot how he'd said those Storad before had been muffled somehow.

One step out of the tunnel, and there it was. Outside. Mythical, denied, a dream of what else life could be. Real. It might have been worth the weight of duty on my shoulders just for the feel of it. Open air. No buildings looming over me, no long drop beneath me to shiver my nerves. The sky, right there above me with nothing to block the moon but clouds; no criss-crossing walkways to hem me in. The pass above us, with vague humped shadows lurking – the new machines, with half an army camped beside them.

That valley wasn't much, I dare say. A steeply sloping tumble of rocks, all shifting shadows in the moonlight, with the road that led to the top of the pass running through it, a couple of warped and knotty trees struggling to survive in the constant wind. That was all. But it felt like something else.

I didn't get the chance to decide what exactly, because the valley still had plenty of Storad in it. Plus Dench was a canny bastard and he knew me too well.

There are two things that will distract me beyond rational thought. One is the sudden appearance of a naked lady, which Dench had sadly failed to provide. The second is the fondness, or slavish devotion, I have for certain foods. Like, nice ones that taste good. Especially at that point when we were all on starvation rations of what had never been very appetising in the first place. We were trying to be quiet but it was hard when my stomach rumbled so much it could be felt, earth-quake-like, in my boots.

The bastard had something roasting. Something nice that

smelled stronger as though it was cooking just feet away. A fat, meaty smell almost choked me in my own saliva, reminding me of long-gone steaks, of gravy I could wallow in for days.

My stomach rumbled again, more a growl this time, loud enough that it echoed off the walls of the tunnel mouth.

"Rojan," Pasha whispered, "we're supposed to be being quiet—" but then his own stomach growled as though in challenge to mine.

I clenched my teeth and told my belly to shut up before it got me killed. "Let's just hurry up and be done with this. Maybe steal the food on the way back, all right?"

"Yeah." He shut his eyes as though he wished he could shut his nose too, cracked a finger and set about trying to see who might be about, who we needed to avoid or overcome.

We waited, and drooled, for a while until the gunshots started – Malaki had arranged for a bit of distraction for us, a small sortie of snipers, his best men with guns. Lise had managed to up the range on a few of the guns, but the Storad didn't know that, so their lights hadn't been dimmed and men stood out clearly against cooking fires and lamps. Bullets pinged off rocks down near the outer gates, a couple of men screamed like Namrat had just bitten their balls, and we had a nice bit of chaos to work with.

I've worked out since that Dench's inquisitor's helm wasn't just a protection against a sudden sword or a whack over the head. It was also a protection against certain kinds of magic.

More specifically, Pasha couldn't hear anything of what went on inside one. He wouldn't even know the wearer was there, as had happened once before. It seemed Dench had shown the Storad just how it did that so that they could incorporate it into their own design – hence Pasha not hearing the guys in the original tunnel too well. This guard, however, had something a bit extra – an exact replica of Dench's helmet – and he had been placed – among others, we later found out – outside where Dench thought the tunnels were, which he had, naturally given his understated efficiency and ability to scare the crap out of anyone who took his orders, mostly found.

I poked my head out of the tunnel and was trying to think clearly rather than gawp at being really, truly Outside and in the nearby presence of food that might even taste of something, when a heavily accented voice to one side said, "Rojan Dizon, I assume?"

My heart nearly had a prolapse, which wasn't helped by the sight of the gun in the man's hand pointed right at my head. Worse, it didn't look like a usual gun but more complicated, which probably meant it was more efficient at killing people. The helm didn't help much – styled like Namrat's head, all teeth and voracious hunger with blank eyes that seemed to judge me.

"And Pasha too, I'm reliably informed. Yes, that's it. Over here where I can see you, hands out. No twisting anything. Dench has warned me all about you. Now, if Jake comes any closer—"

At which point I was glad I'd won the argument about the cantankerous Halina. Two sick wet cracks, a hiss of pain, and the guard lifted off the ground before he slammed into a boulder behind him. The smack dislodged the gun in his hand, but not before it let off a wild shot that made Pasha and me duck as it whizzed over our heads and punched into a scree of rocks.

Pasha grabbed the gun before the guard could react, but he couldn't stop the shout. I grabbed Halina as she stared down in surprise at the stunned guard and, with Pasha behind, we ducked through a crack and between two tents precariously erected in the lee of some house-sized boulders. Not a moment too soon, either. A welter of footsteps as men came running over rocks, hoarse shouts that sounded like gargling with gravel, Dench's name the only word I could understand. Maybe the only one I needed to. The plan had gone tits up before it was properly started. I'm not sure why I expected anything else.

We'd have been done for then, I have no doubt, if the snipers at our gates hadn't started taking pot-shots at the nicely grouped men nearby. Bullets pinged off boulders, slammed through a man's shoulder so that he twirled round and fell in a shower of blood. Everything seemed to happen both too fast and too slow, and my stomach tied itself in knots.

There was only one way out of this, and that was through it.

Cold sweat made my hand clammy as I grabbed Halina's arm and we darted through the tents before anyone could organise themselves enough to try to find us. We'd planned – all right, hoped like hell – to have ten minutes of chaos to work with. Long enough to find a handy little hole to hide in, for me to rearrange the engine of the infernal machine that loomed by the camp, and then get the hell out. Instead of the ten minutes we'd hoped for, the way it looked now we had about two minutes, if we were lucky. Then we had all the time in the world to get killed, because I couldn't see us getting back to the tunnel as things were. Why the hell had I suggested this? Sometimes my own stupidity surprises even me.

All we had time for was trying to live, trying to do what we'd come for and then get out.

I went left, straight to the machine, but Pasha yanked me back. *Four men that way* sounded in my head. He was a handy guy to have around. I nodded and let him lead the way.

Those few minutes so shredded my nerves, I can barely even recall them. I certainly went off going Outside ever again, even if I could get steak or bacon. It wouldn't have tempted me if it was wall-to-wall naked ladies sluiced in gravy. The sheer openness of Outside scoured what little courage I had so that I wished for the comfort of buildings to surround me, for walkways to catch me in their stifling net.

A cry went up behind, in front, all around it seemed. Pasha didn't steer us wrong, knew who was where, when they moved. But a minute – or was it an hour? – later even he conceded defeat. With a sign that we could go no further, not forward or back, we huddled behind a rock that had split, leaving us a tiny hole to cower in.

I could see through the crack a little. The machine, looking squat and powerful and mindless. A jumble of men, of tents and shouting and fires cooking whatever it was that was driving my stomach to distraction. Even through all that, the constant gnawing hunger of the past weeks meant that the smell of cooking meat wasn't far from my thoughts. Just a taste would do. Just a little lick.

I blinked the thought away and carried on looking. Past the tents they'd made a corral of sorts, and in the dim light of the moon shapes shambled about in it, snuffling and making the odd, and I mean odd, squeak. A pair of beady little eyes peered out of the gloom, right at me, and the thing gave an almighty shriek like Namrat had hold of its bollocks and was twisting for all he was worth. I shot backwards into the hidey-hole and tried to press myself into the rock while I processed what I'd just seen. I couldn't be 100 per cent certain – I'd only ever seen them up close in books, or, once, dead and laid out on a slab – but I was pretty sure it was a pig. The bastards really did have pigs. Bacon on the hoof, or trotter or whatever. But I soon had other things to worry about rather than salivate over.

An ominous *whoomph* sound in front, another behind.

"What the fuck was that?" I whispered.

You don't want to know, Pasha thought at me. *Really. If you're going to do it, it needs to be now.*

I peered back through the split in the rock, making sure to avoid the pig's eye. The machine sat there, looking mean and pissed off. Half a dozen men crawled over it with spanners and other tools. Two more had what looked like a sodding great bullet and were loading it into the back of the muzzle.

Someone screamed behind me like their arse was on fire, counterpointed by the subtle crack of dislocating fingers.

Now, Rojan, now!

The crack of my own fingers, and there it was. I tried to ignore the screams around me, inside me, and concentrate on the engine. Too much, it was going to take too much, enough to send me batty but what choice did I have?

At the back there, where a pipe belched out thick, black smoke in oily streamers. Under those steel plates . . . I didn't know if I had it or not, only knew it was something big and complicated, but we were out of time, out of luck. Another twist, another surge, what felt like a vein popping inside my head, and whatever it was, it was gone. I hoped Lise could get some use out of it, and dry-heaved behind the rock.

I stayed there for a while, I think, with the cool rock comforting my sweating face. More meat roasted or burned somewhere close but it had an odd tang to it, one I'd never smelled before that made my grumbling stomach shut up. Someone shook my shoulder and wouldn't let up so I turned to find Pasha. His face was pale, sweating like my own, a touch of panic in his eyes and the jerky way he was moving.

"Thank fuck. Come on, I think I've bought us some time but you have to get us out of here. Rearrange us the hell out."

"Can't do three, you know that," I managed to mumble. Myself and one other, and that was pushing it, especially after what I'd just put my hand and brain through. Even on a good day – and trust me, this was *not* a good day – I'd struggle to do three, in fact I'd never tried it because two was almost enough to burst a blood vessel. I was pretty sure three would leave me good for nothing but the knackers' yard, and I didn't want to test my theory. "Back to the tunnel, that was the plan."

The way Pasha's lips twitched into a grimace said it all, that I didn't want to look, or know; but I looked anyway, or tried to.

"The tunnel isn't an option right now. You don't need to see why. Just get us out before those guards realise what I've made them do, and stop doing it."

He wouldn't let me look past him, but the blood on his hands, splashed over his shirt, was enough. Halina didn't look much better – she looked like she was going to throw up, but she got herself under control quickly enough and tried for a cocky smile that fell flat.

Three – how in hell was I going to manage three?

"Rojan!" Dench's voice cut through everything, all the smoke and blood and the singing in my head. "Come on, you little bastard, you and Pasha, I know you're here."

He sounded ready to split me in two. It was all the encouragement I needed to do something, but I wasn't stupid enough to think rearranging us was a good plan – it was too far and I was too screwed. I was probably too far gone for just me and Pasha, and leaving Halina behind wasn't an option.

I was too screwed for almost anything but I caught sight of the pig, of the rocky slope behind it, and a *slightly* less stupid thing came to mind. Slightly less stupid, with an added hope we might be able to grab a pig too – despite imminent death, my stomach was feeling jealous at getting left out of the planning and kept inserting its own ideas.

"Not rearranging us out. Can't. Not three. Too screwed. But I can do something. Hold on and get ready to help me run." It was a stupid plan really, but all the choice we had apart from die, and I've never been a fan of that.

Pasha tried one of his monkey grins, though it was pretty shaky. "I won't let go, I promise you. You fall in, I fall in."

I managed a nod and he held on to my arm, his voice in my head holding me like he promised, not letting me fall in if he could help it.

It was touch-and-go none the less. The black swooped in like a carrion bird, threatening to carry me off, and I was helpless before it. Only Pasha's voice kept me here, this side of sane. I clung to it, and it was then that I realised how much I'd come to rely on the little sod.

It wouldn't take much, I hoped. I really did. The valley sides were static rivers of rocks, some as big as houses. I wasn't going to manage one of those in my state, but with any luck I wouldn't have to. Take the *right* rock, and all the rest should come tumbling down.

It worked better than I could possibly have hoped for, for once. It was still too much, even that little. Another pop in my head, the gush of something hot down my face. Through some kind of black mist I saw the rocks go, shooting out of the jumble like corks out of bottles and tumbling off down the valley. I heard more than saw the resulting landslide, the grind of rock on rock, a scream, followed by another, and the high-pitched squeal of what was probably a pig. A clatter of trotters on stone as the corral snapped and the pigs made a determined escape attempt, squealing all the way. Halina saw what I was about and joined in the fun – rocks started zipping about, slamming into men, scaring the crap out of some of the pigs so they careered through and over tents, kicking and gouging anyone they found. A bigger rock – Halina grunted in effort – rose straight up and then fell into one of the bigger fires, sending sparks everywhere. A few of those sparks ended up finding a home on the trampled tents, and the subsequent impromptu bonfires had men running every which way.

"Nice," Pasha breathed, then grabbed my arm and dragged me up and away. "Shit."

Yeah, shit was about right. A group of men had stayed steady around the tunnel entrance, ignoring the pandemonium of pigs squealing their way up and down the valley, of men screaming and swearing, of fires and of soldiers turning on each other as suggested by Pasha. Well, I can only assume that's why they were suddenly trying to rip each other's faces off.

I staggered to my feet, wiped at my face and tried again. Another rock or two, another landslide. It might be enough. It was enough to get me another pop in my head, a fresh flow down my face and the voice of the black taking over every rational thought.

A sudden yank from Pasha as a gun sounded right near my ear and the swoosh of a bullet whipping through the air where we'd just been almost fucked it up for good, but I'd got the rocks free, set more tumbling down, end over end, cutting the men off from us, leaving the tunnel mouth blessedly free, for now.

We had to run, but I was barely capable of walking, and I was retching so hard I thought I might actually bring up my stomach.

After that, there was a lot of nothing.

Chapter Thirteen

Sound came back first, little overheard snatches that made no sense. Dendal's papery voice reading scripture. Pasha's worried murmur. Perak shouting, "I absolutely forbid it!" in a voice so strained it almost wasn't his. I kept my eyes shut and let myself drift for a while, not really knowing where, or even who, I was.

All that came back slowly to start with. I was in a bed, and it smelled nice so I could be sure I wasn't in my office, squidged on the sofa that smelled of mouldy stuffed tigers. Not just nice – I could smell proper food cooking, which was beyond nice and into downright heavenly. I turned over, relishing the sudden space, the clean sheets and the promise that smell seemed to give, and discovered an arm draped across me. A feminine one with a delicate hand. Better and better, though it appeared the lady it was attached to was clothed, which was a disappointment.

I was heroically prepared to make the most of it though, until everything else came back with a rush that felt like a mountain in the face and an anvil of weight across my shoulders. Dench – Storad – machines – Halina watching me with eyes like dinner plates in a face pale as winter, all her delicious hatred of the world and everything in it drained away before she snapped back and threw rocks around with an abandon that had scared me. The men I'd seen, whom Pasha had tried to stop me seeing. Half burned, some of them, or with faces ripped and bleeding as they went for each other in a mindless, mechanical way. I sat bolt upright in the bed and leaned over the side to be sick, but nothing came up except pink-tinged bile.

A soft voice, a softer hand on my shoulder that normally I'd have been all over like a rash but I couldn't muster the energy or enthusiasm right then.

"Lie down, you shouldn't be up yet."

I shrugged Erlat off more brusquely than I meant to and tried to stand up. On the third try I managed, and with a shadowy tiger stalking the corner of the room, I found a shirt to put on. "I can't. Not – I can't. Where the hell is my allover?"

"Kersan's still trying to get the blood out."

"Blood? But—"

"Your blood, Rojan." Erlat slid out of bed and came to stand in front of me. I'd never seen her like this before. Maybe it was the hair that threw me, a glossy snake of it that draped her shoulders instead of being kept in its tight coil at the nape of her neck, before it slid on down over the silky nightgown that made me come over all funny. Or perhaps that there wasn't even a hint of either her smooth professional persona or any teasing. I began to wonder how many different women she was. Too many for me to keep track of, especially the way my mind had seemingly turned to mush.

When I didn't say anything, she carried on in a soft, almost bewildered voice. "Your blood, because when Pasha got you here you were covered in it. Out of your nose, out of your mouth, your ears. Your *eyes*, Rojan. Everywhere. Pasha said . . . it took him and Dendal everything they had to keep you here. They told me about this black, that you could fall in any time. That you probably will if you aren't careful, and there's only so much they can do." She took a breath and then the Erlat I knew was back, teasing me, trying to get me to blush with a seductive smile and a taunt, and I thought maybe that was her wall, like mine was cynicism and Jake's was her swords. This teasing, this pretend seduction, was Erlat's wall to hide behind, and that made me wonder what it was she was hiding from.

"Two days in my bed and *still* you won't take me up on my offer. And you're going to stay there too. I promised Dendal that I'd keep you here. Sadly, I also promised him I'd make sure you didn't overdo anything as well. Or you'd be in big trouble, Mr Fancy-pants Mage. By the way, do you realise you're only wearing a quite short shirt?"

I'd managed not to blush through the first part out of long

practice, but then I looked down and noticed that indeed the shirt was very short and I was naked underneath. I blushed enough that it felt like a volcano had sprouted on my nose, sat down before I fell down and grabbed for the sheet.

Once I'd managed to calm my flaming forehead – tricky, in the face of Erlat's delighted laugh – I managed to get out some questions. As much to change the subject from what was under my shirt than anything.

"So, are you going to tell me what's been going on? Did Lise get the engine? It was the engine I got out, wasn't it? Is Pasha OK? What are the Storad up to? Did Halina get back all right? I kind of lost track . . ."

Erlat turned away, but not before I saw a look of sudden fear that dropped a millstone into my stomach. She fiddled with two cups on the table, poured some fragrant tea, and when she turned back she was smooth again, no hint of anything but professional charm as she handed me a cup. Goddess only knew where she'd got it from – the only tasty thing Under, it'd been one of the first things to run out – but then Erlat had some very high-up and wealthy clients. I took a long slug and savoured it. The bacon smell was still there, driving my stomach into giddy knots of anticipation. I began to wonder if Erlat had some and was hiding it, or alternatively whether I was still imagining it.

"Well?" I asked in the end, when it was clear she wasn't going to say anything without me prodding.

She wouldn't look at me while she said it, and instead

turned back to fiddle with the stupid cup. "Lise got what you sent her. Not all the engine, but enough to stop that machine from working. She says it might be enough metal to get another batch of guns, but . . . but that's not going to help much."

"Why not?"

Erlat concentrated on blowing steam from her tea. "After you came back, well, the Storad attacked the inner gate. They've got more than just guns, they've got things that will burn a man where he stands, or so Pasha said. It – we could hear the screams even from here."

That explained the odd smell of roasting meat, and what Pasha had persuaded the guards into doing – turning on each other, burning each other. Turned my stomach too.

"Did they get inside?"

"Not yet. Or not there. But we lost a lot of guards, a lot of Specials. They sent a load of their men up the tunnel too. And not just that one either, all the tunnels they could find. But there weren't enough men left to defend the gate *and* the tunnels, even with them mostly blocked, so Perak sent in his personal guard. Jake knows the 'Pit better than any of Perak's men, and she leads his guards, so . . . "

She clutched her teacup like her life depended on it and I was surprised to see she was holding back tears. Surprised and afraid.

"So?" I prompted as gently as I could, given the ice-pick that had just made a hole in my heart.

"I shouldn't be telling you this. Dendal said not to, that you should be resting, that you'll overdo it otherwise. He said if you fall into the black properly, even he can't save you. That you'll die if you stay in there too long."

"Erlat, please. What about Jake?"

She pressed her lips together as though she was desperately holding in some irrepressible thought, some vicious word, but finally she put the cup down and looked me in the eye at last. "Jake took Perak's guards into the tunnels to stop any Storad coming through. She stopped them all right, but . . . "

The hesitation almost had me screaming. I bit down on it – it wasn't Erlat I wanted to scream at. "But what?"

"Pigs. Pasha said the Storad have brought some with them, that they must have been planning this awhile, or why bring pigs, or have the machines ready? Sorry, I . . .They filled the tunnels with wood. Then they sent in the pigs and blocked them in and set fire to it all. Lise says pig fat burns at higher temperatures, higher than wood on its own. High enough to crack stone. Crack the tunnels."

"They burned pigs?" It explained why that was all I could smell though, why my stomach was doing back-flips at the thought of food, real food, dammit. Then a more sobering thought. "The tunnels – will they hold up? If they're cracked, right under the castle, and the city is built over the castle . . . " Ridiculous as it might seem, the floor seemed to sway under me, as though the city was ready to fall down right now, crumple up like a rotten concertina. Going to the 'Pit in the lift had been bad enough. Going to it via several thousand tons of falling masonry and girders – I was very nearly sick again.

"I . . . I don't know." There was something worse to come, I could feel it. "But that's not – I mean, the tunnel collapsed behind Jake, behind all the guards. She's trapped Outside, and there's no way for her to get back in until we stop the Storad. And not just stop them, beat them."

Chapter Fourteen

Erlat tried to stop me, but I wasn't having any of it. My allover was still wet, but Kersan managed to find a pair of trousers that one of Erlat's clients had, bizarrely, left behind, presumably while in a bliss-like trance. The trousers were too short and way too big at the waist, but I was covered, which was the main thing, especially in the face of Erlat's raised eyebrow.

At least my coat had proved easier to clean. I needed it because night was falling, making the Buzz even darker than usual and dropping the temperature to somewhere around nose-hair-freezing levels. Snow had begun to dust its way down through the walkways. It made a change from rain anyway, made even Under look magical. Mainly because all the crap was covered up.

It didn't take long before I was holding myself up on a handrail. Dendal and Erlat had been right about me needing to rest, but I couldn't. Jake was Outside, trapped there with a few thousand Storad who'd be more than happy to see her dead, actively searching for her, almost certainly. It was odd though. I wasn't struggling my weak-kneed way along a swaying walkway freezing my knackers off for her, or not just for her. What really spurred me on was the remembered sound of Pasha's worried murmur while I'd been out of it, of Perak's shouted "I absolutely forbid it!" I had sudden visions of Pasha the mouse going all lion at the worst possible moment, of him going off on some damnfool suicide run to get her. And he would, I had no doubt, because he was that kind of guy, the kind that heroics come easy to.

The lab windows shone in the dark like the sun, the Glow lights trapping grimy snowflakes in dizzying whirls that matched what was in my head. I staggered inside and the warmth hit me like a brick.

What greeted me stunned me almost worse.

It was chaos, even more so than the usual riot of cables and bits of machinery strewn over workbenches. Half a dozen young mages shivered in one corner and more than one was in tears. Halina was there, looking remarkably poised, all things considered, and she favoured me with a raised eyebrow and a curl of her lip. All cynics together.

Allit stood with Lise, a comforting hand on her shoulder, while Dendal twittered around in the background making vague soothing noises. I knew it was something bad because while Dendal is away with the fairies most of the time, at least he's happy. I know I'm home when I can hear the scritch-scratch of pen on paper and him humming a cheerful tune to himself. He wasn't humming now, and that was akin to the sun not coming up in the morning.

Not as unnerving as the shouts that echoed out of the pain room, punctuated by a lower voice that was still firm, obstinate even as it held a tone of regret. It didn't take much to work out that the shouter was Pasha and the obstinate one was Perak. I couldn't decipher the words, but I reckoned I could figure the gist anyway.

When I came in, Lise jumped to her feet and all but ran towards me, Allit a step behind. She was a study in frustration, her dark hair awry, her face streaked with dried tears but with that stubborn donkey line between her eyes that meant she was damned well determined to get her own way. She and Allit both started talking at the same time, rushed, garbled words that made no sense.

"Calm down and start again," I said and reached for her hand. She grabbed mine in a death-grip. Of the two, Allit seemed calmer, so I got him to explain.

"It's Perak. He says Lise has to destroy the new machine, the shield thing. He says if she can't make it so we can at least test it safely then we need the metal, and he's right, we do. Only Pasha says he wants to use it to help Jake."

"I can't dismantle it, I won't!" Lise burst out. "It's one of the last things Dwarf designed. I know we can make it work, and if we do – if we do, then we won't *need* guns. It'll work, it will."

"And the mage involved?"

She hesitated only a moment. "I can make it work, even that. I know I can. I just need time, and Perak won't give me any and Pasha's ready to use it anyway and he's . . . "

Pasha's gone all lion, I said to myself. I'd known he would. I had to admire the guy's zeal, always so ready to fight.

"All right. Look, I'll see what I can do. But even if I persuade Perak, you need to get it ready as soon as you can, OK?"

Her shoulders relaxed and she nodded before scurrying off to a desk that was covered in incomprehensible drawings and bits of machine.

Allit lingered, and a crash sounded from the pain room so that he flinched, but I waited and it didn't take long for him to come out with it. Never could keep a thought inside, that boy.

"I saw more. When I, you know. When I hurt myself. I've been practising like Pasha said I should. I – I don't know, Pasha says he's not sure if I see the now or past or future. I think maybe it's all of them, because I've been trying to focus like you said and I know I've seen things that haven't happened yet. Not all of them *do* happen either. When you went into the tunnel, I – I saw you die in there, and I tried to get Perak to call you back but it was too late, and then you didn't die so I don't know . . . But I saw – she's out there, on her own. I saw that, and I saw Dench with her, stronger this time, maybe the strongest possibility? She's on her own, no one to help her, but she's not afraid. That's Pasha. But I saw someone use Lise's machine too. I think."

"And did it work?"

His face screwed up in frustration. He was trying, and hard, to help but he was too new in his magic, still figuring it all out.

"I don't know! I only know that someone tries it, and then later – then later there are no Storad. But it's all hazy, like maybe it might not happen if we don't do it right? Does that make sense? Because I saw Storad in Top of the World too. Whatever, I don't know if it's because of the machine, or something else. I thought magic was going to be something useful! But all I can do is see things that *might* happen, or *might* be real, and I can't tell one from the other! What's the use in that?"

He had a point, but even I wouldn't say that to him. I was glad no one had told me he'd seen me die in the tunnel though. *Really* glad. I tried a bit of diplomacy – it came easier if I thought of it as lying, which I could do in my sleep. "You'll find a use for it, I'm sure, find a way to make it work. You just have to think hard and practise a lot."

He nodded glumly. "All right. But you have to make the Archdeacon see, or I won't get the chance because we're screwed at the gates."

I told him I would, but I didn't think I'd have much luck. From the sounds of it, Pasha was already trying very hard, but Perak's got a donkey line too. I opened the door into the pain room, to find the pair of them glaring at each other.

Pasha looked like shit. His eyes seemed sunken, his face more monkey-like than ever with a shrivelled look around his mouth as though he'd just bitten a lemon. Perak didn't seem much better – he looked like if he shut his eyes he'd fall asleep on his feet. As soon as they saw me, they stopped glaring at each other and started glaring at me instead. Not much of an improvement.

"What are you doing here?" Perak asked, the glare dissolving into a worried frown. "You're supposed to be resting."

"Hopefully he's come to knock some sense into you," Pasha muttered. "Rojan, will you tell your brother we need to use the damned pulse machine, the shield thing? Jake – she's . . . I *told* her not to go, told her to keep out of the tunnels, as far from Dench as she could. We have to use the machine. There's no other way."

"I can't let you!" Perak's face seemed to crack at that. "Look, Lise doesn't know what will happen to the mage that tries it. There's a good chance it'll take everything he's got and more. I *need* you. Mahala needs you, every last one of you. Especially you, Pasha, until Rojan recovers. You two are the only ones who can put anywhere near enough power into the generator. It's only been two days without Rojan, and look at you, you're in almost as bad shape as he is; we've had to shut three factories down and the heating's gone in some places. Without power we're sunk, and you know it."

"But Jake – what else *can* we do? Because we're fucking well going to do something. Besides, all the men that have died so far – we could stop it. Stop the Storad right in their tracks, stop them bringing in more men, more machines. Cut the ones already here off from those on their way. Then we'd have a chance. Rojan, tell him."

I was starting to wish I'd stayed in bed. I sat on the pain rig and scrubbed my good hand over my face. Why was it that the further I ran from responsibility, the more it dropped in my lap?

"Look, why don't you tell me everything first?"

So they did, and at least they'd stopped shouting. But the pinch on Perak's face when he told me how the Storad had used their flame machines, had burned so many of his guards and Specials down by the tunnels and where they'd tried to defend the gate, burned them like kindling, the clench of Pasha's jaw as he told me how he'd heard Jake in his head when the tunnel collapsed behind her, I'd almost have rather had the shouts.

"And the machines coming in through the pass," Perak said. "They're slow, but the men with them aren't. They're coming on ahead. Be here by morning, I should think. They've already got twice as many men here as we have guards and Specials left. More, perhaps. When the reinforcements arrive, we'll be hopelessly outnumbered. I'm not sure we can even man the gates properly, let alone keep them out of the tunnels if they manage to get through. The machine you twisted – the first one – they're busy trying to repair it, and when they do they'll have those gates down and there'll be almost nothing left to do."

"What about guns? How many have we got? Things to fling over the wall, I'm sure we've got plenty to give them pause. There must be *something*." Because I had an idea, but I didn't think either of them was going to like it much. "We could unblock one of the other tunnels?"

"No good," Pasha muttered. "Dench has got his men spread out and looking – we're pretty sure he's found the entrances to at least two, and they might be blocked but the Storad have come prepared. They cracked those two tunnels, collapsed them, who says they won't manage to get in this time? If they get through, we're done for – once the Storad are in the 'Pit there's no way to stop them spreading out, no place to really hole them up, stop them. We've got nowhere near enough men to fight both in the 'Pit and at the gates. And if Dench can't get through, he'll probably try to crack those like he did the others, and if he cracks enough maybe there won't be a city left. We're screwed – unless we use the pulse machine."

"Well, we've got more guns than guards now," Perak said. "And Factory Three should be ready with the next lot – the last lot unless we cannibalise that machine – in the next few hours. We've got enough bullets for now, but what we got from the engine you sent wasn't anywhere near enough to last in any sort of sustained attack. It's metal we need, and people."

"Right then." I pushed myself up off the chair. "I think it's fairly clear. We've got plenty of people. You just need to arm them."

"What?"

"You've got more people than you can feed, Perak. A whole teeming mass of them Under. Upsiders, Downsiders, mostly fighting each other. Make them fight something else instead."

"But the guards were all trained and they still died, and all the cardinals will—"

"All the cardinals can kiss my rosy red butt cheeks. Perak, send someone down to No-Hope, or Boundary. I guarantee in under ten minutes you could find a hundred people who can fight just as well as any guard. Better, even. Certainly dirtier."

Perak's eyes were wider than the gaps in my conscience. "And you want me to give them *guns*?"

My brother had been living Over Trade too long. "Yes, give them guns. They'll fight just as well as your guards. Better, maybe. Less to lose. But they live here too, and they'll die just as quick when the Storad get in."

"The cardinals will never agree. I mean, yes, of course, you're right. Should have thought of it myself, but they'll never agree."

"Easy. Don't tell them."

I could see the idea turning over in his head, almost see where he was working out how to persuade all the other Ministry men this was what they needed to do. He had his work cut out there – despite everything, most of his cardinals still looked on anyone from Under as sub-human. But people from Over, well, I couldn't see many of them fighting hand-to-hand, not unless it got right to the end. Over, life was easy and well fed, nothing much to trouble you. Under, life was one long fight from cradle to grave. It'd make a refreshing change to fight someone who wasn't a neighbour.

"What about Jake?" Pasha asked. "I'm not just leaving her out there and hoping for the best."

"Where is she now?"

"Hiding, but there's two thousand men or more walking down that road right now, and that valley isn't big. Soon there won't be anywhere left to hide. Not that hiding comes naturally to her. You know as well as I do what's likely to happen – the first hint of anyone finding her, she'll take out as many as she can, while she can. All or nothing."

He didn't need to spell it out any plainer.

"You can talk to her?"

"Yes, of course. She's a bit far away, so she's faint at times, but I swear I could hear her if she was on the moon."

"Good. OK, look, Perak, you get those guns out to people who might do us some good – vicious, underhand people are who we want right now. But not just any old gang-hand. Get someone down there asking for volunteers – I guarantee there'll be plenty who will if you agree to let them be armed. They *want* to fight."

"And then?" Pasha twitched with impatience.

"And while Perak is picking out who gets to shoot people for Mahala, you talk to Jake. Find out where the men are, where the flamey things are. Who's in charge, apart from Dench, what tent they're in, if she can. Where Dench is too. Anything so we're not going in blind."

"Going *in?*"

My brother can be annoyingly pacifistic at times, and when you've got a bloodthirsty enemy at the gate is one of those times.

"Yes, Perak. It's too late to sit back and hope we can weather this siege. Mahala survived the last ones by being a bunch of conniving bastards, and we're going to do the same this time. This time, we have a Jake in their midst to show Pasha what's what. We've got a load of guns, and a load of bullets. We have a load of people from Under who would be more than happy to shoot a gun, as long as you make sure there aren't any cardinals around. You may want to keep the Upsiders and Downsiders separate though. We take the fight to the Storad, before their mates turn up mob-handed, and when we're done with them, then we bring Jake back."

Perak went to the window, and though he stared out into snow-swirled darkness I don't think he saw anything out there. Finally he said, "All right. All right, I'm going to have some explaining and persuading to do in Top of the World, but all right, I'll persuade them if I can. I can't do a damned thing without them playing merry hell about it anyway. Pasha can concentrate on finding out what he can, from Jake or whatever other way. I'll send someone down to see who they can gather up, if anyone. And you, Rojan. You are going to be resting like you should. Aren't you." Not a question, an order from my archdeacon, from the Mouth of the Goddess.

I couldn't give a toss about what the Goddess wanted.

I sighed inwardly, wishing I *could* rest like he wanted me to. But this, all these Storad outside our walls, Jake trapped out there on her own, people huddling in their homes wondering if tomorrow would come and if it did whether they'd be alive to see it . . . everything came down to me. One little action of mine had brought us to this, and I was getting us out of it too, if I could. "Not a chance in hell."

"So what are you going to do?" Pasha asked. "Not magic. If you do—"

"Ever heard the saying, 'When confronted by a tiger, throw shit at it. Because there will be shit'? I'm going to make sure there's shit to throw."

Chapter Fifteen

The Stench smelled even worse the second time around. I tried holding my breath but by the time I got even a quarter of the way in I was near fainting. In the end I settled for breathing through my mouth and the shirtsleeve that covered it, and trying not to gag. At least this time I knew where to find the Stenchers.

I looked over the vats and felt bizarrely pleased they were full. The scum on top looked even worse today, with a livid green tint to it that screamed "plague waiting to happen", or at least "highly contagious form of the galloping trots". Either one would work nicely, especially if it was fast-acting.

I found a knot of Stenchers just off the corridor where I'd discovered Halina flying and throwing men around. They huddled in a loose circle with the rattle of bones between them. When I got closer, I realised what they were betting on – how many days till the Storad reached Top of the World, with side bets of whether they'd let any Mahalians Under live. No one seemed to be betting yes on that last one.

A gangly face looked my way. He grunted something to his pals, and then they were all looking at me. It wasn't that I didn't like being the centre of attention, but the calculation there sent the hairs on the back of my neck quivering.

One of them stood up, his frown almost hidden underneath the ground-in dirt. Well, probably dirt.

"What do you want?"

I didn't get the chance to reply before one of the others growled out, "Here, that was the one that took our Halina away. She all right? What did you do with her? She's going to be one of them mages, right?"

A low mumble around the circle, from which I gathered that while they didn't really approve of mages as such, anyone who managed to get out of the Stench was on to a good thing.

"Yes and no," I said before I could even think about it. Possibly not the best move, because the circle stood up and it was as tall as me and a lot stronger. I held on to my pulse pistol, and wondered how many people it could take at once, if I had to. Thing was, if I did, there went my chance of getting them to help. And I needed their help, even if I wasn't going to say how much.

"What you mean?" The guy who seemed in charge moved my way and I did my best not to lean back away from the smell. Small breaths through the mouth, that was the trick. Even so, my eyes were watering.

"She came to be a mage, that's true." The urge to lie was almost overwhelming. I've lied my whole damned life, and it's a hard habit to break, especially when the truth might be very painful to my person.

"And? She all right? Why are you down here?"

"You know what's happening up there, don't you? The Storad, the gates."

"Course we know. We stink, we aren't stupid. Be amazed what ends up down here for us to read. That's why Halina went. Couple of us tried to volunteer but they told us to fuck off. Stupid, I thought. We were willing, and that's what counts. But they wouldn't give us no guns, no nothing, and I said in that case the fancy boys from Over can die. Let them wear the Storad down, and when they lose – and they will – less of them for us to worry about. We'd have fought if they'd let us."

"How about if I ask nicely now?"

One of the others started to say something, but this guy glared at him and he shut up. "Oh, you want us now, right? We've got something you want, I'm thinking. I'm also thinking you haven't said what happened to Halina."

"She came to be a mage, and she's good, damned good. She's fine, considering."

Something white appeared in the brown crust of the lead guy's face, and I realised his lip was curled against what he'd just heard. "I know a liar when I see one. She's dead then. Sent her off like they would have done us, no weapons, nothing but a cheery wave I expect. Right?"

"Yes and no. Being able to throw a man across a room counts as a weapon. And she's not dead."

A laugh behind the lead guy – the man who I thought had been with her when I found her. It was hard to tell under the uniform crust over their faces, the identical drab brown of their rags, but the voice sounded familiar. "She could kick the shit out of any one of us. Or at least *throw* the shit out of any one of us."

A slice of the lead guy's hand and the laughter stopped. "So she's not dead, all right. But now you're down here asking us to fight again, I expect, with no weapons. Die when we could be down here, defending our own, not that miserable lot of pious bastards up there. I pity the Storad who makes it down here, though I don't reckon they'll bother us much. No one does. Rumour is, they just want to screw *you* over, not us. No, you just piss off, Ministry boy. You want to save Over, you're going to have to do it yourselves."

The Stenchers weren't going to help us by being a weapon. Bang went another great plan.

The plan to gather together a few men from Under hadn't worked so well either, as I discovered on my way back up.

Halfway through No-Hope, in the most innocuous area full of the kind of proud poor who just worked hard and kept their heads down, I found what looked like a brawl. I began to sidle my way round – one thing Under teaches a guy is when and how to avoid trouble – before I saw who was in the middle of said brawl.

Malaki let off a shot, and the two Specials with him followed suit. They weren't shooting at anyone in particular that I could see, but it was enough to give everyone a bit of pause. Not for long – after their initial fright, the crowd surged in on them again. Specials had got where they were by being the scariest thing anyone knew, but that wasn't the case any more. Now the scariest thing was Outside and on its way in, and from the look of it, Malaki's attempt at press-ganging a few likely-looking lads had backfired in a spectacular fashion.

He wasn't taking the sudden lack of fear from everyone well, but he knew when he was beaten. He caught my eye, saw where I was standing at a nice and handy place to get the hell out of the mess he was in, and headed in my direction. He only pistol-whipped a couple of guys on the way. The other Specials made a line behind him and managed to extricate themselves. The crowd around them dissipated with a mixture of triumphant aggression and sneering catcalls.

I had no love for the slab-faced Malaki, but I did kind of feel sorry for him just then. He looked utterly confused and defeated as we headed up the stairwell.

"Don't they *want* to fight?" he asked.

I looked out over the glowering faces as they crept back into their lives. "You're asking the wrong people. Round here, these are just folks trying to get by, and shit-scared. They'd fight, but not for you, or for Ministry, and most certainly won't if forced. Volunteers, I said. You want to go further down maybe. Find some of the gangs, if you can get that far and still live. They may hate Ministry, and you, but they love a good fight."

Malaki glared at me and shook his head. "Impossible. I have to find men, Perak says, so I'm trying. But I'm with the cardinals on this one. I'm not sure I want to give guns to just anyone who wants one."

"So you're trying to strong-arm some poor suckers who wouldn't know a fist if it hit them in the face? You think those people who just left – the apothecaries, the grocers, the bakers, you think they're the best men for this? That forcing them might work?"

"Better than the alternative," Malaki said. "I don't want men too eager to shoot."

"You don't want anyone so piss-scared that they'll shoot whatever turns up because they've got their eyes shut either. We need to use our strengths, not try to force people into things they can't do."

He grunted at that, but then dropped another little zinger into the mix. "Like your little mages. They'd come in handy too, down by the gates. Cardinals are going to insist on it, and I agree."

I stopped dead and he almost ran into me as I whipped round. "And you can piss right off. They're *kids*, Malaki." *My* kids, I was beginning to think of them as. Too reminiscent of me at that age, mostly not knowing what the hell they were doing. But they weren't going to end up like me, not if I could help it, and they weren't going to blow themselves up trying to be Malaki's secret weapon either. "You get them over my dead body. Or yours, whichever you prefer."

We stood there glaring at each other for a while, but he looked away first.

"What do you suggest then?" he said at last.

I sighed and carried on up the stairwell. "If you won't use the people best suited for the job, at least pick people who might want to do it for what you've got to offer. Volunteers. Try right up under Heights, maybe the bottom of Heights too. Where they're close enough to see what they can't have, close enough to taste it, to want it above anything. Then offer it to them – promotion, a job in Ministry or the Specials, a promise they can believe in, even if it is a load of shit. But no strong-arming them. Or anyone. It's going to be a shitstorm: you know it, I know it. You want people who want to be there, or all you'll have after the first five minutes is a cloud of dust as they very sensibly run like buggery."

He sneered at that, but I got him to agree to at least try in the end. It didn't seem much, but it was all I could do. I left him to it and went to the lab, went to sit with my kids, my little proto-mages, and help them figure it all out as best they could, while we still had the chance.

Chapter Sixteen

The snowfall had thickened till it was hard to see more than ten yards in front of you. A blessing in many ways, because it drew a screen across the crap, blotted out the decay of the walls Under, the flimsiness of the swaying walkways. The city was reduced to orbs of Glow lights shining on whiteness. At least the slush underfoot was a drab grey, else I'd have thought I'd managed to rearrange myself into some weird place where everything wasn't screwed to hell. If I ever found myself there, I dare say I'd be bored to tears in under an hour.

I was screwed to hell too. I'd been a good boy and not used any more magic, but that didn't make a lick of difference to the throb of my poor hand, where the juice built up like water behind a dam. Didn't make a lick of difference to the black either. It was back, had never really been away, was singing sweet nothings in my ear. The trouble with the whiteness of the snow was that it showed up the shadowy outline of a tiger stalking towards me out of the corner of my eye. Then I'd blink and it would be gone, only to stalk me from another direction. I tried my best to ignore it, but that was quite hard.

Above the remaining inner gate, most of the lights were out, leaving only faint reflections off falling flakes to light the grim faces of the men stood behind it. Guards, or what was left of them, but they looked different that day, in that dim light. No longer more arrogant than I was, no longer looking smug and a bit superior in the knowledge that Under, their word was as close to the law as anyone was going to get. They had been all those things and I'd been on the receiving end more than once, but that day, behind that gate, huddled under snow and the gaze of half a dozen cardinals who watched from a nice, warm, safe window . . . with half their number killed or wounded already, the enemy having reinforcements on the way and they were the poor bastards at the brunt . . . that day they looked like any other men. Tired, scared, gaunt from too long without a decent meal.

You'd think the boom-shudders from the machines stopping would have brought some relief, a bit of cheer to them, but no. Those echoing sounds had punctuated our lives, day and night, and now they'd stopped it felt quiet. Too damned quiet, leaving people room to think dire thoughts, to panic. If the guns had stopped, maybe that just meant the infantry were on their way.

Worse, the guards now had reinforcements. Worse because those reinforcements were made up of precisely the sort of people they usually spent their days scaring the crap out of and extorting bribes from – no one very important, though they weren't from Under so the guards wouldn't be too worried about how much they'd jackbooted them in the past. Only a bit worried. Still, it looked like Malaki had taken my advice with who he'd rounded up – these weren't Ministry men: they were from the borders of Heights, the top of Under. I recognised one or two, and the type – merchanters' kids mostly, with the odd priest or factory owner's son or daughter thrown into the mix. It was in the careful way their clothes were cut to mimic a Ministry man's, the sharp look in their eye as they watched for the main chance. Not Ministry, but wishing they were, people who spent their time looking ever upwards, working out how to get there, apologists for the Ministry. Not likely to get funny thoughts about shooting cardinals when no one was looking. Men and women who would volunteer because it might give them an edge the next time Ministry were hiring, or at least get them a weapon if things didn't go to plan, rather than from any sense of helping anyone else.

So the guards weren't just tired and hungry and scared of what the Storad had to offer. Now they had a bunch of clueless people milling about, people who probably had no idea what they were doing and were only getting in the way. But at least they were there, and they'd learn soon enough.

Perak arrived, wrapped up in a couple of thick woollen robes that looked like they could keep out the end of the world. He had that dreamy look to him again. The one that usually meant I was about to get dropped in it.

Pasha was there too, looking worn at the edges. His monkey grin was fixed to his face as though he'd nailed it there, but fresh marks across his fingers, new bruises along his wrists where he no longer took care to keep his cuffs pulled down over his brands, told their own story. Those wrists were thin too, thinner even than they should have been, and his jacket flapped around a frame that had never been big and was now almost skeletal. He looked like a walking corpse.

The three of us gathered under a Glow light in the shelter of an office that usually held the guards checking goods going in and out. At least it had a brazier to warm it, but it was a mean one and all it did was stop my nose from turning blue. Malaki and the last remaining sergeant of the guards looked over our shoulders at what Pasha had brought. A large sheet of thick paper, much creased and filled with pencil markings that had been scratched in, crossed out and drawn over.

"Here's the gate." Pasha's voice cracked, but he swallowed hard and tried again. "And here's Jake. Two of her guys left with her, that's all."

He pointed to what could have been a group of boulders. Or possibly a tree. Whatever Pasha's talents, they didn't include drawing. Whichever, it was on the far side of the valley, where the wind whipped down over the mountains like a knife to saw through your bones.

"Did she have any kind of weather gear?" I asked, but Pasha

gave me a don't-be-stupid-she-didn't-expect-to-be-camping-Outside look so I shut up.

It didn't take him long to point out all the relevant information that Jake had managed to give him. Where the main force was, what sort of weapons they had – at least a third of the Storad had the flamers they'd used before – where their leader was billeted, and where Dench was. He, it seemed from what she'd managed to overhear or otherwise weasel out of some unlucky bastard, wasn't exactly welcome, more tolerated. From what little we knew of them, the Storad had a funny kind of code and to them Dench had sold his own men out. That made him a traitor and, while useful, not to be trusted.

Malaki and the sergeant pored over the map and asked a load of technical questions which Pasha stumbled answers to. Malaki cocked an eye my way and I tried not to flinch. Not very successfully, because old habits die very hard indeed.

"What exactly is our objective here, Your Grace?" he asked.

Perak looked long and hard at Pasha and me before he gave his answer. "Twofold, captain. One: those reinforcements on their way? We want them to find nothing of use when they enter the valley. No troops, no camp. Nothing."

The captain raised his eyebrows at that. Perak never wanted anything done by halves.

"And second?"

"Second, the captain of my personal guard is out there with two of her men. I would like them back."

"That's—"

"What your orders are, captain. This could actually be to our advantage, if we play it right. You know where their leader is billeted. Take him out. And Dench too. Jake and Pasha can also keep you apprised of any changes in the situation as and when they occur. But I want her and those men back, understood?"

I was hard pressed not to grin – someone else was getting dropped in the shit for a change, and it was much more gratifying to see it from the outside.

Malaki threw me an evil look before he and the sergeant left.

Perak deflated after they'd gone, and I realised his commanding tone had been at least half bravado. "All right. Pasha, you go down to the new recruits. I reckon they'll take better to someone who isn't a guard or Special. And then—"

And then it was too late. Any plans we might have made flew out of the window as a big, fat crack reverberated below us, followed by a series of screams.

They'd fixed the machine I'd bent, and it had taken just one shot to break the inner gates. They were in, and killing anyone in front of them.

Perak and I raced to a window. The inner gate was off its hinges and Storad were running amok below, guns firing, flamers burning every man they could reach. Pasha groaned behind us – every man's thoughts were in his head, all their pain, panic, everything. I've never known quite how he managed to stay sane through it all.

The guards fell back, the new recruits in among them, and any differences were forgotten in the face of Namrat stalking through Mahala, his tiger teeth ready to rip throats out, to take the dead and send them where he would.

If I'd thought about it, I probably would have stayed where I was, or moved back in the tactical manoeuvre that is also known as "getting the hell out". I certainly wouldn't have gone charging off the way I did. The old me would have found a handy bolthole and stayed there till it was all over. Not any more, though it was still tempting. But I wasn't the old me any more, or not completely.

Pasha and I ignored Perak's shout behind us and ran, not away, towards. Fuck only knows why, when everything was telling me to get away and quick. Probably because I knew there was no chance of Pasha hanging back, not with Jake out there, and I wasn't letting him take all the glory. I had my pulse pistol out from habit, but sense kicked in and I dragged out my bullet gun instead.

It wasn't just an attack, it was a massacre. The ground was slick with blood and burned bodies, a sight to sicken even the hardest heart, but we didn't have time to dwell on that. The Storad came, and we fell back before them, all of us, Special and guard helping new recruit and vice versa. Before that onslaught, we were all one. I remember thinking at least I'd die quickly, before I got to see Mahala completely destroyed, and wondering how the cardinals would put a Ministry spin on this, make it the Goddess's will.

The Storad came through the swirling snow, flamers out in front. Guns weren't all that much help when you couldn't see what you were shooting, but their flamers – all they needed to do was get in range, flick the switch and watch men burn.

I fired my gun three, four times, fumbling the reloading with my bad hand so that I was alive with juice that I daren't use, making my vision go black in patches, tempting me. That black tiger shape was everywhere I looked. I couldn't see that I was doing any good with my gun, and wasn't sure I wanted to. I've done some messed-up shit in my time, but to shoot a man, even a man who wanted me dead . . .

I wasn't the only one either. All I could hear, in between shots, was people praying, pleading for help, for absolution. The guard next to me kept up a constant litany to the Goddess, even while his shaking hands raised his gun, while he pissed himself when a bullet came the other way and took a chunk out of his cheek before it flew off into the dark.

It was Pasha who turned it. I suppose it was always going to be Pasha, because he wasn't just fighting for Mahala, or for his life. He was fighting for everything that made his life bearable, made it worth living, and she was out there somewhere, and in his head too. Jake would be fighting with all she had; she always did, so that the Goddess would love her, because she had to or die inside.

One second Pasha was next to me and the next he was running forward with a wild scream. His gun wasn't out but he ran with his hands twisting and cracking, holding them out like they were the weapon, and I suppose they were. Before him Storad stopped firing, their faces confused blurs behind the swirling curtains of snow. One of the men holding a flamer turned without stopping his fire, and three Storad gunmen went up in flames. I can hear the screams now, the smell of their skin as it crisped. I can hear the words behind me, from men who would never accept a mage, words that spoke of fear of magic even as it saved their ugly butts.

And I remember the sudden rage at that. How I wanted to take my poor buggered hand and twist it, wanted to rearrange the whole damned place and everyone in it, Storad and Mahalian, wanted to twist their brains and make them *see*. Instead, I came over all sensible for once and lurched after Pasha. Snow and blood made the ground treacherous and I slipped more than ran. Pasha didn't seem to notice, or care, but arrowed straight for the outer gates, or what was left of them. Straight for a bunch of Storad with guns and flamers at the ready.

The thing about Pasha was that he looked like a sulky monkey, he was as jittery as a mouse walking past a cat – but when he had to, when something he cared about was threatened, he turned all lion; and then caution, and indeed anything approaching sensible, went out of the window. Generally at the worst possible moment, like now.

I'd have bet any money you like that he didn't even see those Storad waiting for him. All he was thinking about was where Jake was, if she was safe, whether whatever Allit had seen would come true. Almost laughable, considering she could probably dissect any one of them in two heartbeats. But that was all this was to him now, all these blood and bodies, all that was in front of him. It was all about Jake.

One Storad reacted quicker than the others to this wild-eyed apparition coming for them, and turned his flamer towards the threat. I shot him, managed to hit him too, high up in the shoulder so he half span and his flame scorched the guy next to him. But I couldn't reload on the run, especially with only one hand that worked properly, and there were too many Storad. Pasha seemed to realise where he was then, what he was running into. A gunman aimed at Pasha's head, then inexplicably turned the gun on himself and blew his brains out. "*How far would you go?*" Pasha had asked me once, and I saw it again now, just how far he would. Further than he'd be able to handle, once the lion wore off.

Pasha wasn't the sort of guy who could rationalise it, tell himself he had to, that these men would have killed him given half the chance. Me, I'd shrug it off most likely, at least on the outside. My conscience does what I tell it to, or at least I like to think so, and I was telling it that these bastards deserved everything they got. But Pasha – it would break him; but he didn't care about it right then. He wasn't thinking about tomorrow when this would haunt him, when he'd remember what they were thinking as he killed them, see their wives and children in their heads as they died. It would break him, but he didn't care so it looked like I was going to have to.

I dropped my next bullet into the gathering snow, swore like a motherfucker and grabbed another. Too slow. A Storad, eyes glassy as Pasha rummaged in his head and gave it a nasty suggestion, turned on his neighbour and shot him through the eye. But Pasha wasn't quick enough, not together enough, to brainwash all of them. Not before three men grabbed at him and a gun came round, a finger ready on the trigger.

If I believed in the Goddess, I'd swear on her that everything seemed to stop then. Time stretched, and all I could think of was Pasha. Not Jake, not how I'd have to tell her he was dead, if we found her. Not her, but him. How he'd taken me under his wing once. Talked to me, believed in me, told me not to be such a shit. Been a friend, the best I could recall.

I don't remember telling my hand to bunch into a fist, or recall with any clarity the pain swirling through my head, firing up my juice. I remember the black calling, though, telling me now was the time, right *now*. I'd promised it once, it reminded me. I'd promised that it could have me, and now it was collecting. A voice, not mine or the black's but other than that I couldn't say who, saying, *Not now. Not for this. Not even for this.*

Then Malaki ran a bullet through the heart of the guy holding Pasha. Guards came up, guns ready, and the new recruits were with them. Bloodied and gaunt and terrified, all of them, but they came anyway. I relaxed my hand, willed the juice away, told the black to piss off, it wasn't having me today. I almost succeeded, and got on with the business of shooting at men I'd never met.

Chapter Seventeen

By the time we'd finished at the wrecked gates, all the snow was pink- and red-streaked with blood. Broken flamers lay in bits of tangled metal, fresh snow covering them up as though to hide the fact they'd ever been. Not all the bodies were Storad, not by a long shot. The last sergeant of the guards lay right at the foot of the gates, three Storad bodies in various states of shot-through-the-face around him. Malaki was still upright, though it looked more from stubborn determination than anything else, as blood dripped freely down the left side of his face and off his chin. Something was changed about him, about all of us probably, but it was marked most upon him. A moulding of his features from stiff and uncompromising to grim yet – what? I couldn't say. Only that I liked him a hell of a lot more, especially when he said, "Right, all of you, group up. You're all my men now."

He didn't seem to care that more than half them had never been his, that most had been until earlier today a bunch of men and women from the bottom of Heights, the top of Under, fairly respectable people who were only there because it seemed expedient for their careers to say yes when asked by Ministry. Yesterday, Malaki would have been happy arresting them for standing with intent to look at a Special, and they'd probably have done a runner at the first hint of a Specials uniform within a hundred yards or more. Today, that didn't matter.

Malaki pointed to one of the Heights men, who'd all somehow seemed to accumulate a lot of weaponry. The flamer seemed to ride easy in his hands and two guns poked out of a pocket. The cardinals were going to have a fit.

"You, yes you. You're my sergeant now. In fact, you're all Specials now, got it? You serve me, the Goddess, and the Archdeacon, in that order."

No one argued, though I silently reserved the right to tell the Goddess to go fuck herself if what she wanted was at odds with what I needed to do. All the new recruits looked different shades of stunned – them, Specials? What were left of the guards looked much the same.

"Right," Malaki said. "We hold the gates, and we are going to keep holding them. There will be more men coming, I promise you that. Ours *and* theirs. But these gates belong to us, and no one is going to take them. Got it?"

"But—" Pasha began. He looked worse than ever, grey and

sick, one hand trembling and the other held to him where he'd taken a burn from the flamers. I could almost feel the pain coming off him in waves, feel the juice building in him. Not just juice either – desperation, a touch of panic.

Malaki glanced his way and cut him off. "I haven't forgotten, but holding these gates is primary. I swore to the Goddess first, not the Archdeacon, and this city is hers, and will stay hers." Turning his back on us, he began barking out orders which all the men and women leapt to obey. Funny how the threat of dying together could make all those old arguments trivial. Now, after this, none of those men and women even gave Pasha and me a sideways glance.

Perhaps that's what made it easier for him to slump to the ground, cradling his burned arm. The lion was still there though, under the grey skin and the tremor. It was there in the way his dark eyes bored into mine, the way he gritted his teeth. "Rojan, we have to go."

If it hadn't been Jake out there, if it hadn't been Pasha looking like he wanted to burn holes in the snow with his eyes, I might have laughed. But it was, so I didn't say a damn thing about how I was no use, a mage who daren't use his magic for fear of going batshit, and one who was so strung out on worry and pain he could hardly stand. I like to think it was very restrained of me not to say, "Pasha, what the hell are we going to do?", though I suppose he could hear it anyway.

He could hear a lot, I'd no doubt – his arm was still smoking and the smell of cooking flesh, from him and all the others, mixing together with the smell wafting from what was left of the tunnels, quite put me off bacon for the rest of my life. He had juice enough to hear half of Mahala. But he couldn't hear everyone, and that was the problem.

"When we took the gates," he said in a whisper. "I could hear her up till then. Her and her two men. We came from this side, they were doing what they could on the other. Doing a good job of it too, chaos for a while. Sneak into a tent, take out the men inside, sneak out. And then – I can't hear her now. Her men are dead, and I heard her start to say something, heard her say, 'Dench' and then . . . nothing. She – I – I can't think she's dead. Can't, *won't*. I don't care what Allit saw. Do you see?"

I think I saw more than he thought. That the grey tinge to his skin wasn't just from worry about Jake, though that was part of it. He'd killed men tonight, and Pasha wasn't a killing kind of man. He'd done it for her, as he had once before and that had almost broken him, and yet he'd do it all again, if he had to. Would go as far as he must, for Jake. And now he was asking me to go out there, beyond the gates, out into who knew how many more Storad who were licking their wounds, biding their time till their reinforcements arrived, perhaps. Or perhaps not. But he had to, because if Jake was gone, or if she wasn't and he left her there, then he had nothing except a useless faith in a useless goddess who would do bugger all for him except give him the faint, fool's hope he'd see her again someday after they were both dead.

He laughed, all pity and anger, and I realised he'd seen that last thought in my head. "You'll see one day, you will. Until then, I will not say she's dead. I just can't hear her. Maybe – maybe what Allit saw, only maybe he didn't see all of it? Dench has her, but when Allit saw her she was alive. Maybe Dench got that helmet on her? I swear that's what was blocking me before, at the tunnel. Maybe she's unconscious. Maybe lots of things. But I have to *know*. Are you coming with me, or not? You can walk on your own, and I can use my magic. Between us we make one good mage. What do you say?"

What can you say to a friend who asks you that? Just to find out whether the woman he loves, and you do too, is alive. There is only one thing to say. Of course, I injected my own charm into it, so as not to appear too soppy.

"Fine, but you're paying the cleaning bill to get the blood out of my clothes, and I expect a lot of beer at a later date. A *lot* of beer."

He grinned at that and held out his good arm for me to help him up. But the grin had lion's teeth in it, and it wasn't only a lion that walked with us. A big, gleaming tiger followed in our trail, invisible, silent, watchful, waiting for his chance. Namrat, all teeth and hungry eyes, patient as time, cold as mountains. Namrat the stalker, who would have us all in the end. Death.

I tried telling him to piss off, there's a good little kitty, but it didn't work.

*

We didn't get far. Maybe we would have done, maybe we'd have found Jake, Pasha could have rescued her like the dashing hero he seemed to want to be, whether she needed it or not. Maybe everything would have turned out differently if we hadn't been so screwed, and if the first of the Storad reinforcements hadn't decided to turn up.

Maybe if Pasha had been concentrating on them, rather than on listening in and trying to figure out where Jake was, they wouldn't have surprised us like a pair of children caught stealing sweets. Or if I'd tried a find-spell – but that hadn't seemed the best plan, all things considered. I could have borrowed Pasha's juice, but he was determined to be the hero, the one to find her, so I didn't even suggest it.

As it was, we were huddled out of the wind behind a short row of tents. Pasha was sure he'd found Dench at least, in the end tent, when the tramp of a thousand, two thousand, more feet crunched through the thickening snow towards us and, crucially, between us and the gate. It seemed I only had time for one hurried breath – which I regretted when I realised the frozen puff of it was a giveaway – before there were men everywhere. They looked tired, cold and pissed off, but that would probably only make them meaner if they found us. Which they would, because there wasn't much room in that little valley and those men wanted to find a billet somewhere, preferably out of the wind and snow if they were sensible.

Pasha dismissed them with a wave of his burned hand, but I was thinking a bit more clearly. Didn't matter if we found

Jake if we couldn't get her out, that's what I was thinking. Or if we died trying. I mean, yeah, it'd look good in the history books, men dying heroically to try to save their lady-love and all that, very tragically romantic. But I couldn't help thinking it would be a stupid way to go. Romance I'm all for, but I've never been a fan of tragedy, which, when I think on it right now, is seriously ironic.

Pasha. Pasha! I knew the little bastard could hear me in his head, but he took no notice until I grabbed his arm and shook it until I thought it might fall off.

Shh! I think I—

Most of the reinforcements went straight to the gate, as Malaki had said they would, though at least they didn't launch straight into an attack – they seemed content to dig in and wait awhile, and I doubted Malaki would go on the offensive with the few men he had. But a group broke away from the main force and headed our way. They spoke among themselves and I didn't need to understand their gruff language to know what they were saying, the mantras of soldiers and guards everywhere, I don't doubt: *"Over here, it's out of the wind," "My boots are killing me," "That sergeant's a slave driver," "This is out of the way; we won't get volunteered if he can't see us," "I'd kill for a cup of tea – get the fire on."*

Three more steps then they'd see us and we were dead meat. My hand clenched on instinct and I had to bite back a groan and the sudden, driving need to use my magic, pull all the juice through me and say hello to my madness.

I tried again to get Pasha's attention but he was as lost as I was, only he was lost in trying to find Jake. He hissed a victorious "Yes!" under his breath, but it was almost too late. The soldiers were on top of us.

My hand was itching now, the juice restless inside me – such a change from the days when I was afraid to use it – but it was scaring me more and more too. The black was looming always larger inside me, growing like a cancer, but one I craved and feared at the same time. I was like a junkie after Rapture, knowing what it would do to me but wanting it all the same. I couldn't give in, not now or we were lost, and so was Jake. We were lost if we stayed there long enough to be found too, so I did the only sensible thing I could think of.

I grabbed Pasha's burned hand and smacked it on to the ground between us. His eyes flew open and I could see his tonsils as he was about to scream but he didn't get time. I had hold of his hand and sucked the pain from him, stole it, used his juice not mine, became that bastard I always told myself I wouldn't be. I picked up some of his magic too, I think, because I'd swear I heard one of the soldiers think, *Hey, what was that?*

I had to do this now or not at all, so I sucked out all the pain I could and thought of the lab, warm and waiting for us. A rearrangement, a piece of magic big enough that it brought a fresh scream from Pasha – or maybe that was because we were no longer in the snow, no longer just yards from Jake. We were sprawled on the floor of the pain room and this time

Pasha was throwing up all over the place, looking like I'd sucked half his soul out with his pain and juice. I didn't feel much better myself. Everything kept wobbling in and out of focus like I'd had a fatal amount of booze.

"Bastard," Pasha managed at last. "Jake, what about Jake? I have to find her. Have to get her out of there, she'll . . . Oh, you *bastard*."

He staggered to his feet and stood there glaring at me like Namrat himself, like he wanted to eat my soul.

"Don't you care? I though you at least cared enough about Jake, but no. Obviously not. So to save your own skin, you've condemned her to who-knows-what. She's – they've caught her, you know that's worse for her than if they killed her? Worst thing, for her, to be trapped, to be held. I thought you were better than that, I really did. Looks like I was wrong, doesn't it?"

I staggered to my feet and tried not to imagine using my juice – even using Pasha's had woken up my black, brought it laughing into the back of my head. Pasha's tirade stung too, at least partly because he was right, though so was I, but the sting came out front and centre.

"Us getting shot in the head wouldn't help her any, would it? You want to save her, you need to be alive to do it, usually. And preferably alive to enjoy it afterwards too."

Looking back, I think that was the point where he snapped – but instead of raging further he shut up, stood still as the statues of the saints and martyrs in the temples. His face took on their marbled sheen and his eyes – I've never seen anyone whose eyes looked quite like his then. They were usually dark and angry, spitting sparks at the injustices of life, but now they took on a cool, dead calm that jangled my nerves and made my heart go cold.

"You don't get it." His voice was soft as snowclouds, cold as midwinter on the mountains. "You never did. Never will, too wrapped up in your own head. It's not a sacrifice unless it hurts. If doing it, giving it, is as easy as, as, getting up in the morning, it's not a sacrifice, it's just doing something, meaningless movement. Real sacrifice, like the Goddess tells us, showed us when she gave her hand to Namrat, real sacrifice *hurts*. I would do anything to find Jake and get her back. Anything, no matter what it costs me. You won't because you don't care enough about anything but yourself to hurt like that. You never were willing to go far enough."

We stood and stared at each other, and the sting got worse because maybe he was right. Then again, maybe he was just stupid; I couldn't tell which it was, or whether I'd saved him for me, because he was my friend and I needed him, or for him. Whether I'd ever be the sort of guy who could willingly sacrifice myself for anyone.

I couldn't even tell if I was being sensible or a complete dick when I finally said, "Pasha, I'd have done it, stayed there, died even, if I could have been sure it would have helped, if we could have found her in time, saved her like you wanted to. Dying while saving her, that I can understand, that I'd do.

Yes, I would. Dying while failing to? *Stupid.* And I never took you for stupid. You're too wrapped up in everything *but* yourself, too wrapped up in trying to be her hero to remember she'll want you around to be her hero for a while. And you have that, had her to go home to, and you don't even know what that means. Everything I wanted, you have. And you're ready to throw it away."

An almost silent snort of what might have been laughter, a twist of lips that was a grotesque imitation of his usual monkey grin.

"Throw it away? No, get it back. And not just for her, for all of us . . . " He shook his head and left, silent but intent. On what I couldn't be sure, though "damnfool way to try to rescue Jake" would have topped the list.

I should have followed him, but I couldn't. I envied him like I never had before. Not because of what he had, but because of what he was prepared to do for it, her. I was jealous of the strength he had inside him, even when I thought it was making him stupid.

So I didn't follow him, because all that would have come out and I didn't think he deserved it. Instead I sat and stared at my stupid throbbing hand and listened to that insidious voice inside me, telling me to do it, do it, blow the whole place, you know you want to. And I did want to. Too much. Not for anyone else; for me.

Perak jerked me out of it when he came in, looking wearier than I'd ever seen him. I opened my mouth to ask him something, something important perhaps, I can't recall, but I didn't get the chance. A buzzing zap, familiar but ten times, a hundred times louder than I'd ever heard it before. A burst of something arced past the window, split, pulsed, arrowed down towards the gates.

I knew what it was. Lise's infernal machine. Like my pulse pistol, she'd said, only bigger, stronger, more sustained. Only . . . only . . .

I was out of the room, through a startled gaggle of magelets and banging on the locked door of the machine room before anyone else had even moved. No sound from the other side. Allit and some of the other kids came up behind me. I panicked then, because I thought I knew what I was going to see in there, and I didn't want them seeing it. Bad enough that I had to, and I *had* to get in there and know for sure just how stupid Pasha had been. So I did something pretty stupid myself – gave in to that voice, clenched my hand and let a bit of juice in. Not much, enough to rearrange the lock so I could open the door. Enough that my vision went all black, that my heart stopped in terror as I wondered if this was it, *this* was the thing that was going to take me once and for all.

For a while, it looked like it was. I floundered in the dark of my head, wanting to sink in, give up, fall back, but knowing I couldn't. Not yet, not until I'd seen, until I knew.

I don't know how long I was in there, maybe only heartbeats but it felt as long as the rest of my life. I'd probably still be there now, and none of the rest would have happened the way it did, except for something that felt like it smacked my brain out of my head and brought me back to the here and now. Sitting propped up against the door, which it seemed I'd rearranged behind me. I may have overdone it, because the lock appeared to have melted and then hardened again, and no one was going to be coming in without some very specialised cutting gear.

So I was on my own, except for the machine and what lay on it.

Weird, sometimes, the things you see when you don't want to see anything else, to admit what is right in front of you. That machine is now burned into my brain. I can recall every rivet, every twist of cable, every demented cog and gear. The shine of oil across the top, the little slick underneath where Lise had dropped the oilcan and no one had mopped it up. The faint smell of tangy metal to the air. How everything was lit by the pale swirl of moonlight on falling snow that came through the window and picked out shapes in silver light and black shadow. How those shadows seemed to morph into the shape of a stalking, drool-toothed tiger. The shattered glass of the syringe where it had fallen from Pasha's hand with a few drops of Lise's concoction, the one that amplified magic, still clinging to the pieces. The random thought of *He must have stolen it from her drawer*. I can recall it all, every last detail, because I stared at it rather than at Pasha.

It should have been me on that chair. Would have been, if I'd had half his guts or passion. Then perhaps I'd have been lying there, smoke still drifting from my hair, blood dripping from my hand where I'd brought out my juice, the drips getting slower and slower until finally they stopped. Until I stopped. Lying pale but serene, my eyes half shut and looking . . . triumphant.

I must have sat there for an age, maybe two, just staring at him, but almost all I can remember thinking was, *How can death be triumphant? How?* After a time the room became blurred, colours swam in front of my eyes and the black slipped back in for good. It had never really gone away, but now, with this in front of me, proof if it was ever needed of my own lily-liveredness, its voice had fangs that drove deep.

Chickenshit, it said, and it didn't need to say anything else, but it did. Oh yes. *Chickenshit. If you had any bollocks at all you could have ended this. Gone down to those gates and blown all those Storad sky-fucking-high. Got on that machine and zapped the crap out of anyone you felt like.*

You still can. Then we'll be together. Best friends for ever.

Chapter Eighteen

I think it was Dendal who got me on my feet, patted my back like I was a two-year-old who'd just had a bad dream and said, "There, there." Perak came too; I know that because I heard him say a blessing over Pasha. Not the Ministry-approved bland crap either. A proper blessing, one of the old ones, full of brimstone and anger. I think Pasha would have liked that.

My recollections get a bit hazy after that – just odd sights and sounds. Dendal got me along to the office and I sat on the lumpy sofa and stared at Griswald as though he had any answers. Allit crying, his face all blotchy. Erlat looking frazzled and tearful, cracks in her gemstone façade. Lise swearing, sobbing as we passed through her workshop, rattling her toolbox in frustration and guilt, ripping up the plans for the machine. Snow falling past the window, soft and silent in the dark. Dendal reading some scripture in his dry, papery voice which had a hitch in it now. A cramp in my chest, the sound of the black laughing at me, calling me chickenshit.

It all came back into focus when the door opened and Jake walked in. My first thought was, *How the hell am I going to tell her?* And tell her it should have been me, not him? But the look on her face, the way it had closed off completely, iced over, told me she knew. She hadn't needed anyone to tell her – she'd known anyway, because Pasha was no longer in her head, and I wondered how lonely that would be, to have silence when you'd had the comfort of that voice with you always.

Out of all the faces around me, hers was the only one with no hint of tears. Blood, yes, and mud, frustration and a dead, bone-achingly empty tiredness, but no tears. Pasha had done what he set out to do – somehow, and I wasn't sure how right then, he had saved her. And *boy* was she pissed off about it.

I staggered to my feet, unsure what I was going to say, what I could say that would make any difference. *How far would you go?* How far would I go for her? Not as far as him, it had always been that way. That's why she loved him, not me. Or one of the reasons anyway. But now I thought on what he had said about sacrifice, that it was supposed to hurt or what was the point? The Downside Goddess was big on sacrifice, on fighting the inevitable. If she existed, then Pasha should be getting a damned great reward right about now. But who had his sacrifice hurt more? Because Jake wasn't crying, but there was something fragile just under her surface, obvious in the way she moved, as though she was suddenly made of glass. Like she would shatter if I said the wrong word.

I chickened out, afraid to break her even worse than she already was. My only consolation in all this was that I'd managed to get her a few weeks of happy with Pasha. Not much, but some. And yet maybe that was worse, because now she knew what she'd lost.

So like the coward I was, am, I said nothing and she drifted past me, pale and ghostly, empty of anything. I don't think she even saw me, left us all behind in silence as she went to the machine room. She stayed there a long while.

Perak broke the silence in the end, first with a murmured prayer, and then pulling himself together and speaking out loud. "He bought us some time. He got Jake enough space, enough chaos to get out, and us some time. He did that, at least."

"Time for what though? Arranging our funerals?" I tried not to let the bile out, but it was there and it dripped through every word. The stupidity of it, the sheer waste. *Why, Pasha? We could have done something, could have got Jake out some other way that didn't involve you dying, so why?*

Goddess only knows what Perak was about to say, because Dendal had an attack of lucidity and his voice was unusually sharp. "To do what we have to, Rojan. What *you* have to. And if you don't, I will."

I stared at him, alarmed by the sudden strength of his voice. I half suspected he was going to go on about Goddess-given work, or what she expected of me, so I tried my best to deflect him because that always made me want to blast steam out of my ears.

"What happened, then? When Pasha . . . when he used the machine . . ."

"It worked. Partially," Perak said. "Took out a small area of their men, helped us keep the gates because it scared the rest stupid. Helped Jake get away because the small group was the one holding her, and that's all he wanted, I think. But they won't stay scared, especially if they find out we aren't using it again. And we are *not* using it again."

He said it very matter-of-factly, and his eyes were steady on mine. "Are we clear on that?"

Like I was ever likely to go near the damned thing ever again. I didn't even want to look at it, and I valued my own arse too much to contemplate using it now. "We're clear." And then, because thoughts were swirling around my head that I didn't want to think, "And where are we? The Storad outside the gates?"

"Still there," Malaki said. "They got spooked for a bit, but they won't be long. Not long."

"So what do we do?"

Perak sighed and the captain shook his head. "Whatever we can."

Chapter Nineteen

Perak and Malaki went over what they knew, numbers of men, of guns, where they were, where the Storad had dug in, all the thousand and one details that someone needed to look over and I was glad it wasn't me. Between the guards and recruits and Pasha, we'd held them off. For now.

Allit stirred in the corner of the office as far from Pasha's desk as he could get, twisting his fingers. The pop as one dislocated seemed very loud, but what really got my attention was the look on his face as he saw whatever it was that he saw. Future, past, present? Concrete or shifting? We didn't know for sure, but still, something was better than nothing.

I crouched down in front of him, glad for the distraction. After a minute or two, his eyes came back to here.

"What did you see?" I asked.

"Storad in Top of the World. Storad everywhere. Not as

ghostly this time. I think . . . I think it's becoming more true, or more possible?"

I patted his arm, a pathetic attempt at making him not worry. I mean, we were screwed and it was obvious. Maybe Pasha had got the better deal – quick, probably fairly painless except what he'd used to fire up his juice. Namrat was going to be busy, already was, and many of those he ate would take longer. "Maybe. Anything else? How did they, er, do they get in? Did you see us?"

He frowned, maybe trying to make sense of what he'd seen. "Through the gates, how else? And they cut their way up and . . . and . . . there was blood and something squealing . . . and . . ."

"All right. It's all right, it hasn't happened." Yet, I added to myself. "What else?"

"They all rise."

"What?"

"I don't know. Someone says it, only I couldn't see who, or what they meant. Just, they all rise. You're not there, I don't think. You're . . . I don't know. It seems stupid." He risked a strange look at me. "I mean, you know, what with you hating the Goddess and everything." The way he said it, it sounded like a bewildered accusation.

"How about you tell me, and I'll tell you if it sounds stupid?"

"I don't know exactly. But you were standing in a temple, looking up at the saints and martyrs. You weren't praying but . . . you looked weird."

Well, I would if I was looking at saints and martyrs. I was probably thinking what a bunch of silly sods they were. I didn't say that to Allit, because he looked worried enough as it was.

"I wish I could do stuff like you, or like Pasha – like he did, I mean. *Useful* things. What use is this, when I can't even say for sure it's true, it will happen? It's stupid."

"Hey, look at me." I gave him a bit of a shake, just enough to make him listen past the frustration that was scrunching his face. "You can do magic. You know how many people can say that? Not many, not many at all. It may not seem useful now, but you'll find other ways of using it, maybe find your Minor too. Or maybe this is your Minor and you'll figure out what your Major is. But no matter what, I bet you there's no other kid in this city who can do what you just did. And it *does* help." I wasn't even lying about that, because he'd given me an idea. "If we know, or are pretty sure, that a: they're going to get in and b: they're going to head for Top of the World, then there are things we can do. Not waste men trying to stop them, if we know they can't. Not worry so much about the tunnels – they'd hardly collapse the city if they're going to be in it. Evacuate between the gate and Top of the World, excepting the guards, those with means to defend themselves. Try to get some people out of the Mishan gate, maybe. If they'll take us, which they may not. You did good, Allit. You did good. You keep trying, keep looking. Who knows, maybe you'll be the person that saves the whole city."

Yeah, I know. Doesn't really sound like me. But my brain

seemed to have taken on a wedge of darkness and talking to Allit like that, seeing the worry fade, at least a bit, helped. Not much, but frankly right then I would have taken anything, anything at all to let a little light into my head. Besides, the boy *had* done good. It wasn't much, but it was better than nothing, and he'd seen – he'd seen Pasha use the machine, and he'd been right about that, and listening to him had brought me back a bit of resolve. A bit of light and hope when all had been black and hopeless.

I took him with me to the lab to talk to Perak and Malaki, wanting someone next to me when I couldn't have Pasha, and between us we came up with something. I hesitate to call it a plan, because mostly it was guesswork and hoping, but it was something at least.

There was a fair bit of arguing involved, mainly about me and whether Perak was going to allow me to use any magic. I shouldn't, I knew that. The edges of my vision were dark and blurred, making everyone seem somehow twisted. Faces darkened, eyes shadowed, till I began to wonder who was friend and who was foe. The voice of the black kept up a constant sweet singing in my head, luring me, tempting me. I shouldn't, but Pasha's face haunted me. Triumphant, how could death be triumphant? But he'd done it, even when he knew he shouldn't, that it could kill him. He'd done it for what he believed in, for what he loved, and so I had to too or I was betraying him, or so it felt.

I didn't say any of that, only argued that I was needed, that

I could help, a lot. Perak wasn't having any of it, and neither was Malaki. "No magic" was pretty much all Perak said, apart from "I need you here, Rojan. We've lost Pasha and, if nothing else, I need you because we still need Glow and you're the one who needs to provide it, when you're recovered anyway. We're going to win this thing, and then I'll need you more than ever."

I kind of wished I had Pasha's magic, just for a while, so I could persuade Perak into letting me, but it was hopeless, especially when Malaki threatened to bring in some men to make damned sure I didn't do anything, go anywhere. Talk about feeling useless, helpless.

So I lost the argument, but I was used to that, I'm a past master at losing the argument, and we went on to what we actually were going to do. We went back and forward and got nowhere until Allit piped up with what he'd seen.

"You're sure?" Perak said.

"I – well I'm sure I saw it. I don't know how true it is, or will be."

Perak pinched his lips together, went to stare out of the window, and I went with him. We looked up at the fantastical spire of Top of the World, at Clouds looming over the city like a cancer. Perak had that look in his eyes, the one I'd learned early on usually meant trouble for someone, usually me. It was an unfocused stare coupled with a wistful smile, as though he was dreaming of other worlds, other ways to be. Other ways to blow shit up and get me in trouble.

"Whatever it is you're about to suggest," I said, "the answer's no."

"Hmm? Oh, well." The smile hardened into something more determined. "How likely is it, what Allit sees, do you think?"

"No idea. But he saw someone use the machine and that happened. He saw the Storad bring their machines over the mountain, and we know they're on their way. He saw Dench getting hold of Jake. He says he's seen one or two things that didn't happen but . . . Pretty likely, I think."

"So do I. I can't do it on my own, Rojan. All this, the Ministry, being Archdeacon, trying to change things. It's not about who's in charge. It's the whole damned thing, and it's too big for one man to change."

"First things first. If we can survive the Storad, then you can change things, make Ministry what it should be, *Mahala* what it should be."

Perak once told me I was wrong about him, that he'd changed and that what I called dreaming, he called thinking. I really should have paid attention. It would have helped, later.

"'They all rise,'" Perak said. "What do you think that means?"

"I don't know! Look, it doesn't matter. The Storad are probably going to get in, and of course they'll head to Top of the World. No shock there. The question is, what are we going to do about it? What *can* we do about it? Apart from bugger all, just die. It's not appealing. Maybe we could make a human shield out of cardinals. It might not help, but I'd feel better."

The smile turned into a full-blown grin. "You always hated everything, didn't you? I thought that was just you, that the way things turned out made you like that. Now I'm not so sure."

"Perak, will you tell me what plan you've got running through your head and how it will involve me falling from a great height into the shit? Because it will. It always does."

"Maybe not this time. I'll – I'm not sure, not totally, yet. Not on my end. Top of the World is my domain, where I belong, so you leave that to me. I've got a plan for that, and it *will* work, no matter what I have to do to make it happen. I'll make it damned well work. You, I think, have to concentrate on the 'They all rise' part. Trust me on the rest – if all else fails, I've a plan for Top of the World, especially if I can get around the cardinals."

The thought of Perak having a plan didn't fill me with confidence, but I kept quiet on it.

He rifled in the pockets of his robe and pulled out a slip of paper, scribbled something on it, gave it the official archdeacon seal and handed it to me. "Think about it, what 'They all rise' might mean, how we can use it. In the meantime, Lise needs some help, and perhaps you can give it. Use this if you need anything. Anything at all. And please. *No magic*. Not yet. Dendal was quite firm about it, and I'm not about to lose you too."

With that he went to go and confer with Malaki, and left me more confused than ever. I was never sure, from moment to moment, whether my brother was just a dreamer dreaming ideas too big and too explosive to ever work, or worked way too well, or whether he was so intelligent it scared me. Perhaps both – there's more than one type of smart and it's not always sensible.

Instead of dwelling on whatever crackpot idea Perak had come up with, under the watchful gaze of two Specials who looked like breaking any limbs they happened to find wouldn't bother them one little bit, I went to help Lise like a good helpless brother.

I found her at her desk, scribbling furiously on a notepad, little squiggles and symbols that meant less than nothing to me. She'd stuck the plans for the damned machine back together with tape, making them look more demented and incomprehensible than ever. Every now and again she'd glance up at the picture on her desk, of Dwarf, her mentor and perhaps more. I hadn't liked to ask, especially after he died.

"It'll work," she muttered when she noticed me. "He shouldn't have used it, not yet – why did he?"

"Because he didn't see any other way," I said. Because I wouldn't let him use any other way, I thought.

"I can make it work, I'm sure. Safe too."

"Wouldn't it be better to work on the—"

She glared up at me, the family donkey line firmly in place between her eyes. I was going to lose this argument as well.

"If I can get this to work, we'll be safe, all of us. If I can't, it doesn't matter how many guns the factory puts out, how much steel we can find. Guns won't win this."

And I couldn't help with that, or understand half of what she was actually doing. I felt like one of her spare parts. Funny, I used to loathe my magic, afraid of it, not wanting to hurt myself, or get addicted to it like Dendal was. Well, I still thought hurting myself was a damnfool way to cast a spell, but now . . . I couldn't use it, Perak was right. Not if I wanted to live, stay sane. A mage needs to be well fed, well rested, to get the most out of himself, the most out of his pain, and I was far from both of those things. I didn't fancy dying much, so, Perak's orders or not, magic was out of the question for now, and hell did I miss it.

Up there, in the pain room on the cusp of Trade, I was nothing more now than a hindrance, someone to get in Lise's way or distract Perak from whatever scheme he had in mind. Worse, I had no Pasha. No one to call a little git, no one to rant at me and be my conscience. No more monkey grins, no passionate talk of the Goddess, no turning lion just when it was most awkward or calling me a prick when I needed to hear it.

I had no business being Over because I was Under through and through. I was useless, hopeless, helpless. So I did what anyone might do and went home.

Chapter Twenty

I hesitated at the door to the office. Something didn't feel right and I cursed under my breath. Comes to something when a man goes home to find it isn't what it was when he left.

The office seethed with people – youngsters, magelets. They were perched on Pasha's desk, on the lumpy old sofa, on whatever floorspace they could find. One was even sat astride Griswald, who looked bizarrely pleased, or as pleased as a century-old stuffed tiger can look.

I was about to vent my entire spleen and ask what the hell everyone though they were doing when I caught sight of Halina and Dendal in a cleared space in the centre of the room. Dendal's candles guttered in the breeze of more people breathing than our office had seen, well, maybe ever. The magelets were rapt, watching with avid eyes as Halina cracked a finger out of its socket.

I'd never seen Dendal quite so with it, or not for so long a time, not for more than five minutes or so. Then again, magic and its uses in the service of the Goddess always got him focused.

"All right, see how Halina concentrates, pulls that pain in. You feel it come up your arm like a warmth, a knowledge. Yes?"

Most of the kids nodded, though one or two looked dubious.

"Then you have to show it what to do, lead it along your path, whatever your path is. It will want to go somewhere else, almost always, but you are the master. Remember that. You master it, not the other way around." Ah yes, the start of Dendal's famous "mastery" speech. Soon he'd start banging on about control and I'd start to nod off. Or I would if there was any space to sit.

"Halina?" Dendal murmured.

She favoured us all with an arch and superior smile, half closed her eyes and concentrated. Nothing much happened for a moment, and then a boy gasped as Griswald lifted into the air and twirled slowly round, as though showing off his new boy-coat.

Halina let Griswald down to the floor gently, and Dendal caught my eye before he carried on.

"You all know by now what happened to Pasha. And the warning there is twofold. That is what happens if you can't control your magic, when it masters you rather than the other way around. And also," he held me with eyes clearer than I'd ever seen, "also sometimes it is what you have to do. No matter what the priests say now, they once held that the Goddess made us this way for a purpose. I believe that, with all I have. You have a purpose, and so does your magic, but it's up to you to decide what that purpose is. For Pasha, it was to save Jake and others like her, perhaps to show us the way. It always was his purpose, and he was clear in his mind about what he was prepared to do for her, for them, us, and he did it. Now, Mahala is going to need us, and soon. She's going to need everything you can give it, everything you can give to the people who, whether they like it or not, know it or not, will be relying on us, on the guards, on Lise and whatever genius she can perform. So I need you all to work with me, with Halina and Rojan here to do your best to learn some control. And I need you to think on your purpose, for the Goddess."

At the mention of my name, they turned to look at me, and I couldn't bear it. All young kids, all half starved, half scared to death with not just the siege, the threat of the Storad, but with half-formed magical urges. And with hope. That was the worst. They looked at me like I was giving them hope.

Cabe was there, the boy who'd cut his hand in the Slump, and his look was the worst. "They all rise," Allit had said, and hadn't known what he meant. What Perak had told me to concentrate on, because I was damn-all use for anything else right now. Was this it? These kids, were they going to rise? It didn't seem possible, and even if it was, I wasn't going to be the one at their head.

It was the oddest thing: until a few months before I'd been untroubled by family or friends, except for Dendal, who barely counted as he was away in his head so often. I'd liked it that way too – no one to worry over, or to worry over me. No one to be responsible for, or care about and then see them die, like Ma. Only now I had family, I had friends. Pasha had been right – they were my way back into the world rather than being apart from it. I had these kids, who were almost like a second family because I saw myself in them at every turn, wanted to make sure they didn't make my mistakes. My family, and a weight on my heart, on a conscience that wanted so very badly to be feckless and free. And still I couldn't do that to them, not to these kids who were just trying to figure out what they could do, how they fitted in. Boys like I once was, full of fear. I was still full of fear. I think I always will be.

Cabe said something to me, I don't know what. I couldn't listen. I didn't care if Allit had seen them rising, had seen them going up to take on the Storad at Top of the World. I didn't care what he'd seen, because I wasn't going to let it happen. Not to these kids, *my* kids.

If it wasn't going to be them, it had to be something else, something I hadn't thought of, some*one* I hadn't thought of, and it had to be me doing the thinking because Pasha was gone and Perak had his hands full.

It was down to me.

The thought crushed the breath from my chest like a

tombstone had landed on it. If it was down to me, we were screwed and I couldn't look at that damned hope any more.

I made for the door, ran into Cabe's father, Quillan, pushed past him and out.

It was down to me.

There had to be something I wasn't thinking of, some*one*. There had to be a different way. Goddess's tits, I would have given over a fair part of my anatomy to have Pasha back, just there, showing me how to be the good guy. I had a funny feeling I was going to make a right cock-up of it on my own. I usually did.

The cold air outside slapped a bit of sense into me, but not much. Snow drifted down in little clumps through the mesh of walkways, a dollop here, a cluster there, a blob to wriggle its chill way down my back. It dusted the walkways so that they looked like icing on a fancy cake.

There had to be something. All I had to do was think of it.

Someone came out after me and I whipped round, ready to snap them in two with words, but I came up short when Halina looked at me with half-closed, appraising eyes.

"Running out on them already?" she asked, as though she already knew the answer. "Why am I not surprised?"

"No!" I shut my eyes for a heartbeat, because actually, yes. Until then, until she asked me so baldly. "No. Did Dendal tell you Perak thinks these kids are the answer, the only answer he's got? That we can use their magic, send them down to the gates, only he doesn't know what it's like, how most of them probably haven't a clue what their Major is yet, and would probably kill themselves if they tried anything. Only there has to be something – Allit saw, or rather heard. 'They all rise.' What does that even *mean*? Perak thought maybe mages, but it's not, it can't be. Or not these mages anyway. And the Storad are almost through, and if we don't figure it out now it'll be too damned late and Pasha will have died for nothing. All that sacrifice, all that hurt, wasted, and I can't let that happen. I have to do something, only I can't use my magic unless I want to make another Slump, and what good am I at anything without it? I'm a fair bounty hunter and a world-class flirt. That's about it."

For a moment there, I thought Halina was going to slap me and tell me to pull myself together. I probably deserved it too. She looked out into the deepening snow for a while, and then seemed to come to a decision.

"When you went to the Stench without me – what was it you were really after?"

"A weapon. Actually, shit. Lots of it."

"You wanted . . . oh." She laughed at that, a snide, cynical laugh touched with glee. "You know, I find I like the way you think, at least on some things. Well, I can get you the Stenchers, and the shit. Those scummy bastards will do what I tell them, or they'll feel the slap of my magic. But that won't be enough on its own. What else? *Who* else?"

The answer was, of course, simple.

Everyone.

Chapter Twenty-one

Under wasn't the same place that it had been even a few weeks ago. The snow kept on coming, but by the time it got to No-Hope it wasn't white any more. It picked up all the dirt it could find on its way down, maybe sucked out the corruption of Clouds, the avarice of Heights, so by the time the No-Hopers saw it, it was streaky grey flakes that slapped wetly against the skin before they melted and dribbled down the back of my coat. Even with no rain, my neck got wet.

The streets and walkways were dark, as most of the Glow got siphoned to the factories, and what was left, people were hoarding to keep themselves warm. The walkways were empty too, a watchful, pensive kind of silent that I'd never experienced before, even during curfews and on the brink of riots, when everyone was too damned angry to be quiet. Now the air was like a bowstring stretched beyond all normal tolerance, and it thrummed with fear.

Down here, if the Storad came in, there was no place to run, no place to hide that they couldn't find us in the end. Over wasn't much better but at least there were the gates towards the Mishans for the people with the right connections, the right amount of money. Only someone from Over had any of those things. A chance to beg asylum, to sell yourself off into servitude perhaps, buy your way out. This far down, all there was to look forward to was Namrat silently stalking you, and he might be quick and come by a Storad gun, or he might be slow and let you starve to death, but he was coming and there was no escape.

I hunched my shoulders against it, against the fatalistic feel, and the way my own mind tried to tell me that that was as it should be, because we'd always been told we were worth nothing and sometimes we believed it. I found myself turning to say something to Pasha, faced only snow-swirled air, snapped my mouth shut and carried on.

One building stood out among the rest, and I could see the glow of its lights even from two levels up. Guinto's temple. I hesitated – priests and I have a less than happy history. Basically I loathe them, and they aren't so fond of me, but Guinto and I had come to an uneasy truce. He didn't try to convert me, I didn't tell him he was full of shit. As truces go, it was sort of working. Again, I turned to say something to Pasha, and couldn't, and couldn't bear the crushing weight on my chest either.

Right then, even talking to a priest was better than what

was going on in my head, so I made my way to his temple and, after only a small internal rant about fucking Ministry and sodding priests, went in. If I had something to hate, right there in front of me, I might feel better. Besides, Halina was off firing up the Stenchers, Dendal was away with the fairies again, and Perak was busy with a plan he wouldn't tell me about. I had work to do too, and Guinto might be my best asset.

The temple was packed to bursting, fuller than I'd ever seen it so that it was hard to see the statues of the saints and martyrs, and the murals of the Goddess were lost in a haze of people. A quick inspection showed why – a table with a vat of something that smelled suspiciously like hot water that had once seen a cabbage, somewhere far back in its history. It was doing duty as "soup" for the people who crowded round, thin hands offering up a cup or bowl.

Guinto presided over the squirming, pushing mass of people with his usual – and to me infuriating – serenity. He blessed people, comforted them, told them to have faith, the Goddess would protect her own.

What a crock of shit, but he was doing more than most anyone else, just with the "soup".

He caught sight of me, cocked a questioning eyebrow, and made his way through the hordes of hungry parishioners.

"I won't say it's a pleasure," he said, but he was smiling his superior smile, the one that made me want to zap him with a bit of magic, just to see what he would do. "But you're always welcome, you know that."

I wanted to say something sharp and cutting, wanted to rant till steam came out of my ears and my head stopped thinking all these stupid thoughts, but all I could see was the drip-drip-drip of Pasha's blood on the floor, all I could hear were gunshots and screams. I opened my mouth to tell him why I was here, what Halina and I had decided, and nothing came out.

Guinto dropped the smile, took me by the arm and led me into his office-cum-quarters behind the altar. He didn't say anything, for which I was glad, only bustled about getting two glasses and a bottle of something pinkish and vile-smelling.

"Not much, I'm afraid," he said, and handed me a full glass.

I put it down without drinking, and found my voice. "Pasha's dead."

He sat down behind his stark, darkwood desk and ran his hands over the polished surface. "I know. We held a service for him."

I slumped into the chair opposite. "One he'd have liked, I hope."

"Of course. A full-blown Downside service, with the blood-and-ash devotional and the choir singing one of their hymns. I've always quite liked the Downside hymns, so full of passion, don't you think? Of course, don't tell anyone I said that. But that's not why you're here, is it?"

I hated it when he did that – he claimed it was because the Goddess gave him insight. I say perhaps he was just a shrewd old bastard who only wore the face of a benign and holy priest.

"No, it's not. I can't do anything up there. Can't use my magic, not unless I want to go batshit crazy or die, or I can't use it until I've had about a week's sleep and we haven't *got* a week. Perak won't let me even go out there with a gun. So I thought, if I can't do anything Over, maybe I could do something Under."

I'm sure he only smiled his smug smile just to really piss me off. Worked too. "Who says you have to do anything? I thought Rojan didn't give a rat's backside about anything except money and women and staying alive?"

"Yeah, well, Rojan's changed. Not for the better, I often think – I mean, look at me, I'm talking to a priest and I haven't once wondered what it is you're guilty of. I'm stuck with being responsible, because I am. I'd much rather not be."

"So what are you going to do?"

And there it was, the question that had been rattling round my brain all the way down here. Nothing wasn't an option, not any more. Not after Pasha – it had to be worth something, what the silly sod had done. I owed him that. Without any magic it was going to be tricky, because I'd have to start using my brain. That should have been a warning really.

"You remember Allit?" I said. "The young mage? Well, he's discovered one or two things he can do. One of them, well, we're not sure exactly what it does, but we think perhaps . . . he can see what's going to happen. Perhaps."

"And?"

"And we're going to do something about it. 'They all rise,' he said. I didn't know what he meant at first, and I don't think he did, but . . . they all rise. Under. No-Hope and Boundary, the Stench, anyone in the Slump. Malaki wouldn't take help from Under except what he wanted to strong-arm out of people unwilling to give it. None of them want to take help from Under, except maybe as cannon fodder so they can escape. The cardinals – the ones that are left – are pitching a fit, trying to press-gang people into fighting, the sort of people they usually happily ignore. But they wouldn't give guns to the likes of us, because who knows who we might shoot and it might be them. But I've seen what's Outside, I've seen what's coming and it makes what battered down our gates look like a kid's toy. Against that, we've got guns and bullets and not enough guards Over. But we've got people down here, hordes of them. Nasty vicious people, or just people who want to live and have had to fight their whole lives to fend off the alternative, to stave off Namrat. Which is precisely what you want in a person during a war, and you want them on your side. Right?"

"I don't think I . . . "

"Father, Mahala has got an army down here. They just don't know that's what they are, what they're capable of, because they've been stomped on for too long. We're going to wake them up."

"'We'?"

I allowed myself a smile. "Yes, we. Look, Perak can't do as he wants because he's got cardinals breathing down his neck, cardinals who'd probably keel over with outrage if he even suggested it. He didn't say it outright, he can't, but he'd do it if it was just that, I'm sure of it, but he needs those cardinals, and the guards and Specials. He needs them all willing and on his side if we're to have a hope here, if he wants to come out alive whether we beat the Storad or not. But Perak's known-full-well-to-be-a-pain-in-the-arse brother? He can do a lot of things an archdeacon can't. And a priest who defied Ministry to allow Downsiders in his temple, who allowed the blood-and-ash devotional, who almost any man Under would listen to? Handing out soup or what passes for it is all very well, but what do you think will happen when the Storad get in? And they will get in. What will happen to Under then? I tried before, to get people Under to help, and they wouldn't. All busy trying to get out, or believing some bullshit about how the Storad would leave them be, or, the sensible ones anyway, busy putting up what defences they could. They wouldn't fight for Ministry, and I don't blame them. But they'd fight for themselves. If you asked them to."

He opened his mouth to say something, probably some little adage about the Goddess would provide, but shut it before he could say anything that would incur my sarcasm. He may have been a priest, and we held very different views on things, but he wasn't stupid.

Finally he said, "It would be a busy day for Namrat if the Storad get in. But the Goddess—"

"Will reward you all in heaven with a pat on the head and a biscuit, yes, yes. But don't you think she'd rather you didn't all turn up at once? Did you ever listen to the Downsiders, what they think the Goddess means? The reward isn't for dying, it's for fighting against it every damned step of the way. That's what the Goddess used to mean, before the Ministry sucked her dry."

Guinto sat back and stared at me for a long time, and while he thought I kept my peace and drank the pink stuff, which tasted as vile as it smelled.

"What precisely are you suggesting?" he said at last. "Because I can't go against what I feel the Goddess means to me. I can't condone violence, except in self-defence. And even then it's only a perhaps."

Goddess preserve me from idiots and holy men. I'd have said that if I'd thought it would have helped, or the Goddess was listening. Instead I made an attempt at tact, which, as noted, is not something that came easily. "Perish the thought, Father. And I'm not wanting to press-gang anyone into doing something they don't want to or can't. I just want you to present people with the choice, and a few pertinent facts. Surely, after that, it's up to them?"

"And what are you going to do?"

"Me? If you find me some willing bodies, I'm going to get them the means to defend themselves."

And when they'd done that, when they'd found out they were strong . . . who knew? Maybe we could fend off the Storad, and then take down Top of the World like the black was always tempting me to do, make the Ministry fall, rip open Over and let the sunlight fall on Under. Perak might even help – he loathed the cardinals and all the rest about as much as I did and I was pretty sure he'd give up archdeaconry just the second an alternative presented itself.

Rojan Dizon, defeater of the Storad, leader of the Glorious Rebellion. Got a nice ring to it, hasn't it?

The thing about priests, I've often found, is that they can be right sneaky bastards when it suits them.

Because although Guinto never tired of telling me what good, simple people his flock were, devout worshippers of the most benign Goddess, two hours later the doors to the temple shut behind a group of men who between them had probably mugged, embezzled, scammed, stabbed or otherwise fought their way through half of No-Hope. Well, some of them didn't look too threatening, more disgruntled factory workers, but that covers quite a lot of disgruntled when their workday consisted of twelve hours' humping around a lot of heavy stuff, leaving them with shoulders like battering-rams. Even after a month or more of starvation rations, they were still bigger than me, and intimidating as hell in the wavering shadows of a hundred candles perched along the statues and on the backs of pews.

Good simple people, my backside. They'd been suspiciously quick too, almost like Guinto had them on standby.

All in all, they looked pretty incongruous in front of the nice sparkly Ministry picture of the Goddess with her pet fluffy tiger. They looked *right* at home before the Downside mural of her, in front of Namrat and his death-dealing teeth.

Guinto seemed nervous as hell, and I wasn't much better but I put on a bold front, kept my mangled hand out of sight in one pocket, and the other on the pulse pistol, just in case.

Guinto started, but it soon became clear he wasn't too sure about getting it all into words, or perhaps just not sure how much he should say, whether it might hinder more than help. The men here probably knew crap all. Most of the news-sheets had been keeping it all as quiet and calm as they could, calling for stoic forbearance in the face of this little minor trouble that would soon blow over. The men here knew that for the bunch of shit it was, but they didn't know much else except what the rest of the news-sheets were saying, such as we were all doomed when the baby-eating and defeated-opponent-buggering Storad made it through the gates. What they thought they knew was mostly bollocks, and I couldn't decide which lot of bollocks was worse.

Guinto stumbled to a halt and looked at me. So did all the hulking bruisers. Not a nice feeling. I decided to say, Screw tact. It'd be lost on them.

So I got up on the little dais next to Guinto and said, "We're fucked, well and truly."

As motivational speeches went I could have done better, but I had their attention. So for once in my life I was honest, searingly truthful about just how screwed we were, and why; told them that all that shit about the Storad not bothering Under was a load of old bollocks and how I knew that; and just why they couldn't escape through the Mishan gate. When their faces had begun to look like a bunch of slapped arses, I told them I was fairly sure that the Storad didn't eat babies, and what we were going to do about it anyway.

"The cardinals would have a collective shit-fit at the thought of anyone from Under having a gun, so they're having to rely on Specials and guards, whatever weak-chinned wonders they can dredge up from Over and anyone from Under who's volunteered to be part of a meat shield without weapons. It's not enough – it's not going to be anywhere *near* enough. The Archdeacon can't get around the cardinals. Not officially. But we can. Because I just happen to know where the last lot of guns are. I suspect one or two of you know as well. Factory Three."

A few eyes lit up at that, and I made a mental note to keep an eye on those particular men, but most of them looked thoughtful. One of the bigger guys – belatedly I realised it was Cabe's father, Quillan – said, "And when we have guns, what are we going to do with them?"

"Shoot a few cardinals and priests," someone muttered, adding hurriedly when Guinto looked like he was about to faint, "Present company excepted, of course."

It was hard to disagree with him, mainly because I felt much the same.

"Maybe later," I said, to Guinto's gasping shock. "After we've survived this, if we survive, then things are going to be different I think. They sure as shit will be if I have anything to do with it. But first – you've all got family down here, right? Where will they go when the Storad come? How will they hide? They can't. The Storad will make for Top of the World if they're sensible." I neglected to mention Allit's magic, because that would be a stupid move on my part. It was bad enough Quillan knew what I was, and I could only hope he kept that quiet. "But they won't stay there. Once they're done with the Ministry, where do you think they'll go next? Maybe they won't wait for that, maybe they'll be down here at the same time they aim for up there. One thing's for certain: they want rid of Mahala, in her entirety. They want us gone, so they don't have to depend on us for trade, so they can start selling their own machines, so we won't have a stranglehold on them any more. They'll either come down here and scour us out, or just wait till we starve to death. So, if I give you a gun, what are you going to do with it?"

The guy who'd said shoot cardinals piped up. "Shoot some Storad. We can screw with the Ministry later. All right. But Factory Three – that's sewn up tighter than a gnat's arse. None of us managed to get a working gig there; it's all Ministry. How do we get the guns?"

I grinned at him, and pulled out the chit that Perak had

given me. *I authorise the bearer to requisition any equipment that he sees fit*, followed by Perak's signature and the official archdeacon's seal.

Quillan laughed, and all of a sudden I had my own little army. Better than any Specials or guards, because these were men from Under, used to fighting their way through all the shit life down here had to offer.

Chapter Twenty-two

Getting the guns and bullets, given Perak's back-handed assistance, didn't prove to be too much of a problem. Controlling my army did. It was like trying to herd cats.

The factory workers weren't too bad – they were mostly honest, mostly not too bloodthirsty and mostly sane. Quillan seemed to be their natural leader, so I let him. The rest – well, let's just say I kept my back to a wall as much as I could. But if they were scaring me, I was hoping they'd scare the Storad too.

All in all, we were about thirty men, two guns apiece, which would make it easier because reloading was a pain. I didn't want anyone to pay too much attention to us, not until we were ready, so I had them all drift up towards the Buzz in ones and twos.

"What's the plan?" Quillan had asked. He hadn't said anything about me being a mage, I noted.

"Pretty simple really." Mainly because I was making it up as I went along, but no point mentioning that. "We stick to where we know, what we know. Round the Buzz. If – no, *when* – the Storad make it past the men holding what's left of the gates, we hold them off from Under. Make it not worth their while. Send them up."

"Then what? Once they've fucked over Ministry, we'll still be in for a load of shit."

"Don't you worry about that. The Archdeacon has a plan for Top of the World." I had no intention of revealing the fact I had no idea what the plan actually was. "Maybe it'll work, and maybe it won't. Either way, we need to stop the Storad getting into Under. Even if it's only until we can get as many people out of the Mishan gate as possible. By sheer force if we have to, because we've got some firepower now and the Mishans don't, and a gun in the face concentrates the mind wonderfully. The longer we can stop the Storad, the more people can get out. We'll be a shield, but a shield with guns. Agreed?"

"I don't like that part so much," he said. "Just a meat shield."

"If it comes to that, we're pretty much screwed anyway. But it won't come to that. I'm hoping we can beat the living snot out of them instead." If it did come down to that, to just being a shield while everyone got out of town, then I was going to give in to the black and blow the hell out of everything I could reach. Because if it came to that, I was as good as dead anyway, we all were. Naturally I didn't say that – admitting to being a mage was still a tricky business that might well end up with my head on a stick and, while Quillan knew, I didn't want the rest of them in on my dirty little secret.

"Thirty men with guns though – how's that going to be enough?" he asked.

"It isn't. Which is why, on your way up, you are all going to find a few good men you can trust and bring them with you. Make sure they bring whatever weapons they can find. And when we get there, we are not going to be out in the open, because that would be stupid. I'll meet you there."

"What are you going to do?"

"Find some friends. I hope."

While they were dredging up likely-looking mates to help out, I was pretty busy myself. Now that I had at least the beginnings of a plan, I had all the energy I needed. First I checked with Halina, and she was right where I'd said we'd meet, along with a small phalanx of Stenchers and some suspiciously smelly barrels. I got them going to where I thought we'd need them, and was comforted by the truly evil grin that Halina was wearing.

"You've no idea how often we've dreamed of doing something like this," she said.

I then took the time to slip to Erlat's house, only to find it in chaos. I managed to grab Kersan as he bustled past me, his arms full of various little gewgaws. I didn't even need to say anything before he jerked his head in the direction of Erlat's rooms and scuttled off.

Her room was stripped almost bare, with her at the centre, surrounded by all the others – not all working girls, because Erlat's place wasn't just a brothel but a safe-house too. The younger kids, refugees from the pain factories that I'd destroyed in the 'Pit, ran around picking up anything that was valuable and stuffing it into sacks.

Erlat talked rapidly to two of the oldest women, who still probably weren't over twenty. She held out something that glittered gold and ruby. "Look, this should be enough, don't you think? It's worth more than anything else in the place, and with everything else you should have a chance. You buy your way through, and remember what I taught you – when you get there, you don't let any man run your business. You do the work, you pick your customers, you run yourselves. The Mishans are easy enough to please, from what I've seen of them. Just keep safe, and together, OK? Hopefully you can all come back when it's over."

"If you're not going, I don't see why we should," one of the women snapped back. "And who says there'll be a city to come back to? Or anyone in it? Erlat, please, you come too. If it's not safe for us, it's not safe for you."

Erlat caught my eye, just for a heartbeat, before she turned back. "I'm staying, but I can't ask you to stay with me. The younger ones . . . Someone has to get them out, if we can, and someone needs to look out for them once they're out. Please."

The women went off, muttering about "buggered if I'm going if she's not". Erlat turned her polished smile on me.

"Rojan, a pleasure as always. I'm afraid you find us in a moment of disarray."

I looked around to where a boy a year or two younger than Kersan was rolling up Erlat's favourite rug, while another took a nicely done oil painting off the wall. Within moments, pretty much all that was left was me, Erlat, the bath and the bed.

She noticed me noticing and raised an eyebrow. "Well?"

"Tempting, but maybe now isn't the time?"

"Coward." She dropped the teasing and became serious, as serious perhaps as I'd ever seen her. Another crack in the diamond facet. "They're going to win, aren't they?" and then, before I could say anything, "No, don't answer that. Why are you here? Shouldn't you be out saving the world? Or at least this bit of it?"

There were a lot of things I could have said to that, but they would have been uncomfortably close to the truth so instead I said, "Why aren't you going with the rest of the house? Do you think they can get through?"

A brittle smile that baffled me. "Because I'm not, and nor are some of the others. Probably for the same reason you're not heading that way yourself. And because I have some very wealthy clients who have been very generous, so I can afford to get some of us out. Not to mention some of my girls have been down that Mishan gate every day for the last week, softening up the captain. He's got a real thing for one of them by now and his sergeant is a sucker for a pretty face. Add in a few little trifles worth a month or two of a captain's salary, and the fact I'm sure you can guess who entertained the Mishan diplomats when they were here, and of course my special friend, the Mishan liaison. When we entertain, men don't forget us easily. Which you'd know if you ever let me entertain you. I'd say they've got a good chance. Better than ours."

I knew better than to ask again why she wasn't going. Exhaustion fuddled my brain, made me struggle to think why I was here – I'd come to tell her something. Only now, even here the black was with me. The black never got me at Erlat's, but this wasn't her house any more. This was a room with her in it. I blinked and the world seemed to shift around me. I blinked again and I was sitting on the bed, shadows dancing in all the corners, and not just shadows either – the darkness growled and showed me its teeth.

"You can't stay here," I said at last to the wavering face in front of me. "Storad will be through any time. You should all go, now."

"Rojan—"

"Even if you don't go to the gate, get out, you have to move. I mean it. Go to the lab, or something. It's pretty safe there, I think, locked up tight – Perak had it reinforced when he found out your Mishan friend wanted Lise. It's a damn sight safer than here will be. They've got guns; Lise has booby-trapped the whole place. Dench knows where it is, so they might try for it, but if all else fails, Lise can blow it and them sky-high."

Erlat put a soft hand on my arm and the shadows receded back to where they should be, out of my head so that I could think clearly again. Something – no, some*one* – I should have been thinking of, and hadn't, hadn't dared to because to think of her meant to face my own shortcomings. I didn't have a lot of choice though, because my shortcomings were scattered at my feet like snow.

"Jake, is she . . . " I almost said, "Is she all right?", but that was a stupid question. Of course she wasn't, but I needed to know that she was, well, not all right, but going to be. I owed that much to Pasha. That and not taking advantage of the fact he wasn't around. Only now, now it came to it, that was the last thing I was going to be doing. Maybe I was finally growing up.

Erlat shook her head ruefully, as though I was some little kid who just couldn't quite grasp how to tie his bootlaces. "She's back on duty, up with Perak. What else has she got now? She needs something to keep her mind away, help her lock it all down. Once she had the matches to do that, but now she has this. She blames herself, of course. If it hadn't been for— No, that's not for me to say. But she won't show a damned thing if she can help it, not even to me."

"Blames herself? But—"

A soft knock at the door, as though the knocker was ashamed of interrupting.

"I thought you'd be here." Guinto came in, a flush creeping up his neck because here he was, a good and pious priest, in a brothel. Or what had been a brothel – there wasn't much left by now.

"Look, if you aren't going to the gate with the rest, get to the lab. The Storad will be through here anytime. Please, Erlat?"

I waited for the lash of her words, about how she didn't need big old me to protect her, but she winked at Guinto, making him blush worse than I had, and said, "Maybe, we'll see. I do have a gun of my own, you know. I suppose you're off to save the world now?"

Funny how all the time she talked to me, had her soft hand on my arm, the black buggered off. No quiet voice in my head, no sing-song temptation. It meant I could fool myself into thinking she was right, and that made me grin. "Maybe. Not sure it's worth saving."

She laughed – my reward – and squeezed my arm. "No, perhaps not, but you're going to try." She laughed again, all teasing like she used to, fear pushed back for now. I never knew how she managed to chase the fear away, for both of us. She rolled her eyes and winked at Guinto again, a slow seductive flick of her eyelid that had him blushing fit to burst. "My heroes."

And that thought kept me warm, kept the black at a safe distance, right up until we hit the snow-streaked streets of the Buzz.

Chapter Twenty-three

We gathered in the Buzz outside one of the fake-shabby bars that was now boarded up and looking lonely in the dark – almost all the Glow lamps had faded, with power being diverted to other things. Moonlight made it down here intermittently, slicing over the top of Trade and through a few gaps in Heights. We were close enough to Over, to real true sky, for that, though clouds massed over the pass and after a short time the moon dipped behind them, the wind picked up and it began to snow again. It looked like it meant business this time – not small, bitty flakes all ready to melt at the hint of settling but big, fat dollops that feathered over every surface and stuck there as though they meant to hold out for eternity.

We'd lost two men on the way – they faded out of sight and off into the dark of Under, and I could only hope like crazy I hadn't just unleashed a wave of terror and mugging, aided and abetted by free guns. But we'd gained a load more: factory workers, pimps, gang members, call-girls and street walkers, shop owners, housewives, bouncers who came prepared with brass knuckles and faces so scarred from impromptu glass fights that only their mother could love them. All sorts, more than four hundred all told, and more came in dribs and drabs behind them as word got out. All men and women from Under. All looking a mixture of grimly determined and nervous.

They all rise.

I shivered in the bone-aching cold, and not for the last time I wished Pasha was there too. To rummage in the heads of all these men from Under I'd given guns to, find out what they were thinking. More importantly just to be there, and tell me whether I was being a stupid dick. Yet I had the feeling he'd approve of this – I was going a bit lion, and I think it would have tickled him.

The square was utterly silent, the few scuffles and murmurs stifled by the thickening snow that made it hard to see the whorehouse opposite or even much of the man or woman next to you – Quillan was a dark shape beside me, outlined in melting snow but with his face obscured.

Here it was silent, but vague, disturbing sounds of fighting drifted over from the inner gates. Muffled shots, screams. The rank smell of burning people. An ominous thud that sounded like the gates of hell had just opened.

We grouped together, more or less. In the murk it looked like whole gangs had turned up, and they kept themselves apart. For the best, probably, or they'd have turned on each other way before the Storad could get us.

No one said anything – there wasn't anything to say except the few murmured prayers that hung in the air like a bad smell. All we could do was wait and, in my case, try not to think too hard about not being able to use my magic, about how I would anyway if I had the guts. How I'd probably end up going batshit and blowing myself and part of the city up if I did. About Pasha and Jake and a hundred other regrets, like how I had the stupidest feeling I should have said more to Erlat, though I didn't know what. I only knew I probably wasn't going to get another chance.

Another thud, even more ominous than the first, and the sound of Storad flamers hissed through the air.

"I hope Cabe's all right up there. Sent my other kids down to the Mishan gate," Quillan said. "You think . . . think they might get through? I mean, that's why most of us are here. To give them enough time to get through, if they can."

What the hell do you say to that? "I think they're as screwed as we are"? That they probably didn't have a hope in hell unless he was a lot richer than he looked? Even I'm not that hard-hearted, so I lied through my teeth.

"Cabe will be fine – the lab is the safest place in Mahala right now. And the rest—" Another lie: "They'll get through. I don't think even the Mishans would turn away the thousands of refugees they're going to get, not if it was that or let them die – especially if they can make money off them. The Mishans might fleece everyone, but at least they'll still be alive."

It seemed to be the right thing to say, which didn't make me feel any better about lying to him. Quillan hefted his gun and gave a determined nod. A few others who'd listened in looked much the same.

I'd picked here for a reason. The inner gates weren't far away, and anyone coming through had two choices which way to go. Straight on to the Spine which spiralled its way from Top of the World right down to Boundary, and which I knew from listening in to Perak and Malaki was filled with as many men as he'd thought he could spare. The men at the gates would fall back to the Spine in the event of the gates failing, and hope the Storad followed them. Then they might go down, but I doubted it. If they did, we could be there in moments across a handful of walkways. But I didn't think they would – what was there Under for them? Instead, I thought they aimed to control the Spine from there on up. Whoever controlled that area controlled the city, and from there it would be a matter of working their way to Top of the World like Allit had seen, and then the city was theirs.

The other way from the gates led directly to the Buzz, to this junction overlooked by bars and whorehouses, gambling dens and shops which in better times could have sold you all you could dream of, and a few things you couldn't. Malaki had been of the opinion that the Storad wouldn't bother coming this way, not at first. Maybe he was right – I figured they would want to block it off at the least – but if they didn't come I had ways of making them, at least some of them, or we could move forward and block them off, corner them between two forces, the guards in front and us behind. Halina and I hadn't planned any further than that because once people start moving, start making weird and crazy-arsed decisions, plans go out of the window.

A signal from Halina, who I'd had stand on a walkway by the top of the plushest whorehouse in town, right at the point where the Storad would make their choice on which way to go. The signal was that the Storad had split, and some were coming our way. Every man and woman tensed, and whispered prayers to the Goddess filtered into the silence. I almost wished I believed so that I could pray too, told myself not to be so stupid and said a prayer to Namrat instead. Even I believe in death. My prayer went *Fuck off, you furry bastard, you aren't eating me today.* I can't say I put a whole lot of faith in it, but it helped a bit.

The first of the Storad inched into the faint light from a last lonely Glow at the end of the street. He was big and mean-looking, with a face the colour of curdled milk and hair so dark it dissolved into the shadows around him. Fluttering snow alternately hid and revealed him, making him seem almost imaginary. Bits of metal armour jangled and clanked as he moved – he was real enough. I gripped my gun so hard I almost cracked a knuckle as he crept forward, more and more Storad appearing behind him. Crap, there seemed like a whole battalion of them, watchful and wary, trying to peer into every crevice. They looked like they did this every day of the week, whereas all I had were people who merely tried to stay alive on any given day. I wondered who had the edge in that contest, and then realised I was about to find out.

I waited till I couldn't wait any longer then signalled to the walkways that criss-crossed the little square.

There's one thing about living in a city like Mahala, one that grows more upwards than it does outwards. It gives you a real sense of the possibilities of threats from above and below as well as those on your level – the ever-present threat of being mugged from overhead will do wonders for that. Something these Storad were about to find out.

A series of wild, blood-curdling screams echoed round the square and something very like heavy rain poured down over the Storad. Very like rain in that it was wet, but not like it at all because rain doesn't usually stink that badly, or have lumps in it. The Stenchers kept on whooping and pouring the contents of their reeking vats to the last drop, leaving Storad blind, choking and probably unable to work out which way was up as several were knocked from their feet by the deluge. It was suddenly slippery underfoot, and getting back up seemed to pose them a few problems. If I hadn't been so stomach-clenchingly scared, I'd have laughed till I had no breath left.

As it was, I pulled the gun and as one man we leapt into the fray.

The thing about episodes like that is you can never remember them clearly. That battle flashes across my mind in a series of moving portraits with occasional thoughts as a running commentary. The only things those flashes share are the stench of shit and the gentle fall of snow.

I recall pulling my gun and hoping I didn't need to use it, all while knowing I was going to have to. I kept groping for my pulse pistol on instinct, then remembering: no magic, not if I wanted to stay sane and alive, no matter that the black was whispering to me, the shadowy tiger was stalking across the snow-ridden square, the throb of my hand was filling me up with juice I couldn't afford to spend.

A Storad turned his flamer my way, snow hissing and popping from the heat, and I only just got away in time – half my jacket went up in flames and I had to roll to put the fire out before I started burning too. Rolling in a mixture of snow and shit isn't pleasant, you can trust me on this, but at least I wasn't burning any more.

Halina acquitted herself far better than I did – she didn't seem to give a steaming pile of what she'd just dumped on the Storad who knew she was a mage. Her wild laugh punctuated the gloom like lightning as she used her magic to pick up

Storad and bash them into other Storad, to lob the now-empty barrels down an alley to bowl over men and just generally cause mayhem. She hovered above us, just out of range of the flamers and hard to see in the swirl of snow, and seemed to be enjoying herself immensely. I wished I was.

Gunshots went off all around, the flash of the muzzles searingly bright in the darkness, the sound of the shots deafening, echoing round and round the square, over and through each other till I thought I'd happily go deaf. Other noises – thuds, screams, gurgles. Men and women with no guns doing what they could with what they had. I can clearly recall a man whose ancestors must have been butchers, back when we had animals to slaughter, because he was brandishing two old and rusted meat cleavers like he was Namrat and they were his teeth. Others used kitchen knives or rough clubs made out of whatever they'd had to hand. Swear to the Goddess, I saw a man take out two Storad from behind with a chair leg. It snapped across the back of the head of the first, and then the man used the jagged end to stab the next in the side of the neck.

No one gave a shit who was Downsider and who was Upsider: it was us, Mahalians, against Storad and that was all that mattered. I like to think maybe, after all this, they'll remember that: that when it came to it, when they had to, they fought together and battered the crap out of a common enemy. I don't hold out much hope, but I have some.

But my clearest memory – I hesitate to think on it even now. My clearest memory is when I knowingly killed a man for the first time. I'd let off wild shots before, down at the gates, but apart from one lucky shot to the shoulder, had never known whether they'd hit. I'd once left a man – my father – knowing that if I did he'd die. But never like this. I'd never knowingly shoved a gun in a guy's face and pulled the trigger. *How far would you go?*

He came at me with a flamer and I had nowhere left to turn, nowhere left to run, stuck in a corner between the bar and a neighbouring shop. Even with the heat of the flames singeing my eyebrows I hesitated, but instinct, craven self-preservation took over. I raised the gun, shut my eyes and shot him. A messy wound in the side of his head when I opened my eyes again, surprised I was still in one piece. It didn't kill him straight away, oh no. He had time to stare at me with an almost comical look of surprise before he slid to the ground and bled his life out into the snow and shit. And all I could think was, *Why does death have to be so stupid?*

I didn't think it for long, because there was always another Storad with a gun or a flamer, so I fumbled another bullet into the gun and on we went. The battle – if you could call it that, it was more a protracted brawl with added guns – seemed to last a lifetime, but I don't suppose it was more than fifteen minutes before the square was quiet. Or quieter at least – plenty of moans from the wounded, the occasional scream as someone set a bone or finished somebody off. Bodies all over, slumped and humped shapes on the ground, snow falling again now to cover them over decently, like shrouds. Mostly Storad bodies, but a fair few of ours. I couldn't seem to think, except, *They all rise*. For good or ill, we were rising. All I could do was stare through the whispering snow.

I was still staring when a man ran into the square. He almost got a face full of bullets, but he stopped with his hands up and a startled look and I recognised the Specials uniform. So did everyone else, and the sound of multiple guns being cocked echoed around us.

"Wait!" the Special said, and they did, thankfully. "On the Spine. They're . . . too many of them. We're getting massacred. The Archdeacon ordered me to come and find you. Please."

Funny, how human he looked. Specials had always seemed so, well, untouchable, imperturbable, like nothing could shake them if they didn't want to be shaken. That was part of why they scared the crap out of everyone – they, and the fear they inspired, were the rock we were built on. But this one, the tone of pleading in his voice, the sweat and blood drying in his hair, the wild stare of his eyes – he was a man first. The rest saw it too. They didn't see the uniform, or at least didn't let it blind them to the fact that the man wearing it was desperate. Or most of them didn't.

"Why should we help you?" a voice growled out. "Who cares if Top of the World goes? I might even give them a hand."

"Wait a minute," someone else said behind me. "How does the Archdeacon know where we are and what we're doing?"

All heads turned to me. They didn't look very happy, so I tried a grin that probably came out sickly and weak.

"That's how you had that permission for the guns," one of the gang leaders said. "You didn't steal that order like you said. You're Ministry. You conned us."

That stung me into speaking. "I never said a damned thing that wasn't true." For once in my life.

"Maybe. But you didn't tell us a lot that was."

I was in fear for my life again, only this time from the men and women who were supposed to be on my side. I have such a way with people.

"No, I didn't. But then you wouldn't have helped, and these Storad here" – I kicked at a body within reach – "would right now be murdering their way through Under. Murdering and raping you and your families, and you'd have no guns. You want to hate me, fine, join the queue. I loathe what the Ministry stands for as much as you do. I'll join you shooting a few cardinals when this is over. But that doesn't mean I'll let these fuckers into *my* city."

It was touch-and-go there for a few moments, but in the end Quillan said under his breath, just to me, "You did me a favour, so fair's fair." And then louder, "All right. But don't think I'll let you off later."

Not everyone agreed, but there wasn't much I could do about it. At least there'd be men left in the square should the Storad try that way again. The rest of us followed the Special out on to the Spine.

The waft of cooking bacon wove its way up through the walkways, and I could almost see it in the air. It made me sick, and, a split second later, made all the hairs stand up on the back of my neck. They were burning pigs again. In the tunnels. Trying to crack one, trying to find another way in. I wondered if the Storad in the city realised that no one on the Outside gave a crap whether the city fell with them in it. Because I wondered if the city could stand any more cracks, or whether one burning pig in the right place could make the whole city into one big Slump. They say the superstructure is built to withstand anything. They say . . . I'm pretty sure I only imagined the lurch under my feet, the faint rumble of masonry. Must have done, because no one else seemed to notice.

I kept my mouth shut and followed the Special to the Spine, aware that at my back were many men with guns, and now they had a reason to hate me. To them, I was Ministry. To anyone from Under – hell, to *me* – anyone Ministry wasn't worth shit.

The Spine was empty here, unnaturally quiet. Before I'd buggered everything up, way back a whole few months ago, the Spine had been a bustle of carriages and people, hustling, jostling, Glow-powered adverts blaring out over everything. It had been nothing *but* noise and light. Since we'd got the Glow back on, it'd got back some of its life, but now, nothing. Unless you counted the corpses, but, except in very special and probably mythical circumstances, corpses do not count as life.

"Goddess's tits," Quillan whispered, and I didn't blame him. Just on this one small section of the Spine, on this one little twist of the huge spiral, there must have been two, three hundred dead men gradually getting their fresh new shrouds of snow. Mostly bodies in Specials' or guards' uniforms. The Special who'd brought us here looked sick to his eyebrows.

A murmur ran through the men and women who'd followed, though it was hard to tell if it was shock, sympathy or a small and savage glee that finally the guards and Specials had got back what they'd dished out for so long. Probably a mix of all three.

I tried to think, but my brain seemed to be misfiring like my old carriage had a tendency to do. I wasn't running on all cylinders, because everything kept swirling in my head, a black mass of *Oh fuck*.

I thought of Perak, of where all these Storad were heading, and who'd be top of their list to kill, and that jolted me back into thinking. For a bit, anyway. But not rationally, otherwise I wouldn't have dropped myself right in it.

"Where's Perak?" I asked the Special.

"Wait, you're on first-name terms with the Archdeacon?" Quillan said, and they all took a step away from me.

"Yes," I snapped back, throwing caution to the long drop underneath the walkway. "I am, because he's my brother, my family – just like your family we all just fought for back there. And he's from Under too, like me, and you, and if he gets the chance he's going to change things – but he needs to live first. You," I said again to the Special. "Where is he?"

"They were retreating up towards the lab, but the Archdeacon went up to Top of the World."

The lab – shit, Lise was in the lab. Or had been. Maybe Erlat, if she'd actually listened to me, which I doubted. And the machines – the Storad knew all about the machines, thanks to Dench. Not a chance in hell they'd leave them untouched if they could get to them. I'd have rather blown them up myself than let him get his hands on them. So would Lise, which was my only consolation and no consolation at all.

Quillan came to my rescue then. "I say," he said, slow and thoughtful as though feeling his way through his words. "I say we loot the bodies for any guns and weapons we can, then come up behind and break them from both sides." He gave me the old side-eye. "And I say we keep on eye on this bugger too, just in case. No offence."

"None taken." And I didn't take any, because I don't have to be told when the wind changes. I'm no leader, never have been, never wanted to be, because leadership equals responsibility and we all know how I feel about that. Besides, those men and women were gravitating to him like flies round shit and he seemed a solid enough guy. "As long as we go."

So we rifled through the bodies, which was just as delicious as it sounds, and if nothing else we were better prepared. Had more people too when it came to it, because more and more were creeping along walkways to join us. Never did take long for word to get around in Under, and a loose crowd jostled behind, asking what was happening, or just joining in with getting guns. No doubt some were only nicking them, but by the end we had a decent-sized mob, and Quillan led us on and up.

Chapter Twenty-four

We got to the level under the lab before we encountered any kind of resistance. By the looks of it, the Storad were arrowing straight for Top of the World. Take that and they had the city, or all the parts that mattered to them. Just as Allit had seen – Storad in Top of the World. And here I was, with the rising. That boy had a talent he didn't appreciate, because it was what he'd seen that had given me the idea to try to gather Under together. Perak too, perhaps, though who knew what thoughts it had conjured in his twisting brain?

There was something about that trip, some sort of fraternity that I'd never been part of before. Shit, I'd always kept myself apart from pretty much everyone, and my excuse had been being a mage. But then the core of us had shared things in that square in the Buzz, shared blood and death and kill-or-be-killed. Maybe it was exhaustion, or the thought of having killed a man face-to-face and wanting to know I wasn't alone, maybe it was the black creeping up on me unawares, but it was like nothing I'd felt before and I wanted it to stay. For the first time in maybe ever I felt a part of something, part of other people, part of the city rather than apart and alone, despised. OK, I wasn't exactly Mr Popular and, let's face it, probably never will be. But without Pasha by my side, his solid presence, I needed something to hold on to and they were it.

At the stairwell that led to the lab, there was a knot of Storad. Quillan had taken to this like a bird to air and he knew before we got there. There were gangs that ran Under that no sane man wanted to be up against, and this was a kind of fighting they knew – quick, quiet, take them by surprise. With the men that had joined us, more and more, the gangs were an unexpected addition. Maybe only there for the looting, or perhaps the chance at Top of the World when we were done, but they came, terrifying men with tattoos ringing their faces and eyes that had seen everything and hated it. Luckily, what they were hating right then were Storad.

Guinto asked one why he'd come, and got a growled "This is my patch, and even if it's shit, no one takes it from me without a fight."

With the gangs came their specialists. Men who could dismember another in three easy moves with knives so sharp the point vanished into nothingness; scouts who could blend into a shadow in the wink of an eye, who could communicate with their leaders seemingly without words, just signs and low coded whistles. The gangs didn't get too close to each other, but they were there and that was the important thing. Mahala was theirs, and they weren't going to let her go without a fight, whether the Ministry let them or not. They weren't exactly the sort of people who took orders well, at least not Ministry orders.

Thanks to those scouts – and Halina too, because levitating is a handy way to reconnoitre – we didn't walk straight into the knot of Storad guarding the way towards the lab. Instead, two of the gang leaders approached each other warily, spoke together for a moment and then, with a pair of vicious grins that made me want to drop my gun and put my hands up, beg for my life if I had to, they and their men went in. Not straight in, but from above and below, using arching walkways and shadowed doorways to launch themselves on an unsuspecting enemy that was used to fighting on the flat.

It didn't last long. They didn't even use guns, but their own very extensive collection of knives, clubs and nasty-looking spiky things. The two leaders sauntered back our way, wiping their weapons.

"One–nil to me, I think," the first said.

"Yeah, yeah. Just you wait. My boys'll slice the living crap out of every Storad between here and Top of the World. Bet you ten we get more than you."

"You're on."

I was really quite glad they were on our side, and therefore nominally the good guys. Otherwise I'd have just found a corner to hide in until it was all over because they scared me more than the Storad, if I'm honest. Especially when I saw the mess they'd made. So matter-of-fact about it, like they were discussing the price of pigs.

And speaking of pigs, that distinct smell of burning bacon wafted up to us again on the same breeze that took the snow and turned it into small powdery tornados. Burning pigs, in the tunnels. I didn't imagine the lurch this time, because the men around me felt it too. A walkway ahead of us leapt free of its securing bolts and launched into the void, crashing down, smashing itself to bits as it bounced from building to walkway to building before the sound died away in the depths. No one said anything, but I was thinking, a lot. Mostly about how I'd rather be shot in the face than get dropped, screaming, down fifty levels or so when a walkway crumbled or a crack decided it didn't like it down in the 'Pit and decided to burrow upwards.

The tremor in the city rumbled to a stop as though embarrassed, and I could breathe again. By now the sky was starting to lighten around us. Not much, because snowclouds still hovered over everything, made Top of the World a fuzzy mass above us, but enough to see by. Enough to render half the men speechless. Here we were just Over Trade. Over, and I doubted many of them had been anywhere near this far up. Even the factory workers would never usually get past the very bottom of Trade, at least outside the factories. There was always a guard ready to bounce you back down Under for looking wrong, talking funny, being in the wrong place.

I left them gawping and muttering at the marvel of the sky, grey and lumpy though it was. Quillan, Guinto and one of the gang leaders – the one with black swirling tattoos round his eyes and a snarling grin – came with me to see what had happened with the lab. Quite a lot, by the looks of it.

We'd put the lab somewhere discreet, out of the way, because mages were only newly legal and, well, we'd had trouble. But Dench had known where it was, how to get to it, the best way to get in. Maybe he'd have been better off if he'd stayed with the men he'd sent to try and take it, or perhaps they weren't intending to destroy it, not this time. Maybe they were after the machines, the chemicals, all Lise's devious little ideas for staving off the Storad. Who knew?

We approached the door, and it was obvious why that knot of Storad had been at the end of the stairwell rather than here – by the looks of things they had tried to take the lab, but had been beaten back and had decided to bide their time till they had Top of the World. Scorchmarks from their flamers arced over the door and wall surrounding it, but they'd made barely a dent. There was a small window by the door, smashed in, but the sill was washed in blood and other gloopy-looking things I didn't like to look too closely at. Someone had made an effort to barricade the window while leaving enough room to shoot out of, and it seemed to have worked. Bodies enough littered the ground that it was tricky finding a place to put our boots without finding something soft and yielding – or, worse, squelchy – under them. From my cursory glance, it looked like someone inside was a very good shot indeed.

I conjured a mental map of inside the lab, trying to think if there was any other handy way in, but the rest of the windows had an open view over the top of Trade and even a monkey would have a hard time getting to them. Maybe the Storad would have been able to shoot from a few walkways that crossed that area, but even after that, they'd still have to come through the door. We'd picked the position perfectly. It only remained to be seen if anyone was still alive in there. The fact that it hadn't blown up gave me hope that Lise, at least, was still all right because I knew damn well she had enough chemicals in there to give a herd of rhinos pause, and she'd use them rather than let anyone get their grubby little paws on her precious gizmos.

I got closer to the door, but not too close – whoever was that good a shot might not like me, and there was Lise's expertise with booby traps to take into account. She'd almost killed me with them more than once, back when all this started, around about the beginning of the world.

The barrel of a gun poked through a gap in the barricade, and I heard a whispered "Thank the Goddess," which isn't a greeting I'd ever had before. Behind the door locks ground around, bolts scraped across and other sounds of complicated things being disarmed echoed across the gap. It seemed to take a long time. After Dwarf died, and again after the screwdriver incident, I'd made double damned sure that no one could get in unless Lise wanted them in, and was now glad I'd ignored all her protests about it.

Finally the door opened and a wary face peered round, then Allit shot towards me and almost had me off my feet in what I can only describe as the most enthusiastic welcome I'd ever had. Lise behind him was more reserved, but looked just as relieved as she grabbed for my hand and squeezed.

When I managed to untangle Allit from me, he got himself under control and I wondered at the new look to him. Softness knocked from the edges of his young face, and eyes that . . . He didn't look like the same boy. He didn't look like a boy at all.

"I didn't let them get in," he said, and then he grinned. "I saw them coming, saw where they were going to attack, so I made sure they couldn't get through."

"*You* did? Hmmph," Lise said. "*I* was the one who salted the walkways with traps." She grinned up at me, happy in her work. "Got the bastards a treat. All your magelets helped too, Rojan – good practice for them, and they did well. But the traps were mine."

Quillan looked surprised for a second, obviously taking in Lise and Allit's youth. "You did a good job."

"Very good," I added, and Allit rewarded me with that look of hero worship that I remembered from the days when Perak thought the sun shone out of my arse. Goddess be damned, it felt good. "Is everyone all right? Erlat?"

"Cabe?" Quillan asked. "Is he here?"

"Yes, he's here, came in quite handy – did you know he can bend things just by thinking about it? No? Not quite like Rojan does things, but pretty good all the same. Anyway, we're all fine – well, a couple of injuries," Lise said. "Nothing too much. Dendal used the first-aid kit from the pain lab to patch people up. And Erlat's here – she's good with that gun. I don't think she missed once."

Quillan and the gang leader, Yagin, conferred behind me, then Yagin said, "We need somewhere to fall back, in case. Always have a bolthole, and one you can defend, right? We're going in, up, but if you like I'll leave a few of my lads here. First, a regroup and a plan of attack. A little reconnoitre – I'll send my scouts off, see what they can find, then we'll decide how to go about dissecting these bastards."

The thought of which made my back itch – those "lads" were murdering machines. But I didn't say so. I was only too glad to have someone protecting the lab because I knew, sure as shit stinks, that I wouldn't be able to persuade Lise, Dendal or Erlat to make a try for the Mishan gate.

"Who else have you got?" I said, and followed Allit in, wanting to make sure with my own eyes that Erlat was all right.

Quite a few, was who else. Yagin's eyes almost popped out of his head when one of Erlat's girls wandered past and winked at him. Her seductive dress and elegant make-up were at distinct odds with the gun she had ready in her hand, and the blood splashed all down her front. It wasn't her blood.

Yagin looked at Lise appraisingly, then back at the dead Storad. "You did that?"

Lise bristled, pulled herself up to her not very tall tallest. "Damned right. Well, OK, some of the others are good with a gun. But I was the one who designed and set the quicklime traps."

"Quicklime? I like your style. Could do with a girl like you, after." I saw the look of wicked appreciation spark on his face as he took in her more physical charms, and had to tell myself, Look, she may be your sister, but she's grown up. *And* she's good at being devious and underhand, blowing things and people up. She can handle him.

And she did. "Join the queue, and be prepared to pay a lot for my expertise. Now, what were you planning? I've got any amount of things you might want."

His lips broke into a grin, insolent and waiting, but he didn't look so threatening then.

A few brief words and I left Lise and her new friends at one of the workbenches. I kept an eye on Yagin, just in case, but he behaved himself; in fact he seemed a bit in awe of Lise, as well he might. They cleared the bench of all the detritus of a genius at work and set up a sort of operational base. Perfect place for it too. In the brief snatches when the snow stopped, we could gaze down from the lab over Trade, could see anyone on the Spine from there up to Clouds and beyond, at least until it disappeared into the lowering haze.

Younger lads were sent scampering over walkways to see

what they could find, who was where, and whether the who had any weapons. Others were sent under Guinto's direction to gather who they could, fire them up with his Goddess talk perhaps, get them out of their homes and fighting, as they always had, only this time for ... maybe for nothing. Then again, Under always seemed to fight for something and end with nothing.

I was glad to leave them to it because now I was no more or less use to them than any other man with a gun in his hand. All I had going for me was a pulse pistol I daren't use unless I felt like going the way Pasha had, and a life-long, deep-seated hatred of the world and pretty much everything in it. Hatred and cynicism had got me a long way, but I was tired now. More tired than I could ever recall, and without even the luxury of loathing the Goddess for dumping all this on us from a great height. It wasn't her that had done it, and my hate seemed to have run dry.

It wasn't hard to tell where the Storad had got to – a dark mass on the Spine, moving confidently, but not so quickly that they weren't doing their best to rout anyone to either side. No one seemed to be stopping them. Maybe not much point, if Allit was right. Maybe part of Perak's plan to draw them in. I hoped so. We could see the mangled mess of the gates from here too, just, but the pass, the road and what was coming along it were mostly hidden by Heights and rendered dim in any case by the weather.

I turned to Allit and didn't even need to ask.

"A day, at most, before the really big machines get here," he said. "I can't – I think I can see what they're for. I wish Pasha was here so I could show you."

"So do I," I said, though the picture of them was indelibly printed in my brain, had haunted what little sleep I'd had since Pasha had shown them to me. Machines with teeth and claws. Not guns . . . more like animals designed to pull things to bits. Maybe pull a city to bits. Or people. I hoped like hell that Perak's plan, whatever it was, worked. It had better, because I was fresh out of ideas and didn't have a clue what good this rising was going to do, what *I* could do. Not a damned, Goddess-fucked clue.

I could feel myself sinking then, weighed under the grey of the clouds, under the song of the black, ever calling, ever tempting me. I'd driven it back a for a while as we'd fought in the square, as we'd carved our way to here, but now it was back. It lurked behind my eyes, in the ever-present throb of my screwed hand, coated my mouth when I went to speak.

You could end this. Right now. If you had the guts you were born with, you could blast it all to the moon, lay this city bare, let the sun in Under. If you had the guts. Come on in, Rojan, where it's warm and you never need fear again. Just one little thing, and we'll be together. Always.

My vision had drawn down to a cold hard point, a glimpse of light in darkness, and my hand moved on its own, no thought of mine telling it to bunch, to grind the fractured bones together. Just a little pain and it could all be gone.

The grip on my arm, the voice next to me, jolted me out of it so hard I leapt back and smacked into a wall, heart shuddering at how close I'd been. Dendal was right – right then, the way I was, it would only take one little spell and I'd be lost. And *still* I was tempted.

"Rojan?"

The voice sent it shrieking behind me, lost in the whirl of grey daylight coming in the windows that burned my eyes. Erlat – I never heard the black at Erlat's. My mind grabbed for that thought, for the voice, willed her to speak again so I could hold on.

"Dendal sent me. He said— Are you all right? Rojan?"

A smooth voice, calming, serene like nothing could touch her. Bollocks, of course, because she'd known worse than I ever would, but you'd never know it to hear her speak. Erlat was always strong. Not like Jake, not whirling with swords and anger yet brittle as glass none the less, just strong inside, like a smooth and wickedly sharp blade hidden under a beautiful scabbard.

"I'm all right," I managed, and found to my surprise that I was. Or about as all right as I could be under the circumstances. I stood up straight and tried to look like I wasn't about to keel over or go batshit. "Where's Jake?"

Erlat stepped back a pace and turned away to answer, an oddly taut undercurrent to her voice. "Back where she always used to be. Trying to get herself killed, but too proud to let anyone beat her."

I pulled Erlat gently round to look at me, expecting to find her crying, but she was stronger than that, stronger than me because I wanted to cry. "Because Pasha's gone? And it's all my fault, all of it. I started this whole hot mess, I screwed with what worked, and that action led straight to this, and it should have been me on that stupid machine, right?"

I was kind of hoping for a bit of sympathy perhaps, her to say, "No, no," or because that wasn't really likely, "Yes but you did it for good reasons." Instead I got the full force of her glare and "Yes. You started all this, and I know why, and I think you did the right thing, but it remains that you started all this and Pasha's gone, Jake's sort of . . . shrivelled up inside and won't let anyone see it. But the Rojan I know, or used to, wouldn't be standing here whining about it. He'd be hating everything and everyone and he'd be swearing fit to bust, but he'd be *doing* something rather than feeling sorry for himself. Because this" – she waved her hand at Quillan and his friends as they bickered quietly and not so quietly – "anyone can do that, and yes it needs doing but you aren't even doing anything with them."

She pulled herself up straight and got me right in the eye with her glare. "So what are you going to do, Rojan?"

Sometimes it takes a good verbal slap from someone to really clear the crap out of your eyes. I counted myself lucky she hadn't followed it with a real slap, restrained the urge to kiss her and pulled myself together because she was right. She always was, and it annoyed the crap out of me. Besides which,

I have this in-built wish to not look like a complete chicken in front of ladies.

"Firstly, we're going to find that telescope," I said. "Then we're going to listen to what Yagin's scouts have to say. Then we're going to storm Top of the World. I think."

I was rewarded with a firm nod and a hint of her teasing smile. It was enough, more than enough because I felt a new surge of energy, of hate, like she said. Not for anyone in particular – all right, perhaps Dench but I couldn't even muster much for him – but for the sheer futility of everything, the stupidity of it all.

This was my chance to stop the stupidity, maybe for good, but I needed to know what I was up against first, so Erlat and I went to listen in at the bench where the scouts were reporting back.

"Looks like the Storad are determined to make a go for Top of the World. Bunched up at the top of Clouds for now, and it seems like they're being held off. That's where all the other roads stop, and it's just the Spine, so a narrow place to defend. But the guards won't last for ever. They know it too – they're defending just below the cut-off, and getting out as many people as they can down the side roads."

"Who's defending?" I asked.

Yagin still scared the crap out of me, but I tried not to let it show. "What's left of the guards and Specials. None of the cardinals, obviously, nor any of their men. But the Archdeacon—"

"Perak's *fighting*?" My stomach went cold at that. Perak wasn't a fighter; he'd get himself creamed.

"We think so – hard to tell without getting close. What I can tell you is there is some woman dressed in a uniform we've never seen before and she's laying into those Storad like a drunk lays into a barrel of beer. No guns, but she's got two swords she knows how to use. She's fast and she's devious, coming up on them from the back, the side, any way they aren't looking for her. She's making them pretty jittery."

And messy, with all probability. Jake never killed, or hadn't before. Just enough to wound, to stop them being a threat. But now, without Pasha around, with her comfort gone, all bets were off. I was glad I wasn't a Storad.

"Between us and them?"

Quillan shrugged. "Seems pretty clear on the Spine. Our lot trying to escape, a few of theirs cutting down anyone they find."

"And Top of the World?"

"Emptying fast, and Clouds, though that's been emptying for a while. Pretty good time to kill any cardinals we find, if there are any left," Yagin said, and his men grinned behind him. Men after my own heart, really. Possibly in more than one sense, so I kept my distance. "Why, you got something in mind?"

My mind clicked over everything, all I knew, all that had happened, every corner of me that wanted to blow the whole Ministry to hell and send the Storad after them.

"You know, I think I just might."

Chapter Twenty-five

By the time we left the lab the snow had finally stopped, though the grey clouds lingered and lowered like they wanted to come and play. The light made Clouds into indistinct humps in the greyness, and the snow had turned even the shabby houses we could see Under into magical cottages. Well, magical cottages that some giant baby had decided to stack up like so many toy bricks before it'd got bored and started kicking them about. Underfoot, the passage of the Storad had made the road slippery with slush which had re-frozen into a slick, rumpled sheet, but at least it wasn't rain. Instead it was cold enough to make your knackers clank.

The cold hadn't deterred anyone that I could see. The opposite, in fact. What had started as a few hardy souls doing what pathetic little they could had turned into a fairly organised mob. No torches and pitchforks though: this was a different kind of crowd, brandishing appropriated guns, stolen flamers, kitchen knives, planks of two-by-four, knuckledusters, flick-knives and pretty much any makeshift weapon that a city like this could harbour. Halina was there with her Stencher mates, a wicked grin plastered on her face and not caring who saw that she wasn't so much walking as floating over the ice-stricken way. Lise refused to stay behind and I had no heart to insist – she'd lost as much as anyone, had as much right as I did to be there. With one of Dwarf's weapons in her hand, no one wanted to get too close in any case, although Yagin was making a valiant effort at appearing nonchalant.

The magelets came too, all of them. I couldn't stop them, and I didn't think I wanted to. Cabe was under the protective arm of his father, Quillan. Another boy was bouncing fire on his palm, quenching it, relighting it as sweat popped up on his brow – I could see him becoming very useful, if he managed to stop accidentally lighting his hair. Halina looked exhausted, and her arm was a mass of bruising, but she floated along with one of the others behind her, though every few paces he dropped down to the walkway and had to launch himself again. Halina urged him on with a grim smile. All the rest – they all came, each willing to do their best, whatever that best was. I could only hope they survived the experience. That we all did, but them the most.

The smallest, little Casuco, smiled shyly at me and, with a crack and a hiss, opened his palm to proffer me a sweet conjured out of nothing but his pain. I took it – it tasted even better than it looked – and then Casuco slid his hand into mine. It struck me with a finality that almost robbed me of breath that I was going to have to do something, anything, and when I did it, it was going to be for these little magelets, who were showing more gumption than I'd managed in a couple of decades. *They're your way back in*, Pasha's remembered voice said in my head. I shook it away, because I couldn't bear that it was only a memory.

Along with the diversity in weapons, refugees from the 'Pit mixed with men who'd lived in Under all their lives, gang members walked with priests and housewives, bouncers and businesswomen. Everything else was forgotten in the face of Outsiders, because this was their patch now, their city, and they were scared and pissed off. No one cared which way the other praised the Goddess, or how pale their skin was, what their accent was, because we were all the same.

Erlat came too, along with some of her friends and co-workers. I thought about protesting, but recalled the last time I'd tried, and kept my mouth firmly shut. Instead, I'd asked Erlat if she was any good with that gun. She'd answered by planting a bullet in the wall's plaster about an inch from my face, so I'd taken that as a yes and said no more about it. "Never argue with a woman with a loaded gun" is a nice maxim to live by, if you like to live.

Allit kept up a muted commentary about what was possibly ahead as he walked next to me – we tried to hide what he was doing, but after a few sideways glances no one took any notice. It was a liberating feeling, people not side-eyeing us because we were mages, and one I could only hope lasted after this. If *we* lasted after this.

Heights passed by in a haze of snow and slush and empty houses, discarded shops. They'd had money here, were probably even now trying to buy a way through the Mishan gate. Some of the Glow globes that lit the way were beginning to fade – since I'd screwed myself over, only Pasha had enough juice to fire up the pain room and power the Glow. One mage hadn't been nearly enough, and most of what he'd put out had gone to the factories that lay silent under us now. We had some Glow, but no more was being made. We had no raw materials left either, which, for a city that relied on trade, was almost as bad as the lack of food.

Without anyone saying anything, we slowed as we left Heights. The vast mushroom-shaped estates of Clouds seemed to press down on us, or maybe that was just me. We met with a few straggling Storad, looting and looking for anyone left. They didn't last long.

When the first sounds of fighting echoed down from above, a signal from Quillan stopped us all.

"You're sure about this?" he said to me.

"No, but do we have a choice?"

"There's always a choice."

"Fine, so we all run away and die of starvation. Or wait to get chopped to bits."

I felt pretty bad lying to him, to all of them, especially

Erlat and Guinto and Dendal, who walked with them, humming his happy song. Pretty bad because I wasn't sure in the slightest.

But the very simple plan I'd put forward might even work. If it did, then I wouldn't have to worry about the other one, the one that the black kept on nagging me about, the ultimate one that was feeling more and more the right – and wrong – thing to do. Pasha had shown me the way. It was up to me if I followed. The very simple plan – get in, get Jake and Perak out, blow the shit out of the Storad up there, try not to die – might even work. At least we wouldn't be fighting on two fronts then. If it did work . . .

The low cloud helped – it surrounded the Spine here, leaving me feeling like I was encased in a damp pillow, but it also meant that visibility was limited. At least for those using their eyes.

I took hold of Dendal gently and steered him and Allit into a not-very-private-at-all nook by a pillar which announced these were the gates to Cardinal So-and-so's estates and trespassers would be thrown into the Slump with extreme prejudice, may the Goddess bless them.

Who needs eyes when you've got a couple of mages handy?

Between the two of them we got a pretty clear picture of what was going on, who was where, doing what. Allit could see, and it was probably real and now. Dendal could communicate, a perfect conduit for information when he was lucid. The pretty clear picture they gave me was it was all going tits up. Top of the World was almost empty and so was Clouds, near as they could tell. What was left of the guards were failing miserably against a vicious assault on the Spine just under Top of the World, and Perak and Jake were there with them. Typical Perak: never was with it enough to know when to get out of the rain.

Dendal looked at me sadly, almost wistful. "So what are you going to do, Rojan?"

After I'd got over the shock of him getting my name right twice in a row, and wondering why everyone kept asking me that, I said, "I'm not sure."

"Yes you are." His voice was unusually firm, which meant I was about to get a lecture on the Goddess and my duty to serve her.

I did my best to forestall him. "No, I'm not. There're two options. One: head on up, find Perak, beat the living crap out of any Storad we find, get down to the gates before those machines arrive, and hope for the best. We've got plenty of people now, all willing to fight. Two: two won't be necessary. Even if it is tempting."

His smile was awful, full of pity and sympathy. "You never did really understand, did you? You were saving yourself, your magic, for this, but not just this. It's why the Goddess sent you to me." Then he took Allit's hand and walked off to stand with the rest of them, all the while telling everyone not to worry, Rojan's going to sort it, he's got a plan.

Everyone was looking at me, like I had any answers. Little

Casuco smiled again at me, seeming confident in my ability to get them all out of this, to fix everything, rearrange it all away perhaps. I wished I was as sure.

They were all looking at me, and then they weren't. A tremble at first, just a tremor under our feet. A rumble, far off, though not far enough. I looked out. Heights on one side; on the other, where I'd not dared to look because I was chicken, a fading drop that on a clear day would show the Slump, the lasting reminder of what happens when a mage pushes too far, when he goes fully crazy right before he dies. A tangle of girders, vast blocks of stone tumbled in odd patterns, huge splinters of wood rotting gently into mould. A dumping ground. A moving one.

It didn't register at first – let's face it, at first all I was thinking was, *Crap, the Spine's going to collapse and I'm going to fall to a long and messy death, long enough that I will have time to scream quite a detailed lot of last words*. Once the bollock-clenching panic passed, I realised it wasn't the Spine that was crumbling, moving, sliding.

A block of stone the size of a house teetered, thought about it, and then said "Screw it" and tumbled end over end, rolling down the battered slope of the Slump, pushing friends in front of it until there was what looked like a whole moving mountain. Smaller stones merely the size of men bounced around that first block like puppies taken for a walk, and girders twisted with a tortured screech, all the while reminding me that down was a long way away.

When, after what seemed like about six months, everything stopped moving, the Slump had shifted downwards. Stones that had stayed where they were for years, since that ill-fated mage had gone boom, now looked like a breath would have them shifting and rolling again. I found that I was holding on to the nearby pillar with my bad hand, pain throbbing up and out, leaching into my head, itching at me, wanting to be used. *Do it, do it, take the whole place down. Come on, Rojan, don't be shy.*

Tempting, so very tempting. Only two things stopped me. Just two, but I'm not sure now whether the two I thought of were the real ones. Perak and Jake were up there, that's what the small rational part of my brain said. You can't do it with them up there. You can't. You can't do it at all. No matter how much pain you suck in, you're not going to be able to take it all out, not all of it, and what about the Storad at the gates? The machines even now inching their way over the mountains? Think, for once in your life. Plan.

Whatever we were going to do, it had to be now, before the whole city fell apart and buried us, leaving the remaining Storad to do what the hell they wanted with what was left.

In retrospect it was only the second worst moment of my life, but at the time it was as bad as I thought it could get. Dendal, Allit, Erlat, the rest, they were all looking at me. Perak and Jake were above us, fighting for their lives, and option one – fight on up, take the bastards at their own game – just wasn't going to cut it no matter how I tried to spin it. We had men willing to fight, sure, but not enough and poorly armed, and only trained in staying the hell alive. We'd be hard-pressed to win over the Storad that were in the city now, never mind the rest that were on their way, almost here.

Instead we had option two, Plan B, the thing I had been trying not to contemplate because I couldn't be sure I wasn't going to do it out of personal satisfaction rather than because it needed doing. Because maybe I would, again, make everything worse, which has always been my signature move.

Fucking Dendal and his fanciful notions of what the Goddess wanted from me. That thought of course meant I was going to do it, even if just to stop him looking at me like that.

"All right, Dendal. Tell Perak to get everyone away from Top of the World. Retreat, look like they're running away. Let the Storad in."

His smile was almost worth it. I say almost, because this was going to hurt like a bitch.

Chapter Twenty-six

It took a while, because Yagin and all the rest had been fired up for a fight and all that aggression had to go somewhere. Most of it was aimed at me. But Quillan and Guinto managed to calm them some, mainly by promising them that they'd still have plenty of Storad to batter the crap out of down by the gates, when they got there. The magelets helped more, all bright-eyed and full of hope, saying how they could help, showing Yagin what they could do and giving him a few nasty ideas that made him grin like a shark.

My main problem was Jake.

"What do you mean, she refuses to go?"

The squeak of Dendal's knuckle twisting in its socket as we huddled by the pillar accompanied Perak's faint answer, sounding tinny when channelled through Dendal. I wasn't too keen on the amount of gunfire coming through, either.

"She just won't," he said. "She's like a woman possessed,

and there's no arguing with her. Goddess knows how long we'd have lasted without her, but now she says she'll cover our retreat but she's staying."

Women and my love for them will be the death of me.

"All right, I'll think of something. Just hold on, as long as you can. If it comes to it, you leave, all right? Let the bastards have Top of the World – it's not going to do them any good, not if I have anything to do with it. You just find somewhere safe and try to keep Jake out of it. Remind her she's your bodyguard so she should be guarding your body or something."

I got him to promise, and then Dendal's conduit snapped off and he shoved his knuckle back home.

"Well?" asked Erlat.

"Well . . ." I sucked it up, everything I was about to say, changed the habits of a lifetime and got serious. "You get this lot going. Down to the gates. Those machines will be here soon, and we're going to need all the men we can get down there." *Just in case I can't do what I'm planning.*

"But Top of the World? The Storad?"

"Let me worry about that."

Erlat sat back, her lips pressed thin. "Jake. Always Jake. You're going to swan in and rescue her, be her dashing hero – or try to be." I'm fairly sure the snort was of the derisive kind.

"And that's wrong, is it? Trying to put right what I fucked up by letting Pasha get on that machine, which he did because I wouldn't let him kill himself trying to rescue her?

Stopping her killing herself, or at least letting herself be killed? That's a bad thing, is it?"

At about this point, several things that probably should have been obvious much, much earlier struck me – I am not the sharpest blade in the drawer, especially when my magic kept nagging at me to be used, when I hadn't slept since who-knows-when and I couldn't recall what real food, or indeed anything remotely edible, looked like. Erlat opened her mouth to say something else, but I got in first.

"Erlat, enough. I'm going to make everything right, third time pays for all. Get to the lab, wait for me there. I need you to help me." If I made it, that was, but there was no point saying that part. "*Please.*"

She stood up, dusting her hands down her dress, adjusting where she'd hitched it up to make it easier to move, over the makeshift holders for the two guns she had.

"If this is one of your damnfool ways of trying to protect little old me—"

"It isn't, I promise you that. I need you there to help me, because I can't do it on my own. I think I know what I've got to do, but I need to see Perak and Jake safe first."

She looked at me awhile, speculating, but there wasn't time for more arguing and she knew it. "Fine," she said, and whirled off in a perfect display of high dudgeon.

Quillan soon had the mob moving out and down. The gangs moved with an easy grace, loping down into Heights and taking to the walkways, swinging from one to the other as easily as I might walk one. Easier, because they didn't seem to have any terror of heights. I did, and mine was telling me to not do what I was about to do, no, really, don't.

Quillan frowned my way. "So what is it you're going to do?"

I tried a smile but I got the feeling it came out pretty mangled, because Quillan flinched and took a step back.

Yagin turned up his own grin – I think he'd seen something in me he recognised. "He's going to go and put the screws on someone."

"Hopefully."

That seemed to satisfy him and he followed his men down, flipping on to a walkway with a cheery wave of a knife. Quillan lingered but there didn't seem much I could say. In the end, he put a protective arm around Cabe and said, "You looked after my boy, and I'm grateful for that. And you don't *act* Ministry."

"If I have my way, no one is going to act Ministry after this. If."

He grunted at that, and left finally with a thoughtful frown.

At last it was just Dendal and me – he'd sent Allit and Lise and the magelets back down with the rest. Someone was going to regret the invention of that weapon, of that I could be quite sure.

"I know what you need to do, and I know you can do it," Dendal said. "I've always known that's what the Goddess sent you to me for."

"Enough of the Goddess crap, all right? I've got enough to be going on with without her sticking her fucking nose in."

His glance was reproachful and made him look more monk-like than ever. It struck me that maybe he really was some kind of monk – he'd devoted his whole life to doing what he saw as her work. Sadly, that involved me.

"Don't say fuck," he said. "It isn't nice. And it doesn't matter if you believe in her, it matters if she believes in you."

"Oh, fabulous, buggered whichever way, gee, thanks. Look, can we get on? Only Perak's about to be overrun and there's these big nasty machines Outside on their way to take pot-shots at him, not to mention us, and the Slump's on the slide, hell, maybe the whole city might be about to fall down around our ears if they manage to crack another tunnel. If nothing else, I'd quite like to have a living brother at the end of this, if it's all the same to you."

It's really annoying when you vent your spleen like that and the person being vented at just pats your hand like you're two and having a tantrum, but what could I say? I had to do it. When push comes to shove, sometimes it's best to get a proper run up and say, Sod push, let's fling that shit as hard as we can.

I settled down, not trusting my legs due to them having a tendency to give way at the important moment of a spell. I wanted to hope there wasn't going to be any of my blood this time, but let's face it, hope is for idiots and loonies.

Once I called it, clenched my hand and felt the bones grate, felt the pain run up my arm, warm and red and oh so familiar, the juice came in less than half a heartbeat. The black laughed and clapped its hands. *I knew you'd come to me in the end. You promised.*

I had, and I would, but I had to hold off long enough to do this first.

Deal?

Deal.

The pain built, took over every thought, a thread of red in the black across my vision. Concentrate. Perak and Jake. Could find them both with my eyes closed and half a brain, usually. Hard now though. Very hard, because black was everywhere but I pushed and it came, the knowledge of exactly where they were. Five hundred yards up, forty yards to the east. Push, harder, because Jake's got her back to a wall and four Storad in front of her and Perak's trying to help but looks like he's more frightened of the gun in his hand than he is of the Storad. Push, harder, *harder*, forget about no sleep and no food and being screwed, and that something just broke in the front of my head somewhere with a pop. Maybe my brain exploded – certainly felt like it, but no great loss to the community. Forget the warmth of blood flooding down my face, from eyes and nose, frothing in my mouth with a bitter tang.

At last it came, the sweet rush of juice, up through the black, swelling through me like wine, or sex, or . . . actually there's nothing better, not even sex, and this is me saying that.

Nothing better than juice. Juice is everything, and the black will give me everything I need, I'll be nothing but *juice. When I let it, and that's not just yet.*

I opened my eyes a crack, and Dendal was there, saying, "You can do this, if you try, Rojan." I had just enough time to be gobsmacked that he got my name right three times in a row, which meant things must be getting serious. Then he was fading, I was fading, bleeding through reality, rearranging it around me, a push here, a swift alteration there, swirling the world like dragging my hand through water. Easy when you know how and so, so hard. And then I was right next to Perak at Top of the World and blood was everywhere. My blood.

I threw up a whole load of it, wiped more from my nose and when I could focus again everything was tinged a pinky red. Everything being the inside of a vaguely familiar room up in Top of the World, a cell of sorts, which was plusher than any place I'd ever lived. Or had been till I puked blood all over the carpet, but I didn't think that would be a problem for long. A little Glow-moth, as delicate and rare as the real thing, fluttered sadly around my head, its bright colours dim. No backing out now, no talking myself out if it. All or nothing.

Perak helped me up, looking panicked so I wondered just how bad the blood was. Pretty bad, by the way his hand was shaking and he looked like I wasn't going to be the only one throwing up. "Rojan – I thought – oh, *Goddess*, Rojan, what are you doing?"

"Never mind that," I managed to wheeze out. "You had a plan?"

"Yes, but . . . " He stared at me like I was a surprise naked lady in his bed and absent-mindedly wiped my face with the sleeve of his official archdeacon robes. I kind of liked the pattern my blood made on the cloth, in a funny, dreaming kind of way.

He pulled himself together. "I did have a plan, only it required this being in one piece."

I looked at the mangled mess of wires and metal gizmos he held out, but I didn't have a clue what it was supposed to be. All this new-fangled mechanics was starting to make me feel old.

"Simple words, please. And where the hell is Jake?"

Perak helped me to a chair and I managed to get my breath back properly. "I told her, like you said. To be my bodyguard. This section is locked off – cells for unbelievers. Easy to defend."

"Yes, I recall. Tell me."

"I did what you said. I couldn't see anything else *to* do, so I sent all the guards to retreat, but I couldn't because I had to set this. Only a bullet got it, and now it's no use. So the Storad have Top of the World and there's nothing we can do about it."

"Yes, but what was it?"

"An ignition switch," and then, because I probably looked confused, or perhaps because he was surprised I needed to ask, "a trigger. For everything I've rigged. All the black-powder traps."

I thought back to the sunny-faced boy Perak used to be, wandering around in his own head. A boy who'd blown up the shop opposite by accident, and a guard station accidentally-on-purpose. Who'd invented the concept of using black powder to power a bullet because it had seemed an interesting exercise in applied alchemy, plus it involved a small explosion and hey, who doesn't like an explosion? Perak may have been Archdeacon, but he'd always been a pyromaniac at heart.

Despite everything, or maybe because of it, a laugh forced its way out through a bubble of blood in my throat.

"Well, may the Goddess spank me bandy. You were going to blow up Top of the World, and all the Storad in it. *You* were!" That struck me as so funny, I'd have laughed my socks off if I hadn't been in danger of choking.

"Well, er, yes. It seemed like the best idea, really, when Allit said the Storad would get here, and . . . and hell's teeth, I'm sick of it, of them, of Ministry. Of my own damned cardinals! I was going to blow it all into the Slump – I made sure of where the charges were placed, simple physics really. I was going to blow it all and then we could start again, properly this time. All the charges are in place. Only now I can't, and the Storad have everything up here, *and* more on the way. And now we're trapped too."

Funny how you can know a person their whole life, and still they can just turn around and surprise the air right out of your lungs. Perak, most devout archdeacon and unrepentant daydreamer, who saw the best in everything and everyone, had been about to blow the whole damned place. Blow up the Ministry. It made my head whirl, and then everything became very clear. The whole world was like glass, so I finally understood it. All of it, and what I had to do shone out as clear as a flaming brand in my head. I wanted to be sick all over again, wanted to run away and hide somewhere, be someone else, but I couldn't. Not this time.

"Big brother will take care of it. Always big brother, whether I like it or not. No time now," I said in the end. "Get Jake."

"But she—"

"*Get Jake.*"

As if she'd heard me, a scream echoed through the doorway, and it wasn't hers. No, her sound was harsh breath that hid everything, a clenched-teeth grunt, a vicious swearing. She was killing herself, suicide by battle, I had no doubt on that. Well, she could if she wanted – I wasn't one to stop her – but not yet. Still, maybe discretion is the better part of staying the hell alive, especially when Jake was pissed off and had swords to hand, so I got to my feet on the third try and we went to her.

I left a sticky trail of blood behind me and walking wasn't easy what with my whole body feeling like a very painful wet noodle, but luckily I didn't have to worry about that for much longer. Through the door into a corridor that ended in another, narrower doorway. A whirl of black hair, a flash of sword, the crunch of bone. She was slicked in blood, her own and others', but she didn't seem to notice. She didn't notice anything, I don't think, except the Storad the other side of that door. Didn't notice, didn't care.

Pasha had once said about her, what seemed like decades ago, before they got a little happiness, that she wanted to die on a sword but was too proud to let anyone beat her. That Jake was back, as though the other, happy one had never been. Closed off, dead-eyed, an ice queen but no volcano underneath – the ice went all the way through. She was still glorious, graceful as a cat, but I could see now what I couldn't before, not properly. How could I not have understood?

A lull, a gap between attacks and Perak left me slumped against a wall to insert himself between her and the door. She stopped just short of taking his face off with a sword and blinked back to here and now. It didn't seem to make much difference, because she shoved him back behind her and scanned the outer room for more Storad. There were going to be a lot more.

Perak spoke to her but I couldn't hear what he said because an odd ringing had started in my ears. If I was of a fanciful nature, I'd have said it sounded like temple bells calling me, but that was ridiculous.

She didn't want to leave the door, the certain death that was sure to come through it and soon, that was plain. But Perak talked and cajoled and when that didn't work his face hardened and he ordered. It had much the same effect as the cajoling, to start with. Then he said something that made her flinch back, so I thought she'd just let loose with that sword and hack his face off right there and then. He stood, never wavering, and finally her hand dropped.

Perak took a quick look through the door, slammed it shut and bolted it.

"Rojan? Rojan, can you hear me?"

I was almost beyond talking, but I had a lot to do and I needed to keep my breath for when it mattered, so I just nodded.

"What now?"

Funny how I managed to smile, even then. I beckoned them closer, as though I was about to impart some great plan. Then I grabbed them by the wrists and did the second stupidest thing of my life. It was going to screw me worse even than I imagined, but sometimes you have to say what the hell and do it anyway.

Chapter Twenty-seven

By the time I came to, back in Guinto's temple under the pain lab, I'd managed to make an impressive pool of blood on the floor, the walls were woozing in and out of focus and shadows were stalking me from every corner. Jake swore somewhere off to the left, but her voice had a hitch of tears in it. Perak helped me up, shaking his head like he couldn't understand what I was doing, why I was pushing myself like that. I would have explained, but I wasn't sure *I* understood it, not then.

He helped me to a pew and I rested there a moment, my head on my arms across the back of the pew in front, almost like I was praying. Maybe I was, but it wasn't to *her*. Not to the Goddess.

"Rojan . . . " Perak's voice trailed off into a look of worry that screwed his face up like a paper ball.

Had to look strong even if I felt weak as a kitten, had to be big brother, so I forced myself up. There were still things to do and this was no time to be weak. The plaster statues of the saints and martyrs stared at me, but I didn't have the energy to hate them.

Jake stood glaring up at the two murals of the Goddess, the Upside one, all flowers and happiness and fluffy Namrat and all that happy horseshit, and the Downside one, blood and death and Namrat with his big, hungry teeth just waiting to eat us all up, knowing he would win in the end. Jake had always fought because she wanted the Goddess to love her, because she'd spent half her life being told she wasn't loved, that the Goddess expected more. For the longest time, I'd thought Jake was like that Downside Goddess, had admired her for the way she fought, because for a Downsider it wasn't about shiny promises of an afterlife. No, the fight was the thing, fight with everything you have, even when you know you're going to lose, that Namrat will get you in the end.

Namrat *always* wins.

But when I saw Jake staring up at that mural, I knew what drove her. Fear. Same as me. But unlike mine, her fear was that the Goddess wouldn't love her, would turn her away unless she fought, more and more, always. Brought up in violence, that was always Jake's first reaction to anything. Now she stood there, splashed in blood that wasn't hers, looking more like that Downside Goddess than ever, and it was the fear that was killing her.

She didn't take her gaze from the mural when she spoke,

and her voice seemed very small in the silence, flat and toneless. "Why didn't you leave me up there? I wanted to stay." She scrubbed a hand across eyes that were red-rimmed but dry. "I suppose I'll have to go to the gates then."

"You don't have to," I said. I didn't have time for this, not really. I didn't have the *blood* for it. The Storad wouldn't stay where we'd lured them; I had to get going, but there was always time for this. I had to, not for me or for Jake but for Pasha. "They say it's the fight that's the thing, for her. But you're giving up."

She whirled on me, and her hand caught me a ringing slap around the side of the head, which I really could have done without. With that slap still stinging, I shook my head and spat out another mouthful of blood. I was surprised I had any left.

"What do you know about it?" she snarled.

"Pasha once asked me if I would let you go and dice with death every day because it made you happy. And he did, but it didn't, it won't make you happy because that's not why you're doing it. Look at her, the Goddess, who you want, always, to love you. Always trying to prove to her that you're worthy, and she says the fight is the thing. To *fight*. But you're not fighting, even if you've got swords in your hands and blood in your hair. You're not fighting, because you *want* someone to beat you, even I can see that. You're giving up, and do you think that's why Pasha put himself on that machine? So that you'd die too? He told me, and I get it now, that a sacrifice has to hurt or it's no sacrifice at all. Do you want him to have done that for nothing? Do you want to make that sacrifice useless and stupid? Because I won't let you do that to him. Not to Pasha."

She stepped back and I thought then she might cry at last, but no. No tears, or not in public. Maybe she'd cry later, but not now.

"Bastard," she whispered at last. "What you know about it, about Pasha and me, eh? *Bastard.*"

"Technically no, but I can see why you might think so. You're probably right too. But I can't go and do what I have to up in the lab unless I'm sure about this, about you not trying to get yourself killed. I can't let Pasha dying mean nothing." Or perhaps I was kidding myself, trying to put it off, and that sounded more like me.

Jake's glance flicked upwards, towards the lab, and she flinched. "You're scared. I never thought you were scared. You were always Rojan, who helped us when no one else would, or could. I never thought you were scared."

"I've always been scared. Scared to be alone. Scared to be with anyone, because I'll fuck it up. I thought I loved you once. I still do, in a way. I loved you for Pasha. I loved you because you were safe – I knew I'd never get the chance to fuck it up. I'm scared, but I'm going to do it anyway. I have to. And then I won't have to be scared any more."

I hadn't said what I was going to do yet, but I think she knew. She shut her eyes against the tears that threatened, but even then she wouldn't cry them. "Then you and I are the same – that's why I fight like I don't care, because I don't want to be scared any more."

I wanted to say something – that there was hope, for all of us perhaps, even her and me, screw-ups that we were. But I couldn't because I don't think I've ever really believed in hope. Hope is a crock of shit and never gave anyone a damned thing except a buffer against just throwing themselves down a gap and having done with it. Sometimes it made it more likely. Not the most helpful of things to say, so I didn't.

She turned away, her back rigid, hands on the hilts of her swords, and made for the door. I wanted to stop her, I wanted to tell her . . . what? I didn't know, only that I didn't want it to mean nothing, any of it, Pasha, me, her, everything. But by the time I got my tongue and brain in gear, it was too late. She was gone, and I never saw her again. And funny, I didn't mind, or not much. It wasn't her that drove me after all. All that time, all that mooning as Erlat called it, and it wasn't her. So funny I almost laughed, and instead choked on the blood in my throat.

Perak stared at me, his face as pale as the snow that still piled up in the streets, wherever it could find a way through the warren of walkways and buildings and too many people squashed together. I wanted to say something to him too, but again I couldn't think what and I needed to save my breath so all I said was, "Help me upstairs, Perak."

He wavered, and I looked about at the statues and wondered, were the saints ever afraid? Did the martyrs crap themselves before they did what they'd done? Did they dream of Namrat coming to eat them?

And there, the statue of Namrat himself, his face covered with a black and gold cloth as was proper. I'm not sure what possessed me, to see the face of the thing that haunted me, but I pulled the black cloth off and let it drop. A hungry, snarling face, all eyes and teeth. Namrat always wins, in the end.

Perak got hold of my arm and without another word we made our way out of the temple, away from the silence, from the statues' eyes, away from Namrat. It took a while to get to the lab – walking wasn't getting any easier, and the snow had turned to slushy ice which coated the stairwell, the walkways, every available surface. The air seemed cold enough to snap my nose hairs, but I barely noticed.

We reached the level of the lab, the area where a huddle of dead Storad lay mercifully cloaked by the snow. It seemed quieter than graves. A faint sound echoed in the crystal air – the gates. They were fighting at the gates, in the streets, on the Spine. They'd all risen, but it wouldn't be enough, not to beat them back for good. Because there was going to be more Storad, more machines. More everything, if we didn't do something right now. Of that we could be sure.

"Rojan . . . " Perak's voice, worried and small, like when we were boys and he looked up to me.

I shook my head – saving my breath, and the blood that seemed to float out in misty little droplets with it. I only wanted to say it once, and there was someone else who needed to hear it too.

A shout went up from behind the rough barricade, the door opened and light spilled out. Warm hands grabbed me and took me inside, set me down on a chair by Lise's desk.

Perak crouched opposite me, while Erlat helped me sit up. Even that little thing was hard and I leaned against her, taking a bit of strength from her while she mopped at my face with a cool cloth that seemed like bliss.

"Rojan, what—" Perak said, but I shook my head at him. No words or breath spare to explain.

Instead I used them for Erlat. "Lise's desk. Bottom drawer, at the back. Green."

They both looked at me like I'd gone mad, and perhaps they were right, but Erlat went and got the vial and the syringe that went with it. For once I was going to voluntarily get a jab.

"Perak, open the door." I nodded towards the room that I didn't really want to see again, but had to.

"What? No, Rojan. I won't allow it. I *won't.*"

I levered myself up, and Erlat shifted under my shoulder so I could use her as a crutch. The room swam, colours blurring into black around me, but I managed to stay upright. Just.

"You don't have a choice," I said. "Why were you going to blow Top of the World?"

He looked bewildered at the change of tack, but I needed him to understand even if I didn't.

"I – I—" He pulled himself together. "It's not about the individual man. One man couldn't change Ministry, not on his own, not for decades, unless I wanted to assassinate all the cardinals and . . . the opportunity presented itself. I could have sent Jake away, or tried to and then Top of the World would be empty except for me and the Storad. You gave me the idea, you and Allit when he saw them there, I knew what needed to be done. Take down the whole lot, Top of the World, Clouds, scour Ministry from the positions of power and start again. Most of the cardinals have gone to the Mishans, or tried, and frankly the tribes are welcome to them. I hope they find more use for them than I did. Top of the World is empty, Clouds is a ghost town, except for the Storad. I thought we could topple both, Ministry and Storad, only we can't now. I thought you were going to blow it all up, not bring us down here. If you'd left me up there I could have rigged something, fixed the ignition switch. Could have blown the whole mess into the Slump. Why didn't you leave me, why *do* this to yourself?"

I had to pause in my answer because more blood came up. If this carried on, I wasn't going to have any blood left, but even that didn't matter much.

"You've got a daughter, and she's already without a mother. Even I wouldn't make her an orphan if I could avoid it." Little Amarie, whose kidnap had started this whole sorry mess. A niece I'd never met, who laid flowers at the feet of the saints and martyrs for me, who prayed for me. "Besides, it's not just Top of the World, is it? Machines, down there. More Storad. On way. Just taking out Top of World not going to cut it. Open door. Big brother will sort it."

Perak's gaze went to the windows, to the ominous orange flicker that said everything that needed to be said. Storad in Top of the World, more at the gates, more in the tunnels too, probably, mining, cracking. We had men, we had everyone now, fighting for us. But against those machines, with Storad in place up high, perfectly placed to rain down death on anyone and everything . . .

This was a chance. A chance to put everything right, make a fresh start, do it properly this time. It was the only chance we had and he knew it.

Perak went and opened the door.

I shuffled over, not wanting to look inside, at the machine that I'd last seen with Pasha's body on it. I didn't want to die. I still don't. I had no choice, not really, not if I didn't want to drink myself to death over what-ifs. I wished I'd taken the time to ask Lise if she'd fixed the machine.

Erlat helped me, and I leaned on her. Funny, I'd always admired Jake because she fought back against all that happened to her, fought with everything she had until this last, when it had become too much. She'd refused to stay broken. But up there, in Top of the World, when I'd seen the world clearly, like glass, I'd realised.

I admired her, thought I loved her, because I'd thought she was strong. Then I'd seen, at Erlat's, that perhaps I thought I loved her because she was safe, because Pasha was always there so I wouldn't have to try, and get it wrong in my usual style. Now there was no Pasha, the illusion crumbled.

When I fall for a woman, I always fall hard. But this time, I hadn't realised I'd fallen. Not until now, when there was piss all I could do about it. At least that meant I wouldn't do my usual sort of screw-it-up. No, I was going to do a *different* sort of screw-it-up.

"Rojan, are you sure?" Her voice. Erlat's, soft and smoky, no teasing now but still pushing the black away for me, letting my mind back.

I fell into the chair attached to the demented machine that was going to save everyone. Had to keep my breath for the words that mattered, so I only nodded.

Funny how she always knew the right things to say and do. She held my hand, and I gripped it tight enough I probably almost broke her fingers. She didn't flinch. Strong inside and out. I hoped so, because she was going to have to be. Strong enough for us both.

Enough breath for a few words. Not many. "Perak, first Top of World. Next lot, gates. You'll have to sort the tunnels, I'm not sure I can manage that too."

"Twice? You want to use this *twice*?"

Again, only a nod. Last few words. Make them count. "Erlat." She looked at me, her face dim in the faint light, but

I saw. She'd tried to hide behind teasing, behind making me blush, and I'd hidden behind Jake, behind thinking I loved her. Out of fear. But right then there was no hiding. There was no fear, or not of that at least. I was out in the open, not even any scathing words to hide behind. It was just me, and her. *Use the right words. Don't screw it up.* "You ruined me for other women."

Just for once, because the world is a contrary and fucked-up place, the words were the right ones. But her sudden, radiant smile was twisted, and when she kissed me— Always save the best till last. And it was, my last kiss, my best kiss even if I was covered in blood and had no breath left. It was the kiss that meant the most, out of all the kisses, and there have been a multitude. But none like that, never like that, because I meant that one with everything I had. Finally, when it was too late, I'd figured it out. Typical.

"Come back," she said at last, one hand smoothing my hair back from my sweating forehead. I lied even without breath when I nodded. She knew it too, I was pretty sure, because with a last look she turned and ran. Not fast enough that I didn't see the tears, and they pained me more than anything, more than my stupid buggered hand, more than that machine was going to.

So, at the last of it, it was Perak and me. Brothers to the end. He'd dropped me in it, again, but that was all right. I'd done plenty of dropping myself. If I've learned one thing, it's that responsibility is something you have whether you like it or not. There's no running, only movement that makes you think you're escaping. And when you've fucked up, you have to take the consequences.

Perak held the syringe in shaking hands. "I can't."

"Have to." And then, because he was my little brother and I loved him, "It's all right. It'll be all right. I'll take care of it, I promise. Just a quick trip into the black then back again, right as rain."

Those were almost the last words I spoke. There was nothing else to say and once he'd slid the needle under the skin, once the juice stated flowing through me like electricity, words didn't matter. Nothing mattered but this.

The juice came, of course it did, thundering up my arm, the greatest thing in the world, the most dangerous because I wanted it so much. But it kept coming, the jab doing its work too well, kept coming and coming and I could feel every waft of air on my face as pain, every twitch of every nerve as a searing agony.

Perak plugged me into the machine, surrounded me with wires and blinking lights and whirring noise, and I trusted to him and to my sister, relied on them in fact. Felt the machine take me and twist me, spin out my juice, make it more, make it swell till it filled everything.

I panicked then, thinking I knew why Pasha had died, that he couldn't control it, it was too much, too much for any one man. There was no terror to match that, not even a drop off the edge of the world could compare, a streaming, aching terror knowing that it could only get worse, more, as the green stuff in the syringe took hold. Lise's little concoction to amplify pain. It would get worse, and the pain would explode and I would be gone . . . I had to master it or I was dead, like Pasha. Nothing much left to mourn over, and no one left to mourn anyway, if I got this wrong.

I think I called her name, one last time, said, "Erlat" before I couldn't talk any more, before my mind forgot what talking was.

Then I was home, hovering on the edge of the black, so big now that it was the world. It was everything. It was nothing.

I was light and dark, and the light was life and the black was death. I knew that, I'd always known it, but . . . Dendal had said to embrace the black, know that it was part of me. And the light was too bright, too much life; that was where Pasha had gone wrong. I had to embrace the black inside me if this was going to work. I had to conquer it, be the whisper in its ear rather than the other way around.

So I flexed my hand and relished the pain. Stepped into the black, into the pain and craving and glorious nothing of it.

Welcome home, Rojan. I knew you'd come in the end.

And here I am now, lost in that fearless black, maybe for ever. It's warm in here and I have nothing to fear, no one to rely on me, no worry of making things worse. There is nothing but the pain, and that is far away and dim within my marrow, agony and ecstasy. I watch the brightness of me pierce the gloom of velvet nothing and try to listen for the voices.

Sometimes, when the black fades a little, when I think that maybe, if I tried, I could fight my way out, I hear them. Perak's strong voice, little brother with his head in the clouds no more. The scritch-scratch of Dendal as he reads some scripture aloud to me in his querulous monk's voice. I wish he wouldn't. The other voice, the one I wait for. A face I think I glimpsed once, when the veil was thin, or maybe I only wished it. A pair of soft eyes, an elegant coil of hair at the nape of her neck. I never know what she says, and maybe that's a mercy, but the black is always thinner when she's here, less consuming, less tempting. It's enough that she comes, perhaps, enough for ever.

But I think there's someone in here with me. I think you're here, listening to me. Or maybe I am batshit crazy, finally. I think you're here, but I can't tell if you're real or just my imagination come to play tricks with me. Mostly it doesn't matter. While you're here I have someone to tell my tale to, someone to be with me in the loneliness of the black, even if you are an imaginary friend. I wonder if you look like the Upside murals, flowery and soft, or the Downside ones, full of piss and vinegar, all blood and death and sacrificed hand. And sometimes I wonder if this is the heaven you had planned for me, or if you gave me to Namrat and I'm in hell.

If you're here, you're probably not real. I've never believed in you anyway. But if you are here, if you're really real, there's perhaps just one thing I need to say.

I didn't do this for you. I didn't do this because you said it was right, or because it was my duty to you or I was doing your work. I did it for me, and Pasha and Erlat and everyone else. Because *I* said it was right, because, so help me, sometimes a guy's got to be responsible for his actions, and a sacrifice has to hurt or it means piss all. And sometimes there has to be hope, even if there's none left for me. I learned that if nothing else. But I didn't do it for you.

So I've only got one thing left to say now. Screw you, lady. Screw you.

Epilogue

"What do you think, Allit?"

I looked up at the new statue in Guinto's temple and tried to find some tactful way of saying it. Then I remembered who we were talking about, and just said it. "Rojan would *hate* it."

Perak laughed, but it had a mournful edge to it. "I know, but it was unanimous. Every council on every level, ratified by the main council. Even what's left of the Ministry agreed. Probably because Guinto bullied them into it. I think Rojan may enjoy the irony, at least. And the notoriety."

We both looked at the statue of Rojan, set in place along with the other martyrs, before the aisle led to the statues of saints and on to the mural of the Goddess. The mural was new – neither the Upside sanitised version nor the Downside blood-and-glory version of the Goddess. No longer what Rojan insisted on calling "that stupid fluffy shit", this was a new Goddess for a new time. I caught myself wondering if that's what had always happened – men made her in whatever shape they needed her to be in. Rojan would certainly have said so, and would have gone on to say how moronic it was, because that was people all over, too stupid to live. That thought made me laugh, though I kept it muffled for Perak's sake.

Summer sunlight shafted through the new stained glass of the windows, puddling along the aisle runner, green chasing blue across the altar and a deep red glancing off Rojan's face, making his statue look embarrassed to be there.

You wouldn't be embarrassed if you knew what you'd done. No, he'd have been crowing about it, most surely. He still could, perhaps, though I'd long ago given up hope of him ever coming back. Thoughts of Rojan were now in the past tense, and knowing that made me wish that he was here to see the statue, made me wish I could have heard him swear about it and "all that crap people think they need to believe in". Instead of him and his acerbic mouth, all I had was his old jacket, the one with the burn marks in it, even though it dragged on the floor behind me when I walked. It was almost all I had left of him, except what he taught me, and I treasure it even now.

Dendal often used him as a warning to me and the other young mages, what might happen to them, us, if we gave in to the song that came calling every time we cast a spell. But Dendal couldn't keep the hint of pride out of his voice, or resist telling us too that if we had to do it, then we should, for the Goddess. We were her blessed children, but blessings are put there for a purpose, or so he said. Rojan would have rolled his eyes at that, but I tried my best not to.

I walked out into the sunlight and smiled up at the sky. Guinto's temple wasn't in No-Hope Shitty. Not any more – there was no No-Hope-Shitty. Top of the World had come down in a blaze of magic and blue flame, taken Clouds with it as it tumbled slowly into the Slump. Taken out half the Storad army at a stroke, and Rojan on Lise's machine had stopped the rest with man-made thunderbolts that stunned them where they stood in the valley. The same thunderbolts that even now still flickered around the gates, letting no one in or out all the while he was still alive, still hooked up.

Rojan let the sun in Under and destroyed the Ministry, as surely as if he'd assassinated the Goddess. Most of the cardinals and bishops had run for it, had begged or bought their way through the Mishan gate when it looked like Mahala would fall. Perak had seemed to take a very great delight in denying them the right to return afterwards – he'd told them to go and spread the word of the Goddess among the Mishans, but the smile he'd said it with spoke of another thought entirely.

Six months on, and Under was getting used to seeing the sun on a daily basis. It was still pretty dim down in Boundary, but the tunnels in the 'Pit were shored up – we'd used a fair bit of the Slump rubble to fill them in, and the engineers that had once worked for Alchemy Research were sure they'd hold. Perak had men taking out strategic buildings, making huge light-wells with hanging gardens all the way down, growing what we could, what little would grow after the synth.

I went to see Rojan once, in the room where Pasha died and Rojan did what he did, where he is still hooked up to Lise's machine, keeping any foolhardy Storad out until we are strong enough. I could only bear to go the once, because he doesn't look like him any more. The curl of his lip at everyone and everything is flat now, his face thinner than ever, his body little more than a skeleton despite Erlat and Dendal's efforts with broth and whatever else they can slide between his lips.

He looks like he's dead, but he still moves, twitches and trembles like an old man, his broken hand grinding on itself, more pain, always more pain to keep him in the pain-free black. The doctors managed to stem the bleeding, enough to stop him dying, but they say they'll have to amputate the hand soon. His fingers are little more than purple slugs but still he grinds it out, powers the machine that saved us, that keeps us safe until we're rebuilt. Rojan's in there somewhere, in his black, lost and alone and nothing like the man he was, yet somehow more him than ever, as though this is how he was supposed to be. Looking at him like that was warning enough.

That other concoction could have brought him out of

the black, we were sure – the liquid that could numb everything. No pain, no magic, no juice, no black. But Rojan had insisted it all be destroyed; the doctor who'd invented it, Whelar himself, had either died somewhere down defending the gates or had scarpered through the Mishan gate and wasn't coming back. All his research went up in smoke when the Sacred Goddess Hospital burned; Lise's notes had gone when the pain lab was ransacked in the riots before the siege. If we'd had even a little bit left, she could have resynthesised it . . . But there was no more, and while Lise had tried, had almost torn her hair from her head in frustration, had even found a mix or two that was good for other things, nothing seemed quite able to bring Rojan back. Or maybe it was truly too late for him. Maybe it had always been too late.

Funny, though, how he had twitched less when Erlat came to see him, how he looked less thin, how his lips had moved and tried to form a word. Erlat has changed too, I think, but it's hard to tell. The only change she'll show is when she looks at Rojan, and her face twists, just a little, when he tries to say something, before she smiles a faraway smile. It makes me think, and wonder, and realise that I'll never know what it was that made him do it. What drove such an apparently selfish man to commit the ultimate sacrifice? Or was all that sneering just an act? I wish I could ask him, but I think I know. I wish he was here, being sarcastic and swearing at everyone and caring underneath just the same, though he'd rather die than admit it. Maybe that was why he did it.

In the end, we can only speculate on the why, and many do, endlessly. Priests discuss it in their sermons, men and women talk about him over pints in the pubs, but no one knows for sure. All we know is that he did, and because of it we're safe.

Dendal says Rojan was doing the Goddess's work, that this was why he was here, why he'd been sent, why the Goddess had made his life the way it was, but Rojan would have laughed at that, or spat on it. Me, I think he was showing us, the mages he left behind, who need to know. We are magic, we are strong. But if that strength is needed – it's up to us, whether it destroys us or not, what we do with it. Rojan was strong. Just not quite strong enough to save himself too.

I wonder, sometimes, how so much hate could live in one man and whether that hate was what brought us this – sun Under, Ministry a faint shadow of what it was, now full of good and pious men. People working for themselves, Upsiders and Downsiders not hating each other, even if they don't love each other. Hope, the greatest thing he brought us, and the one thing he despaired of ever finding.

All the time, we were told to love, that the Goddess loved us and that would be enough, our hope, but us loving her back brought nothing but misery. It was hate, and fighting against what we hated with everything we had, that set us free and gave us a real hope. We were told that it was the great and good that would save us, save our souls and make our lives mean something. Maybe that's true, like now, when everything is peaceful. Good men can now do good things. But then, to get that peace, what we needed was a really great old-fashioned bastard.

Acknowledgements

Well if you've read the acknowledgements in the first two books, you'll know what to expect here. My family, for being awesome. The T Party writers group, for same plus curry. Special thanks to Bettie-Lee and Luke, and to Stacia Kane for provoking thoughts (and letting me nick them). Anna for her copious notes that make me slap my forehead and go "Duh!", and Alex for his ongoing enthusiasm. A hairy coo for Scarlett and Lor, just because. McMoo! Is *ma* coo.

And that's about it, apart from whoever I forgot. Except I must acknowledge you, gentle reader. Thanks for coming along for this particular ride.

extras

meet the author

FRANCIS KNIGHT was born and lives in Sussex, UK. She has held a variety of jobs from being a groom in the Balearics, where she punched a policeman and got away with it, to an IT administrator. When not living in her own head, she enjoys SFF geekery, WWE geekery, teaching her children *Monty Python* quotes and boldly going and seeking out new civilisations.

Find out more about Francis Knight and other Orbit authors by registering for the free monthly newsletter at www.orbitbooks .net.

introducing

If you enjoyed
LAST TO RISE,
look out for

THE CROWN TOWER

The Riyria Chronicles: Book 1

by Michael J. Sullivan

Two men who hate each other. One impossible mission.
A legend in the making.

Hadrian Blackwater, a warrior with nothing to fight for, is paired with Royce Melborn, a thieving assassin with nothing to lose. Hired by an old wizard, they must steal a treasure that no one can reach. The Crown Tower is the impregnable remains of the grandest fortress ever built and home to the realm's most prized possessions. But it isn't gold or jewels that the wizard is after, and if he can just keep them from killing each other, they just might succeed.

Chapter One

Pickles

Hadrian Blackwater hadn't gone more than five steps off the ship before he was robbed.

The bag—his only bag—was torn from his hand. He never even saw the thief. Hadrian couldn't see much of anything in the lantern-lit chaos surrounding the pier, just a mass of faces, people shoving to get away from the gangway or get nearer to the ship. Used to the rhythms of a pitching deck, he struggled to keep his feet on the stationary dock amidst the jostling scramble. The newly arrived moved hesitantly, causing congestion. Many onshore searched for friends and relatives, yelling, jumping, waving arms—chasing the attention of someone. Others were more professional, holding torches and shouting offers for lodging and jobs. One bald man with a voice like a war trumpet stood on a crate, promising that The Black Cat Tavern offered the strongest ale at the cheapest prices. Twenty feet away, his competition balanced on a wobbly barrel and proclaimed the bald man a liar. He further insisted The Lucky Hat was the only local tavern that didn't substitute dog meat for mutton. Hadrian didn't care. He wanted to get out of the crowd and find the thief who stole his bag. After only a few minutes, he realized that wasn't going to happen. He settled for protecting his purse and considered himself lucky. At least nothing of value was lost—just clothing, but given how cold Avryn was in autumn, that might be a problem.

Hadrian followed the flow of bodies, not that he had much

choice. Adrift in the strong current, he bobbed along with his head just above the surface. The dock creaked and moaned under the weight of escaping passengers who hurried away from what had been their cramped home for more than a month. Weeks breathing clean salt air had been replaced by the pungent smells of fish, smoke, and tar. Rising far above the dimly lit docks, the city's lights appeared as brighter points in a starlit world.

Hadrian followed four dark-skinned Calian men hauling crates packed with colorful birds, which squawked and rattled their cages. Behind him walked a poorly dressed man and woman. The man carried *two* bags, one over a shoulder and the other tucked under an arm. Apparently no one was interested in *their* belongings. Hadrian realized he should have worn something else. His eastern attire was not only uselessly thin, but in a land of leather and wool, the bleached white linen thawb and the gold-trimmed cloak screamed *wealth*.

"Here! Over here!" The barely distinguishable voice was one more sound in the maelstrom of shouts, wagon wheels, bells, and whistles. "This way. Yes, you, come. Come!"

Reaching the end of the ramp and clearing most of the congestion, Hadrian spotted an adolescent boy. Dressed in tattered clothes, he waited beneath the fiery glow of a swaying lantern. The wiry youth held Hadrian's bag and beamed an enormous smile. "Yes, yes, you there. Please come. Right over here," he called, waving with his free hand.

"That's my bag!" Hadrian shouted, struggling to reach him and stymied by the remaining crowd blocking the narrow pier.

"Yes! Yes!" The lad grinned wider, his eyes bright with enthusiasm. "You are very lucky I took it from you or someone would have surely stolen it."

"*You* stole it!"

"No. No. Not at all. I have been faithfully protecting your

most valued property." The youth straightened his willowy back such that Hadrian thought he might salute. "Someone like you should not be carrying your own bag."

Hadrian squeezed around three women who'd paused to comfort a crying child, only to be halted by an elderly man dragging an incredibly large trunk. The old guy, wraith thin with bright white hair, blocked the narrow isthmus already cluttered by the mountain of bags being recklessly thrown to the pier from the ship.

"What do you mean *someone like me*?" Hadrian shouted over the trunk as the old man struggled in front of him.

"You are a great knight, yes?"

"No, I'm not."

The boy pointed at him. "You must be. Look how big you are and you carry swords—three swords. And that one on your back is huge. Only a knight carries such things."

Hadrian sighed when the old man's trunk became wedged in the gap between the decking and the ramp. He reached down and lifted it free, receiving several vows of gratitude in an unfamiliar language.

"See," the boy said, "only a knight would help a stranger in need like that."

More bags crashed down on the pile beside him. One tumbled off, rolling into the harbor's dark water with a *plunk!* Hadrian pressed forward, both to avoid being hit from above and to retrieve his stolen property. "I'm not a knight. Now give me back my bag."

"I will carry it for you. My name is Pickles, but we must be going. Quickly now." The boy hugged Hadrian's bag and trotted off on dirty bare feet.

"Hey!"

"Quickly, quickly! We should not linger here."

"What's the rush? What are you talking about? And come back here with my bag!"

"You are very lucky to have me. I am an excellent guide. Anything you want, I know where to look. With me you can get the best of everything and all for the least amounts."

Hadrian finally caught up and grabbed his bag. He pulled and got the boy with it, his arms still tightly wrapped around the canvas.

"Ha! See?" The boy grinned. "No one is pulling your bag out of *my* hands!"

"Listen"—Hadrian took a moment to catch his breath—"I don't need a guide. I'm not staying here."

"Where are you going?"

"Up north. Way up north. A place called Sheridan."

"Ah! The university."

This surprised Hadrian. Pickles didn't look like the worldly type. The kid resembled an abandoned dog. The kind that might have once worn a collar but now possessed only fleas, visible ribs, and an overdeveloped sense for survival.

"You are studying to be a scholar? I should have known. My apologies for any insult. You are most smart—so, of course, you will make a great scholar. You should not tip me for making such a mistake. But that is even better. I know just where we must go. There is a barge that travels up the Bernum River. Yes, the barge will be perfect and one leaves tonight. There will not be another for days, and you do not want to stay in an awful city like this. We will be in Sheridan in no time."

"We?" Hadrian smirked.

"You will want me with you, yes? I am not just familiar with Vernes. I am an expert on all of Avryn—I have traveled far. I can help you, a steward who can see to your needs and watch your belongings to keep them safe from thieves while you study. A job I am most good at, yes?"

"I'm not a student, not going to be one either. Just visiting someone, and I don't need a steward."

"Of course you do not need a steward—if you are not going to be a scholar—but as the son of a noble lord just back from the east, you definitely need a houseboy, and I will make a fine houseboy. I will make sure your chamber pot is always emptied, your fire well stoked in winter, and fan you in the summer to keep the flies away."

"Pickles," Hadrian said firmly. "I'm not a lord's son, and I don't need a servant. I—" He stopped after noticing the boy's attention had been drawn away, and his gleeful expression turned fearful. "What's wrong?"

"I told you we needed to hurry. We need to get away from the dock right now!"

Hadrian turned to see men with clubs marching up the pier, their heavy feet causing the dock to bounce.

"Press-gang," Pickles said. "They are always near when ships come in. Newcomers like you can get caught and wake up in the belly of a ship already at sea. Oh no!" Pickles gasped as one spotted them.

After a quick whistle and shoulder tap, four men headed their way. Pickles flinched. The boy's legs flexed, his weight shifting as if to bolt, but he looked at Hadrian, bit his lip, and didn't move.

The clubmen charged but slowed and came to a stop after spotting Hadrian's swords. The four could have been brothers. Each had almost-beards, oily hair, sunbaked skin, and angry faces. The expression must have been popular, as it left permanent creases in their brows.

They studied him for a second, puzzled. Then the foremost thug, wearing a stained tunic with one torn sleeve, asked, "You a knight?"

"No, I'm not a knight." Hadrian rolled his eyes.

Another laughed and gave the one with the torn sleeve a

rough shove. "Daft fool—he's not much older than the boy next to him."

"Don't bleedin' shove me on this slimy dock, ya stupid sod." The man looked back at Hadrian. "He's not that young."

"It's possible," one of the others said. "Kings do stupid things. Heard one knighted his dog once. Sir Spot they called him."

The four laughed. Hadrian was tempted to join in, but he was sobered by the terrified look on Pickles's face.

The one with the torn sleeve took a step closer. "He's got to be at least a squire. Look at all that steel, for Maribor's sake. Where's yer master, boy? He around?"

"I'm not a squire either," Hadrian replied.

"No? What's with all the steel, then?"

"None of your business."

The men laughed. "Oh, you're a tough one, are ya?"

They spread out, taking firmer holds on their sticks. One had a strap of leather run through a hole in the handle and wrapped around his wrist. *Probably figured that was a good idea*, Hadrian thought.

"You better leave us alone," Pickles said, voice wavering. "Do you not know who this is?" He pointed at Hadrian. "He is a famous swordsman—a born killer."

Laughter. "Is that so?" the nearest said, and paused to spit between yellow teeth.

"Oh yes!" Pickles insisted. "He's vicious—an animal—and very touchy, very dangerous."

"A young colt like him, eh?" The man gazed at Hadrian and pushed out his lips in judgment. "Big enough—I'll grant ya that—but it looks to me like he still has his mother's milk dripping down his chin." He focused on Pickles. "And *you're* no vicious killer, are ya, little lad? You're the dirty alley rat I saw yesterday under the alehouse boardwalks trying to catch crumbs. You, my boy, are about to embark on a new career at sea. Best thing for ya really. You'll get food and learn to work—work real hard. It'll make a man out of ya."

Pickles tried to dodge, but the thug grabbed him by the hair.

"Let him go," Hadrian said.

"How did ya put it?" The guy holding Pickles chuckled. "*None of your business*?"

"He's my squire," Hadrian declared.

The men laughed again. "You said you ain't a knight, remember?"

"He works for me—that's good enough."

"No it ain't, 'cause this one works for the maritime industry now." He threw a muscled arm around Pickles's neck and bent the boy over as another moved behind with a length of rope pulled from his belt.

"I said, let him go." Hadrian raised his voice.

"Hey!" the man with the torn sleeve barked. "Don't give us no orders, boy. We ain't taking you, 'cause you're somebody's property, someone who has you hauling three swords, someone who might miss you. That's problems we don't need, see? But don't push it. Push it and we'll break bones. Push us more and we'll drop you in a boat anyway. Push us too far, and you won't even get a boat."

"I really hate people like you," Hadrian said, shaking his head. "I just got here. I was at sea for a month—*a month*! That's how long I've traveled to get away from this kind of thing." He shook his head in disgust. "And here you are—you too." Hadrian pointed at Pickles as they worked at tying the boy's wrists behind his back. "I didn't ask for your help. I didn't ask for a guide, or a steward, or a houseboy. I was just fine on my own. But no, you had to take my bag and be so good-humored about everything.

Worst of all, you didn't run. Maybe you're stupid—I don't know. But I can't help thinking you stuck around to help me."

"I'm sorry I didn't do a better job." Pickles looked up at him with sad eyes.

Hadrian sighed. "Damn it. There you go again." He looked back at the clubmen, already knowing how it would turn out—how it always turned out—but he'd to try anyway. "Look, I'm not a knight. I'm not a squire either, but these swords are mine, and while Pickles thought he was bluffing, I—"

"Oh, just shut up." The one with the torn sleeve took a step and thrust his club to shove Hadrian. On the slippery pier it was easy for Hadrian to put him off balance. He caught the man's arm, twisted the wrist and elbow around, and snapped the bone. The crack sounded like a walnut opening. He gave the screaming clubman a shove, which was followed by a splash as he went into the harbor.

Hadrian could have drawn his swords then—almost did out of reflex—but he'd promised himself things would be different. Besides, he stole the man's club before sending him over the side, a solid bit of hickory about an inch in diameter and a little longer than a foot. The grip had been polished smooth from years of use, the other end stained brown from blood that seeped into the wood grain.

The remaining men gave up trying to tie Pickles, but one continued to hold him in a headlock while the other two rushed Hadrian. He read their feet, noting their weight and momentum. Dodging his first attacker's swing, Hadrian tripped the second and struck him in the back of the head as he went down. The sound of club on skull made a hollow thud like slapping a pumpkin, and when the guy hit the deck, he stayed there. The other swung at him again. Hadrian parried with the hickory stick, striking fingers. The man cried out and lost his grip, the club left dangling from the leather strap around his wrist. Hadrian grabbed the weapon, twisted it tight, bent the man's arm back, and pulled hard. The bone didn't break, but the shoulder popped. The man's quivering legs signaled the fight had left him, and Hadrian sent him over the side to join his friend.

By the time Hadrian turned to face the last of the four, Pickles was standing alone and rubbing his neck. His would-be captor sprinted into the distance.

"Is he going to come back with friends, you think?" Hadrian asked.

Pickles didn't say anything. He just stared at Hadrian, his mouth open.

"No sense lingering to find out, I suppose," Hadrian answered himself. "So where's this barge you were talking about?"

Away from the seaside pier, the city of Vernes was still choked and stifling. Narrow brick roads formed a maze overshadowed by balconies that nearly touched. Lanterns and moonlight were equally scarce, and down some lonely pathways there was no light at all. Hadrian was thankful to have Pickles. Recovered from his fright, the "alley rat" acted more like a hunting dog. He trotted through the city's corridors, leaping puddles that stank of waste and ducking wash lines and scaffolding with practiced ease.

"That's the living quarters for most of the shipwrights, and over there is the dormitory for the dockworkers." Pickles pointed to a grim building near the wharf with three stories, one door, and few windows. "Most of the men around this ward live there or at the sister building on the south end. So much here is shipping. Now, up there, high on that hill—see it? That is the citadel."

Hadrian lifted his head and made out the dark silhouette of a fortress illuminated by torches.

"Not really a castle, more like a counting house for traders and merchants. Walls have to be high and thick for all the gold it is they stuff up there. This is where all the money from the sea goes. Everything else runs downhill—but gold flows up."

Pickles sidestepped a toppled bucket and spooked a pair of cat-sized rats that ran for deeper shadows. Halfway past a doorway Hadrian realized a pile of discarded rags was actually an ancient-looking man seated on a stoop. With a frazzled gray beard and a face thick with folds, he never moved, not even to blink. Hadrian only noticed him after his smoking pipe's bowl glowed bright orange.

"It is a filthy city," Pickles called back to him. "I am pleased we are leaving. Too many foreigners here—too many easterners—many probably arrived with you. Strange folk, the Calians. Their women practice witchcraft and tell fortunes, but I say it is best not to know too much about one's future. We will not have to worry about such things in the north. In Warric, they burn witches in the winter to keep warm. At least that is what I have heard." Pickles stopped abruptly and spun. "What is your name?"

"Finally decided to ask, eh?" Hadrian chuckled.

"I will need to know if I am going to book you passage."

"I can take care of that myself. Assuming, of course, you are actually taking me to a barge and not just to some dark corner where you'll clunk me on the head and do a more thorough job of robbing me."

Pickles looked hurt. "I would do no such thing. Do you think me such a fool? First, I have seen what you do to people who try to *clunk you on the head*. Second, we have already passed a dozen perfectly dark corners." Pickles beamed his big smile, which Hadrian took to be one part mischief, one part pride, and two parts just-plain-happy-to-be-alive joy. He couldn't argue with that. He also couldn't remember the last time he felt the way Pickles looked.

The press-gang leader was right. Pickles could only be four or five years younger than Hadrian. *Five*, he thought. *He's five years younger than I am. He's me before I left. Did I smile like that back then?* He wondered how long Pickles had been on his own and if he'd still have that smile in five years.

"Hadrian, Hadrian Blackwater." He extended his hand.

The boy nodded. "A good name. Very good. Better than Pickles—but then what is not?"

"Did your mother name you that?"

"Oh, most certainly. Rumor has it I was both conceived and born on the same crate of pickles. How can one deny such a legend? Even if it isn't true, I think it should be."

Crawling out of the labyrinth, they emerged onto a wider avenue. They had gained height, and Hadrian could see the pier and the masts of the ship he arrived on below. A good-sized crowd was still gathered—people looking for a place to stay or searching for belongings. Hadrian remembered the bag that had rolled into the harbor. How many others would find themselves stranded in a new city with little to nothing?

The bark of a dog caused Hadrian to turn. Looking down the narrow street, he thought he caught movement but couldn't be sure. The twisted length of the alley had but one lantern. Moonlight illuminated the rest, casting patches of blue-gray. A square here, a rectangle there, not nearly enough to see by and barely enough to judge distance. Had it been another rat? Seemed bigger. He waited, staring. Nothing moved.

When he looked back, Pickles had crossed most of the plaza to the far side where, to Hadrian's delight, there was another dock. This one sat on the mouth of the great Bernum River, which in the night appeared as a wide expanse of darkness. He cast one last look backward toward the narrow streets. Still nothing moved. *Ghosts*. That's all—his past stalking him.

Hadrian reeked of death. It wasn't the sort of stench others could smell or that water could wash, but it lingered on him like sweat-saturated pores after a long night of drinking. Only this odor didn't come from alcohol; it came from blood. Not from drinking it—although Hadrian knew some who had. His stink came from wallowing in it. But all that was over now, or so he told himself with the certainty of the recently sober. That had been a different Hadrian, a younger version who he'd left on the other side of the world and who he was still running from.

Realizing Pickles still had his bag, Hadrian ran to close the distance. Before he caught up, Pickles was in trouble again.

"It is his!" Pickles cried, pointing at Hadrian. "I was helping him reach the barge before it left."

The boy was surrounded by six soldiers. Most wore chain and held square shields. The one in the middle, with a fancy plume on his helmet, wore layered plate on his shoulders and chest as well as a studded leather skirt. He was the one Pickles was speaking to while two others restrained the boy. They all looked over as Hadrian approached.

"This your bag?" the officer asked.

"It is, and he's telling the truth." Hadrian pointed. "He is escorting me to that barge over there."

"In a hurry to leave our fair city, are you?" The officer's tone was suspicious, and his eyes scanned Hadrian as he talked.

"No offense to Vernes, but yes. I have business up north."

The officer moved a step closer. "What's your name?"

"Hadrian Blackwater."

"Where you from?"

"Hintindar originally."

"Originally?" The skepticism in his voice rose along with his eyebrows.

Hadrian nodded. "I've been in Calis for several years. Just returned from Dagastan on that ship down there."

The officer glanced at the dock, then at Hadrian's knee-length thawb, loose cotton pants, and keffiyeh headdress. He leaned in, sniffed, and grimaced. "You've definitely been on a ship, and that outfit is certainly Calian." He sighed, then turned to Pickles. "But this one hasn't been on any ship. He says he's going with you. Is that right?"

Hadrian glanced at Pickles and saw the hope in the boy's eyes. "Yeah. I've hired him to be my... ah... my... servant."

"Whose idea was that? His or yours?"

"His, but he's been very helpful. I wouldn't have found this barge without him."

"You just got off one ship," the officer said. "Seems odd you're so eager to get on another."

"Well, actually I'm not, but Pickles says the barge is about to leave and there won't be another for days. Is that true?"

"Yes," the officer said, "and awfully convenient too."

"Can I ask what the problem is? Is there a law against hiring a guide and paying for him to travel with you?"

"No, but we've had some nasty business here in town—real nasty business. So naturally we're interested in anyone eager to leave, at least anyone who's been around during the last few days." He looked squarely at Pickles.

"I haven't done anything," Pickles said.

"So you say, but even if you haven't, maybe you know something about it. Either way you might feel the need to disappear, and latching on to someone above suspicion would be a good way to get clear of trouble, wouldn't it?"

"But I don't know anything about the killings."

The officer turned to Hadrian. "You're free to go your way, and you'd best be quick. They've already called for boarders."

"What about Pickles?"

He shook his head. "I can't let him go with you. Unlikely he's guilty of murder, but he might know who is. Street orphans see a lot that they don't like to talk about if they think they can avoid it."

"But I'm telling you, I don't know *anything*. I haven't even been on the hill."

"Then you've nothing to worry about."

"But—" Pickles looked as if he might cry. "He was going to take me out of here. We were going to go north. We were going to go to a university."

"Hoy! Hoy! Last call for passengers! Barge to Colnora! Last call!" a voice bellowed.

"Listen"—Hadrian opened his purse—"you did me a service, and that's worth payment. Now, after you finish with their questions, if you still want to work for me, you can use this money to meet me in Sheridan. Catch the next barge or buckboard north, whatever. I'll be there for a month maybe, a couple of weeks at least." Hadrian pressed a coin into the boy's hand. "If you come, ask for Professor Arcadius. He's the one I'm meeting with, and he should be able to tell you how to find me. Okay?"

Pickles nodded and looked a bit better. Glancing down at the coin, his eyes widened, and the old giant smile of his returned. "Yes, sir! I will be there straightaway. You can most certainly count on me. Now you must run before the barge leaves."

Hadrian gave him a nod, picked up his bag, and jogged to the dock where a man waited at the gangway of a long flat boat.

introducing

If you enjoyed
LAST TO RISE,
look out for

CHARMING

Pax Arcana: Book 1

by Elliott James

John Charming isn't your average Prince...

He comes from a line of Charmings—an illustrious family of dragon slayers, witch-finders and killers dating back to before the fall of Rome. Trained by a modern-day version of the Knights Templar, monster hunters who have updated their methods from chain mail and crossbows to Kevlar and shotguns, he was one of the best. That is—until he became the abomination the Knights were sworn to hunt.

That was a lifetime ago. Now he tends bar under an assumed name in rural Virginia and leads a peaceful, quiet life. One that shouldn't change just because a vampire and a blonde walked into his bar... Right?

Prelude

Hocus Focus

There's a reason that we refer to being in love as being enchanted. Think back to the worst relationship you've ever been in: the one where your family and friends tried to warn you that the person you were with was cheating on you, or partying a little too much, or a control freak, or secretly gay, or whatever. Remember how you were convinced that no one but you could see the real person beneath that endearingly flawed surface? And then later, after the relationship reached that scorched-earth-policy stage where letters were being burned and photos were being cropped, did you find yourself looking back and being amazed at how obvious the truth had been all along? Did it feel as if you were waking up from some kind of a spell?

Well, there's something going on right in front of your face that you can't see right now, and you're not going to believe me when I point it out to you. Relax, I'm not going to provide a number where you can leave your credit card information, and you don't have to join anything. The only reason I'm telling you at all is that at some point in the future, you might have a falling-out with the worldview you're currently enamored of, and if that happens, what I'm about to tell you will help you make sense of things later.

The supernatural is real. Vampires? Real. Werewolves? Real.

Zombies, Ankou, djinn, Boo Hags, banshees, ghouls, spriggans, windigos, vodyanoi, tulpas, and so on and so on, all real. Well, except for Orcs and Hobbits. Tolkien just made those up.

I know it sounds ridiculous. How could magic really exist in a world with an Internet and forensic science and smartphones and satellites and such and still go undiscovered?

The answer is simple: it's magic.

The truth is that the world is under a spell called the Pax Arcana, a compulsion that makes people unable to see, believe, or even seriously consider any evidence of the supernatural that is not an immediate threat to their survival.

I know this because I come from a long line of dragon slayers, witch finders, and self-righteous asshats. I used to be one of the modern-day knights who patrol the borders between the world of man and the supernatural abyss that is its shadow. I wore non-reflective Kevlar instead of shining armor and carried a sawed-off shotgun as well as a sword; I didn't light a candle against the dark, I wielded a flamethrower... right up until the day I discovered that I had been cursed by one of the monsters I used to hunt. My name is Charming by the way. John Charming.

And I am not living happily ever after.

Chapter One

A Blonde and a Vampire Walk into a Bar…

Once upon a time, she smelled wrong. Well, no, that's not exactly true. She smelled clean, like fresh snow and air after a lightning storm and something hard to identify, something like sex and butter pecan ice cream. Honestly, I think she was the best thing I'd ever smelled. I was inferring "wrongness" from the fact that she wasn't entirely human.

I later found out that her name was Sig.

Sig stood there in the doorway of the bar with the wind behind her, and there was something both earthy and unearthly about her. Standing at least six feet tall in running shoes, she had shoulders as broad as a professional swimmer's, sinewy arms, and well-rounded hips that were curvy and compact. All in all, she was as buxom, blonde, blue-eyed, and clear-skinned as any woman who had ever posed for a Swedish tourism ad.

And I wanted her out of the bar, fast.

You have to understand, Rigby's is not the kind of place where goddesses were meant to walk among mortals. It is a small, modest establishment eking out a fragile existence at the tail end of Clayburg's main street. The owner, David Suggs, had wanted a quaint pub, but instead of decorating the place with dartboards or Scottish coats of arms or ceramic mugs, he had decided to celebrate southwest Virginia culture and covered the walls with rusty old railroad equipment and farming tools.

When I asked why a bar—excuse me, I mean *pub*—with a Celtic name didn't have a Celtic atmosphere, Dave said that he had named Rigby's after a Beatles song about lonely people needing a place to belong.

"Names have power," Dave had gone on to inform me, and I had listened gravely as if this were a revelation.

Speaking of names, "John Charming" is not what it reads on my current driver's license. In fact, about the only thing accurate on my current license is the part where it says that I'm black-haired and blue-eyed. I'm six foot one instead of six foot two and about seventy-five pounds lighter than the 250 pounds indicated on my identification. But I do kind of look the way the man pictured on my license might look if Trevor A. Barnes had lost that much weight and cut his hair short and shaved off his beard. Oh, and if he were still alive.

And no, I didn't kill the man whose identity I had assumed, in case you're wondering. Well, not the first time anyway.

Anyhow, I had recently been forced to leave Alaska and start a new life of my own, and in David Suggs I had found an employer who wasn't going to be too thorough with his background checks. My current goal was to work for Dave for at least one fiscal year and not draw any attention to myself.

Which was why I was not happy to see the blonde.

For her part, the blonde didn't seem too happy to see me either. Sig focused on me immediately. People always gave me a quick flickering glance when they walked into the bar—excuse me, the pub—but the first thing they really checked out was the clientele. Their eyes were sometimes predatory, sometimes cautious, sometimes hopeful, often tired, but they only returned to me after being disappointed. Sig's gaze, however, centered on me like the oncoming lights of a train—assuming train lights have slight bags underneath them and make you want to flex surreptitiously. Those same startlingly blue eyes widened, and her body went still for a moment.

Whatever had triggered her alarms, Sig hesitated, visibly debating whether to approach and talk to me. She didn't hesitate for long, though—I got the impression that she rarely hesitated for long—and chose to go find herself a table.

Now, it was a Thursday night in April, and Rigby's was not empty. Clayburg is host to a small private college named Stillwaters University, one of those places where parents pay more money than they should to get an education for children with mediocre high school records, and underachievers with upper-middle-class parents tend to do a lot of heavy drinking. This is why Rigby's manages to stay in business. Small bars with farming implements on the walls don't really draw huge college crowds, but the more popular bars tend to stay packed, and Rigby's does attract an odd combination of local rednecks and students with a sense of irony. So when a striking six-foot blonde who wasn't an obvious transvestite sat down in the middle of the bar, there were people around to notice.

Even Sandra, a nineteen-year-old waitress who considers customers an unwelcome distraction from covert texting, noticed the newcomer. She walked up to Sig promptly instead of making Renee, an older waitress and Rigby's de facto manager, chide her into action.

For the next hour I pretended to ignore the new arrival while focusing on her intently. I listened in—my hearing is as well developed as my sense of smell—while several patrons tried to introduce themselves. Sig seemed to have a knack for knowing how to discourage each would-be player as fast as possible.

She told suitors that she wanted to be up-front about her sex change operation because she was tired of having it cause problems when her lovers found out later, or she told them that she liked only black men, or young men, or older men who made more than seventy thousand dollars a year. She told them that what really turned her on was men who were willing to have sex with other men while she watched. She mentioned one man's wife by name, and when the weedy-looking grad student doing a John Lennon impersonation tried the sensitive-poet approach, she challenged him to an arm-wrestling contest. He stared at her, sitting there exuding athleticism, confidence, and health—three things he was noticeably lacking—and chose to be offended rather than take her up on it.

There was at least one woman who seemed interested in Sig as well, a cute sandy-haired college student who was tall and willowy, but when it comes to picking up strangers, women are generally less likely to go on a kamikaze mission than men. The young woman kept looking over at Sig's table, hoping to establish some kind of meaningful eye contact, but Sig wasn't making any.

Sig wasn't looking at me either, but she held herself at an angle that kept me in her peripheral vision at all times.

For my part, I spent the time between drink orders trying to figure out exactly what Sig was. She definitely wasn't undead. She wasn't a half-blood Fae either, though her scent wasn't entirely dissimilar. Elf smell isn't something you forget, sweet and decadent, with a hint of honey blossom and distant ocean. There aren't any full-blooded Fae left, of course—they packed their bags and went back to Fairyland a long time ago—but don't mention that to any of the mixed human descendants that the elves left behind. Elvish half-breeds tend to be somewhat sensitive on that particular subject. They can be real bastards about being bastards.

I would have been tempted to think that Sig was an angel, except that I've never heard of anyone I'd trust ever actually seeing a real angel. God is as much an article of faith in my world as he, she, we, they, or it is in yours.

Stumped, I tried to approach the problem by figuring out what Sig was doing there. She didn't seem to enjoy the ginger ale she had ordered—didn't seem to notice it at all, just sipped from it perfunctorily. There was something wary and expectant about her body language, and she had positioned herself so that she was in full view of the front door. She could have just been meeting someone, but I had a feeling that she was looking for someone or something specific by using herself as bait... but as to what and why and to what end, I had no idea. Sex, food, or revenge seemed the most likely choices.

I was still mulling that over when the vampire walked in.